Praise for *Indiscretion* (winner of the Gold Medal for Romance at the IBPA Benjamin Franklin Awards and Best Romance at the USA Best Book Awards):

'A captivating tale of love, jealousy and scandal.'   ***The Lady***

'*Indiscretion* grips from the first. Alexandra is a beguiling heroine, and Salvador a compelling, charismatic hero … the shimmering attraction between them is always as taut as a thread. A powerful and romantic story, one to savour and enjoy.'

Lindsay Townsend, historical romance author

'Rich description, a beautiful setting, wonderful detail, passionate romance and that timeless, classic feel that provides sheer, indulgent escapism. Bliss!'   **Amazon.co.uk review**

'I thought Ms. Fielding had outdone herself with her second novel but she's done it again with this third one. The love story took my breath away … I could hardly swallow until I reached the end.'

Amazon.com review

Also by Hannah Fielding

Burning Embers
The Echoes of Love

The Andalucían Nights Trilogy:

Indiscretion
Masquerade

LEGACY

HANNAH FIELDING

 LONDON WALL PUBLISHING

First published in paperback in the UK in 2016 by
London Wall Publishing Ltd (LWP)

First published in eBook edition in the UK in 2016 by
London Wall Publishing Ltd (LWP)

A CIP catalogue record for this book is
available from the British Library.

PB ISBN 978-0-9932917-3-9
EB ISBN 978-0-9932917-6-0

10 9 8 7 6 5 4 3 2 1

Print and production managed by
Jellyfish Solutions Ltd

London Wall Publishing Ltd (LWP)
24 Chiswell Street, London EC1Y 4YX

Two shall be born, the whole wide world apart,
And speak in different tongues, and have no thought
Each of the other's being; and have no heed;
And these, o'er unknown seas to unknown lands
Shall cross, escaping wreck, defying death;
And, all unconsciously, shape every act to this one end:
That one day out of darkness they shall meet
And read life's meanings in each other's eyes.

Susan M. Spalding, *Fate*

PROLOGUE

Seven storeys below, the steady hum of mid-morning traffic underscored the fading brassy bellow of a fire truck. Not for the first time, Luna compulsively rearranged the papers on her desk into even neater piles, her gaze straying to the view outside, away from the words on her screen. The tall, arched windows of the converted nineteenth-century spice warehouse that was now the office of *Scientific US* magazine looked out over the smart Hudson Square neighbourhood of Lower Manhattan.

She didn't like surprises. Her editor, Ted Vandenberg, had looked unusually cagey when he had asked to see her in his office in five minutes and now she was in a state of wary anticipation.

Why had Ted been so frustratingly cryptic?

She glanced at her watch and adjusted the blind to let in a fresh breeze from the open window. In the distance, the New York skyline shimmered in soaring peaks of reflecting glass and steel. The glaring sunlight of this crisp, blue-skied, early-spring day was dazzling, as if designed to confront and amaze the onlooker with the cityscape it illuminated: a vertical poem of proud, titanic proportions.

But here, on the western shore of Manhattan Island, where the fresh waters of the Hudson River met the salt waters of

New York Bay, nestled this charming neighbourhood, south of Greenwich Village, a tangle of lower, older buildings and crooked, tree-lined streets. Luna revelled in the chaotic sprawl of its brownstone apartments, bars and jazz clubs, bohemian bookstores and galleries, and how the city's iconic wooden water towers perched on high rooftops like giant Chinese lanterns. There was something fascinating about its clusters of pedestrians packing every sidewalk, a steady stream of human traffic flowing like water around stones in a burbling brook. To her ears, the familiar sounds of the streets were just as pleasing: a background cacophony of buskers' music mixed with the tooting horns of yellow taxi cabs and the rumbling of meatpacking vans making their way from the food markets and warehouses of Tribeca and the West Village to restaurants, stores and hotels.

The anonymity of the huge city suited Luna. New York was a place that made her feel comfortable, like a protective cloak offering to cocoon her within its noisy, bustling chaos. Yet for all its reassuring camouflage, sometimes she felt the elemental forces of life were overwhelming. Something inside her was as chaotic as the metropolis outside, bursting to get out, and she fought to contain it every day.

The dream had come again last night. She had woken suddenly, as she always did, clammy and panting, her deafening heartbeat thumping against her ribs, her own pleading voice echoing loudly in her ears. The nightmare hadn't visited her for a while. She wondered if this time it had been triggered by the intense designer from the art department, who had asked her to have coffee with him; something about his hooded gaze, the intent expression … Luna remembered the panic that had rippled through her at his invitation and now she tried to throw off the feeling of unease that pressed on her mind, combining oppressively with her lack of sleep.

Distractedly, she pushed her long, blonde hair back behind her ears. She was twenty-five but nevertheless still did not feel like a grown woman. Instead, she was trapped in a world of dark, shadowy memories, isolated yet fearing the light. In many ways being alone was safe and so appealing. Why then did this gnawing feeling of restless emotion plague her? It smouldered quietly within her, threatening at any moment to become an all-consuming blaze. On top of that, there was Angelina ... She missed her dreadfully.

'Luna, let's talk now, shall we?'

Jolted from her troubled thoughts, she looked up. A few feet away, Ted Vandenberg was standing in the doorway of one of the side offices on the open-plan floor. Short and rotund, with a shock of almost white hair, his bright blue eyes twinkled behind circular pale-rimmed spectacles. Half in conversation with a gangling male colleague who was shuffling papers back into a leather bag, he smiled and motioned her over.

'Take a seat. I'll be with you as soon as I've finished with Nate, here.'

Luna composed herself and nodded. 'Sure. Thanks, Ted.'

She slipped past him into his office. Inside the frosted glass wall of her boss's inner sanctum, bookcases ran along one exposed brick wall while framed photos lined the white-painted walls. Her eyes scanned the images: covers of old editions of the magazine dating back to the late nineteenth century, journalism awards, colourfully graphic science posters, and black-and-white photographs of famous scientists. Unlike Luna's own pristine workspace, here papers littered every surface, and more books were stacked up on chairs or were arranged in precarious towers on the floor.

As Luna cleared a seat and sat down, she spied a folder on Ted's large, antique mahogany desk and was startled to see her name on it. She glanced nervously back to the empty doorway, still hearing Vandenberg's voice murmuring outside. Sheets of paper were spilling from the folder's side and Luna half stood to take a closer look. The edge of the top page revealed a small profile picture of a dark-haired man wearing glasses. Tempted to get a better view of the folder's contents, she stretched out an arm and had only got as far as touching the edge when the door creaked softly behind her.

'"Curiosity is one of the most permanent and certain characteristics of a vigorous intellect." That's what Samuel Johnson said. Astute man.'

'I'm sorry?' Luna said, returning to her seat hurriedly.

Ted Vandenberg walked behind his desk and sank into his chair, grinning at her. Beneath the tufts of white hair was a kindly face with a low brow, short nose and a broad mouth that was prone to break into a toothy smile, making him look somewhat like an animated turtle, Luna always thought. Full of energy, with a buoyant and congenial demeanour, he also had a sharp intellect that she appreciated. In fact, she liked Ted very much, despite his untidy habits and propensity to be late for meetings, qualities that usually irked her in other people.

She shifted in her chair, deliberately not glancing at the folder.

'That's what I like to see in a scientist,' Vandenberg beamed, motioning towards the folder and pushing his glasses back up the bridge of his nose. 'Curiosity. The best scientists and explorers are like five-year-old children. They never stop asking questions: "Who, what, where, why, when and how?" Curiosity is the well from which we scientists draw our sustenance and energy, Luna, so don't be afraid to use it.' He raised his dark, bushy eyebrows. 'I've always thought you had the makings of a first-rate investigative journalist actually. I'm getting ahead of myself, though … How long have you been with us now?'

'Just over six months.'

What was he getting at? Was he about to say that she was unsuited to the work she'd been assigned? Luna's large amber eyes studied his face for evidence of any disapproval but he simply smiled back with a similarly appraising look.

He stood up and moved towards a side cabinet. 'Coffee?'

'Yes, coffee would be good, thanks.'

Vandenberg poured steaming coffee from a chrome jug into two mismatched bone-china cups. 'I took you on because, with first-class honours in Molecular Biology from Princeton, followed by an impressive PhD in Science Communication, you're a scientist with perfect academic credentials. But it's more than that. You're bold, inquisitive and rigorous. In short, if you haven't yet realized it, you've got all the makings of a top-notch science journalist. You were right not to go into research, far too restrictive for you. In the few months you've been here, I've become convinced you have the kind of investigative instincts I need.'

Luna flushed a little at the compliment, choosing not to say anything, but instead willing him to cut to the chase. Her eyes shone. This was it: the break she'd been longing for.

Vandenberg handed her a cup and sat down. Clasping his hands together, he rested them on his ample stomach. 'Now you know we credit ourselves with impeccable, unbiased research. I've been chewing on this for a few days, as I have a feeling, and I don't want to speak out of turn here, that you have a personal interest in alternative cancer therapies, possibly even an axe to grind, and this might not make you as unbiased as I'd have liked.'

At this, Luna tried to interrupt, but he raised a hand before continuing.

'Having said that, Luna, I think a passionate and focused interest is exactly what makes a great article.'

He paused and though the office was cool he wiped his brow with his handkerchief in a habitual gesture. 'We're wanting a full-length feature done on The Institute for the Research of Natural Remedies, a not-for-profit organization based in Andalucía. I can tell by your face you've heard of it.'

Luna couldn't help her eyes widening. Of course she had heard of it. Her cousin Angelina had been treated in a place like that in California before she died. At work Luna had always fiercely guarded her private life although she had confided in her boss somewhat when she'd asked for a few days' compassionate leave to attend Angelina's funeral. She pressed down her emotions and schooled her features into a look of casual attentiveness.

'Well, good,' Vandenberg continued. 'The Institute is starting to hit the medical press in a big way, with its cutting-edge, although possibly questionable, use of some rather wacky herbal treatments, among other things.'

Luna couldn't help interjecting: 'I bet that's been ruffling a few feathers at some of the pharmaceuticals.'

He smiled and gestured in agreement. 'Indeed. I was talking about that very thing last night with a couple of big hitters in the business. One of those huge dinner parties in the Upper East Side that Professor Henderson throws for the Science Academy.'

For a moment he looked at her pensively, as if about to say something else.

'Anyway, Luna, the guy that runs the operation at this Institute, who likes nothing better than thumbing his nose at Big Pharma cheeses, is the one I'd like you to investigate. He's had all the orthodox medical training, though now he's "gone bush", you might say. Thing is, he's got a brain the size of a bus and he talks a good game. Sounds very credible indeed, a powerful figure. A bit of a playboy too, by all accounts.'

'What's his name? Is that him?' Luna pointed to the page spilling from the folder.

'He's called Dr Rodrigo Rueda de Calderón. And yes, there's some background info for you there too.'

Luna reached for the folder and pulled out the sheets, skimming through the three-page profile on top. It was difficult to tell much from the small photo: though he was clearly younger than she expected, the dark-haired man wearing glasses simply looked groomed and official – hardly the look of a playboy. At first glance the doctor's qualifications and achievements on his résumé appeared impressive.

'So …' Vandenberg looked at her directly, eyes twinkling. 'Does this sound like your kind of thing? A bit of youthful ambition goes a long way in the world of undercover journalism. My instinct tells me you've got what it takes to put in the energy and legwork needed for an assignment like this.'

'I would have to go to Spain?'

'Yes, the clinic is in Cádiz. I understand you speak the language fluently too, which is a plus.'

'For how long?' Luna was already slightly queasy with trepidation. She hadn't been back to Spain since she was a child and, even though she had fond memories of the country and its people, she had no desire to reacquaint herself with her Spanish relatives. That aside, there was also the subterfuge the assignment would necessarily entail. Would that sit comfortably with her? Yet this was an opportunity, in more ways than one, not to be dismissed lightly.

'We were thinking of a month or so. Maybe more,' affirmed Vandenberg. 'We'll apply for an unpaid internship for you, which shouldn't be too difficult to secure. Get one of our contacts at Princeton to send over your résumé, so the Institute doesn't find out that you're working for us. The magazine will cover your expenses.'

Luna's mind was already formulating the perspectives. 'So you want a carefully researched exposé of the Institute and its charismatic, rebellious leader?'

'I expect that's what we're looking at, yes.' Vandenberg dropped two lumps of sugar into his coffee and stirred, regarding her. 'Nothing that might discredit the magazine, though. Proper research.'

'So you think there's an added angle here? Pharma companies hacked off with a flaky treatment programme that's stealing their media space?'

'There might be a story there. I can't believe the good doctor is affecting their revenues to any great extent.'

'I'm presuming the medical establishment has been loudly dismissing his treatments as just another example of pseudo-science?'

'Of course, but that doesn't mean your article has to toe the party line. Like I said, unbiased.' He sipped his drink and chuckled. 'But no harm in adding a bit of spice to the pot, is there? In fact, your uncle was there last night at the dinner. He has a lot of cash tied up in his research and patents, as you can imagine. Doesn't take kindly to the herb peddlers who try to pass him on the inside.' He chuckled again. 'Actually, it's usually water off a duck's back. These guys are normally small fry but there's a rumour Dr Rueda de Calderón is raising money for trials, which means he might be on to something with one of his treatments. And, as you so rightly pinpointed just now, your uncle is downright ornery at all the press the doctor's been getting.'

At the mention of her uncle, Luna's face had become impassive, though her fingers tightened on the papers. She picked up her cup and tried to sound casual.

'So what is Lorenzo doing in New York?'

'He's over from California for a few days before he heads off on his tour of Europe. Impressive man, Herrera. A lot of drive. It's easy to see how he's managed to make his pharma company the largest in Spain. He's really started making his mark over here too. Good luck to him.'

Luna took an overly large sip of coffee, wincing slightly as the heat scalded her tongue. 'Yes, Uncle Lorenzo has always been single-minded in getting what he wants.'

That's an understatement, she thought, glad that California was almost three thousand miles away.

She quickly changed the subject. 'How long do you think it would take to get everything in place?'

A smile spread across Vandenberg's face. 'I've already made enquiries to fast-track an application to the Institute. You could be in Cádiz this time next week.'

Luna put her cup down carefully on the desk, then looked at him intently for a few moments.

'Okay, Ted. I'll do it.'

*   *   *

A couple of hours later, Luna left the building and headed up Sixth Avenue to her favourite lunchtime deli. She had almost flinched when Ted mentioned alternative cancer therapy. It had been less than a year since Angelina's death. Only twenty-one, her cousin had been so full of what she wanted to do with her life, her plans for the future. Luna's grief was still so raw that whenever a recollection hit her, it was like a tooth coming into contact with something ice-cold, a pain that would jab away at her like a knife when she least expected it.

Pulling out her phone, she dialled a number and took a steadying breath. She listened to her aunt's warm, enquiring voice at the other end.

'Hi Aunt Bea. Yes, it's Luna. I've got something important to tell you.' Choosing her words carefully, she filled her aunt in on her conversation with Ted Vandenberg.

'So, you see, this is a chance for us. Maybe there's something positive we can get out of what happened to Angelina, if only to try to stop other people and their families falling prey to these charlatans,' she continued, then waited, listening to the trembling voice of her aunt, before replying: 'Yes, I agree. Clinics like this can't get away with peddling false hope.'

CHAPTER 1

Northern Spain, a few weeks later

Ten o'clock at night and Barcelona was just coming to life. Luna made her way along the crowded pavement, heading for Las Ramblas, the city's well-known promenade. A few hours before, the aircraft that had brought her to the 'Old World', as some Americans referred to Europe, had landed. The flight had been delayed and the journey had been tiring, but Luna needed to stretch her legs. In New York it would only be late afternoon and she was still wide awake.

When she had arrived at her hotel, the Casa Montaner, Luna had deposited her luggage in the lobby, lit alluringly by the soft yellow and pink glow of Gaudí-inspired lamps. It was an elegant art-nouveau building in the Eixample district, just north of the old part of the city, with marble and stone pillars sweeping up to a vaulted ceiling. Despite the hotel's welcoming atmosphere, Luna had immediately asked the way to the seafront. The friendly young concierge, recognizing she was American despite her fluent Spanish, had given her clear directions to Plaça del Portal de la Pau and Port Vell, Barcelona's oldest port.

'*Hay una magnífica estatua de Cristóba Columbu en la plaza*, there is a magnificent statue of Christopher Columbus in the square,' he told her. His appreciative gaze took in Luna's long, champagne-blonde hair and the amber eyes that shone through a fringe of dark lashes under perfectly arched brows. 'You'll find Port Vell at the end of Las Ramblas. It's a pedestrian-only street with plenty of restaurants and bars. You can't do better in Barcelona for entertainment. In fact, nowhere in the world are the nights as lively as in our *tascas*,' he added with pride. 'But take care of your wallet, *señorita. Hey muchos carteristas en todo*, there are many pickpockets around. Late at night, the southern end of the street in particular becomes less respectable, shall we say.'

Luna smiled. She had no intention of taking any unnecessary risks. Besides, she was from New York so she figured she could take care of herself well enough. 'Thanks for the advice. Is Las Ramblas far?'

'*Diez minutos a pie en la mayoría de los*, ten minutes' walk at the most.' The concierge pushed the registration book across the gleaming teak desk. 'May I ask, are you in Barcelona for business or pleasure?'

'I'm here for the conference tomorrow at the hotel,' Luna confirmed, signing her name. 'Then I'm travelling on to Cádiz.'

The concierge nodded politely and offered her a broad smile. 'Ah yes, a very prestigious speaker, apparently, Professor Goldsmith. Well, have a pleasant evening, *señorita*, and enjoy your stay with us.'

'*Muchas gracias*, you've been very helpful.'

It was a fine spring night and the roads were teeming as Luna walked through the Gothic quarter. Curious and exciting smells, not one in particular but a succession of warm and spicy aromas, hung in the still air. She tried to single them out: garlic, seafood, pimientos, saffron, hot oil, fried tomatoes and a host of others that she did not recognize. Occasionally she would catch the scent of flowers from neighbourhood gardens, a heady mix of roses, jasmine and tuberose. There was the unmistakable imprint of city life on every street corner that echoed New York, and yet the sheer exotic, foreign nature of the place was exquisite.

Everybody was out. By the looks of it, the credit crunch had not crushed Barcelona. Shops were still open at this late hour, doing a roaring trade. Restaurants and cafés with bright awnings spilled out on to the pavements. Crowds strolled to and fro at a snail's pace, refusing to be hurried, seeking bargains and looking at everything. Traffic crawled and fumed, nose to tail along the one-way street, and from time to time Luna would pass a stationary car blasting thumping music out of its open windows. She was in Spain!

She walked with the self-assurance of someone who has grown up before her time. Comfortable in her flat-heeled pumps and stretch-denim jeans that moulded themselves perfectly to the contours of her trim figure, Luna was oblivious to the interest the easy, swinging movement of her hips was attracting. Men's heads swivelled and their gaze lingered, following her with fascination, but she was immersed in her own thoughts.

She felt light-hearted. More than ever, she knew she had done the right thing. Yes, a part of her had been undeniably reluctant to go to Cádiz in case she should bump into her Spanish relatives yet such was her fascination for Spain it had overcome any other concerns.

And now here she was: Luna Emilia Ward – youngest daughter of Montgomery Ward, the well known American business tycoon, and Adalia Herrera, the beautiful Spanish socialite – back in Spain for the first time since those faraway childhood holidays. That evening, soaking up the unique atmosphere of the city, she wished she'd returned to her native country earlier, that she had been braver and had given in to the complicated tug of her roots.

Even though she was Spanish on her mother's side, Luna had only been to Spain for short vacations when she was a child. What maternal coldness she had experienced in her early childhood had at least been offset by the joy of those holidays. The memories still glowed warmly inside her like a tiny, unextinguishable flame. They returned to her mind more vividly now than ever: playing in orange groves under the Spanish sun; the white hilltop villages; taking boats out in the perfect azure sea; the haunting sound of flamenco guitars; the endless festivities, and the friendly Spaniards, who were always so passionate about eating, drinking, making music and being happy. Something of the country had embedded itself in her and had slumbered all these years. She had kept up her Spanish, perhaps with the unconscious intention of returning one day.

Her parents had suffered an acrimonious divorce when she was seven. Adalia had taken the daughter from her first marriage, Luna's half-sister Juliet, with her to Spain, while Montgomery had kept Luna in California. He had immediately packed her off to boarding school but she had, at least, the solace of holidays in California with her paternal grandparents. She also saw her cousin, Angelina, whenever she could. But she had never seen her mother again.

Luna had been twelve when Juliet, who was seven years older than her, died in a car accident while studying at a university on the east coast of America. Adalia, already an alcoholic by then, drank herself to death shortly afterwards. Adalia's brother, Lorenzo, sought out Luna and, from then on, visited her and Montgomery twice a year in California.

As Luna later saw it, her Uncle Lorenzo, always astute when it came to serving his own interests, had made full use of her father's business connections during his trips to the West Coast. Lorenzo Herrera owned a pharmaceutical company on the Costa de la Luz in Andalucía that was expanding into the rest of Europe, and his eye was firmly fixed on the US as his new base for Farmacéutica Corporationas. It was this, as much as his efforts at being an influential presence in his niece's life, that had drawn him to California, though he always maintained he was chiefly there to ensure Luna never forgot her 'proud Spanish heritage'.

His visits stopped abruptly around the time Luna was entering her teens. She had never found it in herself to accept a single one of her uncle's invitations to his hacienda in Granada or his house in Cádiz. The very thought of having anything to do with her mother's family had made her stomach churn. In fact, she ignored Adalia's homeland altogether, just as her mother had mostly ignored the young Luna for the first few years of her life while in her care. When Luna grew up and started travelling the world on her own, she went to Egypt, Peru and China, never Spain.

It was not that she particularly minded spending most of her time alone while growing up. It meant that she could indulge her burgeoning intellectual curiosity unhindered. Fascinated by the precision and predictability of science and its quest for new discoveries about the universe, at high school her academic achievements soon stacked up, leading to places at Princeton and then Cornell. After that she had her pick of university research posts but, before she had a chance to decide on which offer to take up, Ted Vandenberg called. He'd read an article she'd submitted to his magazine, and now her investigative impulses switched direction. It had taken little persuasion to tempt Luna into journalism at *Scientific US*.

'You have a nose for a story, scientific or otherwise,' Vandenberg had told her.

Now she was to write her first big story for the magazine. Her hard work had paid off. As promised, the magazine had organized an internship. She would be assistant analyst and researcher at *El Instituto de Investigación de los Recursos Naturales*, The Institute for the Research of Natural Remedies. She gave a shiver of excitement. Tomorrow, after the conference, she would be on a plane to Cádiz, to a strange new life, albeit temporarily.

In Cádiz, she'd be near the sea. Maybe there she would sleep more soundly. Already she could feel an unexpected sense of freedom that seemed to permeate the air around her. Exhilarated by the vibrant surroundings, Luna walked quickly towards the main street, soaking up the atmosphere. She took a right turn and suddenly Las Ramblas was there. For a moment she stood, taking in the scene. The brightly lit promenade, adorned with plane trees, was seething with a river of people.

As she joined the cosmopolitan throng, it felt like all of the action – Barcelona's entire nightlife – was centred on this wide, tree-lined street, from cosy traditional Spanish bars and restaurants to clubs lit up with neon. The hubbub was indescribable. Although seventies disco had become largely a thing of the past back home, it seemed to thrive in Barcelona and the pulsating music reverberated in the warm night air. Decaying movie houses, abandoned garages and long-closed vaudeville theatres had all been turned into colourful nightlife venues.

Luna could barely take in the staggering parade of diversions. There were booksellers, souvenir stands, flamenco dancers, clowns and acrobats. A dozen street performers, painted bronze or white like statues, wowed the crowds in a fantastic array of costumes, some standing or sitting, others moving in jerky mime. Luna found them somewhat eerie and, unlike other tourists, didn't stop to take their photograph.

She passed a bank, whose façade was decorated with a huge model of a dragon and an umbrella, the fairy-tale flamboyance of which made her smile. Interrupting her brisk walk, this time she allowed herself a few minutes to pause and take some snapshots of its eccentric charm. Further down, people were having their portraits painted by street artists. A caricaturist approached Luna, offering to draw her. '*Incluso en la caricatura no seria menos bella*, even in caricature you would not look less beautiful,' he told her. But she merely smiled and shook her head politely. '*Tal vez en otro momento*, maybe some other time,' she said as she moved on.

The lights turned red when she reached the edge of Plaça del Portal de la Pau. Traffic roared around the colossal, brightly lit Columbus statue, which stood proudly in the middle of the square overlooking the sea. Here, the crowds suddenly thinned and the pavement was almost deserted, except for a group of shell-game touts. They gathered around Luna, jostling for her attention, standing too close: 'Which shell is the pea under? Where are you heading, *señorita*?' The red light flashed to green and, with a sigh of relief, she crossed over to Passeig de Colom and the sea.

Slowing her pace, she glanced around her, wondering which way to go next. The wooden swing bridge of Rambla del Mar was visible ahead, heaving with crowds. Standing under a streetlamp, she pulled a small map from her pocket. Despite the noise on this wide avenue of palm and orange trees, she could hear the vague hissing roll of the Mediterranean as it licked the expansive shoreline and knocked against the smart yachts docked in the marina. Above the yellow glow of the city, the sky was a deep sapphire blue. The playful night breeze lifted Luna's blonde mane, gentle, constant and cool. The air was sparkling, flavoured with the tang of the sea. Luna inhaled deeply, taking in the freshness of the night air. She passed her tongue over her lips and tasted salt.

Soon she was besieged by hawkers with a variety of cheap wares. She hung on to the small leather shoulder bag swinging freely by her side and clasped it firmly under one arm as she quickened her pace. The concierge at the hotel had warned of pickpockets in this part of the city; if she lost her bag, she would have only herself to blame.

She was about to turn back when she caught strains of music and bursts of clapping coming from a narrow side street to her left. Flamenco music … her favourite.

Luna hesitated, pondering whether to go off in search of it. It wasn't part of her plan. The distant frenzied notes vibrated on the night air, sending a delicious hum through her body. She had been to a few flamenco shows in Las Vegas and in other parts of the US, but had always wanted to see a live show in Spain. The sensible voice inside her head told her that she would have plenty of opportunity to see flamenco over the coming months, and that it was foolish to follow a whim when she should be getting back to the hotel, but right at that moment Luna was tempted to give in to her curiosity and follow the sound. In fact, something stronger than curiosity beckoned, something more alluring and seductive, that seemed to stir her soul – a call of enchantment drifting through the night air. In answer, she stepped quickly into the alleyway.

The sinuous passage was paved with cobblestones and was badly lit. It was empty, save for a few couples that stood in the shadows, absorbed in each other. Both sides were lined with the colourful façades and beautiful wrought-iron balconies of secretive houses, their drawn-down *persianas* and wooden doors jealously guarding the lives of their owners. Luna wondered about the hidden inhabitants, just as she had done a few years back when gliding in a gondola past the magnificent but eerie shuttered palaces of Venice. Here, just as in the streets of the Gothic quarter, the air was laden with fascinating smells; this time the piquant aroma of cooking mingled with wood smoke and the ozone of the sea.

With rising anticipation, and ignoring her better judgement, Luna moved along the narrow lane into deeper darkness. The distant music and the rhythmic clapping and tapping of feet came to her in waves; sometimes it seemed nearer, then farther away. A cat crept noiselessly out of the shadows, making her jump, and flashed its phosphorescent eyes before scampering away and disappearing into the small, gated entrance of one of the houses. Suddenly she was aware of the sound of her footsteps on the cobblestones and she felt a frisson of fear. She knew she was being reckless by persevering down this maze of dark alleys but, having gone so far now, she was not about to turn back.

Unexpectedly, at an abrupt bend in the narrow street, the sound of live, full-blooded flamenco music burst out once more, echoing through the night. It came from a nightclub a few yards away, its façade painted with warm sunny colours under the flashing fluorescent sign *El Cabo de Oro*.

Now, as she approached the tavern, Luna could clearly hear the loud clapping of hands, the *olés*, and the clinking of glasses. She hesitated outside the bright walls a few moments longer, a curtain of beads the only thing separating her from the exuberant sounds of the show.

Finally, she pushed it aside and went down the few steps leading into the dimly lit room below. Anti-smoking campaigns had obviously not reached this wild little world, she noted, engulfed by the hazy atmosphere.

Here, the *cuadro flamenco* sat in a semicircle on a platform at the far end of the room with that part open to the night sky. The troupe played its music at a fast tempo, while the audience clapped their hands and stamped their feet in rhythm on the tiled floor with cries of *olé* to encourage the young dancer. A girl was singing hoarsely, seductively, and her castanets marked their own syncopated rhythm.

Lamps on the red painted walls threw out a warm amber glow, illuminating an assortment of bullfighting posters, advertisements, and photographs of *toreros* and flamenco dancers. On one side, to the right, stood a long, wooden bar lined with endless bottles of different shapes and colours and topped by a row of gleaming glasses. Tended by a scraggy-looking waiter chewing a quid of tobacco, most of the clientele sat on cane stools along the bar, eating tapas or drinking around low tables made from empty wine barrels. To the left of the stage, an arched roof opened out on to a walled patio, where a small number of people sat drinking and chatting in the balmy evening air.

Luna made her way deeper into the room, looking for a table nearer the patio where she would be less affected by the fug of smoke. The tavern was packed. The audience was mostly men and what women there were, were all accompanied. Luna was the only single woman in the place, and it made her feel uncomfortable. She began to regret her rash decision. Back in New York she had never been to a bar alone, so why had she suddenly decided it was a good idea to do so on her first night in Barcelona? Her pale blonde hair and pearly complexion caused her to stand out starkly against the darker colouring of the Spaniards who filled the club.

There was a drop in the level of noise as she became an object of interest. Men's eyes were drawn to her like a magnet. Some of them whispered to each other, casting sidelong glances. Women also stared, their eyes narrowing, reflecting quite a different sentiment altogether. The *cuadro* had stopped playing while the musicians sipped their wine and a new dancer emerged from the background to take over the lead. Luna stood at the side of the seated audience and glanced around.

Maybe I should go back, she thought, feeling distinctly out of place.

And then it happened … their eyes met across the room and held for a long moment. The effect was electric and hit Luna like a bolt of lightning. His gaze, fringed by long black lashes, burned with a fire that scorched her as it moved slowly and deliberately over her face, then her body, with frank admiration, as if drinking in her every feature. Though she could not see the exact colour of his eyes at this distance, she knew they were paler than his tanned complexion – brilliant and alive with passion.

The man before her was mesmerizing in his perfect male beauty. His bold, open stare should have made her want to turn and run but something more powerful than she had ever experienced, a shot of pure adrenaline in her blood, had her rooted to the spot.

In that split second of silent meeting, Luna's heart seemed to turn over in her breast and her pulse accelerated to a wild beat.

'*Puedo llevar a la señorita un vaso de sangria y unas tapas?* Can I bring the *señorita* a glass of sangria and some tapas?' The solicitous voice of the waiter brought Luna back down to earth with a bump. As she hesitated, still a little confused, he smiled at her. 'I've got a free table, down at the front. It's a hot night and you'll have a perfect view of the band.'

'Yes, thank you.' In a daze she followed the waiter and took her place outside, under the starry sky, as the fiery music started up again.

Luna's gaze was drawn back to the stage, to that sculpted face.

He was one of the musicians, and a gypsy, she had no doubt. Now he took up a mandolin and began to accompany the two other guitarists and a drummer who was beating a tabla, a type of drum she remembered having seen in Egypt, with an opening at one end. A couple of girls from the audience had joined the *cuadro* and the dancer on stage. The atmosphere was spontaneous and wild.

From her vantage point, Luna had a full view of her gypsy and she could survey him without it being too obvious. His hair was black, thick and shining, swept back from a broad forehead. The hair was rather long, she noted, but perhaps not that long for a *gitano*. A few tendrils fell across his brow from time to time as he moved his head to the music. His chiselled features were strong, with high cheekbones and an aquiline nose that seemed more aristocratic than gypsy, though this was belied by the crackling aura of raw danger that seemed to emanate from him.

His mouth was wide and inviting, with smooth, slightly bowed lips that prompted illicit thoughts in Luna, thoughts that raced uninvited through her head and made her shiver despite the warmth of the night. Now she could see that the eyes that had met hers with such intensity were blue, a deep, unfathomable blue, like the skies and the seas of his country. Luna wondered at his age: mid-thirties, maybe a little younger.

As the dancer finished her set and retreated, the gypsy stood up, came forward and murmured an announcement of the next song, making a fresh thrill ripple up Luna's spine at the husky, masculine sound of his voice. He started the rhythmic clapping of a *toca de mano*, and the waiter went round refilling glasses while the audience joined in, working up to a crescendo of hand-claps until the whole tavern shook with cries of '*olé*' and '*anda*'.

The gypsy was much taller than Luna had guessed – over six feet, with a perfectly proportioned, lithe body. Wide shoulders and a broad chest, narrow hips and muscled thighs clad in a pair of jeans that hugged his form so well it left little to the imagination. She was aware of his intense magnetism, which was just as powerful as his steely physique. At this distance, she could detect the dark, curling hair lightly covering his chest just visible at the neck of the faded T-shirt he wore with surprising panache.

The muscles of his arms flexed as this time he picked up a guitar and strummed a rapid cascade of chords. He gazed down into her eyes. The dazzling white smile he gave her almost stopped her heart and she lowered her head to hide her confusion.

As the rhythmic clapping subsided, he began to sing. His voice was rich and mellow, warm with vibrant tones and tingling with emotion, beguiling and beckoning like a *filtre d'amour* that scrambled her thoughts and stirred primitive and alarming desires within her. The music was plaintive and feverish, and as Luna watched his long fingers alternately strum and flick across the strings of his guitar, first lightly and then harder at lightning speed, she found herself wondering how those hands would feel on her skin. His songs were in *Caló* so she could not understand the words, but she could sense the intensity of feeling that went into the full, vigorous notes and although he sang to the audience, she knew from the sensuous intimacy in his eyes that he was singing for her alone.

Luna sat breathless, her gaze fixed on his expressive face, stirred to the depths of her soul.

He was applauded madly as the last notes of his passionate melody faded and his fingers lay still on the guitar. Luna clapped as long and loudly as everyone else. New customers were now piling into the tavern, and she shook herself out of her trance and tried to wrestle back her grip on reality. She glanced at her watch: it was past one o'clock in the morning. The gypsy guitarist was surrounded by fans, young and old, and was obviously enjoying the attention. She must be thinking of getting back, she told herself, her eyes lingering on the broad, muscular back of the guitarist as he headed for the bar. She wondered if she would find a taxi at this hour. After signalling to the waiter she paid her bill, leaving a generous tip.

Then, on impulse, she took out of her purse a fifty-euro note. '*Por favor dar a este al guitarrista que acaba de cantar*, please give this to the guitarist who just sang,' she told him.

The waiter grinned broadly. '*Gracias, muchas gracias, señorita*,' he said, giving a curt bow. 'But things are only warming up. Are you sure you won't stay and enjoy the dancing?'

As if on cue, the musicians still on stage took up a fast, syncopated thrumming on their guitars and the whole crowd whooped and broke into wild stamping again.

'You see, *señorita*, the night is still young, as they say.'

Luna stood up and smiled, calling on all her self-discipline. 'Not for me, I'm afraid. But thank you, the music has been wonderful,' she said, and started to make her way back through the room as the waiter hurried off to deliver her tip.

People jostled past Luna in their eagerness to join the dancing, which by now had spilled out on to the patio. The relentless rhythm of the music seemed to grow louder as if calling her back. And then she looked up at the bar.

He was there with the waiter, who was saying something in his ear and pointing in Luna's direction. The guitarist ran a hand through his hair and looked at her. He nodded his thanks for the tip, and held up two glasses filled with what looked like fino. A quizzical expression danced in his bright eyes.

Luna's mouth went dry: he was inviting her to stay. Conflicting emotions flashed through her, none that she could quite grasp but every one of them making her heart pump faster as the music continued to vibrate through the tavern.

Part of her wanted to succumb to the heady atmosphere and wished she could be like all these people – sensual, passionate, uninhibited. But something told her that if she stayed any longer she would be stepping into unfamiliar and dangerous territory, and that unnerved her far too much.

She took a deep breath and smiled back at him, shaking her head apologetically as she kept moving through the crowd. He watched her go and took a swig from one of the glasses, his gaze unwavering.

Luna made her way to the door. She went up the steps and turned at the entrance to catch a last glimpse of the man who had disturbed her equilibrium so powerfully.

Over the heads of those around him, he was still watching her intently. His lips quirked as their eyes fused again. Luna focused her camera on him and clicked, blushing at her own nerve as she did so. Her thoughts in turbulence, she stepped out abruptly into the night.

*   *   *

The taxi that had picked up Luna on the Plaça del Portal de la Pau sped through the narrow streets towards the hotel. Still intoxicated by the singing, Luna stared out of the window, gazing at the glittering night with eyes scarcely aware of its beauty. After she had left the tavern, the haunting strains of the music had lingered on the still air, threading through the night like a love call as she had made her way back to the square. There was plenty of life on the boulevards even at this hour, but what Luna had found so fascinating earlier, now she hardly noticed. The events of the evening absorbed her whole being.

She closed her eyes, trying to etch on her mind the flamenco singer's features that were already beginning to fade in her memory. Glad that she was tucked away in the back of a dark taxi where no one could witness her sense of almost teenage foolishness, she scrolled through the photographs saved on her camera and found his picture. Even though it had been taken from afar, the gypsy's intense and charismatic personality leapt from the device to collide with her emotions. Nothing in her carefully guarded and uneventful life had prepared her for an assault of such concentrated masculinity on her senses.

Luna had an odd realization. Suddenly she was aware of all the things a man and woman do together. For the first time, the fact that she was twenty-five and had never had a lover struck her like a blow to the head.

Sure, she had had plenty of opportunities. Since she could remember, men had looked at her with something more than interest, the very thing that put her off. On a few occasions it had even filled her with nausea and not a little panic. Though she had a natural desire to feel attractive, like any woman, and enjoyed the odd flirtation at parties, sometimes she wished she was just Plain Jane: loved for herself and not as an object to be possessed.

Despite that bruised, fragile place inside her that she hid from the outside world, she had deeply buried yearnings and desires but they were ringed by fear and guilt.

She had dated now and again, and had even had a few crushes but these had been merely flashes in the pan. Disillusioned, she had simply moved on. Luna's inclination towards solitude meant that her circle of friends was small, but they were close and carefully chosen. She had never understood the need for superficial acquaintances and hated small talk. To her it seemed like nothing but a waste of time.

Many of her close friends had tried to set her up with good-looking, eligible men, but somehow they always fell short in Luna's estimation. Perhaps her impossibly high standards were an act of self-sabotage but, even if that were the case, she couldn't seem to help her reaction. Nonetheless, she persisted in attracting admirers, whether or not she wanted to.

Luna paid off the taxi. The euphoria of the past few hours remained with her, intimate and exciting, while she climbed the steps of the hotel in a daze and crossed the grand lobby. She retrieved her key and went up to her room on the fourth floor. It was only when she switched on the light and the magnificent wrought-iron chandelier flooded the place with its luminous glow that she came back to reality. The room was stylishly *moderniste* with tall French windows but it now seemed empty and lonely. She threw her shoulder bag on the bed and opened the windows wide to let in the night.

What was this *coup de foudre* between the gypsy and herself that had struck her so forcibly? It had released emotions in her that were completely unfamiliar and uncontrollable. Always Luna liked to be in control.

Though she scarcely dared to admit it, this gypsy had the features and physique of the man of her dreams – a man whose existence she had given up on as a weak and immature fantasy. The passion he radiated was a compelling magnetism she had secretly searched for all her life. His stare had invaded every fibre of her being. An affinity had established itself between them – a powerful attraction of which he had also been aware, of that she was convinced. It was a strange thing to have one's entire reality turned upside down as soon as one set foot in a new country. The world would seem a brighter and more exciting place if she thought for one minute that their paths would someday cross.

This admission threw her. She shook her head as if to dislodge the idea, suddenly shocked at the ridiculous sentimentality of it.

The man was a complete stranger. What on earth was the use of indulging in romantic hopes when it was unlikely she would ever meet him again?

The chances were nil unless she was to go back to the tavern that night, which, anyway, her pride would prohibit. Anyhow, she was only in Barcelona for another twenty-four hours. Surely he was married – she'd heard that gypsies married young – and even if he didn't have a wife and half a dozen children, he most certainly had a life in a world so remote from hers that it was naïve to envisage any sort of relationship between them.

A long, shuddering sigh escaped her as she blinked back the tears that trembled at the edge of her eyelids as she ruthlessly tried to suppress her foolish longing. Love at first sight only existed in romantic novels. She prided herself on being a level-headed scientist and yet tonight she had let herself get carried away like a teenager. The sooner she realized that these emotions were simply prompted by unruly hormones and an unfulfilled need for physical intimacy, the quicker she would rid herself of the hollowness and desolation assailing her.

Though covered with plump cushions, the bed for some reason looked singularly uninviting. She suppressed another unhappy sigh. Anticlimax, she thought. It had been such an exciting night and now she was alone again. She would have a hot bath to unwind and then try to get some sleep.

Luna lay back in the warm water, unable to shake off these bittersweet thoughts despite her self-remonstrations. She was still cherishing the memory of the gypsy's eyes as he sang to her. In truth, no man had ever succeeded in arousing real desire in her. One boyfriend had angrily called her frigid when she had rebuffed his advances. She'd believed him … until tonight.

If this man, this gypsy, asked her to, she could imagine unashamedly giving herself to him; and she found the whole idea of it reckless in the extreme. The new fever that set her on fire and made every inch of her body pulse with desire for a stranger was more frightening than the prospect of never knowing fulfilment through lovemaking.

Twenty minutes later, she was in bed but not asleep. Her laptop was on her knees and she was reading her emails. One was from Ted Vandenberg, with a list of addresses and telephone numbers of colleagues from the magazine she could contact if she wanted. Then there was one from Aunt Bea, hoping she'd had a good flight and was enjoying Barcelona.

Luna sent a brief reply to her aunt. With it, the reason for her being in Spain returned, bringing back a wave of sadness about Angelina that heightened her pensive mood. Her cousin had been in Barcelona when she was first diagnosed with cancer. Luna could almost picture her now, walking briskly – almost dancing – along the Spanish streets, copper hair swinging in tune with the lilt of her hips. Always laughing, always joking – never really serious about anything, not even her illness at the beginning. To Luna, it had felt as if a light had been extinguished with Angelina's passing and, since then, she had found the world a darker place.

Sighing, she closed her eyes briefly and took a deep breath. Enough of these maudlin thoughts … Thinking constantly about the darling cousin who was lost to her, and the gypsy she'd never have, was not going to do her any good. She needed to forget any might-have-beens and start adopting the right mindset for the job that awaited her in Cádiz.

She glanced at her diary. At three in the afternoon she was due to attend the conference at the hotel on orthodox and alternative pain management. Professor Arthur Goldsmith, one of the speakers, was a visiting American from Johns Hopkins University and hailed worldwide as an authority on the subject. Hopefully, it would offer some useful background information before she started at the clinic. In the evening, after the conference, she planned to go to the reception and book signing.

She would be leaving Barcelona the next day.

Her mind flitted back to the bar and the gypsy singer. A surge of regret washed over her again but she steadfastly ignored it.

Finally sleepy, she closed her laptop and turned off the lights. She hoped that tonight she would not dream.

*   *   *

Luna woke at noon, relieved to have slept deeply. The flamenco singer was still at the forefront of her mind like the lingering refrains of the music she could not forget either.

Rising from her bed, she went to the French windows, full of midday sun, and opened them. The warm rays of spring sunshine poured pleasantly into the room and she stepped out on to the balcony, fascinated by the panoramic view that extended to the horizon like a hazy coloured postcard. The hotel was on the edge of Eixample, a residential part of the city surrounded by magnificent villas and, from her vantage point, she could see their riotous gardens, tall cypresses needling into the blue sky. There were palms along the promenades and, in the side street immediately below, jacaranda trees spread their beautiful branches, laden with purple flowers.

It had not yet been twenty-four hours since she'd arrived in Spain and already she was surprised by how much this country was getting under her skin.

Luna asked room service to bring up some coffee and a bowl of fruit. She had a few hours before the conference started so she sat in an armchair next to the window, savouring a bunch of juicy grapes and drinking her double espresso, flicking through her notes as she did so.

She was looking forward to Goldsmith's talk. It had meant a detour before flying to Jerez, the closest airport to Cádiz, but she felt it would be worth it. The man was one of the few proponents of alternative medicine that she had any time for, and she had read his book on hypnosis in pain management and thought his arguments persuasive. Coming to Barcelona for the talk had another benefit too: hypnosis, she knew from her folder of notes, was one of the interests of the man she was about to secretly profile.

She flicked through her file on Dr Rodrigo Rueda de Calderón.

Since she had accepted Ted Vandenberg's assignment, Luna had researched her subject. She had learnt what she could about Dr Rueda de Calderón from the internet. He too had written about hypnotism – mostly in press features and online articles – and it formed part of his programme of alternative cancer therapies. Although she didn't agree with many of his theories and had thought the tone of his articles arrogant, his arguments were intriguing and persuasive. In fact, his entire résumé was intriguing, she had to admit.

Dr Rueda de Calderón's reputation was built upon his work as a brilliant, but somewhat renegade, oncologist. His medical career had begun with the conventional treatment of cancer with chemo- and radiotherapy; but then his work had very quickly diversified, before he became almost wholly taken up with his own herbal treatments, the majority of which, Luna presumed, hadn't been near proper trials. Of course, it made sense that in the fight against cancer you have to build the body's natural defences but, when it came to peddling hope in some arcane Amazonian jungle root or gypsy herbs straight out of folklore, Luna believed that a very firm line should be drawn.

Psychological support and healthy foods alongside conventional treatments were all well and good, she thought, but some of his wayward treatments could be a one-way trip to disaster for a cancer sufferer, especially if they were led to believe that they offered an actual cure, thereby encouraging the patient to ignore traditional medical treatments. The man was passionate in advocating his programme's potential, but such passion could be dangerous. It was unclear whether he was in it for the money, but no doubt that would become apparent once she started digging.

Luna closed the file and rested it on her lap. She looked forward to challenging him on some of his more dubious practices.

Discreetly, of course: she was supposed to be at Rueda de Calderón's clinic as a researcher and, though privately she might regard his theories as pure quackery, it wouldn't do to let her real opinions slip out in an unguarded moment. Opinions she must try not to cloud with emotion.

No, Luna assured herself, Angelina's death had not made her any more biased. As a true disciple of evidence-based medicine, she had long held strong views on alternative therapies.

*   *   *

Luna took her time to shower and dress. She loved clothes and refused to compromise her femininity where they were concerned, even if she attracted unwanted male attention as a result. She chose a pure silk, crepe-de-Chine suit in light pistachio. The design was classic, feminine and chic, with pointed lapels and gold buttons. She put her hair up in an elegantly simple ballerina chignon and kept her make-up to a minimum. With jewellery, likewise, Luna's motto was 'less is more', so she wore a pair of classic button-style earrings in twenty-four-carat gold with a subtle web pattern, which were discreet without being apologetic. A wide gold bangle adorned her slender wrist, giving the finishing touch to a very slick outfit.

Glancing in the mirror before leaving the room, she ran her hands over the matt silken surface of her suit and slipped on a matching pair of Charles Jourdan signature high-heeled pistachio pumps. Her reflection was professional and elegant – exactly the image she wanted to portray. She lingered for a few more minutes, giving her notes a final look, before finding her way to the conference hall on the first floor of the hotel.

The noise of the hall enfolded Luna as she paused momentarily in the doorway to gaze across the wide, crowded room. With its tall, broadly arched windows, a characteristic of the whole hotel, the interior was bright and sunny with interesting paintings on the wall and a ceiling whose shape gently undulated like a wave. Her eyes flicked around, searching for a seat at the front. There were a couple of empty places on either side of the central aisle in the first row. She walked purposefully to the front of the room. '*Es este asiento reservado?* Is this chair reserved?' she enquired of the grey-haired gentleman who was sitting next to one of the empty seats.

He looked up at her amiably and shook his head. '*No, estado esperando por ti*, no, it has been waiting for you,' he gallantly told her. She smiled back at him in appreciation. Very nicely put. Spanish men were so courteous, she thought, as she sat down and took out her notebook.

There was a stir in the room and the noisy chattering whittled down to a gentle murmur as Professor Goldsmith took his place on the platform. He smiled and nodded to the crowd, tapped the microphone and cleared his throat.

'Ladies and gentlemen, thank you for inviting me to speak today …'

Still absorbed in her notes as Goldsmith began his talk, Luna felt a rush of air brush past her as a latecomer took the empty seat on the other side of the aisle.

'So, how does hypnosis work to tackle the pain and side-effects of cancer treatment?' Goldsmith continued. 'To put it at its simplest, imagine a patient believing they can see, feel and taste the cool refreshment of a mint leaf whenever they are beginning to experience the unpleasant feeling of nausea and that new sensation simply replaces the unwanted sensation. Or, how visualizing their favourite cottage by a lake might take away the pain of the needle biopsy in their physical body because a pleasant detachment has taken place …'

But Luna did not hear the rest of the professor's remark, which disappeared in the haze of her confused mind as she lifted her head. She froze, startled, then embarrassed. For a second, imagining her eyes were deceiving her, her thoughts swam in her head, a strange and disconcerting mixture of dream and reality.

She stared in disbelief at the man who had taken the seat a few feet away from her and was now pulling a pen and notebook out of a leather briefcase: the man who, only hours ago, had sent her pulses racing. All sound in the room had faded abruptly, replaced by the heavy beat of her heart resounding loudly in her ears.

He had swapped his clingy jeans and discoloured T-shirt for a superbly tailored beige suit, crisp white shirt that emphasized his deep tan and a maroon Jacquard silk tie. The impression was casual, laid-back elegance. His glossy dark hair seemed slightly shorter, neatly combed back behind his ears, its wavy inclination kept in check. There were no unruly tendrils over his forehead today, she noted, but the aura – the powerful sexual charisma that transcended ordinary good looks – was still there.

Her brain tried to grapple with what she was seeing. The gypsy singer was here – *but why?*

Now, as he propped one ankle on the opposite knee and leaned back in his chair, his eyes, darkly blue as the Aegean Sea, swept around the audience and fell on Luna's face. They flashed with surprise and then deepened to curiosity. Time stood still as she felt herself the captive of their shimmering azure depths. Her facial muscles tightened and she caught her lower lip between her teeth as her heart melted in her chest. Still, she held his gaze almost defiantly. Pride would not allow her to betray how flustered she was feeling.

He raised an eyebrow, those sculpted lips curving into a slow smile. His dark head gave her a nod of acknowledgement.

With enormous difficulty, she managed to drag her gaze from his, focusing on her notes, her heart thumping.

From then on, Luna spent most of the lecture in total turmoil, from time to time casting furtive sideways glances at him through her lashes, her scrambled brain unable to concentrate on what Professor Goldsmith was saying. Each time she looked over at the dark-haired stranger, she noticed a shadow of a smile pass briefly over his features as if sensing he was being watched.

She was impatient for this agony to end and at last Goldsmith reached his conclusion. 'Ladies and gentlemen, speaking as both clinician and open-minded researcher, I hope I've been able to shed some light on the complex issues surrounding hypnosis and visualization used in the palliative care of cancer patients.'

Applause broke out and the professor gestured his thanks as the clapping calmed down. Meanwhile Luna sat rigid in her seat, furious with herself for having managed to take in almost nothing of his lecture.

'And now for any questions,' he said, looking around the room expectantly. 'Ah, my esteemed colleague! I thought we might hear from you.' Goldsmith smiled and leaned forward on his lectern.

Luna turned her head to see that the professor's 'esteemed colleague' was her gypsy-turned-gentleman.

She had the perfect excuse to look at him now. If he had been exceedingly handsome in her memory of him at the tavern the previous night, today he was impossibly so. In fact, 'handsome' came nowhere near describing him. Just looking at him again, seated with languid ease, his ruggedly perfect features in profile, made her stomach execute another alarming somersault. She wanted to look away but couldn't, every nerve ending crackling in anticipation of hearing him speak.

The dark-haired stranger grinned and nodded courteously. 'Professor Goldsmith, your arguments are fascinating, of course. I would be interested to know where you stand on those cases where hypnosis is used as a frontline defence in itself, helping to instigate the necessary battle against cancer cells when chemotherapy isn't used at all? Mind over matter, if you like.'

His voice was warm and compelling. It filled Luna's head like the slow, deep resonance of a bass string.

She looked away, glancing around the room. The audience seemed to hang on to his every word. He had a dominating presence, not merely because of the confidence of his statements, but from the sheer strength of his personality.

Goldsmith nodded. 'It's true to say that mainstream medical researchers have never gone far enough, perhaps, in their assertions.'

'Yes, Professor. And isn't that because it's simply not in the pharmaceutical companies' interest for the relevant trials to be held?' replied the stranger, without missing a beat. 'I'm not sure whether anyone else in the audience has an opinion,' he added.

He looked around and sought Luna's eyes, then stared at her thoughtfully.

Luna tried to steady herself. Her head was starting to ache as if it were stuffed with cotton wool, making it impossible for her to think straight. The stranger's eyes were piercing and intense. He really did have the most sensual lips. Moments passed which seemed like years – precious seconds filled with vain longing, during which Luna sent up a silent prayer for help. All the questions and answers she would normally have fired back at such remarks had gone out of her head. She felt her face burn as a light flush crept up her cheeks.

And now his stare slid away from her and more members of the audience were taking up his question. Luna wryly noted almost all the remarks came from females. Women were flocking to him in the same way they had in the tavern. Oh yes, women clearly liked him … loved him passionately was more like it. She had no doubt more than one heart had been lost to his dazzling magnetism.

Rebellion stirred. She was not going to be one of the pack; she had seen how some of her girlfriends' relationships had ended when they had been blinded by good looks and charisma. Whether this man was a gypsy or a scholar, she would not sit here stupefied, losing all sense of pride and letting her dignity melt in a puddle on the ground.

Luna waited for a female member of the audience to finish her breathily earnest agreement with the gypsy-scholar and then cleared her throat.

'But surely our knowledgeable speaker here admits that hypno-therapy has drawn its fair share of critics over the years for good reason,' she ventured in as strong a voice as she could muster. 'Without rigorous trials to assure the public it is safe to use in the field of cancer, who knows what side effects might present themselves. Besides there may be a danger of masking the actual symptoms of pathology.'

The gypsy-scholar had turned his gaze on her. That faint shadow of a smile returned to his lips and Luna fancied she saw a gleam of gratification in his eyes.

'All very good points, *señorita*.'

At the sound of his addressing her directly, Luna swallowed.

He was agreeing with her?

'But where is the funding?' he enquired drily. 'Rigorous trials are exactly what we need to show how successful the practice has been and to convince the medical establishment, but they can't be done without money.'

'But something that depends on the suggestibility of the subject is hardly going to be taken seriously enough to warrant funding, surely?' interjected Luna, holding his gaze.

He shook his head. 'Hypnosis is not simply a matter of suggestibility. The theory behind medical hypnosis is that the body's brain and nervous system cannot always distinguish between an imagined situation and a real one.'

At this Luna felt *herself* falling into an hypnotic state, mesmerized by his ruggedly chiselled jaw.

Stay focused, an alarmed voice warned inwardly. His gaze seemed to concentrate on her even more intently, as if he knew what she was thinking and was challenging her not to look away.

'For example, as Professor Goldsmith has already described, a hypnotherapist may ask a patient to change their perception of pain. So a burning sensation on your skin feels instead like cool water.'

His gaze dipped momentarily down to her bare arm then back to her face. Her skin instantly tingled in response. This infuriating insurrection by her own body caused Luna to tilt her chin up defiantly.

'So why isn't it used more?'

She gave herself a mental kick – a stupid question.

Again, his expression was unreadable. 'Because people are nervous of it and the hardest part is getting other doctors to accept it, not just a sceptical public.'

'No wonder they're sceptical,' Luna shot back. 'There have been studies that show that hypnosis rarely eliminates chronic pain and only provides short-term relief that lasts for a few hours, let alone being a frontline defence, as you call it.'

His eyes sparkled with challenge. 'You are welcome to your views, *señorita*.'

At this he became more animated and shifted in his chair, turning his body towards her. He lifted a perfectly muscled leg to rest on his other thigh; in so doing making his trousers stretch tightly across it in a way that made Luna will herself not to look.

'But I have conducted my own trials and have encountered some truly remarkable effects, ones that repeat themselves in patient after patient.' His lips twitched almost imperceptibly. 'You seem to need convincing, and I'd be very happy to show you results of our findings myself.'

Luna's eyes widened slightly at this veiled provocation. He was clearly enjoying himself at her expense and she found herself scrambling around for a suitable response, annoyed that he was besting her. However, just at that moment, Goldsmith intervened to wrap up the lecture.

'I see we have run out of time, though we could carry on this fascinating discussion for many hours, I'm sure.'

Luna was left frustrated. Her arguments, martialled now and at the ready, were never aired. She was determined not to look at the gypsy-scholar, as she now thought of him. She did not want to see what expression he had on his face. Was he laughing at her? Did he sense her humiliation at feeling so exposed, so foolish? All she wanted now was to get away as quickly as possible and so without a further glance, Luna hurried out of the conference hall with a few frayed shreds of her self-possession still attached, unaware that his intense blue gaze followed her.

*   *   *

Ten minutes later, Luna sat in her room cogitating, furious with herself.

She was a normal, reasonable person; she had never been shy or introverted. On the contrary, she had always prided herself on being sociable and outgoing, with a fair amount of self-confidence and guts that had carried her through the various tragedies in her life. So why had she behaved earlier this afternoon like a lovesick teenager, nervous, tongue-tied and coy? It was so out of character.

She had spent hours pining after her gypsy singer but, as soon as she had been given a second chance to meet him, she had blown the opportunity by first letting her intellectual pride get the better of her, and then losing her nerve into the bargain. Her gypsy singer had turned out to be a gypsy-scholar. It should have been a perfect scenario. She could have used their debate as an excuse to go and speak to him afterwards.

Luna stared at the blue file that was taunting her on the table, witness to the amount of time she had devoted to reading up on this subject. No, she told herself, indulging her naïve fantasies was exactly what she should *not* have done. What had she been thinking? Her mind should never have been clouded by such whimsical emotions when she needed to focus on a professional situation. She had collected controversial articles on hypnotism and could have confronted him far more competently with her knowledge than she had just now. If she'd managed to destroy his point of view it would have been a confidence-building warm-up for the assignment she had been given. How could she have let herself down so completely?

Outside the light was fading to the soft pastels of early evening when Luna finally got up. Distant evening traffic noises and the strange smells of the night wafted in through the open window, bringing with them nostalgic memories. Yesterday she was still light-hearted. The cool breeze touched her cheek. She shivered and closed the window. She felt numb and lonely, a new feeling to her. She thought of the reception in honour of the publication of Professor Goldsmith's book. No doubt *he* would be there.

She would see him again.

An alarming sense of expectancy swirled through her veins, an altogether frightening and enthralling feeling that made her edgy.

A hot bath eased some of the tension, sheer heaven to sink into the scented water and play with the bubbles. It brought back memories of childhood bath-time in California. She recalled how intrigued she was by the various bottles of scent, creams, shower gels and cosmetics on her grandmother's bathroom washstand. Grandma Ward, whom she adored, used to allow her to choose her own fragrance of the week and, with bath-time becoming instantly more exciting that way, Luna had been less reluctant to come up from the beach at the end of those sun-soaked days.

The alarm of her mobile phone made Luna jump, reminding her that there was a reception to attend and she must get dressed. At lunchtime, she had asked room service to refresh the dress she had chosen for the occasion. It was now hanging on the cupboard door. A couple of months back she had bought it at a sale in one of the boutiques on Sixth Avenue. The simplicity of the pale-peach, brushed-silk garment displayed in the window had caught her eye. She loved its knife-pleated, tiered and scalloped skirt and its square neckline. Spaghetti straps had always suited her.

Though still angry about her foolishness that afternoon, the hot bath had been soothing and had restored her calm composure. With a fresh wave of enthusiasm she began to dress.

She was going to put her hair up but then decided to let it fall loosely around her shoulders, so she brushed it until it was silky and shining. Though quite pale in colour, the chamomile shampoo she had used brought out her hair's summer-wheat highlights. As usual, she kept her make-up to a minimum but gave her eyes a smoky look.

She stepped into the dress. The dropped waist with its gathered detail at the front gave it a 1920s twist. To accentuate the look, she took out a long string of pearls that once belonged to her mother and had been left to her in Adalia's will. They were beautiful. She paired the necklace with a matching set of cluster-pearl earrings and slipped on some pale-gold stiletto sandals.

Luna glanced at herself in the mirror; she liked the image it reflected. If she was going to see her gypsy-scholar again, above all else she needed to feel confident and now she was more than ready to meet him again. She glanced at her watch: 7.30pm. The reception was already under way.

After turning off the lights, with a swell of anticipation she went downstairs.

CHAPTER 2

He was sitting in a comfortable alcove in the hotel lounge, waiting for her. At least it felt like he was waiting. What he was meant to be doing was concentrating on the discussion going on around him.

He and a handful of colleagues were assembled for an informal meeting in the spacious lounge that opened out from the lobby, with papers strewn over the low table they encircled. The pale marble pillars punctuating the sumptuous room rose to meet a shimmering orange rib-vaulted ceiling, forming discreet areas that afforded a degree of privacy and creating the sense of being in a colourful, Romanesque temple. Previously, it had seemed convenient to schedule a string of appointments in the hotel following Professor Goldsmith's lecture.

Now it was frustratingly ill-timed in every way.

He moved a hand restlessly through his hair. Leaning back in his plush velvet armchair, he followed the conversation with one ear but his eyes kept straying to the stairs on the right, which led to the upper floors, and then over to the left, where the gated, art-deco lifts opened out on to the lobby.

He had been too caught up with people demanding his attention after the lecture, and had kicked himself for not seizing the moment to approach her before she was gone. He could only hope that she would be attending the book signing. Perhaps she was staying in the hotel. In any case, when he'd finally joined his colleagues in the lounge, it was a profound relief to see they had chosen a place with such a good vantage point.

He was hoping that any minute she would appear.

After years of casual dalliances, of noticing beautiful women, pursuing and then conquering them, he had reached the point in his life where this had become a game of hollow rewards, giving him only a fleeting sense of excitement. These days, it took a lot to rouse him beyond an aimless interest. But this woman – this exquisite creature with her bewitching gaze and haunting beauty – had captured his attention.

After she had left El Cabo de Oro, he had been awake most of the night trying to get her out of his head. He had never been so distracted by a woman.

It was her eyes that had entranced him even more than the wildly feminine shape he had discerned beneath them. The previous night, her watchful, honey-brown irises had shimmered with so many expressions, they had hypnotized him. Intelligent, wary and questioning, they also held a surprising innocence. He wasn't used to being attracted by such a lack of guile in a woman's face. It was normally the knowing, voluptuous sort who found their way into his bed.

In that hazy bar, the room had contracted to just the two of them. Their mutual attraction was sensual, demanding and real. When the music had taken hold of him, he'd felt compelled to play only for her and she had listened to every note he sang as though she knew the song intimately. Something new then came alive in the intriguing depths of her eyes. Suddenly they had brimmed with hidden fire and temptation, with invitation and promise, and so many things he sensed she was trying to conceal. The way she had stared at him sent electric pulses through his blood. The memory of it still did.

There was a world of mystery behind that gaze that he was aching to explore and, judging by his body's emphatic response at the mere thought of her, his exploration didn't want to stop there. Those shimmering caramel eyes made him want things that would send a blush to that smooth, porcelain skin if only she could see inside his head.

It was a good thing she could not.

And now he knew there was a sharp intelligence behind her delicate beauty, and that enticed him even further.

At Goldsmith's lecture, the moment of realization that they were just a few feet away from each other had detonated the air around them like a small explosion. The shock in her expression had given way to a dignified coolness he couldn't fathom but it was a tantalizing invitation to his curiosity. Knowing she then watched him from time to time made his blood heat and his thoughts stray to places to which they should not be venturing in the middle of a lecture room.

He'd nearly lost his concentration.

Yet, once she'd challenged him, his mind had never been so focused. Before that, he had almost been willing her to speak so he could glean any clues about her, even just to hear her voice. When she had, he had neither expected her confrontation nor her tenacity. Given the obvious electricity they had shared the previous night, he wondered what had triggered such a combative response. Still, her unpredictability only served to fascinate him more. He had to admit, he had enjoyed trying to ruffle her feathers during their verbal duelling, watching her eyes flash with spirited intensity.

He smiled to himself. Oh yes, she was a challenge indeed. Something primal and urgent in him responded to the memory of it with unprecedented force.

Who was she? A foreigner, of that much he was sure: she spoke good Spanish but he had detected an accent: Scandinavian or American maybe. Why was she at the conference? Was she a doctor, a journalist, a researcher? He had noticed she wore no ring. He could not believe such a beautiful woman was single; yet there was something of the unattainable about her. So many questions swirled around in his head.

He looked up quickly again and she was there. Emerging from the gated lift with two men and a woman, with whom she was deep in conversation.

He drew in a breath, once more struck by her fresh beauty. Now he had the chance to take in all of her at his leisure. She had a slim and energetic frame. The silky dress she wore delineated her feminine curves, its thin straps showing off the pure lines of her slender neck, the delicate wings of her collarbone and her beautiful, elegant shoulders. He imagined peeling that dress off her slowly and letting his hands claim every exquisite inch of her. Blood rushed to his groin and he struggled to master his reaction but, captivated, he was unable to look away.

She glanced up and her perfectly shaped caramel eyes met his gaze and locked with it for an instant, bringing a pink rose to her cheeks before she turned away. He was surprised to find that her aloofness did not discourage him but, on the contrary, spurred on his fascination and stirred his blood uncontrollably.

His thoughts turbulent, he tried to participate in his colleagues' discussion, a fixed smile frozen on his features. He did not want to be caught openly staring at this alluring creature who had suddenly walked into his life, filling his head like lightning across an unsuspecting sky.

Every time he looked up, his eyes were drawn to the young woman like a magnet, feasting on her loveliness as, still talking to her companions, she slowly crossed the lobby, graceful and lithe as a nymph. A long, elegant string of pearls hung down between the soft swell of her breasts that, though they were small, he guessed were full, taut and feminine. Her legs were long – dancer's legs.

She was perfect. Everything about her resonated through his being, like the sweetest arpeggio of a viola or the whisper of the sea at dawn.

Perfect.

He watched her straight back as she moved towards a glass-fronted side room to the right of the lounge. Waiters were giving out champagne at the door as guests began to arrive for Goldsmith's book-signing reception. A consummate *mujer de mundo*, she was self-confident and at ease, talking and laughing with those around her as they joined the lazy flow of bodies into the room. For once he wished that he wasn't working, and regretted he had scheduled these meetings to overlap with the start of the reception. He would have to wrap things up fast in case he missed his opportunity again to speak to her.

'Would anyone like some more coffee?' The sound of his colleague's voice disrupted his absorption.

'What a good idea,' he smiled. 'Let me take care of it.'

*   *   *

Luna had spotted him in the hotel lounge as soon as she walked out of the lift. His gaze had shot up when she had appeared and she had sensed his eyes on her, as though turning her inside out and laying her bare … in every respect. It had stirred a sudden and obscure yearning, totally foreign to her body. Hot colour rushed to her cheeks, and she had quickly turned away, her nerves taut with the awareness of him.

From what she had seen, he was engaged with a group of people who didn't look like they were in a hurry to leave their table. They appeared to be in a meeting.

Perhaps he was too busy to get away, and wouldn't be coming to the reception after all. Now that he was staring at her with those sea-swept eyes, glinting with dangerous appeal even from this distance, she wasn't sure whether she was disappointed or relieved at the prospect of his not being there. It was a struggle not to look back to where he was sitting, though she knew his gaze was following her and the thought sent a tingle down her spine.

People were milling around the lobby, drawn to the tables of appetizing canapés on either side of the glass-panelled, arched doorway that led into the reception. Even though some guests were beginning to move inside, many were still chatting and mingling here, enjoying the food and drink.

Luna was caught between staying where she was and following the other guests. She didn't want to seem intimidated by the gypsy-scholar's presence, though it would have been far more comfortable to escape his view. In truth, part of her thrilled to the idea that he was watching her, only a short distance away.

She allowed herself the most furtive of glances towards him. He was resting his elbow nonchalantly on the arm of his chair, thumb and forefinger on his chin. Then, at one point when she was compelled to look over again, at the same time so did he, sending an electric wave through the room as their gazes collided. Warmth bloomed between her thighs and for a moment she was mesmerized by the intensity of his stare. Wild, mutinous passions stirred deep inside her, before she dragged her gaze away and regained her composure.

Soft music wafted from the room, just audible a notch above the many voices and sounds, the combination of which reminded her of the continuous buzzing of starlings in the early evening. A waiter carrying a tray of drinks stood before her and she helped herself to a glass of champagne in the hope it would settle her nerves. She sipped it gratefully, letting the chilled bubbles refresh her dry throat.

Guests drifted into circles and other people engaged her in conversation. Luna was too on edge to really enjoy talking to anyone, but she had learned how to circulate. There was no need to enter into a long conversation: a few strategic questions and all she had to do was listen. It always amazed her how people loved to talk about themselves. She listened and smiled and laughed, always aware of his intent gaze following her around and, though she tried to avert thoughts of him, her mind's eye was filled with the stranger. There was that same tension between them that had been there from the moment they had set eyes on each other. It made her dizzy, hollowing out her stomach, and sent her pulse racing at a terrifying pace.

She knew that if he approached her now, they would talk and their connection would be exciting. Exhilarating. Dangerous. She would surrender to this mounting passion that could destroy her and therefore reason dictated she must not stick around. She must run now, she told herself in sudden panic, and set down her glass.

He looked up abruptly and trapped Luna's gaze as she threaded her way through the ebbing crowd, which was now moving more concertedly into the reception room. She noticed he had already summoned a waiter and was scribbling something on a scrap of paper. He gave it to the young man, speaking urgently. She could see that he was impatient and annoyed.

The waiter caught up with her at the lift. There was no escaping now. He grinned broadly. 'The *señor* over there has asked me to give you this note.'

Luna took it and turned to look at the gypsy-scholar, the note unopened in her hand. His eyes searched her face for answers and he saluted her with his glass. She smiled and nodded a polite acknowledgement, and was going to move on when the waiter prompted: 'The note, *señorita*. He would like a reply to his message, *por favor*.'

She unfolded the small piece of paper, on which was written: *Will you do me the honour of having dinner with me tonight? It seems we have much to talk about.* It was signed: *A humble gypsy.*

Her eyes lit up as the thought of being with him brought an uncontrollable surge of excitement. She turned again and met his bold gaze slipping over her in silent appreciation, and her face fell.

Rationality reasserted itself and doused her like a shot of cold water.

It was the same old story with her and men. An easy seduction, she thought. *So that's what you're really after? I don't think so!* She was not about to leave herself open to the attentions of a hot-blooded Spaniard, who was only waiting for a chance to get her into bed. What a blind fool she'd been, thinking there was anything other than physical urges at play here.

Luna put up a hand to express her thanks and smiled, a pale smile, nothing broad and warm: he might mistake that for encouragement. She turned to the messenger. 'Please thank the *señor* for his kind invitation, but tell him that unfortunately I am otherwise engaged tonight.' Then on impulse she added: 'Maybe some other time.' Thereupon she hurried into the lift, closing the gates on the bemused waiter, who shrugged and walked off.

Once in the sanctuary of her room Luna went to the window and stepped out on to the balcony. She was hot and needed air, but she was trembling from head to toe and had to hold on to the balustrade as if her knees might fold under her.

She did not understand herself. What was she doing? If she gave in to these confused emotions she would burst into tears and cry her heart out. She had just thrown away an opportunity to meet someone she had last night labelled the man of her dreams. *That's precisely what you wanted, to see him again*, a little voice at the back of her head nagged incessantly. *But he made you feel cheap, like all men do*. Her mouth gave a wry tilt: no, he hadn't, not really, she admitted wistfully. Instinct told her he was different. *This* feeling was different. She was simply running away.

Luna had no doubt he wanted her, he had made no secret of it; but she was also aware that this overwhelming rush of sheer sensuality, which had invaded her mind and body ever since she had set eyes on him, was a reaction so alien to her, she was terrified. She half wished she hadn't come to Spain, or that she knew how to break free of this intoxication, which bombarded her with so many new emotions she hardly recognized herself. Or perhaps it was the idea of not giving in to these unleashed feelings that troubled her more.

She remained still as she leant against the balustrade, breathing in the night. The beauty of the scene stretched out soothingly into the distance. It was like a picture in black and gold, with the dusky sky making a dark canopy over her head; and golden stars, so much larger, it seemed, than the ones back home. A deep orange glow spread over the lit-up city, making it seem as if life were going on everywhere else, vibrantly, adventurously … passionately. She sighed and stared out over the luminous landscape. Tonight, she had coped with the situation in the only way she had known, and that was to flee: to put miles between her and the risky business of getting hurt.

This was a beautiful place but she was happy to be leaving Barcelona the next day. It had been an intense forty-eight hours, and she looked forward to quieter times in Cádiz.

*   *   *

The Jerez flight was already boarding, Luna noted, glancing up at the departures board as she hurried into Barcelona El Prat Airport. She had already checked in online and thankfully the queues were short. After speedily dropping off her bags at the check-in desk, she passed through the half-empty security hall and jogged down to the departure lounge. She was panting a little as she joined the long line of passengers at the gate waiting to board the plane.

It had been one of those mornings. Still jet-lagged, she had woken to find she had missed her wake-up call and that it was already past ten. Showering and dressing had been a hasty affair with no time for breakfast or even a cup of coffee. Reception had forgotten to book her taxi and, to top it all, there had been an accident in the city centre before they reached the motorway. Twenty minutes in a traffic jam added to the delay, during which she'd had to put up with the noise of horns blowing, brakes grinding, and gears scraping while the *Guàrdia Urbana de Barcelona* diverted the traffic, finally resulting in a race to the airport at breakneck speed.

Now, Luna gradually cooled down as the queue to the plane doors dwindled to the last handful of passengers. She was glad she had dressed comfortably: a pair of white linen cropped trousers with a white-and-pink polka-dot poplin blouse, a white linen jacket and sensible pink ballet pumps. She had no hand luggage, apart from the oversized Havana shoulder bag that held everything she might need for the journey.

'*Buenas tardes, señorita. Bienvenidos a bord.*' The steward flashed her an appreciative smile as she handed him her boarding pass. '*El asiento de la ventana, la segunda fila a la derecha*, the window seat in the second row on your right,' he added, and winked at her.

The flight was full. It was a small, regional plane, hot and cramped. A woman carrying a child and a large bag, coming close behind, jostled Luna as she was putting away her jacket in the overhead locker. Luna jerked forward and banged her head. She winced. It simply wasn't turning out to be her day at all.

Finally she took her place near the window, tidied her bag under the seat in front of her, fastened her seatbelt and tried to relax. She had barely shut her eyes when the voice of the pilot announced over the intercom that take-off would unfortunately be delayed due to the late arrival of a passenger.

Luna glanced at her watch. She was meant to be meeting the estate agent, Diego Montez, that afternoon to pick up the keys to her house in Cádiz. Rather than leaving it to *Scientific US* to arrange her accommodation, Luna had searched the internet herself for a place. She wanted control of her surroundings while staying in the city, and had found a two-bedroom house right on the beach that seemed ideal. Given the failure of the Spanish property market, it had had not been difficult to negotiate a short-term lease with the estate agent that suited her purposes. If the day continued the way it had started, she would be late for her appointment. She had better ring Montez before the plane was ready for take-off and let him know.

Her bag was full. She rummaged in it for a few moments, but couldn't find her mobile. Her whole life was contained in it and, she wondered distractedly as she checked again, how anyone ever managed before mobile phones. A growing sense of panic stole over her. Could she have left it in the taxi? That was the last time she remembered using it. Thankful that the seat beside her was empty, she began to take things out of her bag, one by one.

'*Es esto lo que busca?* Is this what you're looking for?' she heard a smooth, confident baritone ask in Spanish.

Startled, Luna's head shot up, a grateful remark on her lips, only to have it freeze, unuttered. With a plummeting heart she met the dazzling cobalt eyes of the gypsy-scholar. He was looking down at her intently, a smile playing at the corners of his mouth. So absorbed in what she was doing, Luna had been quite unaware of his approach.

Speech seemed to desert her and all she could do was stare at him. The eyes that flashed back at her with amusement were like brilliant blue flames.

'Is this what you're looking for?' The enquiry, this time in perfect English, was spoken with a seductively Spanish lilt.

'Yes, thank you,' Luna managed finally, though evidently too stunned to move. Her hand was still hovering over the contents of her bag, strewn over the seat.

He smiled, his gaze never wavering from her face. 'I found it just here on the floor, at the edge of the aisle.'

It must have fallen out of her pocket when she got bumped against the overhead locker. 'Thank you,' she repeated, summoning a faint smile and taking the phone from his hand.

His lips gave that now familiar quirk, and she caught a glimpse of gleaming white teeth as he stood there, shrugging off the jacket of his expensive-looking beige lightweight suit and laying it in the overhead locker. Her eyes strayed automatically to the open-neck shirt that clearly delineated his broad shoulders and torso. It revealed the same triangle of dark hair that had been so appealing under a T-shirt before, and she wondered how the rest of his chest might look beneath that crisp, white cotton. The thought sent every cell in her body firing to a new level, acutely aware of his nearness.

His eyes held hers again. He signalled the place next to her, which still had the pile of her paraphernalia sitting on it. 'My seat,' he murmured.

Mortified, and with a breathless apology, she began piling her belongings back into her bag, conscious of the other passengers' mild curiosity and a few glares of disapproval. The air stewardess came up to ask if there was any problem, but he dismissed her easily with his charming smile. Then he slid into the place next to Luna, laying his small briefcase under the seat in front of him and fastening his seatbelt.

Near or far, this man represented a danger Luna was incapable of handling, she thought, as hammer-beats thundered in her blood; and now he was much too close for comfort. Their arms were almost touching and she could feel the heat of sheer male energy radiating from him. Her keen awareness of his smouldering presence an inch away was a sweet nightmare, but a nightmare nevertheless. With unsteady hands she managed to send a brief message to the estate agent and, turning off her phone, she tucked it into her bag.

The stranger leaned towards her and she was conscious of the faint musky scent of his aftershave. 'Would you like a mint?' he offered with a warm smile, half reaching for his briefcase.

Luna shook her head. 'No, thank you,' she murmured politely. If only she could think of something to say.

He saved her the trouble, though she almost wished he hadn't. Settling back in his chair, his smile was still on her. 'It seems fate is determined to throw us together.' His voice was a little huskier this time.

She tried not to dwell on the images that provocative remark conjured in her head. If she'd been the sort of person to believe in fate then, right at this moment, she would have railed against it. It was certainly determined to undermine her resistance. Still, she should show more constraint now, she reminded herself. She hadn't forgotten the openly appraising look he had given her in the hotel lounge as she'd read his note. The sheer arrogance of it still smarted.

Just like other men.

Well, perhaps he was not like other men, she admitted reluctantly. Certainly he was different in ways that confused her. In fact, this gripping, powerful attraction was like nothing she had ever known.

She shook the thought loose. No matter how attractive or charismatic he might be, he was not the kind of man she should be getting mixed up with.

'I don't believe in fate, just extreme coincidences,' she said, less confidently than she would have liked.

'Not even luck then?'

'Isn't that the same thing?'

He grinned. 'In any case, as extreme coincidence has made such an effort on our behalf, we should at least know each other's name.' He turned slightly, his hand outstretched. 'My friends call me Ruy.'

Ruy. He hadn't offered his full name, which gave her the perfect excuse not to volunteer her own.

'Luna,' she said, reaching her hand towards his.

When their palms came into contact, it was all she could do not to gasp at the strange exhilaration that spread to her nerve endings. Like the rest of him, his hand was strong and well groomed. Once again, her stomach performed an unwelcome feat of acrobatics and she ignored the accompanying squeeze of disappointment when he released her hand.

'Luna,' he murmured, as if tasting the sound on his tongue. From his sinfully perfect lips, her name sounded positively decadent. 'A Spanish name. The moon, Queen of the Night … Yes, of course.' The plane was moving on to the runway now, lining up, waiting for instructions to take off. He studied her silently for a few moments. 'Where are you from?' he ventured.

'The USA,' she said. She slanted him a half-smile, noticing how his cropped curly dark hair lay in fetching wisps against a tanned neck. She cursed herself for letting her gaze wander again. If his appearance made her lose the power to think, then she would have to keep her eyes on something else. Luna reached for the inflight magazine tucked into the pocket in front of her, opening and raising it hastily to her face, not even seeing its contents. Perhaps this would give her a few moments to compose herself. She could tell that he was watching her flustered manoeuvrings with interest.

Damn him. Why didn't he just find somewhere else to look?

Leaning a little towards her, he gently took hold of the edge of the magazine and turned it around, his fingers lightly brushing against the back of her hand. The tiny shock of his touch shivered through her body and she sucked in her breath.

'Maybe this way, you'll find the article more interesting,' he whispered, his eyes dancing with mischief as she flushed bright red, realizing that she had been holding it upside down.

Luna felt an instant desire for the floor to open up and swallow her whole. She bit her lip and turned to him in a dignified manner, despite herself.

'Thank you.'

Safety procedures began over the intercom, much to Luna's relief. Having politely listened to the air hostess's instructions in case of emergency, Ruy said no more as the plane rumbled along the runway, picking up speed. Their eyes met for a split second, making her turn away abruptly from that intense and penetrating look. There was nowhere to run here.

What was wrong with her? Where was all that calm self-confidence, on which she always prided herself? Luna was not a woman who became flustered so easily. Then again she was not a woman who read her magazines upside down either.

Why was she being so coy? Deep down, she had dreamed of seeing him again. *Ruy.* The name echoed in her mind. *The man of her dreams was called Ruy.* Fate, luck or coincidence, whatever the cause of their chance meetings, she now wondered at her own maddening prevarication at every one of them. After all, she was sure he was conscious of the chemistry between them; there was no point in trying to hide it, her awkward manner had given her away. The answer to her questions came loud and clear: with dreams there must come a time of awakening, and she was protecting herself.

So she steeled herself for the flight ahead. This was going to be the longest plane journey of her life. Take-off was smooth. The jet lifted slowly, climbing gradually over the clouds before it levelled.

Inevitably, he spoke again. 'I thought I detected a twinge of an American accent,' he said. 'Your Spanish is impeccable. Are you here on holiday or for business?'

She inhaled slowly, determined to handle a simple conversation.

'Yes, and no. I was in Barcelona only for Professor Goldsmith's lecture.' She deflected his question. 'Do you live there?'

'No, I'm not from Barcelona. I was there just for a few days for the same reason.'

'And are you in the habit of singing in bars in places you're not from?' The question had popped out of her mouth before she had time to stop it …

Careful, Luna. It will seem as though you're flirting with him, she chided, appalled at herself. *Think before you speak.*

Ruy chuckled. 'It has been known to happen but I travel to Barcelona now and again. I have friends there. So are you staying in Spain for long?'

'I'm taking up a job in Cádiz on a short-term contract.' That was the truth. Besides, it was probably wise that she start practising her story so that she could settle into her undercover role.

'I'd guess you have a science background. At least from your incisive interrogation of me at Goldsmith's lecture.' His mouth twitched.

'Yes, I'm a researcher.'

'Ah, that figures.' His smile broadened at her reply and something brightened his blue gaze. 'So, Luna from the USA, you're a scientist travelling to Cádiz.'

'Yes, that's right. And so, Ruy, who isn't from Barcelona,' she said, now determined to give as good as she got, 'you're a scientist who's a gypsy singer in his spare time.'

His mouth curved devilishly, clearly enjoying her response. 'In a manner of speaking. Did you like the music?'

'Yes, I love flamenco.' Luna didn't add that it was *his* performance of flamenco that had her spellbound, that sent a shiver through her and made her feel gloriously alive.

'But you didn't stay for more.' The gleam in his eyes deepened. They twinkled at her with a bold intensity that made it almost hard for her to breathe.

'No. I needed to be up early to get some work done before Goldsmith's lecture,' she lied.

Ruy paused as if he was going to say something else but had thought better of it. 'So tell me,' he said, 'you seemed to be highly sceptical of the benefits of hypnotherapy at the lecture, despite my arguments. Does that scepticism extend to all alternative medical practices?'

'On the contrary, I'm very interested in hypnotherapy, which is why I was at the lecture,' she said, sincerely. She paused. This could be an opportunity to try out her new professional persona. Once she took up her new post, she would need to show sympathy with these ideas.

Let's make this believable.

She lifted one shoulder in a shrug. 'I think it's important to play devil's advocate, don't you? It's not about knee-jerk scepticism, but constantly questioning to find the truth. How can one strive for excellence in any discipline without truth?'

'Well put.' He grinned. 'In other words, you were testing me.'

'Perhaps. I couldn't see that anyone else in the audience was going to.'

He let out a throaty laugh. 'You have an interesting way about you, Luna. I'm sure there isn't much a man could get away with where you're concerned.'

Luna blinked. That was a rather arrogant remark. Was he implying that she was surprisingly clever for a woman, or something else entirely? She had meant to show him that his charm did not faze her, but her determination to stand up to him was not having the desired effect; instead, it seemed to be making him deliberately provocative. Maybe she had played this all wrong. Annoyance bubbled inside her.

'I'm interested to know,' Ruy continued, 'where your question-ing takes you when it comes to non-orthodox treatments. Have you ever been hypnotized, for example?'

Only by you, she thought warily. His expressive eyes seemed to shift in colour and now were almost aquamarine in this light.

She slanted her gaze to the magazine on her lap, wishing there was more space between them.

'No, I've never been hypnotized myself, but I find the idea interesting,' she went on, keen to move the conversation away from herself. 'Whether or not you agree with its benefits, though, it's been bundled with other "alternative" therapies, many of which, like so-called energy healing, get a bad press with the medical community.'

'True,' he agreed. Luna couldn't help but notice the line of his smooth-shaven jaw as he rubbed his chin. 'But being from a gypsy family, I've come to realize that there are definitely more things in heaven and earth, as they say.'

So he was a gypsy. Suddenly she was fascinated to know how a man from gypsy stock had come to be the elegantly besuited person next to her. She knew little about the *gitano* culture apart from the stereotypes that painted them as a socially isolated people. But perhaps it was best not to show her interest by questioning him further, she decided.

'Would you like a drink?' he asked. 'A glass of wine or a gin and tonic perhaps? I think the stewardess will be heading in our direction soon.'

'No, thank you. I never drink on planes.'

'Nervous of flying?'

'Not at all,' she said, glancing at him. She *was* feeling nervous, though not of flying. 'I just can't really see the attraction of alcohol at thirty thousand feet. This isn't a bar or a club. An airplane is a functional space, designed to get you from one place to another as fast as possible,' she continued, shifting uncomfortably in her seat. 'Why would you want to drink during the journey?'

'Some people find it relaxing,' he pointed out. Then, with a glint in his eye, he lowered his voice: 'By the way, massage is one of those complementary practices that I'd put high on my list.

It's been proven to alleviate many discomforts. You might find it useful yourself to relax.'

'I don't need to relax,' she said, her voice brusquer than she intended. As if to demonstrate, she tilted her head back against the headrest and scanned the switches above, darting a single look at him in annoyance.

He gave another deep chuckle. 'Oh, but I think you do.' His gaze perused her face, then momentarily skimmed down further, before locking on her eyes again. 'Your body is tense and you're frowning.'

He had noticed her body. Now she was burning with self-consciousness. An all-too-familiar hot sensation pooled deep down between her thighs, melting her centre of gravity. Disturbed by the unwelcome reaction, and remembering his bold regard of her before, she became defensive.

'Well, perhaps it's because you keep looking at me in a strange way.'

Ruy stared at her intently. He certainly didn't seem to mind scrutinizing her with open curiosity whenever he liked, Luna thought, struggling to ignore the sensual effect he had on her, to the extent that she was forced to distract herself by feigning a sudden interest in the contents of her bag. Maybe all Spanish men were like this, she speculated, even the sophisticated ones. Yet beneath the polished exterior that Ruy now presented, there was still a sense of contained recklessness about him, a smouldering fire in his gaze that spoke of the gypsy in him. Its alarming power made her lose the ability to think straight.

'It's your hair and your eyes, against your skin,' he said, jolting her from her reverie so that she looked up quickly. 'You must forgive me if I find the arresting combination of light-gold silk, brown honey and alabaster skin fascinating. It's very rare over here. *La Luna*. Fair and perfect, like moonlight.'

Now he was openly flirting with her. The thrill of it sent a renewed wave of awareness rippling through her body but she smothered it with an inner warning to remember her resolution. She was responding to him when she should be resisting. Whether she was flattered or alarmed by Ruy's attention, one thing was certain – she had failed to discourage him.

You've only yourself to blame, Luna thought.

She kept her voice steady. 'Do you do this often?'

'Do what often, fly?'

'No, deliberately provoke women you've never met before and then pay them absurd compliments.' There … she'd done it again – prodding him; she was the one being provocative … almost rude. She didn't recognize herself. Luna wasn't normally susceptible to this sort of male charm. Usually she just ignored it but Ruy had got under her skin and made her say things she didn't mean to say.

Ruy looked surprised at the rebuke and laughed. 'Well, possibly.'

Yes, she had thought as much. *Just like other men*, her mind intoned. The worst of it was her own attitude had encouraged him.

He gave her his most disarming grin. 'But with you, Luna, I do actually mean them. Besides, we have met before. Twice, as I recall. And both times have given me many reasons to pay you compliments.' He wrestled a serious look back on to his face. 'But I don't think I've ever enjoyed provoking a woman as much before, so you're mistaken in that assumption.'

Insufferable man!

Ruy leaned in, and Luna caught the intriguing scent of his aftershave, mixed with clean masculinity. 'Perhaps it's your unusual self-possession,' he murmured. 'It's a provocative thing for a man. It makes him want to undermine it somehow, and see what lies beneath.'

Luna silently caught her breath. If she had hoped to hear an apology, clearly she was to be disappointed. He found this an amusing game and she was merely another in a long line of women, no doubt. Still, she deserved it for having indulged herself this far.

She replaced the magazine and leaned down to retrieve her bag from under the seat in front. Her pulse was thundering.

'Well, I'm sure some women find being undermined by a man highly attractive,' she said as evenly as she could, without looking at him. 'But it's not a sport I find particularly interesting.' She fished a notebook out of her bag and made a show of flicking through it. Hopefully this would signal to him that the conversation was at an end.

'I was teasing, Luna. Just ignore me.' She could hear the grin in his voice.

She looked over her book at him, fixing a polite smile on her face that said, *I intend to.*

Ruy seemed finally to cede defeat. He reached for his briefcase and swung it on to his knees, pulling out his laptop.

She kept her eyes on her notebook, hoping he would not try to talk to her again. The sun was shining. Luna momentarily shifted her attention to the small oval window. They were flying above the clouds, which were like a bed of cotton wool below them.

Ruy made no further attempt at conversation. His mind and energies seemed to be wholly absorbed by his laptop, his face taut with concentration, his fingers moving on the keyboard with practised ease.

Though a lack of communication was exactly what Luna had intended, it disturbed her slightly that Ruy no longer appeared to have any awareness of her. When the hostess came round with the trolley of drinks, he ordered a neat whisky, which Luna noticed he downed in one gulp. As much as she tried to ignore his presence, it was difficult when all she wanted was to sit there and stare at him, taking in every detail of his face, and from time to time her gaze strayed in his direction, observing the lean line of his jaw and the clear moulding of his lips.

Putting her notebook away, she took out a travel guide on Cádiz she had bought at the airport in New York, but had not yet looked at. She might as well learn about the town in which she would be living for the next few months. For the rest of the flight, Luna paid studious attention to her book, battling with her wavering concentration.

Finally, after what seemed an eternity, the pilot's voice came over the intercom. 'Ladies and gentlemen, we are making our descent towards La Parra Airport. The weather in Jerez is seventeen degrees centigrade, with sunny, clear blue skies.'

Luna looked out of the window. The clouds were beginning to scatter in different directions into wispy trails and she could see the pattern of the earth. Above the edge of the Atlantic Ocean, they flew over white cities with avenues of trees and a jungle of apartment blocks, and hillsides clothed in green.

The perfect azure sky mirrored in calm, blue sea.

As the plane continued its slow descent and they came closer to land, she could see the frill of foam left by the rhythmic break and fall of the waves, delicate as lace against the sable sand. The Bay of Cádiz was alive with craft of all sizes. Then there were vineyards, and houses with turquoise swimming pools shimmering in the afternoon sun.

'Is this your first visit to Cádiz?' The warm tone invaded her thoughts once more.

She turned and was faced with Ruy's sparkling gaze.

'I noticed you were reading about the city,' he explained, gesturing towards her book. A smile flitted across his face, reaching his eyes. She tried not to find them fascinating and bewitching still as she met their magnetic caress.

'Yes. I've not been to Cádiz before,' she admitted reluctantly. Luna didn't want to tell him that she'd not been back to Spain since she was child – that would only invite more conversation. She wondered how she was going to brush him off politely once they were off the plane, even though part of her regarded that idea with deep regret.

'I'm going to Cádiz myself,' he went on, 'and would be delighted to give you a lift in my private limousine.'

Luna's eyebrows shot up as her heart rate accelerated. He was actually making a pass at her.

'Sorry?'

He mistook the incredulous look in her eyes. 'Oh, it's not a big, luxurious one, just an old vintage model, but it's very comfortable and there's plenty of space,' he told her, hopeful eyes fixed on her face.

The arrogance of the man! This Ruy whatever-his-name-was had really got the wrong idea about her. Did he actually think that she would allow herself to be picked up by a virtual stranger, even one with a comfortable limousine? Again she chastized herself for being duped by foolish hope and naïvety. She was merely a challenge to his male ego.

Luna, you're an intelligent woman. Why did you let yourself be seduced by a foolish dream?

She had to put a stop to this before it got out of hand; especially now he knew she was going to Cádiz. It had already gone too far.

Luna squared her shoulders, refusing to let him see how disconcerted she was, all self-consciousness having vanished into thin air and replaced by rising hackles to combat his audacity.

'*Señor*, we hardly know each other. Don't you think you're being a little presumptuous, thinking I'd get into a car with a virtual stranger?' Her amber eyes glared at him, scarcely concealing her indignation, but her voice was calm. 'What makes you think that having refused to have dinner with you yesterday, and today having made it quite clear I'm not open to overtures from a stranger, however charming, that I'd be so naïve as to accept a ride in your limousine, luxurious or not?'

Ruy's cobalt eyes burned into hers as he spoke in low, soothing tones. 'I don't feel like we're strangers, Luna.' He gave a slight tilt of his head and looked at her searchingly. 'You're going to Cádiz and so am I. Again, you must forgive me, but I can't pretend not to find you fascinating. Neither can I ignore that you are as beguiling as moonlight, living up to your name. But trust me, I meant no offence.'

To her horror, Luna found herself blushing. This man's words had a stride of their own, coursing through her veins in bewitching temptation. It made her feel vulnerable, and that was the last thing she wanted to project.

She tossed her head and arched an eyebrow in an attempt to seem contemptuous. 'Your looks and your way with words no doubt make it easy for you to twist women round your little finger. Unfortunately for you, this particular woman is not taken in at all. I'd be grateful if you left me alone. And please don't think of trying to seek me out in Cádiz to change my mind.' Her voice was firm, even cold, and she had somehow managed to look him straight in the eye without flinching, she noted with satisfaction.

He froze. For an instant, a strange emotion flashed across his face. It was so brief she could have imagined it. His mouth quirked in a grim smile.

'And now who is being presumptuous?' he said dryly.

It was a simple response but it was as if he had hit her with a bucket of icy water.

The aircraft wheels landed on the runway with a dull sound, echoing the thud Luna felt in her heart at Ruy's words. Her thoughts blanked off. The plane slowed to taxi to the terminal. She gave him a sideways glance. He had leaned his head back against his seat and his eyes were closed. Dark lashes fanned out on a tanned face. It was really unfair that a man should have such long, thick eyelashes. His hands rested on his closed laptop; strong hands with long, tapering fingers and beautifully groomed nails.

Having burned her boats, Luna's eyes moistened infuriatingly as the impact of what she had just done hit her.

The plane ground to a halt and the seatbelt sign switched off. Ruy opened his eyes and passed a hand over his head, fingers raking through his thick, black hair. Unfastening his seatbelt, he pulled his hard, lean frame up out of the seat with one arm. He looked completely relaxed. Bending over, he pulled his briefcase from under the seat in front of him, slipped his laptop inside and, without so much as a glance in Luna's direction, stood at the edge of the aisle, lending her a view of his broad shoulders.

He forged ahead to the front, leaving her behind. Having recovered her jacket in the overhead bin, Luna disembarked with the other passengers. Once in the baggage claim area, waiting for her suitcases, her eyes eagerly scanned the crowd milling around the carousel. She looked for his tall, elegant figure, but he had disappeared altogether.

*   *   *

Ruy was out of the plane in no time. He had no luggage, so he made his way immediately to the exit of the small, neat airport building and out into the afternoon sun, looking for Chico.

The thought of seeing his old friend usually put a smile on Ruy's face, but that afternoon his mood was unusually pensive.

He had tried to ignore the wild emotion that had taken over his senses since he first set eyes on Luna and now he had bumped into her three times in twenty-four hours. Seeing her suddenly again on the plane had provoked an immediate rush of desire and for a while he had found it difficult to drag his gaze from her. She had tied her hair back carelessly into a ponytail and her skin, devoid of make-up, was luminous.

So young, so innocent, and so indescribably beautiful.

Normally, innocence was not something that beguiled him but with this woman it was enticingly combined with a feisty defiance that did strange and wonderful things to him.

She may not have believed in fate but he did. Particularly when he'd learned her name.

Luna. It had to be the same Luna. He'd detected the American accent and then found out she was heading to Cádiz. At that point, he had quietly acknowledged that the game was on, taking a mischievous pleasure in having the advantage. Granted, she wasn't the kind of woman who was likely to find his spontaneous ruse amusing, but he would cross that bridge later. Perhaps he shouldn't have indulged himself, but he'd enjoyed their banter all the more for it. Besides, something about this surprising, intoxicating woman made him curious to know what made her tick.

He wanted to know so badly, it almost alarmed him. So he was disappointed that Luna had remained stubbornly cool and had insisted on misinterpreting his intentions. She had reacted as if they were complete strangers and he was trying his luck. True, his past was not blameless. With any other woman he would have made a much more obvious move and then enjoyed the gratification that swiftly followed. He wasn't sure what to call this unfamiliar feeling that unfurled swiftly in his chest, alongside the unparalleled heat in his loins, when he thought of her, but his intentions towards Luna were honourable. Something about her had held him back, even though he recognized the spark of fire in her eyes and what it meant: the attraction was there.

He'd seen the signs of female interest before, but Luna was far more difficult to read: she was complicated, unpredictable. There was a story behind her hesitant gaze that piqued his fascination. She was different to any other woman he'd ever met – as fresh as a spring morning, with a lively intelligence that excited him as much as the bewitching amber pools of her eyes or the alluring curves of her body. As for her attempts at proud self-control, the vulnerability she sought to hide slipped through at the edges, tinged with sadness …

Why did she not trust him? Maybe she had been hurt. Obviously a woman with those angelic looks must have numerous men after her. Yet she seemed so innocent, so fresh, so untouched.

Now that he had found her, he was determined not to be put off, no matter how tough the obstacles. So he strove to control his rising passion, instinctively aware that if he frightened her at the outset, he would damage his cause irreparably. Still, it had all gone wrong. She had slammed the door in his face.

Ruy scanned the outside of Jerez La Parra Airport; the building was fronted by a neat line of palm trees, partly shading a long row of cars. His eyes found the waiting vintage 1947 Austin limousine, its maroon and black body shining in the afternoon sun. Leaning against it was a tall man, built like an ox, his long black hair tied back in a ponytail. He was smoking a cigarette, which he flicked it to the ground when he saw Ruy approach. A broad grin split his weathered face, revealing a couple of missing teeth.

Ruy dropped his bag to the ground.

'Chico!'

He clapped his hands on his friend's shoulders.

Ruy had known Chico since they were boys and looked upon the gypsy as the older brother he'd never had. In fact, they were more than brothers, and Chico was one of the only people in whom he ever confided.

'Ruy! It's good to have you back, *hermanito*, little brother.' Chico grabbed the younger man's neck in the crook of his arm and gave him a rough embrace, before ruffling his hair with one massive hand. He gave a quick pull to the lapel of Ruy's tailored jacket. 'I keep forgetting how good you always look in fancy clothes.'

Ruy pushed away from him with a playful jab to Chico's solid wall of stomach. He gestured at his friend's ripped jeans and loud

Hawaiian shirt. 'And I see you've put on your best outfit to meet me from the airport. I'm touched.'

Chico's coal-black eyes, a little close together, made him appear slightly inscrutable, though he managed a comically indignant look. 'What can I say, eh? My chauffeur's uniform is at the drycleaners. Besides, this is my lucky shirt. I wore it when I asked Morena to marry me.'

'Lucky for you, unlucky for Morena,' Ruy laughed, dodging a swipe from Chico, who grinned.

'Even Morena isn't immune to my charm and good looks. Come on, give me that bag, you little brat,' he said, throwing him the car keys. 'You can drive.'

As the old limo sped away from Jerez, Ruy leant his forearm on the edge of the open window, enjoying the warm breeze rushing in and watching the honey-brown fields pass by. Under a hot cobalt-blue sky, the scenery gradually gave way to clumps of dark-green juniper trees and lines of olive groves laid over the softly undulating landscape.

He was glad to be going home.

'So, Ruy, when will we be seeing you at the camp?' Chico lit up a cigarette and blew the smoke sideways out of his mouth. 'Carmencita is big now and due in a couple of weeks. She and Juan want to see you before the birth.'

'Sure, I'll come. Just as soon as I get a few things sorted.'

Luna will be in Cádiz, Ruy thought. It was only a matter of time before they met again and this time he would not mess things up.

Chico drew on his cigarette and stared out of the window. 'Your father said he would pay a visit too but we haven't seen him in a while. The business seems to take up more of his time these days.'

Ruy sighed. 'He should make more time. I sometimes wonder if *Papá* remembers where he came from.'

Chico glanced across at Ruy. 'Of course he does. If he didn't, he wouldn't have let you run around the camp since you were knee-high. Exposed you to your *Caló* roots.'

'Yes, I suppose.'

'No "suppose", Ruy. *Gitano* blood still runs strong in his veins. Make no mistake, as the gypsy queen's eldest son he did his duty, sure enough. But times have changed now. Every man makes his own way in the world. You and your father are not so different. You've always followed your star, ignored what other people have said.'

There was a silence while Chico eyed his young friend between drags on his cigarette.

'So, *hermanito*, spill the beans.'

Ruy looked sideways at Chico and then back to the road. 'What do you mean?'

'You think you can fool me? I know you too well. Did something happen in Barcelona? If I didn't know better, I'd say it was a woman.'

Ruy frowned. He should have known that he could never get anything past his *gitano* friend.

Chico let out a rumbling chuckle. 'But no woman ever made you look like that.'

'Okay, okay, you win.' Ruy smiled ruefully. 'Yes, it's a woman.'

'But not just any woman.'

'No.'

'In that case, I'm assuming this woman has succeeded in evading the famous Ruy charm?'

Ruy shrugged. '"I'm not looking for male attention" is certainly written all over her, if that's what you mean.'

'You want to know your problem?'

'No, but I have a feeling you're going to tell me.'

'It's that women have always fallen at your feet,' Chico continued, without drawing breath, 'because you're a handsome, charming rascal and they've always let you know it. Though I can't see it myself.' He turned his head, grinning, gap-toothed, at Ruy.

'But you've been spoilt by these women who've come and gone, and all that can make a man arrogant.'

Ruy sighed, his eyes on the long straight road of the Autopista del Sur, now flanked on either side by stone pine trees. 'You know what, Chico? You're at your most annoying when you're right.'

Chico flicked his cigarette out of the window. 'It's a burden I live with every day.'

Ruy paused. 'Anyway, it's not idle adventure I'm looking for this time. It's not as simple as that.'

Chico raised an eyebrow. 'You're a hunter, Ruy. You love women and you love the chase … and the victory. You've never wanted to be tied down by one woman.'

Chico was right. Again. Over the years, there had been a couple of long-term liaisons that had led to nothing, because Ruy could never envisage a lifetime with the same person. Now, women still came and went but the excitement, the sexual emotion he had felt with some, had deserted him. He was blasé about it these days and, whenever he was intimate with a woman, he just went through the motions, taking physical pleasure from the encounter but nothing more.

Yet suddenly, now, the sleeping beast had been aroused. It was like a fever burning within him. He had not been rebuffed by Luna's coolness, but instead consumed by an insane drive to try and melt the wall of ice about her.

Yes, Ruy admitted it: he was a hunter and, unknowingly, by pushing his advances away, Luna had only increased his mounting ardour. Some raw, primitive instinct within him wanted to conquer her, but he was forced to realize that he wanted to break down her defensive barriers in more subtle ways.

'She's different from any woman I've met before, Chico. All those women I've known can be tagged instantly, but there's no label on this one.'

'So, do you think she likes you too?'

Ruy remembered the way she had looked at him in the bar. She'd skilfully kept her shield up, but he had felt it in the way she'd shivered when he accidentally brushed against her hand.

'Yes, but she told me to leave her alone.' His brow furrowed at the memory of Luna's scathing remarks. He rubbed his face with one hand and returned it to the wheel. 'In fact, she thinks I try to twist women round my little finger and pay them absurd compliments.'

Chico barked out a laugh. 'Hey, *hermanito*, I like her already!'

Ruy's expression relaxed into a grin. 'Okay, so maybe I deserved it a tiny bit, but she isn't going to get rid of me so easily.'

Chico reached for the cigarette packet in his top pocket. 'Heh, you see? There's the Ruy I know and love. Comes out fighting.' He tapped a cigarette on the dashboard. 'Sounds like you'll just have to watch yourself. But you're a clever man, you'll figure it out.'

Ruy watched the signs for Cádiz flash past as he joined the long access road from the mainland to the city. Yes, the next time he saw her he would have to be more careful. He would tell Chico the rest later, after he'd seen Luna again.

She had gotten under his skin. It wasn't just the hot surge of desire that gripped him whenever she was near. The swell of some deeper emotion lurked beneath. Was he heading for trouble? Some foolish part of him didn't care, and he wasn't sure whether to greet this unfamiliar feeling with joy or apprehension.

*   *   *

Luna slowed the metallic blue Mercedes as she rounded the bend looking for the beach house. The instructions Montez had given her said to look out for a house behind a pink wall with a tiled top.

There.

Luna saw it in the distance on the right and breathed a deep sigh.

Throughout the whole drive from Jerez airport, she had berated herself. She could not remember ever having acted so foolishly with a man. Why did Ruy have this effect on her, making her perversely uncivil, even in the face of her outrageous attraction to him? She didn't know which was worse, the fact that she'd told him so insultingly not to look for her in Cádiz, or that he had implied he'd not thought of it.

Maybe it's all for the best, she decided.

Anyhow, she'd been relieved not to have to face him again once she'd collected her luggage. Despite her rude behaviour, apologizing was not something she wanted to do, even if she had been in the wrong. Maybe she had misjudged his intentions … but had she really? She would never know. Yes, it was definitely all for the best. In a few days, this small mishap would be filed away to join other painful memories buried in the depths of her mind.

She turned the hire car off the main road, on to the gravel parking strip outside the house. A bank of pine trees behind it extended along the top of the beach, separating it from the road and interspersed with low shrubs, which gradually thinned out down towards the golden sand.

Diego Montez was waiting for Luna, leaning against the coral pink wall, smoking under the shade of a flamboyantly giant palm tree. He was dark blonde, well built and deeply tanned, which was all the more accentuated by his informal, open-necked white shirt with sleeves rolled up to the elbow that was tucked into a tight pair of jeans. In the afternoon heat he looked cool. As he watched Luna pull up, he threw away his cigarette, raised his hand in salute, and ambled towards her with the air of a man who had the day off.

'Señorita Ward, welcome to Cádiz,' he said in strongly accented English. 'I hope you had a pleasant flight, and the car journey wasn't too tiring.' He wore dark glasses so she could not see his eyes, but she got a glimpse of even white teeth as a warm smile spread across his face. He opened the car door to help her out.

'Señor Montez, good to meet you,' Luna answered him in English. For some reason, she felt like playing the tourist to maintain some distance. She stepped out of the car and briefly shook his hand. 'It's been a long day, but the drive was straightforward. The directions you gave me to the house were perfect, thank you.'

It was then that she looked out across the sea. The beauty of the landscape took her breath away.

Her new temporary home was situated directly on an isolated stretch of beach, offering spectacular views of the ocean and Puerto de Santa María. In the distance she could just make out the outline of the Sierra de Cádiz, that range of densely wooded, rugged hills with whitewashed villages, *los Pueblos Blancos*, clinging to its side. The white beach house itself looked as though it had sprouted out of the sand like the wild pine trees and fig bushes that grew around it.

It couldn't be more different to the urban chic of her redbrick, federal-style townhouse back in Greenwich Village, she mused. The endless vista here was exhilarating.

Diego Montez gestured towards the car. 'Would you like me to help you with your luggage now or would you prefer to have a look at the house first?'

'Don't worry about that, Señor Montez. I'll take it in myself later on, thank you.'

'Please call me Diego,' he said as they walked to the wrought-iron gate.

Luna merely smiled politely and read out the tiled name on the wall, '*La Gaviota*, The Seagull. That's a pretty name.'

'The house was designed to look like a bird,' he told her as he pressed down the latch and pushed the small gate, which opened with a creak.

It was a small, two-storey, unusual-looking building with whitewashed walls, interspersed with floor-to-ceiling sliding windows, a domed roof and three terraces. The one at ground level led down to the beach, while the two on the upper floor jutted out on the north-east and south-east sides of the house, like wings of a giant bird about to take flight.

Montez inserted the key in the lock of the front door and held it open for Luna, who found herself in a large whitewashed room, bathed in early-evening sunlight. He drew back the silk voile curtain and pushed open the sliding glass doors. The fabulous view of the dazzling white beach, which seemed to run to infinity alongside the indigo sea, greeted her in a flash of splendour as she stepped out on to the wide terrace.

'This really is a magical corner of the world,' she murmured.

The luminosity of the air sparkled like champagne, making Luna inhale deeply. The breeze was fresh and laden with the scent of seaweed and salt. All the tiredness and the troubles of the last forty-eight hours vanished. For two days she had been another woman, an unsophisticated, gauche stranger to herself. Here, she felt revived and happy again.

'It's a quiet, undisturbed patch of beach, a very private place,' the estate agent said, following her out on to the terrace and leaning against the iron balustrade. 'Many artists and writers have come here to work, and have found it an inspiring haven.'

'I'm surprised the rent is so reasonable. You also mentioned in your email that it's up for sale, didn't you?'

'Sí. The past few years have been difficult in this business. The property market and the tourist industry have been at an all-time low. The proprietor, Señor Alvarez, owns many villas and has been unable to let them as well as he used to. He built La Gaviota for his personal use about sixty years ago, inspired by the work of a well known Andalucían avant-garde architect, Eduardo Rafael Ruiz de Salazar. You're paying a minimum rent for a unique creation. I'm sure if you made an offer today, you could acquire this house at a very interesting price.'

Luna raised an eyebrow and laughed. '*Today*? I've only just got here!' She was amused at his overt attempt at hard sell. 'Though I can see the views alone make it tempting for anyone wanting a permanent home here.'

'You are not considering staying in Cádiz permanently?' He had taken off his sunglasses and was looking at Luna intently, his emerald-green eyes surveying her appreciatively.

She noticed that his irises were quite striking, and he was definitely handsome, but she was in no mood for male scrutiny just now. Besides, she was used to this look. It only ever seemed to take in the pleasing outward package, or see a cool challenge to a male ego. No man had ever looked at her and seen the real Luna, she was sure of it. She gazed out to sea, scanning the horizon, trying not to think about Ruy.

'No, I'm not in Cádiz permanently,' she told him.

'I must admit, I was surprised that you chose La Gaviota,' he continued. 'This place is isolated. Not many people like to be cut off like this. The next set of *casitas* is about three hundred metres away.'

Luna shrugged. 'I'm fond of my privacy.'

'If you don't mind me saying so, you're a very beautiful woman. Most women would think twice about living in such a deserted place.'

At his suggestion, an instinctive twist of nerves caught in her stomach, but she ignored it. If Montez was interested in selling her the house, he wasn't exactly helping his cause. Nevertheless, she was not going to be condescended to as a helpless female.

She gave him a questioning look. 'Does the house have an alarm system?'

'Yes, I will show you the two systems before I leave.'

Luna smiled tightly. 'Then I should have nothing to worry about. Isn't that so?'

He laughed, his gaze sweeping over her, up and down. 'You're a courageous woman, eh?'

She turned away again to look at the ocean. 'Not really, I've lived alone before. Isolation doesn't frighten me, provided I've the necessary protection.'

'The alarm systems here are good. There's one for the outside, another for inside, but we'll come to that at the end. Shall I show you the rest of the house?'

The living room was modern, simple and furnished with tasteful, basic furniture. The décor was blue and white, with a profusion of indoor plants. 'It is all designed to reflect the beautiful atmosphere of Cádiz,' Montez pointed out.

The whitewashed beamed ceiling was high, with recessed lights; the floor was of polished white marble. Facing the sea view was a large sofa, covered in thick white linen fabric with plump feather cushions in various tones of blue, two armchairs and a good-sized square coffee table, upon which a large conch shell had been placed in lieu of an ashtray. In a corner, at one end of the room, four bamboo chairs painted white were set around a circular dining table with a blue-and-white checked tablecloth and a bowl of yellow roses in the middle. In the opposite corner, a small wrought-iron spiral staircase clung to the wall.

They entered the narrow kitchen that ran the length of the house, and Luna was pleased to see it was well equipped and light, with the same spectacular views. A small cloakroom to the right of the front door had a stone basin and a long mirror with an antique wrought-iron surround.

'Shall we go upstairs?' Montez offered as he started up the ornate staircase that spiralled in an elegant curve to the bedroom.

Here again the windows were floor-to-ceiling sliding sheets of reinforced glass on three sides, allowing unobstructed views and ensuring a large amount of natural light during the day. Two of the windows opened on to terraces with fabulous north-eastern and south-eastern views over the countryside. Luna couldn't help but gasp. From this vantage point, she had an almost 180-degree perspective of those far-off dark green hills and the harbour's lighthouse, which had just begun sweeping its powerful and comforting beam over the Atlantic twilight.

She took in the oversized bed with its beautiful Spanish wrought-iron headboard. It was covered with an old-fashioned bedspread of thick white lace and was draped with a snowy mosquito net, secured by a satin tie-back. The dressing table and chair were also antique-looking. Its oval, free-standing, Murano glass mirror with silver inlay in its frame, combined with the beautiful cobalt-blue Murano glass chandelier hanging from the beamed ceiling, lent a touch of bygone charm to the room, which she found an attractive contrast to the downstairs living area.

Leading off the bedroom was a dressing room with a walk-in wardrobe, and a white marble bathroom, which had a skylight ceiling.

'The house is air-conditioned throughout and the system is reversible, so in the winter months you won't be cold,' Montez explained.

They went back downstairs and he showed her how to use the alarm systems, which Luna satisfied herself were more than adequate.

'In addition, all the rooms have shutters. I would recommend you close them whenever you leave the house, and maybe on the ground floor at night as an extra security precaution,' Montez advised her.

'Thanks, Diego, you've been very helpful. I'm delighted the house has such adventurous architecture. It's wonderful! I've fallen in love with it already.'

Luna looked around. She wasn't just being polite – this was a perfect haven. She could imagine taking walks on the beach and spending hours on the terrace, reading or just gazing at the view.

The estate agent beamed. 'I hope you'll be very happy here. I'll help you bring in your suitcases now.'

'You really don't need to,' she assured him quickly.

He flashed her a chivalrous grin. 'I insist, *señorita*. It's the least I can do.'

Luna thought of the narrow spiral staircase and the fact that she'd not yet learned how to travel light. She smiled. 'You're very kind. Thank you.'

Montez carried her luggage up to the bedroom and then Luna walked him back to the gate.

When she held out her hand, he took it and kept it in his. 'Forgive me if I sound too bold,' he began, 'but will you have dinner with me tonight? It would give me great pleasure to show you the town, as you're new to Cádiz. Maybe we could discuss the house further. La Gaviota is unique, and it can be yours for half its real value.'

Luna stifled a sigh. All she wanted was to be left alone now. True, Diego Montez was attractive and charming and, although he'd made an immediate move on her, she did not feel threatened. For once, it wasn't that.

Instead, her head was full of a darker, more charismatic man. A frustratingly bewitching one who sang to her with the tormented soul of a gypsy, who intrigued her with his words and bewitched her with eyes as deep and blue as the roaring sea. How could she think she could get him out of her head so easily?

Montez had a certain smoothness about him that she found too obvious. No doubt he could make a woman feel indulged and pampered, but he wasn't really her type. Latin men were flirts, it was second nature to them – she should just enjoy the attention and leave it at that. Luna hesitated. Did she want to be distracted just for one evening? Her fridge was empty and she hardly relished the idea of going to a restaurant on her own that night, but she knew where this spontaneous invitation was leading.

She noticed he was still hanging on to her hand and released her own quickly.

'I'm rather tired,' she told him. 'It's been a long day and I need to get some sleep. But that's very kind of you. Perhaps another time,' she added, not wishing to seem rude.

He smiled and nodded. '*No hay problema*, no problem. You need your rest. *Sí, sí*, another time.'

'Thank you, Diego. I do appreciate your kindness.'

He beamed and winked at her. 'My invitation, *señorita*, has not been prompted by kindness. It would give me immense pleasure to take out such a beautiful lady as yourself, whenever you decide.'

Luna waved to him from inside the gate and as she closed the front door, she heard his car move off with a roar.

Finding her bag, she headed back out to her car, deciding she would stock up on groceries from the small supermarket she had seen on the main road not far from the house.

Inside the *supermercado*, she marvelled at the foreignness of it all: the Spanish food labels, the music playing in the background, the profusion of colourful fruit and vegetables, even in this small, local shop. But it was the particular smell of cured meats and fresh cheeses, an earthiness and something else sweet that she couldn't identify, which instantly triggered memories of being in Granada as a young child. She had forgotten that smell and now images flashed in her mind of accompanying her mother's round and jovial housekeeper on trips out shopping and being given an ice cream because she'd been good. As far as she recalled, her mother had never once bought Luna an ice cream anywhere. The friendly Spanish servant often looked after her when her mother was out with her sister Juliet, though where they went, Luna had no idea. She wondered where that kindly housekeeper was now.

Luna filled her basket quickly with enough food for a light supper and breakfast the next day. Tomorrow she could stock up with more for the weekend. It would be her only day before she started her new job at the Institute on Friday, and it would be lovely to spend the afternoon in town, shopping and looking around.

Half an hour later she was back at the house, sitting on the terrace with a chilled glass of wine and some bread, cheese and olives, absorbing the vast beauty of the landscape and the sounds of the sea.

The velvety light of dusk was approaching. The port of Puerto de Santa María glowed in the distance, accompanied by the steadfast wink of the lighthouse. Fishing boats were still out on the ocean and to the east, the faraway Sierra de Cádiz was edged with the fading sky, making *los Pueblos Blancos* dim to a soft violet.

Even though it was still early, Luna was feeling sleepy, her body clock disorientated by the time difference. Added to that, she was exhausted by the emotionally eventful day.

Yet, every time she let her eyes close, she saw him.

Ruy. The image of his unforgivably handsome face tormented her. The sound of his smoky voice, singing to her, murmuring to her, seeped through her veins. Even the memory of those bold aquamarine eyes sent a tingle down Luna's spine now. Perhaps he wasn't like other men, she conceded. They only took in the polished surface she chose to show, and were uninterested in what lay beneath. The way Ruy's gaze penetrated her layers of defence was frightening and intoxicating. It was as if he could see all of her.

Had she been wrong about this particular man? Had she just pushed away the one opportunity she'd been waiting for her whole life? Other men seemed to pale by comparison beside Ruy – after all, she had just turned down dinner with a perfectly handsome and charming man – Diego Montez, a typical Spanish Romeo. Somehow, it brought home to her that the bolt of lightning she'd felt as her eyes had met Ruy's that night when he'd sung to her meant much more than she had been prepared to accept.

When she thought of it, the impact of that first, unspoken encounter still overwhelmed her self-control, as much physically as mentally. Unsought, in the most unexpected manner, something had happened to her then, something unusual and wonderful. Something that, deep down, perhaps she needed, even if she found it hard to understand.

But what use was that now? Why should Ruy wish to seek her out after her unjustified rudeness? How petty and immature she'd been. From then on he had completely switched off – he'd made that quite plain, leaving the aircraft without a backward glance. Even though Luna knew she was being unfair and illogical, she was hurt.

She sighed. *Stop dramatizing*, she admonished. *You're not likely to see him again, anyway. You don't even know his last name. Just forget him. Let's face it, he's probably forgotten you already*, she told herself disconsolately.

This problem she had with men lay with her, not them. The dream that haunted Luna's nights came from something deeply rooted in her psyche. She had to deal with it, she realized, before it blighted her life. Perhaps she should try hypnosis, she mused wryly. After all, according to Ruy, hypnotism cured a multitude of ailments. Still, she knew she would find it so hard to admit to anyone how vulnerable she was.

Luna sat up a while longer, looking out into the falling night, thinking about all that had happened since her arrival in Spain. Hopefully the nightmare wouldn't return tonight. However, there was no use delaying her bedtime, she thought finally, clearing her things away. Already she was fighting sleep.

CHAPTER 3

When Luna woke up, the morning was blue and gold – a poem of warmth and sunshine, the atmosphere light. The first thing she did was to go out on to one of the terraces and look around her. The sky was high, pale and serene, and the bay shimmered like silver. There was not a soul in sight. Silence was deep except for the dull, rhythmic sound of the surf breaking along the shore.

There had been no nightmares, no anxiety, and no terror. Luna's night had been peaceful in that respect and, if she had woken hot and breathless, it was not with fear. Ruy had been with her all night in her dreams. Obscurely aware of a tangle of limbs and the racing of her blood, she surfaced from sleep, needy and aching, tormented by the lingering sense of his mouth on her body. The fading memory of the dream left behind it half-echoes of whispered words and wild, untamed emotions.

Luna stared out over the glittering sea and breathed in the tangy air, letting her thoughts settle. Even if her heart was full of him, at least she could try to put him out of her mind.

She hadn't unpacked properly and so she spent a leisurely hour or so putting her clothes away and finding a place for everything. Normally, she would have made efficient work of such a task, but she was relaxed in the house and felt like taking her time to familiarize herself with her new home. It captivated her attention so much that Luna found herself unusually distracted and reluctant to tear herself away from the mesmerizing sight and sound of the sea. Finally, she flicked through her guide to Cádiz, debating where to go shopping for the rest of the morning.

Aware that time was getting on, she showered and dressed speedily, pulling on a pair of denim shorts and a short, white, sleeveless V-neck top. Armed with her guidebook, she went into the city. It was too hot to walk so she took the car and, anyhow, she had only bought a few provisions the night before and needed more for the next couple of days.

The many pedestrian zones of Cádiz made finding a parking space tricky at first, but Luna was finally able to leave the car in one of the long, shady streets in the centre, off Plaza de Las Flores, not far from the covered marketplace. As she turned a corner into the broad, noonday glare, her first impression was one of a radiant atmosphere in the dry heat. The intense blue sky was growing molten as the sun approached its meridian.

The heart of the city was animated by a voluble and good-humoured crowd. There was movement everywhere as people shopped, walked and whizzed by on scooters, or sat and drank coffee in pavement cafés. The effect was kaleidoscopic and bubbling with life. As she walked further, pretty pink and yellow houses came into view, their narrow balconies decorated with hanging baskets overflowing with fuchsias and red begonias. They framed Plaza de Flores itself, which opened out into a triangle, rather than a square, and was lined with trees and ornately curling iron streetlamps. Luna ambled past the fountain at one end, stopping to look at the shops and stalls, topped by pale awnings. Most were crowded with flowers, which spilled in every direction in a riot of colour. Unable to resist such beautiful blooms, and thinking they would make the beach house look even more homely, she asked one of the stallholders to make her up a bouquet of carnations, marguerites and roses.

One street away, the covered market was also teeming. Housed in a large, Neoclassical, rectangular building, edged with Doric stone columns that provided a welcome shaded walkway, it was obviously the meeting place for local housewives and restaurant chefs, shopping for their daily needs. Luna passed through the impressive arched entrance, noticing only a handful of tourists, looking but not buying. It was brightly lit, and everybody was talking at once.

Stall after stall was heaped with fresh, colourful local produce from land and sea. Luna paused to admire the day's catch of fish lying on slabs of ice, their silver scales glistening under the neon lights; some of which were specimens she had never heard of. She wondered how they were able to keep them looking still so appetizing in the heat.

'We have the best red tuna in the world, fished locally in Tarifa,' the fishmonger proudly told her. He grinned broadly. 'Only for you, beautiful *señorita*, I will make it half price.'

Luna laughed. Even the fishmongers here turned on the charm. 'I'll come back in a few days, and you'll have to tell me how to cook it.'

'*No problema.*' The fishmonger gesticulated enthusiastically. '*Yo iré y cocinar para ti, si te gusta*, I will come and cook it *for* you if you like.'

One merchant offered large white eggs – so rare, as he took pleasure in pointing out. 'They're fresh today from my own farm. *No usamos ningún productos chemicos*, we don't use any chemicals,' he assured her. Luna bought six, as well as some butter and a bottle of milk. She would cook an omelette for her lunch with organic red vine tomatoes, crunchy yellow peppers, and wonderful spindly green chives that she picked out from an array of colourful vegetables. These ranged from incredibly thin beans, tender spinach, young petits pois, baby carrots and globe artichokes, to large cabbages, enormous potatoes, oversized tomatoes that looked more like small pumpkins, and thick asparagus fingers, the like of which she had never seen before.

Everything smelled delicious. There were stores selling Serrano ham, chorizo sausage and the famous *chicharrones* – fried pork rind – from the coastal town of Chicalana. A woman nodded to Luna, gesturing at her to try a sample from a small bowl. Luna smiled and thanked her, popping a piece into her mouth. It was delicious, but rather heavy and rich. Maybe another day. Instead she chose a bunch of black grapes and a couple of juicy-looking peaches and nectarines, whose sweet fragrance filled the air.

As Luna strolled through the market, happy to browse among the huge array of stalls, soaking in the vibrant atmosphere, her mind couldn't help straying to Ruy and speculating where in the city he might be at that moment. The notion that she might round a corner and come face-to-face with him again made her stomach flip, and she admonished herself for not pushing all thoughts of him out of her head.

She stopped at the dry foods stand that offered a vast assortment of nuts, glazed fruit and jars of cocoa and ground coffee, and bought a couple of jars and some pistachios. At the next-door counter, the region's cheeses were on display, so she selected some *queso de cabra*. On the way out, she picked up a medley of olives, a bottle of olive oil, and a loaf of bread from the bakery. Delighted with her morning's shopping, she headed back to the car, just as people were starting to fill the restaurants.

It was already two o'clock. She was looking forward to a quiet afternoon at the house, and a swim in the peacock-coloured waters of the bay once the heat had died down a little.

By the time she got home, she was ravenous. She cooked up an omelette with the ingredients she'd bought that morning, made a cup of coffee and sat in a shaded place on the terrace, looking at the view.

The small waves of the bay swept in majestically, roll after roll, gently dying out on the white sands, clear and brilliant, leaving behind long, curling lines of white foam. She could see the harbour in the distance displayed picturesquely in the afternoon haze. A liner had arrived and was waiting out at sea to enter the port. It hooted once or twice, its eerie, raucous sound breaking the pervading silence. Her gaze shifted and she spent a moment watching a woman and her dog, a black spaniel, paddling down on the beach.

Luna was happy and at home here. She loved the house. It was perfect; she could find no fault with it. Perhaps she should think about buying it. Diego Montez was right: it was a rare jewel. She could easily see herself settling down here. The more she came in contact with Spanish people, the more she felt akin to them, and that surprised her. Spain was a passionate land and its people were made in its image: colourful, volatile, flamboyant. Luna had always hidden a passionate nature beneath her ordered, fastidious exterior. It was so much easier to control the fire burning away inside her than to expose it. That way, danger lay.

Still, she couldn't help thinking of Ruy and how much that dangerous impulse in her was drawn to him like a magnet. Even while she had been shopping he had monopolized her thoughts. He was a nagging obsession, unsettling her mind in a mass of confusion and contradiction. One minute she wished she would see him again, the next she was thinking she had done the right thing in rejecting him and was better off this way. She could not remember all of her dream but she knew that, alongside all the fevered abandon, he had been gentle and loving.

After lunch, Luna spent the next hour on the shady terrace, reading over her notes on the Institute in preparation for her first day. The Institute would have been happy for her to wait until after the weekend, but Luna had told them that she was keen to have a look round tomorrow and meet everyone. That way, she reasoned, she could use the weekend to devote some uninterrupted thinking time to how she might shape her article.

The afternoon sun was still high and hot in the sky when Luna closed her laptop and looked out over the beach. The white-gold heat of it was vibrating, the colours startling. The beach was fawn and amber with patches of white foam; the sea a deep blue, calm and silent as a lake, a few sails sprinkling its scintillating surface.

Nothing's going to stop me from having a swim, she thought, gazing at the water lapping limpidly on the burnished sand.

In no time, she had slipped on her bikini and made her way down the dunes to the water's edge. She stepped into the sapphire water, which, further on, shadowed to cobalt beneath the rocks of the wide bay. As she looked back, the peninsula of Cádiz appeared in all its splendour, outlined on the horizon, a white dream of domes and towers, thrusting out like a pearly hand into the dark blue Atlantic.

The sparkling water and view of the pale, climbing buildings of the city reminded her of holidays gone by. Images of playing with other children on the sand flooded back into her mind. Some had been friends of her parents, she supposed, and others she knew were the housekeeper's family. Those she remembered a little more distinctly: running wildly up and down the beach with her, burying each other in the sand. She was happier then than she had ever been.

As she came out of the water, the waning heat of the sun on her wet skin, Luna passed the same woman and dog she had seen earlier, paddling on the beach.

The stranger smiled at her. She was dressed simply in a black skirt and a rather garish flowery blouse; a working woman of imposing stature, with a burnt copper complexion and vivacious, but tender, dark eyes. Her hair was magnificently black and curly even though she was clearly beyond middle age. Luna couldn't tell exactly how old she was: late fifties, early sixties perhaps.

'*Buenos días, señorita.*' The woman gestured towards La Gaviota at the top of the beach. 'You have rented this house?'

'*Buenos días, señora.* Yes, I have.'

'I'm glad. It seems such a lovely house. You know, for two years it has been looking so sad. It has been empty, you see. Cádiz, like the rest of Andalucía, has gone through difficult times. Like people, houses need love and care.' She sighed then smiled again, knowingly. 'This is a quiet, isolated place. So you're a writer, *ey*?' She had a rich and powerful voice.

'No, no, I'm just a tourist.'

'You speak good Spanish for a tourist.'

'I'm half Spanish.'

The woman nodded. 'You look Scandinavian.'

Luna smiled, amused by the roundabout way she was being interrogated. She was obviously an object of interest and what struck her most was the Spanish woman's entire absence of self-consciousness in her curiosity.

'No, I'm American.'

'*Americana, ey?* You are staying long in Cádiz?'

'A few months. Do you live near here?'

'*Sí, sí,* I live on the beach too,' the woman said cheerfully, reaching down to the black spaniel, who had been sitting patiently at her feet. She ruffled its ears and unclipped its lead, watching it race off down the beach after a seagull. 'I've lived here all my life. Cádiz has the best people, the best fiestas and, of course, the best food in Spain.' She let out a sunny, infectious chuckle and patted her ample hips. 'Though sometimes I wish it didn't. But it's a little late for me to be watching my figure, and life is for living, *ey*?'

Luna grinned. She was instantly taken by this engaging, charismatic woman and thought it would be entertaining to bump into her often if she was close by. 'Yes, *señora*, I suppose it is. I've already seen a little of Cádiz's amazing food at the market this morning.'

'Ah yes, the market is very good. The freshly cooked *churros* there are almost as good as mine! I see you like to swim, *señorita*, and there's nothing of you, so luckily you can eat what you like. My trouble is, I like my own cooking too much, so have to walk my dog Lobo here every day,' she chattered on happily, her sparkling, dark eyes sweeping the beach. 'But it's one of the most beautiful spots in Cádiz, so why should I complain?'

They began to walk up the beach together.

'May I ask what brought you to Cádiz, *señorita*?'

'Someone close to me died recently.' The answer came out instinctively. Perhaps it was the maternal, easy manner of this woman that prompted Luna's confession, but for some reason it seemed more appropriate to speak of Angelina than her assignment at the Institute. 'She lived in Barcelona for a while and truly loved Spain.'

'*Ay Dios*, I'm very sorry for your loss, *señorita*. My husband died not so long ago too and, may the saints be my witness, I know it's not easy to lose someone you love. The sorrow is always there somewhere, but *no hay nublado que dure un año*, a clouded sky does not last a year.' The woman smiled sadly and paused to study her young companion. 'So you are here to pay your respects?'

'In a manner of speaking, though she died last year,' Luna replied without elaborating. Nice as this stranger was, right now she didn't feel like going into lengthy explanations about her job in Cádiz.

Luna glanced down at her own bare feet sinking into the wet sand as they walked. 'It was my cousin. We were very close and grew up together in the US. My mother had returned to Spain with my half-sister when my parents divorced, and my father wasn't around much, so my cousin and I spent quite a bit of time together.'

There came a sympathetic tutting sound from beside her. '*Madre de Dios*! She took your sister and not you? A girl should not be left by her mother.'

Luna shrugged. 'I've done fine on my own.' Yes, she had, she reminded herself. It's true, she often wondered what it would have been like had Juliet lived. Would Luna have been persuaded to make the trip to Spain earlier to build a relationship with her older sister? As for her mother, Adalia Ward had clearly been nothing but a selfish, vain socialite and, even if she were still alive, they would not have been close, nor would she have given her daughter the kind of guidance that Luna secretly craved from time to time.

The other woman seemed to read her thoughts. 'Mmm, perhaps the mind can find its own way alone in the world, but the heart …?' Her reflection seemed to trail off. 'So your mother and sister are still in Spain?'

'No, they both died when I was in high school. But that's another story.' She gave a half-smile.

The woman stopped in her tracks and crossed herself. '*Benditos sean los dulces nombres*, Holy be the sweet names!' She clasped Luna's face gently between her hands, her dark eyes full of compassion. 'My poor child! Too much sorrow for one so young.' Her arms dropped to her sides and her frown softened. 'One day, you can tell me the story and I will bake you some of my *churros*. A story like that needs something sweet to help the telling.' They began to walk again. 'So I'm thinking your cousin was more like a sister too, no?'

Rather than being disturbed or embarrassed by the woman's questions, Luna felt perfectly comfortable. 'Yes, she was, though we were nothing like each other really. She was a complete livewire, always getting into scrapes, whereas I was always the sensible one.' She looked up and smiled sadly, surprised at her own unreserved response to this stranger.

The woman patted her arm in a comforting gesture. 'Well, *señorita*, you've come to the right city to smile again. Cádiz is a bewitching place. It will soothe your troubles and its magic will heal your heart.' She paused, then looked askance at Luna, a twinkle appearing in her eye. 'Did I also tell you that it has the best men as well?' Another appealing chortle escaped her lips and Luna found herself joining in.

'Well, I've certainly witnessed the charm of Cádiz in more ways than one,' she laughed as they reached the dunes separating the house from the beach.

The sun disappeared behind a cloud. Luna shivered.

'Go in, go in, *señorita*, don't let me keep you,' the woman said apologetically. 'You'll catch cold, and I need to walk off the chocolate I ate this afternoon.' She chuckled again. 'Though my husband, the angels protect him, never seemed to mind my extra inches. He said that being curvy was nature's way of saying: "You're so good, I'll just make more of you!"' She smiled a little sheepishly this time. 'Listen to me, I'm babbling on as usual. If you need anything, I live further down the beach.' She pointed at the cluster of cottages in the distance. 'The first *casita* covered in red bougainvillea on your right. You can ask for Señora Sanchez. Everyone knows me around here.'

'*Gracias, muchas gracias, Señora Sanchez.* I'll bear that in mind.' Luna smiled at her and before she could offer her own name, her new neighbour was bustling off, calling to her spaniel.

Luna made her way back up to the house. How wonderful to have someone like Señora Sanchez for a neighbour, she thought as she let herself in and headed for the shower. They said that Cádiz was known for its generosity and warmth, and nowhere had the kindness of strangers been more evident than in this ancient, beautiful, laid-back city, she mused. Once again, she felt an affinity with these people. It made something deep within her sigh with relief, like the weary traveller lost in a dark wilderness who finally discovers the light to guide him home.

*   *   *

The next morning, Luna pulled the car up in front of the gates of El Instituto de Investigación de los Recursos Naturales. The elegant iron barriers opened automatically, and she drove into a narrow parking area.

During the drive to her new job, she found herself wondering if she was going to find this professional deception almost too hard to carry off. Although she had strong views on alternative medicine, Luna had a positive nature, and the idea of pretending to be someone she wasn't for the sake of her article – even if it was a prestigious assignment – made her all the more nervous now that she had arrived. Still, as she manoeuvred into a space in front of the Institute, she reiterated her resolve that she was doing this for all the right reasons.

She was early. Switching off the engine, she stepped from the car and looked around her. The Institute for the Research of Natural Remedies was a spectacular converted old *casa señorial* in the north of the Old Town near the port, set back from the road behind a grassy strip of palm trees. Attached to one side of the imposing mansion house stood a couple of long, single-storey dwellings, perpendicular to each other, which formed an open courtyard, edged with arches of pale stone. It had been constructed in keeping with the style of the main building: a stately combination of whitewashed walls and terracotta stone, with Moorish embellishments.

Luna took in the tall, open windows looking out through the palms to the harbour beyond, their soft marquisette curtains fluttering outwards in the breeze on to the wrought-iron balconies that adorned the façade. *What wonderful surroundings to work in*, she thought, lingering outside. The overall impression was magical.

Now the sun had risen, as it always did here, with a kind of burst. It was going to be a hot day. The sky burned an electric blue above the turquoise sea in the harbour. Inside the shady courtyard, jacarandas, flame trees and frangipani spread their fragrance, filling the air with sweetness and invading her senses. Luna glanced at her watch: it was time to go in.

She made her way from the car park, following signs to the reception. Inside the building, she paused to get her bearings. The white interior and giant potted plants lining the short corridor created a calm and pleasant atmosphere. Soothing seascapes hung on the walls. Luna could see the reception desk straight ahead in a large, bright, open space but there was no one manning it. She peered into the first room on her right. It was empty, save for a few comfortable armchairs and a rack of magazines set in one corner.

'Can I help you?'

Luna swung round to find herself staring at one of the most beautiful women she had ever seen. Obviously Spanish from her dark colouring, and a little older than Luna, she was a vision of sophistication and elegance. Striking midnight-black eyes looked down a perfectly proportioned nose at Luna, surveying her sharply. Her eyes travelled up from Luna's beige, leather-belted pencil skirt to her practical, short-sleeved white shirt, and lingered momentarily on her blonde hair.

The disdainful goddess arched a perfect brow. 'I presume you are the new researcher,' she said haughtily. She reached out a perfectly manicured hand to grip Luna's. 'I am Vaina Jiménez Rivera, managing director of the Institute.' She enunciated every syllable in a patronizing tone, suggesting Luna should neither forget the name nor the status.

Luna's amber eyes brightened to a burnished gleam, levelling a steady gaze at the Spanish woman.

'Bull's-eye!' she replied. When it became apparent that joviality was totally wasted on the other woman, in a clear voice she parried: 'Dr Luna Emilia Ward.' Luna couldn't help giving a slight emphasis to the word 'doctor', while still holding Vaina's stare. If the woman insisted on being superior, she too could play that game.

From that moment, as their eyes locked, an immediate antipathy settled between them.

Vaina turned on exquisite stilettoed heels and walked with brisk, confident steps towards the reception area at the end of the corridor.

'Please follow me. I will take you to Señorita Rosario Martínez. She will show you around the premises.' She spoke without looking at Luna, nose in the air, her tone condescending. 'As a researcher you will be assigned to one of our practitioners, who you will assist with the various assignments they set for you.'

Luna followed her, admiring the trim figure clad in a classic grey suit, which clung in all the right places, and the elaborate twisting chignon that held her shiny, thick black hair at the nape of her neck. There was something obvious about her groomed, sleek beauty, but there was no denying she was stunning. Stunning, but territorial. Luna knew that Vaina had instantly sized her up. She wondered at the cool – no, downright hostile – welcome and hoped the rest of the staff would not be so unfriendly.

As they approached the end of the corridor, a woman of about thirty emerged from a side room opposite the reception desk.

'Ah, Rosario, there you are. Just the person I was looking for.' Vaina turned towards Luna for the first time since they had left the front room. 'This is Dr Ward, our new researcher with whom you'll be working. Would you please show her around and give her the usual documents to sign, plus the Institute's manual so she can familiarize herself with our systems and procedures.'

'Of course, Doña Vaina. Everything is on Dr Ward's desk. Dr Rueda de Calderón asked me to allocate her the office next to his, opposite the lab in Casa Vistaria, as they'll be working together. I have—'

Vaina's lips tensed. 'That is most unsuitable,' she interrupted. Flames flared in her dark eyes as they darted towards Luna before fixing on Rosario. 'He never mentioned this to me. I had given you different instructions. You will do me the favour of remembering that I'm the one managing this Institute. Dr Rueda de Calderón may be a genius in his field but, like all men, he is most impractical when dealing with administration and management.'

'But …'

'Leave it for now. He's coming in this afternoon and I will deal with the matter myself.' The arrogant glare was back as she breezed past Luna and marched off, her high heels resounding on the marble floor.

Rosario rolled her eyes. 'Impossible woman!' she grunted. 'One day I'll tell her just where to get off.' Turning to Luna, she grinned. 'Don't take any notice. Welcome to our turbulent little world.'

Luna smiled back and shrugged. 'I really don't mind where my office is. The buildings and the grounds all look so beautiful. Really, Señorita Rosario, if it will keep the peace …'

'Don't give it a second thought, and call me Charo – short for Rosario. Everybody here calls me Charo.'

'And you must call me Luna.'

Charo blinked. 'Is that normal in America? In Spain, it's the done thing to call the doctors and researchers by their surname; in the office at least. Though it's not the same the other way round.'

'Well, Charo, that hardly seems egalitarian.' Luna looked at her askance. 'Why should I respect you less than you respect me? Please, we'll be working together closely. I insist you call me Luna.'

The woman beamed at her. 'Well, if you insist – *Luna*.' She had a beautiful smile with large, laughing blue eyes that twinkled mischievously. Charo was petite, with chestnut hair that framed her heart-shaped face and strong, expressive eyebrows that seemed to have a mind of their own. Luna warmed to her immediately.

As if encouraged by this unexpected show of informality, Charo gave her a conspiratorial look and lowered her voice to a whisper. 'I should tell you, Doña Vaina is temperamental, to say the least. Especially where Dr Rueda de Calderón is concerned. Those two have had a stormy on-off relationship for years.'

'I find it hard to see how any two people can work together under those circumstances,' Luna observed wryly. 'Anyhow, I suppose it's no business of anyone's but their own.'

Still, Charo wasn't about to be stopped, and no doubt read the glimmer of curiosity in Luna's eyes. 'They've been going through a bad patch for a while now. They met when he was doing his medical training. Her father's a director of one of the biggest hospitals in Barcelona, and she's been after him ever since. At one time there were rumours that they were going to get engaged. Then suddenly it all went cold. Anyhow, he's been very busy lately and, what's more, he hasn't showed up for almost a week. She's been going crazy, she hates it when he's not under her nose.' She grinned. 'But he just does his own thing, however much she pouts and complains.'

Luna's eyebrows went up. Charo was imparting rather a lot of personal information about Dr Rueda de Calderón, though she was admittedly fascinated by the young woman's endearing indiscretion. If he succeeded in thwarting the supercilious Doña Vaina, she was beginning to like him, despite his playboy reputation.

As if reading her thoughts, Charo gave a sheepish look, accompanied by a giggle. 'Oh, I'm a terrible gossip, I know, but I can see by your face that you're totally trustworthy. Life is simply too boring without a bit of spice, don't you think?' She waggled her eyebrows comically.

Luna laughed. 'Oh, quite right. My lips are sealed. Doña Vaina will hear nothing from me.'

'There, I knew you were a decent sort. Come, I'll give you a quick tour of the premises and then we can deal with the boring paperwork.'

They walked through the spacious and calm main building, which seemed such a haven of peace. Luna almost had to remind herself that her assignment was to write an article that she imagined would end up denigrating all the things that this beautiful place seemed to hold sacred. Was this haven just an illusion created for the benefit of gullible rich people, or was there more to it, though?

'I'm looking forward to studying the reports on your successes,' Luna told Charo in the library. She plucked a large tome from one of the shelves and leafed through it.

'Oh, our therapists have achieved phenomenal results and the most impressive is Dr Rueda de Calderón's programme. He's completely inspirational.' Charo's voice was warm with admiration. She nodded at the book in Luna's hands. 'Herbalism is a particular interest of his.'

Charo suddenly glanced at her watch. 'We'd better get going or you'll collapse with hunger before lunch,' she said, grinning.

Next, she took Luna to where they would both be working. A whitewashed dwelling covered in purple wisteria, they had to reach it via the sun-filled courtyard Luna had glimpsed from the car park earlier. Here, the intense brightness threw into contrast the shadows cast on to the walls of the building from its slanting, tiled roof. A burbling fountain and a cluster of terracotta planters, brimming with pink and red carnations, lent the space a peaceful tranquillity; and the scent of orange blossom floating in the air, emanating from the small orange trees planted in the borders, was a delight.

Inside, the building was cool. The reception area was large, with chairs neatly lined up against one wall and a small desk with a computer and telephone against another. 'This is where I sit,' Charo told her. 'I prefer working here. At least I'm not interrupted all the time. I'm so lucky I get to do project work with a single researcher. Much better than being one of the secretaries in the main building, who get switched from project to project the whole time.'

She showed Luna the lab, where she could run tests and work on small projects. 'For more complicated analysis, you would need to use the larger labs in the main building.' Then they went through to Dr Rueda de Calderón's office. It was a vast room, stark and sanitary, apart from the beautiful surrealistic paintings that adorned its walls in a wild splash of colour and drama. Other than this almost confrontational decoration, the interior didn't give away much about its owner: just a plain desk, with a neat row of writing utensils and a pair of reading glasses.

'You will be working next door,' Charo said, shooting Luna a glance that looked almost amused.

The office Luna had been assigned was filled with sunshine. It overlooked the small courtyard and beyond to the harbour. Through the slits of the windows' elegant wrought-iron balconies, she could just make out patches of the scintillating sea, and colourful yachts bobbing up and down in the bay. Next to the window sat a smart oak desk, accommodating a computer and a couple of telephones. A series of prints of various herbs threw splashes of colour on one of the whitewashed walls. Another was lined with files and medical journals. As her eyes moved round the room they came to rest on something almost fantastical standing in a corner – enchanting, she had to admit, but definitely out of place in a researcher's office. It was a large sculpture of a young gypsy holding a basket brimming with what looked like wild flowers. Something about the statue stirred her, but the scientific researcher in her was tempted to reject it as caprice.

Luna turned to face Charo and smiled. 'I'm lucky to have such a beautiful room. I'm still trying to get my head around the idea that this is a medical centre. It feels like an elegant old family hacienda, but then you've got all the state-of-the-art labs.'

'That was the vision for *El Instituto*. The idea is if the staff are happy then the feeling spreads to our patients. Do you really think there's anyone in the world who wants to be treated in a concrete-and-steel block? I think not!' She grinned. 'I love it here, and I just know you will too.'

Luna regarded Charo thoughtfully. Whatever delight the young woman took in being indiscreet about its employees, clearly the Institute itself inspired her unwavering respect.

'You should find everything you need in here,' Charo added breezily, 'but if there's anything else you want, just let me know.' She paused. A mischievous little devil danced in her bright blue eyes.

'Actually, you're very lucky to have been assigned to Dr Rueda de Calderón. Wait until you meet him. He's swept through this place like flu. There isn't a woman at the Institute who doesn't secretly fancy him. He can be a terrible flirt. It drives Doña Vaina crazy, I can tell you.' She shot Luna a sideways look, then gave a little chuckle. 'Though I've known him long enough myself to get past all that. Besides, I only have eyes for my boyfriend, Miguel.'

Luna smiled but offered no comment. Human nature was the same, whether in Cádiz or New York, and she had learned a long time ago that to survive the gossip mill, it was sensible to adopt the prudence of the three wise monkeys. Her thoughts drifted reluctantly back to Ruy – another Spanish alpha male who seemed to make all women go weak at the knees.

Charo seemed in no hurry to go to lunch.

'Are you married?' she asked.

'No.'

'Boyfriend?'

'Not at present.'

'Wait until you see him. I'll bet my last euro you won't be immune to his charms. You know, I have a feeling he won't be indifferent to yours either. You might just get on like a house on fire.' She winked conspiratorially. 'It would really drive the Virago completely out of her mind. She's already furious he's given you this office.'

Luna laughed. 'Not a hope in hell! I'm not into Casanovas, and certainly not relationships at work.' She tried to visualize the thumbprint photo of the bespectacled man she was going to work with, an image that didn't seem to tally with his reputation as a Don Juan. From what she remembered, it was unlikely that he was going to get under her skin. 'Anyhow, I'm finished with men.'

Charo paused. 'If you don't mind me asking, are you gay?'

Luna gave her assistant a guarded look. 'No, I'm just not into that type of man. Not at all my cup of tea.' She shrugged. 'Besides, I've got better things to do with my time than to take up with some idle womanizer.'

'Womanizer maybe, but Dr Rueda de Calderón isn't idle. Far from it,' Charo protested vehemently. 'I've worked with many medics over the years and, I can tell you, I've never come across a more dedicated person. Totally devoted to his research, so passionate about it. You'll enjoy working with him, believe me.'

'Let's hope so,' said Luna.

She looked up at the clock on the wall. It was nearly one o'clock. Where had the morning gone? 'I'd better sign those papers Doña Vaina was talking about, and then I'll head off for my lunch break.'

Charo opened a desk drawer and took out a pile of documents. 'Here, take your time reading them over the weekend, if you like. I can pass them to the Virago on Monday.' She grinned. 'Do you have any lunch plans? I could show you the local deli, it's just across the road.'

Although Luna would have preferred being on her own for a while, she didn't want to seem standoffish on her first day. 'Sure, why not,' she replied. 'I was just going to grab a quick sandwich so I could catch up on some things before Monday, but it would be good to go out for a while.'

Charo's blue eyes were inquisitive. 'You're new to Cádiz, aren't you?'

'Yes, that's right.' Luna replied as she flipped through the contract in her hand.

'I expect you don't know anyone in the city.'

'Mmm? No, I don't.'

'There's a Vargas exhibition next week. A few of us have tickets,' Charo ventured. 'If you'd like to come along as my plus one, you might find it fun. A few drinks, canapés, a bit of culture, you know.'

After the frosty attitude of Doña Vaina this morning, Luna felt a sudden glow of appreciation. 'That sounds lovely. Really kind of you.' She smiled. 'You're right, I don't have any other plans. I'd love to come, thank you.'

Charo beamed. 'Wonderful! Right, I just have a letter to type before lunch. I'll pick you up as soon as I'm done,' she said, and slipped out of the room.

Luna read through the lengthy contract. It was quite a complicated document with umpteen provisions and stipulations, one of which was a particularly detailed confidentiality clause.

She had spoken to Ted Vandenberg about confidentiality and her editor had pooh-poohed it as something he would take care of when the matter arose. She could easily scan and email the agreement over to him to check before Monday. Yet she hesitated. Wasn't this assignment partly about proving to Ted she could be independent? She needed to show some initiative, use her own judgement. Besides, there was no room for procrastination if she wanted the job.

She wanted the job too. It wasn't just her ambition it spoke to. Everything about it was so novel, and it appealed to the adventurous side of her personality – the side she was discovering more and more; the side of late so expressive that she hardly recognized herself. Still, she was uneasy with the role she was meant to play to fulfil the assignment.

She reread the clause a few times. It definitely stipulated that all information was the property of the Institute, whether new discoveries made by her or other material. If the worst came to the worst, they could just pull the article. Ted wouldn't endanger the magazine by inviting a lawsuit. Even if her article never made it to print, the assignment would still be a leaf added to the notebook of her professional experiences. To see a clinic like this in action – how it functioned and whether the health programmes served its clients – all that was invaluable.

She signed her name on the dotted line.

*   *   *

An hour later, Luna was walking back through the gates of the Institute with Charo. Their lunch had taken longer than she'd planned but given how entertaining Charo had been and how charming the surroundings, she found herself not minding one bit. In the colourful deli on the corner of the next street, its window piled high with mouth-watering cheeses, chorizo and jars of appetizing sauces and pickles, she had watched the cheerful man behind the counter as he prepared a *bocadillo* with serrano ham for her, using a rustic *barra de pan*, drizzling olive oil and rubbing a cut tomato on the inside of the bread. These small details made Luna revel in the difference of everyday life here. Even compared to the Jewish delis of New York, the rituals of sandwich preparation seemed more exotic in Andalucía.

Charo seemed to know half the customers who came and went, chatting animatedly with those who stopped at their small table. She introduced each one to Luna, who watched her new colleague's carefree spirit with amused admiration. When they were left alone to carry on with their meal, though the young woman tried to fish for more personal information, there were enough interruptions to make it easy for Luna to field Charo's evident curiosity.

Now, as they crossed the car park and Charo expounded enthusiastically on the gastronomic and cultural delights of

Cádiz, a vintage-looking black-and-maroon car pulled into a space in front of them. The door opened and a familiar dark head came into view. Luna's heart leapt – she would know that profile anywhere.

It was *him*. Again.

Ruy emerged from the car looking his usual infuriating, stunning self in a lightweight pale-blue suit and tie. His sparkling aquamarine gaze fell on Luna and his mouth curved into a slow smile. If he was surprised to see her, he didn't show it.

Luna, on the other hand, was staring at him, almost frozen to the spot. Once more this man was appearing out of nowhere when she least expected it. Her emotions ran riot. A million thoughts crashed through her head, jostling for prominence. The longer she stared at him, the more mockingly handsome he became. His dark hair still curled in a devilish wave behind his ears. His shoulders looked more magnificently defined than ever; and his eyes glinted like crystals, making her feel lost, set adrift in a sea of confusion. Had he followed her, despite his cool denial of such intent at the airport? Was this some kind of joke? She was torn between anger and excitement, indignation and curiosity.

For a few seconds the air around the two of them crackled with electricity; one could almost hear the undercurrents crepitate, waiting to explode at any moment.

'*El gran doctor en persona*, the great doctor in person!' Charo exclaimed with an impish smile, which Ruy acknowledged, arching an indulgent brow. 'Dr Rodrigo Rueda de Calderón, let me introduce Dr Luna Ward, all the way from the United States. She arrived this morning and I've been showing her around.'

'Thanks, Charo. What luck! I believe we've already been introduced … briefly,' Ruy declared, his eyes glinting with humour.

Luna blinked at his arrogance. Could that small, grainy photo of the short-haired, bespectacled Dr Rodrigo Rueda de Calderón really be the same man? *Him?* The jigsaw of coincidences fell into place: Ruy, short for *Rodrigo*, of course ... the knowledgeable 'gypsy-scholar' in Barcelona for Goldsmith's talk ... His presence on the same flight to Cádiz the next day. Was there really such a thing as fate after all?

Then for a moment, as their eyes met, a flash of empathy passed between them and, without thinking, she responded to his smile.

'We'll have all the time in the world to get more acquainted,' he carried on as he continued to observe her, his blue eyes teasing. 'Since Dr Ward has been hired to help me in my research, I'm sure we'll achieve great things together. Isn't that so?' His gaze held hers steadily, scanning her face as if trying to gauge her reaction.

Luna swallowed and nodded, aware, too, that Charo's eyes were darting back and forth to watch their exchange, almost as if she were at a riveting tennis match. He must be enjoying this moment immensely; and she was finding it all too easy to let down her guard, faced with those bewitching blue irises. Well, she wasn't going to look like a dumbfounded fool.

'I'm sure it is,' she managed, forcing a polite smile. 'What surprising luck we've already had the chance to meet! Then again, my first few days in Spain have been full of surprises, Dr Rueda de Calderón,' she added pointedly.

'Please, it's Ruy.' His gaze was unwavering.

'Yes, of course it is,' she retorted, trying to keep the sarcasm from her voice. Underneath her contained exterior Luna was panicked, wondering if it wasn't too late to back out of her assignment. Her feelings about having to investigate the doctor – working undercover – had been uncomfortable enough, without the fresh complication of that doctor – her new boss – turning out to be Ruy. She had signed the contract, though, and she squirmed equally at the thought of retracting now.

Charo, who had been casting speculative glances at the pair of them, finally piped up: 'Well then, I'll leave you both to get *re*acquainted.' She raised an eyebrow at Ruy, then said to Luna with a knowing smile: 'I'll see you back in the office.' At this she bounded off, turning to give them one last mischievous look as she disappeared through the main entrance.

'Charo is a breath of fresh air to work with,' Ruy observed after she'd gone. 'Charming, good-hearted and a dreadful matchmaker. Now she'll be quizzing me about how we already know each other.' Luna turned to catch him grinning shamelessly at her. He shrugged. 'Doesn't fate work wonders.' It was more of a statement than a question. 'You know that saying: "When God closes a door, he opens a window?" Well, sometimes he'll do you one better and kick a wall down.'

'Do you know what Lemony Snicket says about fate? That it's like "a strange, unpopular restaurant, filled with odd waiters who bring you things you never asked for and don't always like,"' she answered, her dry tone valiantly trying to mask the feeling of shock.

Without warning, his hand reached out and covered hers. She stared down at the long, brown, elegant fingers. When she looked up again his eyes were boring into hers and suddenly the atmosphere was emotionally charged again. 'We have to talk properly, don't you think?' he whispered sheepishly. 'My dinner invitation still stands. How about tonight?'

Shock now made way for anger. Luna pulled her hand away and glared at him, her lips setting in a belligerent line. She ignored his question. 'Was it really just coincidence that we kept bumping into each other so conveniently?'

He nodded. 'Yes, absolutely. It was rather convenient, I'll give you that.'

'But you knew who I was on the plane, didn't you?'

'Not at first.' His lips twitched with a mixture of amusement and contrition. 'It wasn't hard to put two and two together once you told me your name was Luna.'

'Though you, of course, deliberately kept *your* name from me.'

Now he had the grace to look guilty. 'Yes, I suppose I shouldn't have. It was unfair of me.'

'Downright manipulative and obnoxious, I'd say. Do you get off on playing mind games?'

He raked a hand through his hair. 'I didn't mean to play games with you.'

Luna lifted an eyebrow and shook her head. 'Oh, please! I'm not a fool.'

He was still standing by his car and now locked it with a click of the key. Her expression seemed to make him thoughtful as he leaned his back against the door and folded his arms.

'Listen, Luna,' he said, smooth and low. 'I meant what I said to you on the plane. I can't apologize for being drawn to you but I am sorry for not divulging my identity. When I found myself sitting right next to you, I suppose it was too good an opportunity to miss, after letting you go twice before. I wanted a chance to see you unguarded.' He raised an eyebrow. 'Though clearly I failed miserably on that front. If I had told you who I was, you might have behaved differently, given we were going to work together. As it was, you made it very clear that you weren't interested in talking to me, so I thought it best to leave you alone and hope we could start again.'

Their gazes tangled and his was direct and sincere. At that moment she believed him. Yet she also knew it was only half the truth. Whatever this electricity was between them, it was charged with a dark, competitive edge and he had revelled in having the upper hand.

'So you thought it worth lying to me?'

He rubbed his jaw. 'Technically, I didn't lie to you about anything.'

Luna stared at him. Was she overreacting? Yes, probably. Her own hypocrisy wasn't lost on her either; after all, she was here under somewhat false pretence. Still, something about Dr Rodrigo Rueda de Calderón made her lose her grip on reason. This man seemed to make her feel either stupid or furious.

Ruy scanned her determined face, her stubbornly lifted chin. 'You're right, of course,' he added. 'I should have admitted who I was. It was ill-judged.' He pushed away from the car door and took a step towards her.

Luna felt his gaze travelling over her face, burning, scorching, and the male vibrations of his nearness on her skin. An invisible thread was drawing her back to him. Her senses were whirling dizzily, electrifying heat stirring through her veins. She had the impulse to touch him, to rest her hand on his sleeve, anything to have some sort of physical contact with him. Her heart hammered like crazy as she fought not to give in to that overwhelming need.

'We've got so much to talk over, Luna.' He was employing every weapon he possessed, caressing her with his eyes, his voice. She could read the desire in his steady gaze; he was using it to manipulate every nerve in her body and every cell in her brain with masterly expertise. His blue irises swept down and she cursed her own automatic response as her nipples tightened to firm points beneath her bra.

Please don't let him notice.

His gaze returned to her face, now focusing on her with unnerving intensity.

Luna held herself still, battling with her own weak will. How could she work with this man, day in, day out, and submit herself to such powerful, disturbing feelings? He was standing too close now and, although the rest of her was in turmoil, her light amber eyes were unblinking.

Suddenly, she said: 'I don't think this is going to work. I should quit now and save us both the bother of realizing it later.' Her voice was defiant, hiding the havoc his proximity was wreaking on her emotions, but she held her ground.

Gratified, she saw his face suddenly register surprise. 'You can't do that. You've just signed a contract. You owe me six months.'

'I owe you nothing. If I owe anybody, it's the Institute's board of directors.'

'Of which I'm one.'

Changing tack, she said: 'Given your attitude to me so far, and with your reputation, I'm likely to either hit you or sue you within the month. I'm sure you'd welcome neither prospect.'

Ruy laughed aloud, but then gave her a curious look. 'What do you know about my reputation?'

'Enough.'

'Really?'

'Your reputation has preceded you.'

His perfect lips curled on one side. 'You mustn't believe everything you hear.'

'I don't need to believe; I just need to go on what I know of you. That's the problem.'

Ruy sighed. 'Luna, come on. We really need to talk. I apologize for misleading you. We need to work together, and for that to be a success ...'

'Don't worry about the job, Doctor. *I'm* quite capable of being professional when needed. I'm good at what I do.'

Saying this out loud made Luna come back down to earth. Abandoning her assignment was not an option. Never mind her boss had turned out to be the man who'd tormented her dreams and waking hours for the past few days. The fact was this was something she needed to do for herself although, when she contemplated the stark reality of working with – and investigating – Ruy, she realized this job was going to be tougher than she'd ever thought possible. Still, she wasn't one to run away.

'I'll take up the post,' she declared, 'and I can assure you that you'll never have to complain about my work.'

Ruy considered the grave, challenging gaze that met his.

'So, where do we stand with each other now, Luna?'

As if to mark his point, he took a step closer. At this range she could see the darker cerulean outer ring of his irises surrounding the cool myriad flecks of turquoise and bright blue. The ready flush rose to her cheeks.

'Just as I said, you have nothing to worry about. I will do my job conscientiously and professionally.'

'So you'll give me a second chance?'

Luna took a deep breath. 'I really do need to get back to my desk now, I have a lot of notes to catch up on.'

He inclined his head slightly before stepping back, continuing to watch her reflectively. 'Of course.'

As she hurried down the pathway that led to the courtyard and Casa Vistaria she felt his gaze on her. Trembling slightly, she stopped at the entrance to collect her wits. Would she ever get used to this strange turn of events? Was this going to happen every time she spoke to him? She needed to get a grip on herself.

The door to the building was wrenched open. Charo stood on the threshold, frowning. 'Luna, are you all right? You look rather pale.'

'I'm fine, I just have a bit of a headache. Perhaps I had something for lunch that didn't agree with me.' She gave a small laugh, trying to sound light-hearted. 'I'm not used to having such a big meal at this time of day. In the States, I usually eat a sandwich on the run.'

'Well, next time, I'll show you our café. You can grab a quick salad, if you prefer something lighter.' She grinned. 'So now you've met your new boss.'

'It seems I have.'

'And?' Charo's bright, bird-like eyes would miss nothing, Luna supposed.

'And what?' she replied defensively.

Charo laughed aloud, but then gave her a curious look. 'Are you sure this headache of yours isn't the first symptom of flu?'

'I'm immune to flu. I always have the jab every year.'

'There are some viruses impossible to fight.'

'Don't worry about me,' said Luna, pressing on towards her office. 'I know how to take precautions to protect myself.'

CHAPTER 4

That evening, returning from the Institute, Luna was full of pent-up energy despite her long first day. She had meant to leave earlier but had not got as much reading done as she'd hoped. It was just past seven o'clock, too late for a swim, but she wanted to at least get in a long walk on the beach before dark. Changing into a loose lilac dress, she remained pensive as she let herself out of the back door of La Gaviota and made her way down through the dunes.

If there truly was such a thing as fate, then it had a perverse sense of humour, she mused. In the last forty-eight hours, her path had repeatedly collided with a charismatic, disturbingly handsome stranger whose very presence excited her more than any man she had ever met. Secretly, she had yearned to see him again. Now her wish had come true with the cruellest of twists: he turned out to be her new boss, the man she had been assigned to expose. She no longer knew what she was doing, or even who she was any more. It was as if the whole world had gone into free fall, leaving her reeling, grasping for a foothold to anchor her spinning thoughts and emotions. Where was the order and certainty that she was used to?

The heat had died down; the beach was deserted. Right and left, the magnificent coast stretched to oblivion, while the restless ocean swirled and eddied round the small rocks jutting above its surface, blowing spindrift off the crest of small waves. A gentle breeze rippled playfully along the tops of the sand dunes. Once again Luna was conscious of the intense silence surrounding her.

She had been walking briskly for twenty minutes, lost in thoughts that were mostly about Ruy, when she saw a figure coming towards her in the distance. At first it was only a black smudge on the landscape, then as it approached she realized it was a jogger – a man – still some way off. He was moving in her direction with a steady, rhythmical pace.

As he came nearer, Luna's heart started to thud; there was a drumming sound in her ears, and her breath caught in her throat: it was Ruy.

It was hard to believe her eyes. He was slowing down as though weighted to the sand by a strong counterforce, and Luna instinctively quickened her pace. No doubt he had also recognized her. She tried to look elsewhere as he approached, but her gaze was totally focused on him, mesmerized. He wore black compression shorts that were moulded alarmingly well to him, and a vest in the same colour, outlining those powerful shoulders. Locks of hair fell over his forehead in a sinfully touchable way as he moved, and beneath, his dark eyebrows and masculine jaw were set in concentration. It was a devastatingly handsome combination. Even at this distance, he really was Apollo reincarnated.

A few metres away from Luna he began walking, casually pulling up the edge of his vest to wipe his face and exposing a glimpse of chiselled muscle. Luna's eyes widened as her gaze fell helplessly to that tantalizing patch of stomach, and she had to focus hard on putting one foot in front of the other in case her knees gave way.

She stopped, bracing herself to meet him. Instead of halting too, he carried on closing the distance between them. Strong, warm hands went straight to her shoulders and before Luna had time to register what he was doing, he had pulled her towards him and his lips were on her cheek, greeting her with a kiss. She felt a shiver of excitement, sensing the delicious proximity of his strong jaw and the heat of his skin as he moved to the other cheek and did the same. He smelled of cool wind and fresh masculine sweat and the faint aroma of pine. His breath was only slightly laboured and the warm feel of it on her neck sent jolts of electricity shooting through her, settling in a hum deep in her belly.

When his hands slid from her shoulders, she could barely manage to say hello. Distracted by this onslaught of virility, Luna's mind wildly sought suitable words that might break through her own stunned embarrassment. Why was she consumed by such contradictory impulses? When he wasn't around, she thought about him all the time but when he appeared, she wanted to run in the opposite direction.

Ruy, however, seemed totally unabashed. His sharply defined brows lifted a fraction as he regarded her closely, then he chuckled. 'Luna, are you sure you don't believe in fate?' he asked, in his rich and deep voice. 'It seems we're destined to meet, whatever we do.'

At that point she made the mistake of glancing down at his thighs, which were long, tanned and muscular.

'You've been for a run,' she finally said, nonsensically.

'Yes, it appears that way.'

Luna dragged her gaze back to his face, and was met with an amused smile. She tried to regain some composure. 'I ... What I meant was, is this where you always go jogging?'

'Sometimes. This beach is one of the best in Cádiz. Do you live nearby?'

'Yes,' she replied elusively.

When it was clear no further information was forthcoming, he gave a half-smile and began stretching his lean, powerful leg muscles, lifting one foot and holding it behind his thigh. 'So, how was your first day at the Institute?'

Luna blinked, trying to concentrate. 'Fine, thank you. I caught up on some note-taking in the afternoon.' Although the truth was she'd been so distracted by her meeting with him in the car park that her mind had frequently wandered from the page. Luckily, he had not reappeared for the rest of the day.

'Your new office is to your liking?' He bent the other leg back behind him.

'Yes,' she agreed warily. Whether or not she liked being right next door to him, she wasn't yet sure. Then the thought of her assignment returned abruptly. At least it would make it easier for her to keep tabs on him for her article, she told herself.

He planted his foot back down on the sand and fixed her with a knowing look. 'Good. You'll find Charo excellent to work with. She's decided she likes you so, of course, you'll have to put up with her constant interference.'

Luna shot him a quizzical glance.

'I told her that we had run into each other in Barcelona, and Charo can be like a puppy with a new toy when she makes up her mind about something.' His mouth curved into a devilish, conspiratorial smile. 'It now seems we are her latest matchmaking project.'

'Is that so?'

He shrugged. 'We've become friends over the years. She likes to tease me about …'

'Your reputation?' she interjected, wryly.

'… the reasons I've not settled down,' he said simply. 'Of course, I told her that I had no designs on you whatsoever.' His eyes glittered. 'That would be presumptuous, would it not?'

So he was admitting his interest in her was frivolous and nothing serious would ever come of it. A treacherous wave of disappointment swept over Luna, leaving her adrift for a moment.

'Well, yes, we've already agreed that our relationship is a purely professional one,' she conceded, trying to put some conviction in her voice.

'Then again, it doesn't do to be too frank with Charo.' He cocked his head to one side with a half-smile. 'I'm perfectly capable of looking after my own love life.'

Luna tamped down the hopeful stirrings, trying to replace them with caution. Certainly, that kiss he'd given her, however chaste, was not entirely innocent. The imprint of his lips on her cheek was still tingling under her skin.

'Why did you kiss me just now?' she blurted out. It appeared she had formed the habit of asking him stupid questions.

'Should I not have done?'

'It's not appropriate. It's ... unprofessional.'

He grinned and gestured nonchalantly to his state of dress. 'We're not in the office now,' he pointed out. 'Besides, that is how Spanish men greet women they know. It's no big deal.'

'It is, if we are to work together properly.'

'It's only an issue for you because you find me attractive and for some reason you don't want to admit it.' His eyes gleamed a daring, provocative shade of blue. 'I, on the other hand, have no such problem.'

His arrogance was so blatant it almost made her laugh. Yet he was right and it was almost a relief to hear him voice what she couldn't deny.

'You're very sure of yourself, aren't you?'

'About some things, yes.'

He looked so boyishly pleased with himself that finally she did laugh. 'I suppose it's that kind of staggering self-assurance that makes every woman fall at your feet.'

His eyebrows went up. 'Clearly, not every woman.'

'It may surprise you, but some women require a little more subtlety.'

He laughed low, and some indefinable emotion flashed in his eyes. 'I've never had a use for it before.'

Luna shook her head. 'The flaw of many an attractive man.' Her flirtatious response came all too easily and because she was beginning to enjoy their exchange and because that sensual mouth of his looked so devastating when it broke into a wolfish grin, she smiled back at him.

Ruy folded his arms across his broad chest. 'So you think I'm attractive?' he teased.

Ever since childhood Luna had been a terrible liar, so she decided to be direct. 'Yes, of course. I won't deny it. You're also very upfront about what you think. I'm not used to it. It's, well, very … Spanish.'

He laughed more loudly this time, a deep throaty sound that made Luna's toes curl and shot warmth to all her secret places. 'Yes, we say what we think here. We are passionate, reckless, proud and sincere about all of it. It's the Spanish way. What you call an argument we call *una discusíon*, what you call lack of subtlety, we call *la franqueza*.' He dropped his voice in mock seriousness. 'And let me tell you, in Cádiz we are even guiltier of all of those things.'

Luna chuckled, unable to resist his playfulness. 'In that case, I'll have a crash course in Spanish culture living here.' From that moment, she found herself softening. It was really no use trying to maintain any kind of defence with Ruy. He was determined to charm his way around it.

'You know, you're a different person when you relax,' he said, regarding her. 'I know you're apparently immune to absurd compliments but did you know that those honey eyes of yours turn gold when you smile? It's enough to bring a man to his knees.'

She felt a warm blush rise up her chest and throat. *I'm certainly different with you. No matter what I do, I don't seem to be able to control myself.* She held his gaze. 'No wonder you have a certain reputation with women.'

'I'm merely stating the truth.' He looked mildly affronted. 'And my reputation, as you call it, is exaggerated, largely rumours and gossip these days. Anyone who knows me well knows that.'

'That's just it, I don't know you well at all.'

His proximity seemed to make the air between them gently pulsate and Luna hugged herself, as if needing some kind of protection against it. She could not tear her eyes away from him.

'So why not let fate do its work,' he murmured, 'and that will be remedied quickly enough.'

He had moved closer and was studying her thoroughly, intent blue eyes warmly stroking, setting her heart racing with excitement. Spellbound, Luna felt a flame sweep through her and she shrugged shyly, struggling to stop its effect from surfacing.

'Am I allowed to tell you that you are *encantador*, ravishing, in that lilac dress? Pastels suit your delicate beauty.'

He was smiling down at her, meeting the obvious confusion in her eyes with open, uncomplicated desire. Luna's pulse hammered in her ears.

No other man had ever made her feel this feminine. Her whole life had been spent in wary observation of the opposite sex, never wanting too much attention. She would never have believed her whole being could revel in one man's scrutiny. Now, the way Ruy was looking at her, she never wanted it to end.

Luna managed to laugh, trying to lighten her own awkward emotions. 'That's what it is about you Spanish men. You're so suave and engaging.' She held her hands up in defeat. 'I admit it. You always find just the right words to say to a woman. Back home, women are not used to this kind of treatment.'

His eyes darkened as he gazed at her. He was serious now and for a moment she wondered if her remark had offended him in some way.

'But you are not at home, Luna, you're in Spain, the land of love and passion.'

Indeed she was. Over the past few days her thoughts had often touched on that, but she did not tell him so.

'Look over there.' He gestured behind her with a nod. 'Have you ever seen such incandescent sunsets?'

Luna turned and was met by a festival of red, gold and blue exploding like fire in the sky. Together they stood side by side, silently watching the close of day, only half-absorbed by the sun sinking rapidly in blazing glory just above the horizon, each strongly aware of the other.

Ruy was the first to break the silence. 'Twilight is brief here. It gets dark very quickly. Can I walk you back to …?' he hesitated.

Luna answered his mute question. 'My house is on the beach.'

'Ah, yes, one of those cottages?'

'No, a little further along.'

He frowned slightly. 'I didn't know there were houses at the far end of this stretch.'

'There's only one house. I've rented it.'

For a few moments Ruy remained where he was, contemplating her, his head on one side. Then, without a word, he held his hand out to her. She took it automatically, confidently, and was aware of a comfort in his firm clasp, which she hadn't realized could exist between a man and a woman. It gave a new, unspoken intimacy to their friendship. As they strolled back across the sand, it was as if she were walking in a dream. All clarity of thought deserted her and she had no idea why she was letting him accompany her back to the house, possessively claiming her hand as he did so. The only sense she had as they walked back, neither of them speaking, was of that warm, strong grip that made her feel almost giddy with exhilaration.

By the time they reached La Gaviota, the breeze blowing in from the sea had somewhat intensified. A brilliant, almost theatrical-looking full moon sailed up above the distant hills, and millions of stars were scattered like irregular diamonds on the sapphire velvet sky.

This time it was Luna who spoke first. 'We're here,' she said as the house came into view above the dunes.

Ruy turned to face her and finally released her hand, smiling that lazy, enigmatic shadow of a smile which, in the moonlight, made him look even more dramatically handsome and mysterious.

At this moment she knew nothing else except that her heart was beating furiously, her knees threatened to fold under her at any moment as sensuous shivers rippled over her entire skin and she longed for him to take her in his arms and kiss her. Was she going mad? This was so out of character. It would be crazy to embark on an affair with this man.

He was much too close to her again, his body too barely clothed for her sanity. Then she watched with a thrill of arousal and panic as his gaze dipped to her mouth. Slowly his head began to draw nearer to hers.

Luna had wanted this so much but a warning voice managed to rise up through the hazy intoxication of the moment. *Stop. Think. You can't let this happen.* She shook her consciousness back to a stunned awareness and placed both hands on his chest, feeling the solid wall of muscle beneath.

'No, Ruy. You know this isn't a good idea.'

His sensually shaped lips quirked as he continued to gaze at hers. 'I'd say it was a very good idea.'

Gently she pushed her hands against him and played the best card at her disposal. 'We've discussed this. We have to work together.'

For several moments Ruy contemplated her, his face inches from her own, his eyes burning with intensity. Finally, he sighed and nodded, his gaze still locked on her. 'The moon does funny things to men, didn't you know that?' he said huskily, pulling back.

She swallowed hard. *Oh, you're in trouble, Luna. This man is dangerous indeed. It could all go terribly wrong.* She wasn't there to fall for anyone, let alone Ruy Rueda de Calderón.

The soft breeze ruffled her hair and a few blonde wisps fell across her eyes.

'Don't look so alarmed, *querida*, I won't turn into a werewolf at midnight,' he murmured as he lightly brushed back the pale strands from her face. She sucked in her breath when his fingertips came into contact with her skin and looked up into his face with only the moon to guide her gaze.

They were bathed in pearly light and shadow. Around them, the sound of the sea rumbled on, as the waves broke rhythmically on the narrow stretch of shingle with a rustle and drag in their ceaseless ebb and flow.

Ruy's deep-set eyes were so dark they seemed almost black as they gazed at her, soft and eager. 'Will you accompany me to a masked ball tomorrow night?' he suddenly asked, his sensuous lips curving into a disarming smile.

Luna blinked in surprise. This was the last thing she had expected him to say. She replied with the first sentence that came into her head: 'I've never been to a masked ball.'

'My grandparents give one every year at their hacienda in Jerez. Will you come?'

Luna hesitated. A masked ball ... with Ruy. What should she say to that? Stepping on to his home turf rang so many alarm bells yet, despite all the personal reservations lining up to agitate her better judgement, another part of her stirred. A powerful and unknown part of her enchanted at the exotic prospect of a masked ball with all its attendant glamour, intrigue and romance. She stared into Ruy's eyes that had darkened to blue obsidian as they watched her expectantly in the moonlight, and knew that part of her also thrilled at the thought of being alone with him at such an event.

That's hardly the point, a sterner voice inside her piped up, shaking her out of such frivolous emotions. Pure logic stepped in like a neglected, interfering old friend. She must remember why she was there, and that was to complete an assignment … and her assignment was Dr Rodrigo Rueda de Calderón. There was a lot riding on this job, both professionally and personally. Ever since they met she had been behaving like hunted prey. Heaven knows how she was going to do it but, from now on, it was her turn to be the hunter.

Accepting his invitation would be the perfect opportunity to get to know her quarry better. After all, she was an investigative journalist doing an exposé. Presuming they would travel together to the ball, the journey time to Jerez would allow her to quiz him about his medical background, the clinic and its treatments.

Still, the ball was tomorrow night. To her, such spontaneity was completely alien and rode roughshod over her need for order.

'What shall I wear? How would I get hold of a costume at such short notice?'

The question was as much to herself as to Ruy.

'Live in the moment, Luna.' He smiled at her and, despite her previous inner pep talk, she felt the warmth of it ripple all the way down to her toes. 'Besides, it shouldn't be difficult. Mascaradas has everything you can possibly think of. It's a shop in Jerez that has supplied costumes for the El Pavón annual masked ball for a century. I can take you there.'

'Thank you, I'm sure I'll find it. Mascaradas, in Jerez, you said?'

'Yes, off Plaza del Arenal, the main square. It's half an hour's drive from Cádiz.'

'I've already driven that route, coming back from the airport.'

'Yes, of course.' He grinned. 'So will you come with me tomorrow?'

Luna inhaled deeply. 'Yes,' she answered. 'Yes, thank you. I'd love to go to the ball with you.'

'I'll pick you up at nine o'clock.'

She smiled back at him, still wondering at her own intrepid spirit. 'I'll be waiting.'

'I'll walk you up to the house,' he said. 'La Gaviota, a very apt name,' he remarked as they cleared the dunes and went through the gate. 'The house really does look like a large bird. It's a very unique design. Quite a find, I would say.'

She didn't take in his words or make a rejoinder, as it had suddenly dawned on her that he had walked half a mile to escort her safely back to the house. Was his own home far away? He might live in one of the cottages he had mentioned, but it seemed unlikely, otherwise Luna would have seen him around the beach more. How would he get back? Of course he could always call a taxi, she supposed.

It was night, and the temperature had dropped dramatically. In that skimpy running outfit he must be cold, she told herself. As her gaze slid involuntarily downwards again, Luna was glad that her infuriating blush was largely hidden by the night.

She quickly stooped to pick up her keys from under a flowerpot beside the path. 'How are you getting back?' she asked. 'It's quite chilly tonight.'

He smiled faintly. '*No te preocupes por mi*, don't worry about me. My car is parked just off the beach road, not far from here. I was jogging back to it when we met.' Amusement danced in his eyes as she looked at him furtively. 'But thank you for your concern.'

They walked up the couple of steps to the front door.

'This is a very isolated spot. Do you live alone here?'

'Yes.'

'I'm surprised that your *novio*, your boyfriend back in New York, doesn't object,' he ventured coolly.

Not a very subtle way of finding out whether she was single. Nice try, she thought, and smiled inwardly, busying herself with opening the front door so she would be saved from making a reply.

Luna stepped inside, switched on the light and turned off the alarm. Ruy stayed on the threshold, and her senses throbbed with the awareness of him standing just behind her. She didn't ask him in.

'Thank you for walking me back,' she said as she twisted round to face him. In the bright overhead light of the room, his good looks were even more overwhelming as he leant a forearm against the doorjamb. Their eyes met, words trembling unspoken between them. She stood motionless, her senses transfixed by his hypnotizing irises that gleamed with cobalt intensity; and he knew just what he was doing to her. It was written all over that infuriating Cheshire cat smile. He was tantalizingly close, watching her silently with a caressing, heated gaze that made liquid heat flood her, spreading wildly down between her thighs. Luna felt a powerful urge to widen the gap between herself and Ruy, away from that smile, away from those tauntingly muscled arms and legs. She took two steps back. He wasn't playing fair. How was she supposed to relax with him when he looked at her that way?

His eyes drifted briefly over her taut body, poised to flee, then back to her face. '*Buenas noches*, Luna, Queen of the Night,' he murmured. He flicked her an amused wink. '*Hasta mañana*, until tomorrow.' Thereupon he turned on his heel, jogged down the steps and out of the gate.

Luna closed the front door and pulled back the sliding window to let in the soothing night air. She needed to sit down. Taking a deep breath, she tried to think, but confused thoughts bumped against each other in her overexcited brain. Her limbs were trembling, the sensation of quivering heat still coursing through her body. She leant her head against the back of the sofa, closed her eyes and though she knew she should not, she let her fantasy run free.

Ruy hadn't left. She invited him in for a drink – red wine. She brought the bottle and a couple of glasses on to the terrace, where he was waiting for her, looking out to sea. The full moon was shining, turning the restless ocean to silver and the rocks at the side of the bay to velvet. He turned, and moonlight fell on his handsome face. His eyes were dark and intent, charged with pent-up feeling. All for her.

They sipped their wine, never taking their eyes off each other. He took the glass from her hand and put it down on the table. Words were irrelevant. Electric crosscurrents of emotion seemed to spin and spread between them with the intricacy of a spider's web. Then he was kissing her with single-minded urgency – his lips, his hands, tasting, touching, exploring, purposeful and possessive in their relentless hunger. As excitement undulated through her in delicious waves, she felt dizzy with yearning, eager to be totally possessed by him, until her body and his were one …

Suddenly Luna was startled from her sensory dream by a dull thump on the sofa next to her. She smothered a scream and her hand flew to her chest as she stared into the yellow-green eyes of a large black cat, a beautiful creature with a bushy tail and a small white patch on his chest. He must have come in through the open window.

Once she had recovered from her surprise, Luna noticed he wore a collar around his neck with a silver medallion. She peered closer and read *Gitano-Negro*, black gypsy, with a telephone number underneath. 'Your owners must be looking for you,' she whispered to the creature, which was watching her now with half-closed eyes.

She lifted herself up from the sofa, still a little dazed from her erotic reverie, and staggered to the telephone. Then she glanced at her watch. It was not yet ten o'clock and, by Spanish standards, still early. Luna dialled the number and let it ring for a few seconds, but there was no answer. She looked at her uninvited guest. 'I suppose I could put you up for the night. I'll bring you some milk and then we'll both turn in early. What d'you think?' The animal scrunched up its eyes a few times, hopped off the sofa and followed her into the kitchen.

Milk was a good idea. She wasn't hungry enough to eat anything more than a few biscuits, and needed something soothing to help her to sleep. The day had finally caught up with her and, although she was now tired, part of her mind was still whirring.

Luna heated some milk for herself and filled up a bowl for Gitano-Negro. 'Come on, cat,' she said, turning round, but he had deserted her. She went back to the living room, but he was not there either so she called out his name. No sign of the creature. Sighing, she looked for him upstairs and again on the ground floor.

This was the sort of aggravation she could do without. The house was compact; there weren't many places to hide. He must have gone back to his home, she thought. His owners were probably inhabitants of one of the cottages further down the beach.

Luna closed the window and made sure the shutters were securely shut. *That's taught me a lesson.* She should be careful not to fall asleep with the ground-floor windows open. What had got into her? She would never have taken that kind of risk before. This time the intruder was a cat, next time she might not be so lucky. Both Ruy and the estate agent Diego had commented on her living alone in such an isolated place. Still, she loved this house and if she only remembered to be vigilant about security, she'd be fine.

Her milk was lukewarm by now, but she was too weary to heat it up again. She carried it to her bedroom, and once upstairs turned on the alarm.

Luna ran a bath and lay in it for half an hour, delighting in the gentle strokes of hot water on her tense body, feeling the strain of the evening gradually seep away. No matter how much she tried, she couldn't stop her mind from wandering back to the erotic daydream she'd had after Ruy's departure. She had never fantasized in this way before. Every detail was still alive in her memory, the yearning and the intense ache in her loins. A heat suffused her body that had nothing to do with the bathwater, and she was aware that it would not take long for her to conjure up those forbidden delights again; they were still quivering on the edge of her imagination, alive in every erotic detail … but to what end? Even if Ruy hadn't been off limits, he still would not be there to satisfy her hunger. Oh God, what use was there denying it? How she longed to make love with him. She made a determined effort to push away images of his tanned skin sculpted with muscle and the bulge of virility between his thighs, enhanced by the form-hugging shorts stretching tight across it, where more than once her eyes had fallen quite inadvertently.

It was extraordinary how something always seemed to conspire to make the two of them meet again. She was almost tempted to believe there was such a thing as fate that played with people's lives like pieces on a chessboard. First, the nightclub in Barcelona, quite off the beaten track, to which she had not planned to go. Then he had turned up at the conference the following day. The next thing she knew, he was claiming a seat next to her on the plane to Cádiz; and to top it all, when she arrived at her new job, he turned out to be Dr Rodrigo Rueda de Calderón, the man whom she'd been sent to Spain to investigate.

Luna put a soapy hand over her eyes and groaned. This was truly terrible. She'd had fears enough about getting mixed up with such a dangerously attractive man before she even knew who he was. How could she possibly get involved now?

Expect the unexpected – that's what she should have warned herself when it came to Ruy. That way, perhaps she would have been less dumbstruck this evening at their chance meeting on 'her' stretch of beach. The probability of this happening again was low, her logical mind reasoned, rinsing herself off, stepping out of the bath and enveloping herself in a soft, fluffy towel. Yet everything about Ruy – and her reaction to him – was intriguing. Even his invitation to a masked ball added ambiguity and mystery to their encounter. She felt reckless. Within her there was a surging, oblivious excitement over which she had no control. Somehow, she was being drawn into a game, the rules of which she didn't know, but for the first time in her life, Luna found she didn't mind at all.

*   *   *

After leaving La Gaviota, Ruy had jogged briskly up the beach road to his car. He had a free evening and, although it would have been wise to get straight behind the wheel and drive away from there, he hadn't fancied going home just then. Besides, when had he ever done the sensible thing? It had grown chilly. He'd put on the tracksuit he always kept in the boot, let out his black cat from the back seat where it often liked to doze and strolled back to the beach with the creature at his heels. He'd sat down on the sand, gazing at the glittering path of moonlight on the ruffled waters of the bay, not far from Luna's house, though far enough for her not to see him if she came on to the terrace. He had a strange need to be close to her.

Ruy breathed in the spicy sea air and gazed into the dark sky, streaked with silvery-edged clouds. He thought he'd reached some kind of equilibrium these days, made more bearable by the easy solace of forgettable women. The past was a shadow that always followed him, but kept an obedient distance. For the first time in his life, a light had pushed through that darkness, and its delicate flame was glowing invitingly. It was so clear. He wanted it; he wanted *her*.

Yet Luna puzzled him.

He knew without doubt that she was aware of the irresistible attraction between them and felt threatened by it. Perhaps it was just professional prudence, as she claimed. Maybe she had a point, as they would be working closely together. Yet, why had she persistently held him at arm's length before she'd even found out they were to be colleagues?

Was she a private person, cautious or just shy? Perhaps all three … No, shyness was not one of her traits, he decided, remembering her challenging talk at their every encounter. Still, intuition told him there was more to this startled rabbit manner than met the eye. One minute there was a spark of warm humour in her eye or the darker promise of flickering passion beneath; the next, those same bright amber eyes were edgy, vigilant … almost fearful, it seemed. He had learned to look beyond typical characteristics when analyzing a person; human beings were ambiguous and complicated creatures, personalities multifaceted.

Luna was a bundle of contradictions – a shapely and bewitching one that had begun to haunt him.

He ran a hand through his hair. It had been foolish to try to kiss her; it was too soon. Though she had thawed towards him tonight, he sensed she was still wary. Professional partnership or not, he had to see where this unfamiliar, exciting feeling would take him. He needed to spend more time with her; get to know her better. Now that he had manoeuvred it so that her office was next to his, that would make it easier.

He evoked her delicate features: the pert nose, that lovely mouth, so sensitive and perfect it might have been carved by a sculptor, yet so curved, soft and inviting … he really had to get a grip on his urges. If she had let him kiss her, what would she have tasted like? Of simmering wildness, and sweet honey. Those almond-shaped golden eyes that had looked up into his, so warm and limpid, had stirred him more than if she had been lying naked at his feet. Luna naked … It was an image he was becoming used to picturing during restless nights. Naked beneath him while he threaded his fingers through her long silken hair, spilling over her breasts. He wanted her so badly, he ached. Ruy shuddered with frustration.

The temperature had dropped even further. It was time to go home.

He looked for Gitano-Negro. 'Damn the cat!' he muttered softly. What was he up to now?

His eyes strayed to La Gaviota. Light was streaming through the ground-floor window. She was still awake. High above, the golden stars were shimmering against a navy blue canopy. Determinedly, he tried to make out their patterns.

It was no use. His mind slipped back to her.

What did she wear in bed? He could just imagine her beautiful blonde hair scattered around her face like a pale mantle on her pillow. His body tightened; he felt its growing anticipation.

Damn the woman and damn the cat!

He wrenched his clothes off and ran down to the sea, embracing its iciness with relief.

*   *   *

That night the dream revisited her, more vivid and frightening than usual. He was in the room, she could tell. It was dark, with shadows falling across her bed from the open window. A hot night. Too hot.

The sound of her door was a slow creak, closing shut with a click. She couldn't move. Why couldn't she move? It was as though she were paralyzed from the neck down.

She tried to speak but no sound came out.

Panic gripped her throat as she tried to shout. She could hear him moving around the room, getting closer. Was she in Cádiz or at home in California? All she knew was that he was coming for her.

Her head thrashed from side to side as the footsteps moved softly towards her.

'Sshhhh, Luna.'

No. No. No.

Luna woke, gasping from the nightmare. She sat bolt upright, her chest heaving, then slumped forward, head in her hands. After a few moments, she reached for the water by her bed and gulped it down until it was all gone. She ran her fingers through her damp hair.

Although this was no new experience for her, she couldn't sleep for hours after the nightmare, terrified it would haunt her again. She was not surprised that it had finally caught up with her. Perhaps it was to be expected after the roller coaster of emotions she had been through.

Turning off the house alarm upstairs, she padded downstairs to the kitchen where she made herself another hot drink. Finally, as dawn stretched its flaming fingers through the sky, she went off to sleep, exhausted, wondering how she was going to have enough energy for the ball, but grateful that it would at least be masked.

CHAPTER 5

The sun was already lowering in the sky, casting long shadows in Plaza del Arenal when Luna arrived in Jerez late that afternoon to search for the costume shop.

An uninterrupted sleep well past lunchtime had revived her, though she wished there was more of the day left. That way there would have been more time to explore this impressive square, she thought, walking along the wide boulevard lined with tall jacaranda trees, and taking in the colourful food shops, street vendors and craftsmen.

Her gaze picked out an odd-looking place.

Ah, this must be it.

Luna stood for a few seconds outside the glass-fronted shop and lifted her gaze to the tatty gold-painted sign above the window. *Mascaradas*: she was definitely there.

Mascaradas was by no means a smart shop, especially compared with the luxurious boutiques with which it was competing for attention along the long stretch of pavement. Yet the faded panelled wood of the façade spoke of a bygone elegance that was both endearing and fascinating, like a glamorous old lady imparting secrets from her youth.

Luna pushed the red door and let it clang behind her. The shop reeked of turpentine combined with the heady scent of jasmine, attesting to the fact that, inside at least, the whole place had recently been painted. From floor to ceiling the interior was coloured burgundy. It was lit with bright neon lights, and a kaleidoscope of costumes hung higgledy-piggledy on long black rails and spilled out of large, yawning leather trunks. Mannequin heads that had seen better days stared out from shelves, some with garish-looking hats, others held false beards and wigs. Everything seemed gaudy; Luna was not impressed.

A young woman in faded jeans and a white lacy blouse emerged from a curtained-off room at the back of the shop, behind the counter. She smiled her greeting. '*Bienvenida, señorita? Puedo ayudarle?* Can I help you?'

Luna had no doubt the woman was a gypsy. Her fierce, raven-black eyes and the swathes of wonderful jet-hued hair that undulated down her back like waves of dark water were evidence of her blood. Long golden filigree earrings hung from her ears and dozens of bracelets clanked on her wrists.

'*Buenas tardes, señorita.* I've been invited to a masked ball tonight at rather short notice and I'm looking for a costume,' Luna explained.

'The ball at El Pavón, *ey*?'

Luna's eyebrows went up. 'Yes, that's right. How did you know that?'

'What other ball could it be?' The gypsy woman scooped up some feather boas that had escaped their boxes on the cluttered shelves behind the counter and carefully put them away. 'The masked ball at El Pavón has been going on for generations. It's a well known tradition and very exclusive.' She turned back and winked. 'You're a lucky one to have an invite.'

Nerves skittered in Luna's stomach again, reminding her of the glamorous event she would be attending in just a few hours – and the man whose guest she would be. She smiled faintly. 'Yes, I suppose I am.'

'Then again I'm not surprised,' the other woman added cryptically. She noticed Luna's momentary look of confusion and gave an enigmatic smile. 'So, what do you have in mind?' The *gitana* was friendly and laughter lit her strong features.

Luna relaxed. 'I'm not sure. Something simple, I think. Nothing too flashy.'

The Romany woman peered at her curiously. 'You're not Spanish. *Inglés? Americana?*'

'I'm half Spanish and half American.'

'Ah! That's why you speak our language so fluently. You look foreign but, of course, you could have come from Castilla. The people there are as fair as you are.'

Luna smiled politely. She didn't want to seem rude; still, she ignored the *gitana*'s speculations and tried to bring back the conversation to the task in hand. 'You seem to have a large choice of costumes,' she ventured, her eyes travelling round the shop.

The *gitana* tossed her head proudly and pulled back the long green-and-gold curtain behind her. 'Don't bother with the fancy dress things in the front of the shop. They're for ordinary parties, just a bit of fun. You'll want our VIP selection, the vintage costumes. The disguises are divided into four categories: history, tales and legends, costumes of the world, and miscellaneous. I can help you.' She beckoned with her hand to invite Luna behind the counter. 'Come. *Sí, ven, ven!*'

The shop was more organized than Luna had thought at first. As she followed the woman through the thick curtain, she could see that the space back here was tidier. It was a large square room with dark-green walls and ornate gold cheval mirrors at one end. Neat rails of clothes lined three sides, interspersed with mahogany chests of drawers, on top of which stood black mannequin heads displaying a fantastic array of masks. A few faded velvet chairs and stools occupied the centre of the atmospheric room.

'This is quite an Aladdin's cave you have here,' Luna remarked, walking up to one of the chests and picking up a gold-and-silver feathered mask. 'How long have you had the shop?'

'Oh, Mascaradas doesn't belong to me. I just stand in for my friend, the owner, when she goes on holiday,' the woman explained, rearranging some clothes on the hangers. 'It was her uncle, old Jaime, who used to own it before her. He took years building up the collection. I like it here, though. These four walls have *buenas vibraciones*, a good spirit. The people who come here always have a story or two to tell as well.' At this she smiled warmly at Luna, who wondered if this was a fishing remark. She carefully replaced the mask back on its mannequin.

With the *gitana*'s encouragement, Luna began to rifle through the rails. Some of the costumes were fabulous but, even though she was spoilt for choice, she found most outfits too bright. Red, orange, green and violet alternated with electric blue, fuchsia pink and other colours of the rainbow; and while they were all beautiful, none took her fancy.

Luna was beginning to lose heart when she pulled out a dress of such fine and silky fabric that it appeared almost unreal. The light muslin panels that made up the skirt were woven with a silver yarn that shimmered each time it caught the light, as though minuscule diamonds were encrusted in the material. It was a daring dress that, if worn, would reveal the greater part of her thighs and legs when she walked. Not only that, the fabric was virtually transparent. She would have to wear a flesh-coloured bodice underneath it.

'You like this one?' the gypsy asked.

'Yes, I think so. Though I'm wondering whether it's not a little provocative.'

The shopkeeper nodded. 'It's an exquisite and unusual piece. It wouldn't suit everybody, that's why it has never been worn.' She gave Luna a frank stare and then glanced at the pale green vintage dress that clung to her slender frame. 'God has given you a rare beauty, *señorita*, and a delicate figure to match. You must not be ashamed to show it off. I think it's the perfect choice for your colouring and physique.'

Luna smiled shyly at the woman's compliment. The *gitana* had an intense way of speaking, warm and direct, and a look in her eye that seemed wise beyond her years.

'That's very kind.' Luna held the costume up again, thoughtfully. 'What does it represent?'

'It can be turned into all sorts of different disguises depending on the accessories you choose to go with it. We have ones for the Snow Queen, various nymphs and fairies of the rivers and seas – and of course for Luna, the Queen of the Night. The items which complement that costume are not for hire, only for sale, because they're expensive and very fragile, too.'

Luna was suddenly beside herself with excitement. Ruy had called her 'Queen of the Night' and now here was a costume that represented just that.

'Can I try it on?'

The woman nodded with a knowing smile. '*Si, por supesto*, yes, of course. Would you like me to bring down some accessories?'

'Yes, please. The Luna ones.'

The gypsy returned carrying a diamanté tiara topped with the carving of a crescent moon at its centre, a shawl made of fine silver threads, a pair of dainty sandals, a round, sparkling clutch bag and silver dust to sprinkle over Luna's hair. She gasped admiringly as Luna, who had slipped on the dress, came into the fitting room and then stared transfixed while she stood in front of the mirror.

'This costume was made for you, *señorita*. Such otherworldly loveliness. It has been waiting for you.'

Luna regarded her own reflection with a combination of surprised pleasure and wariness. Normally, she dressed in an understated but feminine way for parties from the habit of carefully measuring the attention she would attract. However, this was a masked ball and no ordinary party – and she was not her usual self these days. A kernel of impetuosity in her nature was growing shoots that were pushing their way determinedly to the surface.

'I think it does suit me. Can I buy it?'

'We don't usually sell our costumes, but this one is meant for you. I can see that now.' The *gitana* gazed at her. 'What is your name, *señorita?*'

'Luna.'

The Romany woman's eyes widened. 'Ah, Luna … But of course! *El Destino te ha traido aqui hoy*, destiny has brought you here today, Luna. Though I can tell by looking at you that you do not believe in such things.'

Luna glanced sideways at her. 'No, not really.'

The other woman chuckled. 'Do you think *El Destino* is bothered by what we think? Its wheel carries on turning, no matter what we believe.' Her bracelets jangled on her arm as she gestured towards the diaphanous dress moulding itself to Luna like a second skin. 'You think it was pure chance that you found this costume today? Or perhaps I should say that the costume found *you.*'

'You really believe all that, even in this day and age? I mean, in a force beyond our control?'

The *gitana* tutted and shook her head. 'We *gitanos* know from our own history that however long your legs, there is no running from *El Destino*. For good or ill. May the sky fall upon me but it's true.'

Luna's curiosity gave another kick. '*Being from a gypsy family, I've come to realize there are more things in heaven and earth, as they say.*' Ruy's words came back to her from their conversation on the plane. She wanted to ask the woman what else gypsies knew about, but didn't know how to begin such a conversation.

As if reading her thoughts, the *gitana* smiled and raised her chin slightly. 'My name is Morena. I am the granddaughter of Paquita, the great Romany fortune teller, whose words never failed. Like her, I have the gift. Give me your left hand, *y té dire tuo destino*, and I will tell your fate.' She broke into a broad smile, revealing perfectly white teeth in her gold-hued face.

As little as a month ago, Luna would have found a polite excuse to decline such an offer. Her logical disposition didn't lend itself to this kind of superstitious indulgence. After everything that had happened since her arrival in Spain, she found, to her slight irritation, that she was curious, though. Besides, she secretly found it quite romantic to have her palm read by a gypsy. This new, irrational aspect of herself was clearly to blame. She held out her hand to the other woman.

As she touched Luna, Morena flinched and her magnificent dark eyes blazed like those of a tiger. 'You have been endowed with *la gracia de mano*.'

'*La gracia de mano*, what does that mean?' Luna peered down at her own hand, as if trying to discern what Morena had seen in it. 'I don't understand.'

'It's a healing power. God in his kindness blesses one woman in a thousand with it. Like I have been given the gift of reading the future, you have received the power to cure.' Morena nodded, deep in thought. 'Most of all, when you are with a man your touch will be unforgettable. It will bewitch the one who falls in love with you.'

Luna's former scepticism reared its head against the *gitana*'s words. Wasn't this what every woman wanted to hear? Still, she kept her thoughts to herself.

Morena took Luna's left hand in her own and smoothed its palm flat with her thumb. 'You have a sensual hand,' she noted. 'Yes, the pleasures you can give a man are infinite and, with the right partner, you yourself will reach the highest levels of fulfilment.' Then her keen sable eyes concentrated on the lines of the palm and she began telling Luna of the past. Her remarks were largely generalized – a separation from her parents, loneliness, great academic achievement, a need to prove herself … Overall what she said was remarkably true, however.

'Now for the future, *señorita hermosa*, whose heart is wrapped in night, a night so deep and so dark that it's making you blind. Monsters and demons inhabit it. It's full of fears that make you timid, like a *paloma*, a dove.'

At this the gypsy looked up. In her dusky face, her eyes, dark and mysterious, met Luna's. They revealed nothing of what she was thinking. She lowered them again. 'There are stars of hope in your sky, though. One in particular shines strong and bright. Still, its beauty dazzles you, and you turn your eyes away, afraid of its brilliance. Reach out for it. You are Luna, Queen of the Night. You are not made for dusk, half-measures and compromise. Let yourself be healed and do not settle for less than you are worth. You inspire great passions. You are made to love and be loved.'

Again she lifted her head. Luna tried to read her face, staring into the gypsy's great charcoal eyes, reluctantly drawn in by her words, but Morena would not relax her fixed expression.

The gypsy's voice was deeper and richer, almost cavernous, when she took up her reading once more. Suddenly, her eyes closed. She was like a statue of copper towering over Luna's delicate, pale hand, her perspiring face glistening as if heated by fire. Suddenly she seemed ageless, her face an inscrutable mask.

'Beware,' she rasped, her speech seeming to cause her much effort, 'beware; fate is a two-sided coin, and this opposite side to your destiny can endanger all the good and allow evil to prevail … Beware of shadows, and of murky waters. Your heart is kind and pure, pure as the pearly light that shines through your skin, so trust your judgement and only your judgement. Your conscience too.'

Luna watched, mesmerized, as Morena seemed to plunge deeper into her strange trance. Nothing about it looked affected. She had never seen anything like this before.

'Someone close to you is dangerous, and you keep running, but run towards the dazzling light. The one you need must find his own forgiveness too before you can stand still.' Her words were an incantation that she chanted again and again – a kind of low, hoarse melody that fascinated Luna. As the trance ended, the *gitana* looked up at Luna's troubled face.

'What does all this mean?' Luna said after she had finally let out the breath she'd been holding. 'I don't understand the significance of any of it.'

For a moment the *gitana* fell silent before saying, 'Listen to your heart, beautiful *señorita*, and it will guide you.'

'Are we talking about the near or the distant future?'

Morena considered Luna, her gaze suddenly alert and penetrating. 'The wheel of fate is already spinning fast.' Her expression relaxed and the youthfulness of her face returned. 'Come, I will wrap the dress for you. You don't have long before the ball at El Pavón starts. I don't want to be the one to make you late.'

It was clear that the *gitana* was going to remain cryptic. As she disappeared behind the curtain into the main shop, Luna quickly changed and carried the dress out to the counter. She paid for the costume and the accessories.

'How much do I owe you for the palm reading?'

Morena shook her riotous ebony curls and a strange light flashed in her dark eagle eyes as she fixed them on Luna's face.

'Your payment, *señorita*, will be lifelong, and to all my brothers and sisters under heaven.'

Luna's eyebrows crinkled in a frown. 'I don't understand.'

'Soon, very soon, it will be clear to you. As black ink on a virgin page of white paper.'

Luna remained perplexed. More than ever, she felt a great question mark hanging over her future. Still, the gypsy's words had stirred in her an illogical sense of excited anticipation. She collected her things and warmly thanked Morena. As she reached the door, the gypsy called out: 'Beware of flames, *señorita* … of fire.'

Luna turned, appalled. 'Fire? Am I to be burnt in a fire?' she croaked.

'Fire has many facets, *señorita*. It can take many forms,' the *gitana* stated obscurely. 'Just remember, the Queen of the Night has it in her power to triumph over anything.' She smiled and nodded as Luna hesitated at the threshold to Mascaradas, before slipping out into the street, carrying the glittering costume neatly packed in a box under her arm.

*   *   *

The sun was melting slowly towards dusk when Luna began preparing for the ball. A sense of anticipation and foreboding floated in the air, making her heartbeat flutter. The prospect of seeing Ruy again – for a romantic, glamorous event at a Spanish hacienda, no less – made goosebumps rise on her arms. Added to that, Morena's ambiguous words still resounded in her head, even though it was not like her to entertain the idea of some cosmic plan controlling everyone's destiny. Yet, strangely, she *was* giving it her attention. Despite herself, Luna had cogitated on the gypsy's predictions, trying to decipher her obscure ramblings about the future. Some of it she found herself holding on to like a light at the end of the tunnel, but most of it remained disturbingly dark.

Luna took out the Moon Queen costume from the cupboard, removing its transparent dress protector. It shimmered as the fine, silky fabric captured the rays of the dying sun that bathed the room in golden twilight. As she passed her hand over the delicate material, not for the first time marvelling at the celestial quality of the garment, she found herself wondering how Ruy would feel about her choice. She wanted him to be proud of her in front of his family and friends and hoped he wouldn't think she was deliberately trying to be provocative. After all, it was a very revealing outfit.

Her cheeks burned as she recalled the outrageously bold and infuriating habit his eyes had of sliding over her. Yet they were wonderful ocean-blue eyes, eyes in which she could drown. A deep surge of adrenaline lit up her irises from clear honey to heated amber, and her heart clamoured with excitement. She was both expectant and afraid. At El Pavón she would be under scrutiny from many quarters and in Ruy's company all evening. Never before had she felt so painfully unsure of herself. She knew so little of this man who had suddenly taken such a large place in her thoughts. Tonight it was her desire, as well as her job, to find out more.

Luna wallowed in her scented bubble bath, washed and dried her hair and brushed it until it fell like a shiny silk cloak down her back. She rubbed her whole body with a delicious, fragranced cream that left her skin smooth as satin. Her nails and toenails were painted silver to match her outfit and the character of the Moon Queen. After days of walks around town and on the beach, the sun had touched her skin with a honeyed radiance, so she didn't need to apply more than the faintest touch of make-up for her face to glow.

Tall and slender, her body veiled in silver georgette, woven in a yarn that appeared to be from another world, Luna looked the part. The close-fitting bodice was the colour of her skin, giving the illusion that she was naked underneath her costume, dressed merely in lunar vapours.

Luna sprinkled some fairy dust on to her hair before placing the small tiara on the crown of her head. The diamond teardrop earrings given to her by her father for her twenty-first birthday sparkled in her ears and the matching pendant shimmered just above her deep cleavage, drawing attention to the perfect curve of her breasts.

She was just slipping on her clear stiletto sandals when the doorbell rang. Her heart lurched wildly and her pulse accelerated. A last glance at herself in the mirror and even she could see the way her eyes glowed. She tried to compose herself and, taking a deep steadying breath, she went downstairs to open the door.

Ruy stood on the threshold; a commanding presence, magnificent in an Eastern sultan costume made of pure ivory silk. His head was clad in a turban, totally concealing his raven black hair, which meant that attention was immediately drawn to his deep-set eyes, which tonight were dark blue and glittering down on Luna with unconcealed appreciation.

As she gazed into them, Luna felt trapped in the invisible net they cast. Before she knew it, his head had come down and his lips brushed against hers with a kiss as light as a breath of wind. Warmth flooded her at their contact and she could do nothing to stem the colour it brought to her cheeks.

'Ruy,' she uttered, her heart skipping wildly and her voice barely above a whisper. 'How lovely to see you.' A bit of a cliché as greetings went, Luna thought, but her paralyzed brain had not found anything better to say. Instead, she accepted it in a daze, forgetting her resolution to keep things at a distance with him.

'You look amazing. I found you beautiful from the first moment I set eyes on you, but tonight you are stunning,' he told her.

Luna moved aside and he came into the house.

'Let me look at you ...'

Acutely self-conscious, she executed a twirl, finishing with a mock curtsy. Cocking an eyebrow, she tried to make light of his bold perusal. 'Well? Do I meet with your approval?'

Luna was fully aware that he was devouring her, his eyes almost the colour of night and dark with desire as they roamed every curve of her body – a look altogether frightening and exhilarating. She still felt the imprint of his feather-light kiss on her lips. All her previous resolutions seemed to be melting in the heat of his gaze. Her nipples were growing taut, thrusting against the silk of her underwear, and she knew that their outline was etched on the fine fabric of her costume.

Ruy's sensuous lips curved into a languorous smile. 'Luna, you look as beguiling as your name … the Queen of the Night.' His gaze lingered over her face. 'An enchanting beauty, so ethereal that tonight you actually appear to be made of moonlight.'

'Thank you,' she said, still mesmerized by the intense blue of his eyes.

He was exaggerating of course, in the charming way Latin men had of paying compliments to women, but at his words a thrill of pleasure invaded her veins like a heady wine. Many people had commented on her name before and she had often wondered why her parents had chosen it until her father told her that the full moon was shining through the hospital window when she was born. It had surprised her to find that the name had been her father's romantic suggestion; in every other way he was so practical, logical and pragmatic – a lot like her, she had to concede. Though for a man who was so compelled by his work ethic, and who never seemed to have any time for the playful or whimsical side of life – or, for that matter, for her – it had provided a tiny insight into a whole different side of him. Still, before Ruy, no one had ever made her name sound quite so exotic. Mentally, she gave herself a shake.

'You look quite spectacular yourself,' she countered, her eyes dropping to take in the rest of him. 'A romantic character from ancient times … That's a wonderful costume you're wearing.'

'It's an heirloom. It's been in the family for almost four generations. My grandfather wore it on the night he met my grandmother. There's a romantic legend attached to it. I'll tell you later tonight.'

Slowly, he ran his eyes up and down the length of her again, this time studying the detail.

'Your costume is stunning, it suits you to perfection. Did you get it at Mascaradas?'

Luna flashed him a radiant smile. 'Yes, the young gypsy who sold it to me said that it seemed made for me, and I think she's right.' She then assumed an expression of mock seriousness. 'It seems the power of *El Destino* extends to fancy dress and fashion accessories too.'

Ruy gave a shout of laughter. 'It warms my heart to see that you're finally grasping the mysterious workings of the universe,' he chuckled.

Luna grinned and walked over to the side table, picking up her shawl and clutch bag, and the black silk mask she had bought from Mascaradas.

When she turned back to him, his mirth had faded and Ruy was staring at her intently. 'I've been so dazzled by you that I nearly forgot to give you this,' he said. From under his wide belt, he pulled out a narrow, white velvet mask, decorated with silver moons and stars and covered with a sprinkling of minute diamonds.

Luna let out a faint gasp. 'My goodness, it's beautiful! So suited to my costume too,' she murmured. 'How did you know?'

She was conscious of Ruy's gaze searching her face, but he didn't answer. Instead, he moved behind her. 'Here, let me put it on for you,' he said in a deep warm voice, as he placed the mask over her eyes. It fitted snugly around her head.

Then he took the shawl from her hand and laid it around her shoulders. His fingers brushed against her skin and a throbbing sweetness quivered through her, almost eliciting an involuntary gasp of pleasure from her lips. She drew away, recognizing yet another tantalizing flicker of treacherous attraction, one her subconscious was urging her to resist.

'Shall we go?' he murmured as she looked up at him, wondering if he had sensed her reticence, but not a muscle moved in his face.

'Yes, yes, of course,' she said with a faint smile as she led the way out of the house.

With every step she took she could feel Ruy's eyes searing her back. Again, that mixed feeling of dread and delight invaded her: dread because he was a man who wanted her, and delight because it was Ruy's eyes burning her. Somewhere amid all of that, there was the worst complication of all. A warning voice whispered she was risking so much more by letting this overpowering electricity between them take hold. One day he would find out who she really was. What would happen then? He would despise her for her duplicity. Oh, she was playing a dangerous game. She blinked slowly and smothered her confusion.

The maroon-and-black Austin limousine was parked under the giant palm tree. He pulled the passenger door open for Luna, who gathered up the spangled panels of her gown in one arm.

'Here, let me help you,' Ruy said, taking the delicate swathes of fabric from her as Luna gingerly manoeuvred into the seat. He leaned in over her to help tuck the dress panels into the car. They slid open as she moved, baring a long strip of shapely leg and she heard his breath catch.

Suddenly she felt almost naked. His face was only inches away; she could feel the warmth radiating from it. The light fragrance of his aftershave was spicy and masculine.

She mumbled an unintelligible 'thank you', provoking a smile that did magical things to his eyes. The door shut with a gentle click and he moved round to the other side and eased his lengthy frame behind the wheel.

'I'll find it easier to drive without this on,' he said, removing his turban and tossing it on to the back seat in such a relaxed manner, it harked back to the scruffy gypsy singer she had first encountered. His mussed-up hair flopped boyishly over his forehead, making her mouth go dry. She almost flinched, as if she had been seared, when his hand gently reached over to her face and took off her mask. 'I think you can do without this right now,' he said with a smile. 'I want to be able to see your expression while we talk. You're enigmatic enough as it is.'

The engine purred into action and the car pulled away from the gravel strip in front of the house. 'It's not a long drive to El Pavón,' Ruy explained as they joined the main road. 'It'll take us about half an hour if the roads aren't too busy. My grandparents' hacienda is on the outskirts of Jerez.'

They drove in silence for a while as the violet streaks of the dusky sky sank into evening. The moon was high and the soft night cast a faintly luminous veil over the even landscape.

'Are you always so quiet?' Ruy asked.

Luna glanced at him, suddenly aware that she'd been distracted. 'I don't think so. Why?'

'Then it must be the effect I have on you.'

She smiled broadly despite her brooding unease. 'I'm just wondering why you asked me to your home tonight,' she said matter-of-factly.

'Why shouldn't I?'

'We've only just begun to work together.'

His mouth twitched as he stared ahead at the road. 'So, it'll make getting to know each other easier.'

'We're virtually strangers. You know nothing about me.'

'True, Señorita Ward. You're a complete mystery.'

'Oh, there's nothing mysterious about me,' Luna said dismissively, yet she knew there were plenty of things about her that she didn't want Ruy to know.

His eyes darted sideways at her. 'Oh, you think so? I never know what's going on behind those amber eyes of yours.'

'It's a good thing they'll be behind a mask tonight, then, so you'll have double the challenge,' she quipped.

'Exactly. So in answer to your question, the enigma of your personality makes you the perfect guest tonight,' he laughed. 'Masked balls are so mysterious, so romantic, don't you think? And the El Pavón ball is the most romantic of all.' He flashed a mischievous smile at her. 'But the simple truth of why I asked you tonight is that I'm enchanted by you. Haven't you noticed?'

Luna didn't answer. Her eyes shifted away from his dark gaze. He was altogether too flirtatious, too roguishly confident; and he knew it. Handling his charm was difficult enough but, most of all, it was his sexual aura that made her nervous.

A slight smile played about Ruy's lips as his gaze returned to the road, now signposted to Jerez. They slowed to join the traffic on the motorway, each side of it bordered with low, scrubby bushes that were lit by the beams of cars moving, as if in gleaming convoy, through the night.

'I know you're new to Cádiz, but is this your first visit to Spain?' he asked. 'Your accent is very good for an American.'

'No, it's not my first time here. I'm half Spanish. I used to come to Granada for holidays as a child. This is my first visit for a long time.'

'Don't you like Spain?'

'I wanted to explore other countries. There are so many beautiful places to discover in the world.' The half-truth rolled off her tongue surprisingly easily. After all, she had spent most of her adult life telling herself the same thing.

'And now that you've done your exploring, you have come to settle down here?'

'Maybe for a while,' she said guardedly. 'Obviously, once I've worked my contract, I'll review my options.'

Ruy's eyes skipped over her with amusement. 'Your options, I see. What made you come all the way over here to take the job at the Institute?'

Luna shifted slightly in the soft leather seat. She had blurted out to Señora Sanchez that Angelina's death had brought her to Cádiz, but there was no way she was going to invite Ruy's questioning on that subject.

Instead, she gave the answer she had rehearsed many times in her head, though the deceit rankled. 'I thought it was time to explore my Spanish roots. Besides, the Institute is getting a lot of press. I was fascinated by the work that you do here.' That much at least held some truth, she told herself. This was the opportunity she needed to switch the spotlight on to Ruy now.

She continued: 'What about you? It takes great conviction to turn your back on conventional medical training and do what you're doing. How did that happen?'

For the first time, Luna saw a shadow pass over Ruy's features. 'It's a long story …' He rubbed his jaw with his hand. 'Let's just say that my gypsy heritage had something to do with it. Even as a small boy, I was always interested in natural and traditional methods of healing. Just like you: exploring my roots, I suppose.'

On the plane he'd mentioned being from a gypsy family, Luna remembered. She instantly forgot that she should be quizzing him about his work at the clinic. His family background was something she found far more compelling.

'Were your parents gypsies?' she asked.

He smiled and shook his head. 'Not exactly. My father, Andrés de Calderón, discovered he was half *gitano* when he was a teenager. His real father was Eduardo Raphael Ruiz de Salazar, the famous Spanish Surrealist painter, his mother Marujita, queen of the sea gypsies here in Cádiz – though originally she hailed from Jerez. My father was taken away from his mother at birth and brought up as a *gajo* – what *gitanos* call non-gypsies – by Eduardo's sister and her husband. When he discovered his true parentage, he went to live with the gypsies and stayed with them, on and off, leading a double life for many years.' Ruy's hand raked through his hair in the restless motion Luna was becoming accustomed to. 'By then he was a very successful businessman and a little troubled by his identity.'

Luna's eyes widened. 'I'm not surprised. That's a very dramatic story.'

'Yes, it is, and one day I'll tell you the whole tale when I've found out more about you.' He grinned at her.

'But we're still talking about you,' she persisted, neatly side-stepping his comment. 'So, did you know your gypsy family?'

He chuckled as if appreciating that he'd been elegantly out-manoeuvred. 'Oh yes, my father took me to the camp regularly from when I was a young boy. He always encouraged me to spend time there. He wanted me to feel that I have *gitano* blood in me. Yes, he was always drawn to the gypsies …' His brow creased. 'That seemed to change as I grew older, though. Most of the time I was left to go there on my own. These days, he seems more preoccupied with his business. I'm the one who spends most time with the *gitanos*. They're like my extended family.'

Luna recognized the tiny nuance of disappointment in his voice when Ruy spoke of his father. Wasn't that a feeling she knew all too well? She'd spent a lifetime persuading herself that she liked being alone, that it was fine that her father was preoccupied with work, but now that she was in Spain it was as if the tight bud of her emotions, so long held in check, had somehow loosened and unfurled. Suddenly she was not afraid to admit to herself that although she had been self-sufficient – all her life, it seemed – she had been lonely … and with the loss of Angelina, that feeling of isolation had only intensified.

It was funny how Ruy could touch a chord in her like that. Their relationship, what it was, was full of revelations. Indeed, it delivered surprises about herself. For instance, Luna had never regarded herself as particularly intuitive about people, but now she sensed with absolute certainty that something troubling had happened in Ruy's past, some story that lay behind the edge in his voice – and the stirring of tenderness she felt deep inside disturbed her.

'Perhaps your father simply trusts you to carry the torch, to keep up the connection with your gypsy family. If he can't be there, at least you can do it for him,' she offered.

Ruy turned to her, surprised, with that same searching glance which always made her feel turned inside out. 'Perhaps … I always find it odd that even though he has more *gitano* blood in him than I do, I think I feel a stronger bond with them.'

By now, Luna was engrossed in this side of Ruy that was emerging. He seemed to be able to switch on the suave, sophisticated intellectual when he wanted to, as he had done at the conference and on the plane; but since then, she was seeing more glimpses of the wild, restless gypsy beneath.

'What is it that attracts you to the *gitanos*?'

Ruy looked thoughtful. 'Many things. Their lust for life, their unique customs and traditions … the fact that they live close to nature. Their unparalleled capacity for having fun,' he added with a grin.

A smile tugged at her lips. Oh yes, she could see how he would find that appealing. 'Which no doubt partly accounts for their unfortunate reputation,' she said.

He nodded. 'A centuries-old reputation and not always deserved. It's true, their nomadic lifestyle, as tinkers, musicians and fortune tellers, lent itself to begging and stealing and now modern gypsies, who are hard-working and honest people, get tarred with the same old brush.'

He glanced at her and shrugged. 'Yes, they have traditions that involve drinking and going wild, but their hearts are as full as their brandy bottles and bursting with fiery passion.' His gaze continued to follow the road. 'Growing up, I couldn't keep away from that explosive energy. It used to draw me like a hypnotic flame.'

She studied his strong, handsome profile, wondering distractedly about those perfect noble features and from which parent he had inherited them. Tonight she would find out soon enough and the thought made her slightly edgy. Still, her curiosity was proving stronger than her nerves.

'What about your mother?'

'My mother?' he repeated with a warm smile. 'What do you want to know about her?'

'Is she from Cádiz?'

'Yes, she was born here, though she was educated in England. She's from one of the oldest aristocratic families in Spain, the ones you'll meet tonight, who own El Pavón.'

Ruy explained that his grandfather, Salvador de Rueda, had come from a dynasty of winemakers and stud owners, though horses were his main passion – that is, until Ruy's grandmother, Alexandra de Falla, had arrived in Spain in 1950. A cousin of Salvador's but not by blood, she had grown up in England before being reunited with her estranged Spanish relatives. Her independent ways had been a constant challenge for the conservative young Salvador, not to mention the *Duquesa* – Salvador's great aunt and the matriarch of the de Falla family. As Luna listened to Ruy she could tell that he loved his grandfather deeply and, despite differences in outlook, their relationship was smoother than the one he shared with his father.

When Luna steered the conversation to his mother, Luz de Rueda, Ruy's face became instantly animated. He was quick to laugh about her outspoken comments or how she had so much energy he was always telling her to slow down. It was clear that the rebellious streak Luna saw in Ruy was threaded through the generations of women in his family and not just a result of his gypsy blood.

'My mother is beautiful. Fiercely independent, of course. She's always given my father a run for his money,' Ruy chuckled. 'She met and fell in love with him, not knowing he was half *gitano*. It's a complicated story and theirs wasn't an easy path. It seems to be a theme in my family,' he added wryly. 'Then again, as the

Bard himself put it so aptly, the course of true love never did run smooth. Again, it's another story for another time.'

Ruy's head was still facing forward, and now his expression was unreadable. He shifted his weight behind the wheel and there was a moment's pause. 'Have you ever been in love, Luna?'

Her gaze fixed on him. 'No, have you?'

He laughed and shook his head. 'No, I haven't. So we both have much to learn.'

Luna wasn't sure where he was going with such an ambiguous remark and kicked herself for firing back her response without thinking. She had allowed the conversation to stray in quite the wrong direction.

'I think we've become sidetracked,' she interjected hastily. 'You still haven't really answered my question about why you moved away from mainstream medicine and developed alternative practices.'

He cocked an eyebrow and smiled. 'Luna, I believe it was you who asked me about my gypsy family.'

'*Touché*,' she conceded. 'And so …?'

Ruy glanced at her and then stared back at the road. 'There was never any doubt in my mind that conventional medicine would be my starting point. When I was just out of university, I came across a very wise gypsy, who first introduced me to herbal remedies and hypnotherapy – of course she didn't call it that, but it amounted to the same thing. I could see how powerful they both were.' Ruy drummed his thumb lightly on the steering wheel. 'She taught me everything she knew and when I began my career in oncology, that knowledge took root in my mind. I began to study the effect of herbs on disease.'

'I wondered if the herbalism had come from the gypsy part of your background,' noted Luna. 'Go on, tell me more.'

'As you probably know, I'm interested in stimulating the immune system naturally. Our clinic has developed quite an arsenal of nutritional supplements and herbs to support the body. In fact, they do much more than that. They're actually able to direct and charge the body's own immune responses.' His eyes shone with energy. 'The more success cases we can build up, the more we'll be able to push for funding for further trials.'

'The press has certainly been taking an interest in your work. Of course, the scientific community will only counter that the media are always gullible, prey to slick marketing.' She glanced at him quickly. 'Then again, I'm sure I can guess your answer to that.'

'Whoa there!' he said, cocking an eyebrow. 'I hope you're not trying to ruin my evening …'

She smiled quickly. 'No, not at all.'

'So, why do I get the feeling I'm being interrogated?'

Luna snapped to attention under his speculative stare. 'How can you arm yourself against the sceptics unless you learn to think like one and anticipate their arguments?'

'Fair enough, I suppose. But this is my night off from all that.'

She had the grace to look rueful. 'Sorry, I just can't help looking at things from every angle.'

'Including me, it seems,' he grinned.

'Especially you,' she said wryly.

He laughed loudly and the rich, husky sound of it shot heat straight through her.

'You know where it all started for me? It was the history of plant remedies that was the first hook, if you like. I learned a lot from my wise gypsy friend and her herb garden.'

'I can see the fascination in that,' Luna agreed. 'I loved that part of our general science course at college … quinine from cinchona, morphine and codeine from poppies, and aspirin, of course, from white willow.'

Ruy nodded. 'Exactly. The list is huge and we're still discovering more. Take mistletoe …' He paused, slowing down as they approached the Carranza Bridge, where the traffic was becoming heavier.

'What about it?' Luna replied. She gazed out of the window for a moment at the silvery-lined clouds, lit by the moon. Fascinated as she was by what made Ruy tick professionally, it was becoming increasingly difficult to focus her attention on probing him about his work when her mind was wandering to the glamorous evening ahead that they would be sharing.

'*Viscum album* … European mistletoe. Used for centuries to treat various ailments. Only now it's becoming one of the most widely studied alternative therapies for cancer. Now there's a tonic for the immune system, not to mention its most important therapeutic function.'

Luna turned back to him. 'And that is?'

'Making it far easier to steal a kiss from a young lady at Christmas.' The roguish grin was back again, and with it Ruy's demeanour had reverted to boyish mischief.

She couldn't help but laugh and studied him surreptitiously, her eyes tracing his profile from his perfect brow down to his sensuous mouth that moved so easily to laughter or a devastating smile.

His eyes sparkled at her provocatively. 'The Druids viewed it as a sacred symbol of vivacity and fertility because it could blossom even during the frozen winter.'

'A hardy plant,' she agreed, amusement still playing on her lips. 'One noted for its worrying toxicity too.'

'Ah, Señorita Ward, such cynicism! Did you know that in eighteenth-century England the kissing tradition first caught on among the servants? The custom was that men were allowed to request a kiss from any woman caught standing under the mistletoe, and refusing was viewed as bad luck.'

'Then I have a feeling it's a good thing for you this masked ball isn't at Christmas,' Luna laughed, taking her chance to tease him for a change, rather than the other way round.

'You wound me, Luna.' He exaggerated a crestfallen look.

'Oh, I think it would take a lot for a woman to wound you, Ruy.'

'That depends on the woman,' he said, his gaze shifting to her momentarily. The silence hung in the air. Then Ruy's mouth curved into a smile. 'Now, isn't it my turn to play interrogator? I'm intrigued to know more about your background.'

Luna suddenly wanted to forget who she was and enjoy the fantasy that it did not matter. 'Let's just talk about something else for a while.'

'So you're intent on preserving that mystery you've been denying.' He grinned. 'Very well. Then I'll keep my questions for another time. Tonight you are Luna, Queen of the Night, or maybe Princess Budur from *A Thousand and One Nights*, and I will be Prince Kamar Al-Zaman who fell in love with her.'

'You said you'd tell me the legend.'

'Haven't you read the famous Persian stories of *A Thousand and One Nights*?'

'No, unfortunately not,' Luna confessed. 'I wasn't given many stories to read when I was little. My father bought me a leather-bound set of *Encyclopaedia Britannica* but seemed to forget a child needs stories too.' She paused, remembering she'd never actually been read to as a child either. 'Looking back, sometimes I feel I missed out on part of my childhood. Only once was I treated to a weekend of fairy tales and legends. It's actually one of my fondest memories of Spain.'

'Go on. I'd like to hear about it,' Ruy coaxed her.

She gave a self-conscious laugh, before continuing. 'I was probably about six. We were invited to a hacienda in Jaén … Olivar. One of the most romantic places I'd ever seen. It was a converted old olive mill in the hills, with hectares of olive groves. How many, I don't know. The owners were American, friends of my father. The evening we visited, we sat in the garden, next to a man-made lake with a waterfall, while our hosts told us myths and legends about the olive tree.' Luna gave a little wistful laugh. 'Images of that evening remained a long time with me, and I remember crying bitterly when I heard that the house had been sold. You see, I'd always hoped to go back. It's funny how relatively small things can mean so much to a child ...' She paused and then added pensively: 'I often wonder what's happened to it ... who lives there now.'

They had climbed away from the coast, having finally crossed the congested Carranza Bridge, and had just joined the queue at one of the toll booths for the A-4 motorway to Jerez.

Ruy was a good listener. She could sense his natural-born intuition, as he probed: 'Was it the setting or was it the legends that touched you most?'

She shrugged. 'Oh, I don't know. The whole evening was magical. It still brings an odd lump to my throat when I think about it.'

'Children are very impressionable,' he agreed. 'When I was a child, my father used to tell me these wonderful stories at bedtime.' He chuckled. 'My favourite was that romantic legend of Prince Kamar Al-Zaman and Princess Budur. Both names mean "moon" in Arabic and ever since I've been fascinated by the moon ... the fairest star in heaven, as the story says.'

He took his eyes off the road for a second to look at her and, even in the dark shadows of the car, she could see they glittered like sapphires. 'And tonight, dear Luna ... tonight, the moon is within my reach.' The vivid blue of his eyes grew more intense and he stretched out a hand and gently trailed a warm finger down to the curve of her chin. He met her wary amber gaze as a wave of helplessness threatened to engulf her ...

How could she ever protect herself from the hypnotizing enchantment this man had over her?

The car behind hooted suddenly, bringing them back to earth. Ruy waved an apologetic hand out of the window, paid the toll and they were off again.

Now the traffic had cleared and the road stretched straight ahead, lit only by the beam of the car's headlights and the pale moon above. They travelled in silence for a long while, each lost in their own thoughts as the car shot through the night. Ruy was a fast but not reckless driver and Luna was surprised at the speed of the vintage Austin. He manoeuvred the old car with smooth, masterly skill. No doubt as he did the legion of women that swooned at his feet, Luna guessed. Her father once likened women to cars in a way that had made her feminist hackles rise, saying they needed to be treated gently but with a masterful hand.

'Do you have a boyfriend, Luna?' he asked suddenly, without preamble.

Luna blinked before curbing the sharp retort that quivered on the tip of her tongue. 'No,' she replied truthfully. 'I don't.'

'Why? I can't believe a beautiful woman like you could still be single.'

She was used to this line – a cliché many had used before him, but no one made her heart beat as fast as this when they had asked her.

'What about you?' she asked, turning to look at him.

He grinned provocatively and glanced back at her, mischievous devils dancing in his eyes. 'Likewise … A bit of luck, isn't it?' A dark eyebrow lifted interrogatively, inviting her answer.

He was either being presumptuously forward, or else he had a strange sense of humour. Was he teasing her? Or was he one of those men who sailed on life's vast ocean without anyone ever challenging their behaviour? She decided to ignore his question and change the subject. 'I thought you were going to tell me that romantic legend.'

Ruy eyed her. There was a touch of amusement in his irises. 'Is that what you want? I thought we were doing pretty well.' He smiled at her innocently.

Luna raised a challenging eyebrow. *Now's my chance to warn him off*, she thought. She smiled back sweetly, though there was the faintest note of reproach in her voice. 'Don't push your luck.'

He allowed his gaze to flicker over her for a moment. Then he laughed, a frank open laughter, deep in his throat. 'You can't make up your mind about me, can you?' It was more of a statement than a question. 'I'll tell you the tale of Kamar Al-Zaman and Princess Budur, but you'll have to wait until later. We're about to turn off for El Pavón and it's a long, romantic story.'

CHAPTER 6

The ball was in full swing when, a few minutes later, the Austin swept through El Pavón's imposing gates.

'We're here,' Ruy whispered as smoothly they made their way up the winding drive.

Weeping willows bordered the sides of the gravelled approach, their stooping branches trailing in the slow waters of the canal that irrigated the grounds. In the distance, the imposing ancestral home stood out among the surrounding shadows like a dazzling jewel, bathed in moonlight. Lights blazed a welcome from its elegant windows and, together with the carriage lamps mounted on its whitewashed walls, competed with the star of the night and other constellations. Sweeping violin music drifted out from somewhere inside the house while guests had spilled on to the open terrace at the front to enjoy the evening air. A kaleidoscope of lanterns hung like fireballs from arbours and twinkled softly through the thick foliage of shrubs in the beautifully landscaped gardens. Fountains were dotted about, and their fine spray sparkled with a million rainbows as though spouting a rain of little gems. Clothed in mystique and timeless romance, the hacienda glowed in festive mood, greeting its guests with open arms.

Luna was used to homes of the rich in California, where her father had a sprawling ranch-style house, but the understated sense of history that El Pavón exuded was singularly impressive. As the car followed the curve of the lawn and neared the entrance, her appreciation of this beautiful scene was suddenly usurped by butterflies invading her stomach. She tried to calm herself. Fixing her gaze on the ancient portico, she attempted to determine whether its neo-classical columns were seventeenth or eighteenth century.

By the time Ruy had pulled up in front of the house, Luna had abandoned her distraction tactics so she breathed deeply and resolved to pull herself together. The car's discreet throb of power died and Ruy switched off the engine. A valet hurried towards them. Ruy gave him the keys, then reached into the back seat for his turban and mask, and jumped out, coming round to open the door for Luna.

He held out his hand – it was large and firm and the feel of it made her tremble. '*Encantador*, ravishing,' he murmured under his breath as he helped her out. He smiled lazily as his gaze settled on her, brilliant with life.

Luna's body tingled with that fearful excitement again. The force of Ruy's personality was casting a spell on her as it always did and, suddenly, looking at him dressed as a mysterious prince, more exotically masculine than ever, not only did she doubt her ability to hold him back, she wasn't sure she really wanted to. With unsteady fingers she made certain the narrow, glittering, white velvet mask was tightly fastened across her face. At least this way, she hoped the emotional hurricane assailing her would be safer from his scrutinizing gaze.

Ruy halted on the step as if frozen in place. 'Perfect,' he murmured huskily. 'A heavenly moonbeam.'

He paused to don his turban, then his strong hand was at her elbow again as he led her through the handsome wooden doors, above which the family's coat of arms was sculpted in the form of a peacock, in relief. They entered a vaulted hallway where a wrought-iron and marble staircase curved majestically up to the two storeys above. An old grandfather clock on the far wall had just begun to strike ten, and its organ-like chimes echoed loudly in the vast space, despite the sound of music and voices emanating from an adjoining room.

Entranced, Luna gazed about her, admiring the rich decoration on the ceiling and embroidered tapestries on the walls, as well as the heavy, ornate Spanish medieval furniture. Great urns of flowers displayed at each end of the room scented the place with their cloying sweetness, and everywhere candlelight shimmered on the walls.

Slowly she walked forward, her high heels resounding on the huge flagstones, her eyes eager to be everywhere at once. 'What a magnificent home your family has! Back home we have grand houses too, especially in the South, where they've the old colonial plantations, but they lack history. I mean, it's not the same as the castles of Scotland, the *palazzi* of Venice or the great *châteaux* of France.' She waved a hand admiringly at her surroundings. 'I mean, look at those wonderful Moorish carvings in the stonework. You have hundreds of years of history here.'

A slight smile curved Ruy's lips. 'Did you acquire all this knowledge during those travels that kept you away from Spain?' The gleam in his eyes was openly teasing.

'No, I just like to read.' Her crystalline laughter filled the room. 'I'm definitely guilty of spending all my holidays exploring far-flung places, though. It's probably an American thing, a craving to see different cultures, immerse ourselves in history ... I've always loved the history of art – European, Asian or African. Now that I'm in Spain, I intend to see more of it up close.'

'One day I'll take you to visit Puesta de Sol, the house of my grandfather, Eduardo, the one I told you about, who was an architect as well as a sculptor and painter. The style of La Gaviota looks very similar to his. I'm sure it must be a homage to his work.'

'I've not heard of him but, if his other work looks anything like the beach house, then I'm sure I'd love it,' said Luna, who had moved to the nearest wall and was studying a large painting of an aristocratic young Spanish woman.

Ruy came to stand behind her. 'My great grandmother, the Duquesa, Doña María Dolores de Falla,' he explained. 'A formidable woman by all accounts.'

'Yes, I can see that,' mused Luna, looking at the intelligent, dark eyes staring back at her. 'She has such an air of dignified authority for someone so young.'

Ruy chuckled. 'She needed it, given the history of the de Fallas. In fact, we have a rather colourful family on both sides.'

Luna glanced at him. 'Why does that not surprise me?'

He grinned. 'Yes, it's a miracle I'm sane, quite frankly. We'll talk about architecture and my eccentric ancestors some other time, though. Let's find the party.'

He took Luna's shawl and bag from her and gave it to the major-domo, who appeared suddenly out of the shadows, as if summoned by one of the genies of *A Thousand and One Nights*. Luna could hear the hum of voices and laughter coming from a doorway on the right, at the far end of the hall. A band was playing an achingly romantic Russian waltz, and her heart responded with a foolish twinge that made her dare not look at Ruy in case he somehow intuited her emotions.

'Ah, there you are, Ruy! We were wondering what had happened to you,' called out a distinguished-looking man in formal dress without a mask, coming slowly down the marble staircase. Tall, with a shock of snowy-white hair, his stature was imposing despite his advanced age. He must be in his eighties, Luna thought, but he still had plenty of charisma. His grey eyes, strikingly pale in a bronze complexion, were still lively and smilingly tender as he walked across to meet them.

'Grandfather! I'm sorry we're late, but the drive from Cádiz was slow. We really need a second bridge. It'll be better once La Pepa is built.'

'Well, you're here now, Ruy. That's the most important thing,' his grandfather said cheerfully. 'They're a lively lot in there. I guess most of them are your friends,' he added, as he slapped Ruy affectionately on the back. His attention moved politely now to Luna and he smiled at her benignly. 'I don't think we've met. Welcome, my dear.'

Turning to his grandson he added: 'I'll not ask to be introduced to your very beautiful escort just now. The rules of the game are "*incognito hasta la medianoche*", in disguise until midnight.' His grey eyes twinkled at Luna with genial curiosity. 'After that, I insist on knowing all about you.'

Luna gave a gracious nod. 'And I'd be delighted to return the compliment, Señor de Rueda.'

He beamed at her. 'Ah, the game is up already! Then again, it's the host's prerogative to be recognizable.'

Ruy turned to Luna. 'May I present my grandfather, Count Salvador de Rueda.' He gestured towards Luna. '*Abuelo*, my guest for this evening. As you say, after midnight I look forward to divulging her identity.'

'You will have to retain the advantage for a few more hours, *señorita*,' said Salvador de Rueda, lifting Luna's hand to kiss it.

Luna raised an eyebrow to Ruy, as if to say teasingly, *Are all your relatives so outrageously charming?* Ruy answered silently with a mischievous cocked eyebrow of his own: '*Of course, what did you expect?*'

Salvador held on to Ruy's arm, patting his cheek playfully. 'Don't think I won't be asking this charming young lady for a dance later, so you'd better not keep her all to yourself. There's life in these old legs yet.'

Ruy chuckled. 'I don't doubt it, *Abuelo*. You're still strong as an ox and just as contrary. Speaking of which, when are we going to have lunch again? I'm missing your diatribes about the socialist government and how we're all doomed.'

His grandfather gestured with good-natured impatience and told Luna: 'Oh, this one enjoys baiting me, and he knows it.'

Luna smiled widely. 'Ruy? Surely not.' She made a show of innocent surprise, already deciding that she liked Salvador de Rueda very much indeed.

Her host laughed in a throaty way that had a familiar ring to it. 'I see she has the measure of you already,' he said, nudging his grandson. 'I mustn't keep you from the party, though. Go and join the fun. *Vamos*, come now. On with your mask, Ruy!'

Ruy grinned and pulled on his narrow black velvet mask. 'What about yours, *Abuelo*?'

'Oh yes, here it is.' Salvador reached over to a handsomely carved hall table. 'I took it off to read something upstairs and forgot to put it back on. This ball always brings back wonderful memories,' he mused, fixing a moulded white-and-gold Venetian mask to his head. 'Don't forget to go and kiss your grandmother after midnight, Ruy. By the way, your parents are here. They were whizzing around the dancefloor when I last saw them.'

He turned to Luna. 'Welcome to El Pavón, *señorita*,' he said, bowing his head a fraction. 'I wonder if the legend of Kamar Al-Zaman and Princess Budur will be triggered again this year.' He gave Ruy a knowing look and, with that, strode off, chuckling away to himself.

'Your grandfather is rather wonderful,' said Luna, watching Salvador walk away.

'Yes, he is. Not bad considering he's over ninety now.'

'Really?' Luna's eyes widened. 'He's very sprightly for his age.'

Ruy moved to stand closer. 'The men in our family are full of vitality,' he said in a deadpan voice.

She turned to see his expression alive with amusement. The band had struck up a tune in African-Brazilian lambada-style, with sizzling rhythms. He smiled into her eyes.

'Come, let's dance. My grandmother has only allowed us a few modern dances, and this is one of them.'

'Doesn't she approve of current music?' asked Luna, watching a sudden influx of young couples hurry past to get to the dancefloor.

'She's rather old-fashioned and romantic. Usually insists on traditional dancing.'

'In that case, why is she making an exception?'

Ruy grinned. 'Because I requested it, and she can't refuse me anything.'

Luna found herself smiling back at him. 'Another thing that doesn't surprise me.'

He bent his head towards her. 'I know I'm not supposed to say this, but I've been wanting to hold you in my arms since I first saw you at the taverna in Barcelona. Seeing you tonight, looking the way you do, has only increased that urge by an alarming ratio.' His voice dropped. 'If you don't believe me, feel …' He took Luna's hand and held it to his heart. It was racing, thumping as hard as hers.

She met the midnight-blue eyes that gazed back at her: dark, dangerous and loaded with the same pent-up desire that had haunted her too these past few days. Desire that she had steadily tried to deny. His hand settled in the small of her back and a shiver of anticipation rippled up her spine as he guided her down the hall towards the music.

Luna and Ruy paused just for a moment in the arched doorway of the grand ballroom, watching the flamboyant spectacle spread out in front of them. Sparkling chandeliers and mirrored walls reflected a kaleidoscope of moving colour. Heavily masked men and women, their imaginations unleashed, each of them dressed in a magnificent costume, spun and swayed on the polished oak floor, taken up in a whirlwind of fantasy in which romance and mystique merged with a contemporary festival of eccentricity and delight.

Without another word, Ruy dragged Luna into the midst of the twirling couples, joining their wild pace, swift and light as leaves caught up in a tempest of wind. Luna was as airy and delicate as thistledown, her long pale hair smooth and shimmering under the lights, the soft panels of her skirt billowing about Ruy's legs as they wheeled around. Even though she didn't know all the steps, he led her effortlessly, twirling her around him, and then, with a flick of his arm, bringing her back to the heat of his chest. His strong, inescapable arms held her tightly to him, so close the two of them seemed fused together.

Luna was aware of the ragged beating of his heart through the silk of his tunic, the power and muscular dominance of his frame, his hardness pressing against her softness. It felt good; it felt right. When she looked up at him, she thought his eyes had flamed an even deeper blue behind his black velvet mask and she was hypnotized by the rapt intensity she read in them. Her face half-covered by her own shimmering disguise, she could almost imagine she were someone else, her inhibitions and fears forgotten in the magic woven around them.

Instinctively, her body moved with his in a wanton responsiveness to his erotic command. His hips were in startling contact with hers, swaying fluidly and suggestively; sending her senses into mayhem. He crushed her breasts against his broad chest, and pressed the heat of his arousal against that part of her that wanted him most, his hand moving caressingly over her bare back. He wasn't letting her go now, keeping her flush against his hard length. The mass of people on the dancefloor were a blur of whirling figures, the music a relentless rhythm. She closed her eyes and swallowed. Images crowded her mind. Her heart fluttered wildly at the thought of what that hard, sculpted body might feel like naked against her: his hot lips covering her in scalding kisses, his wonderful hands roaming inch after inch over her flesh, his long fingers sensually exploring, sending thrilling tremors through her body.

Luna had never felt this rush of desire for any man. She was trembling, the vivid fantasy of him stirring her emotions to the core. Surges of unknown, overwhelming sensations invaded every part of her, sweetly agonizing. They were building uncontrollably inside; now the next wave rushing in, threatening to engulf her. Somewhere in her fevered mind, another part of her whispered a warning, but she was too faint with longing and too overwhelmed by an urgent need that she couldn't control. There was only the call of Ruy's power over her now, the feel of his warm cheek on her brow and the scorching heat between their bodies.

Her head was spinning; her breath was coming in short pants and her limbs were turning to water as her loins flooded with delicious heat. Jolts of wild sensation rocked her, making her cling to him tightly. She was soaring in a heavenly, delirious dream and a moan escaped inadvertently from her lips.

Trembling, Luna forced her eyes open. They were on the veranda, she realized, and Ruy was watching her, still holding her against him, his gaze smouldering. Transfixed, she looked directly into the attentive depths of his eyes, her stunned mind still reeling. Her face, that part of it which was visible below the mask, was white as ivory.

'It's alright, *querida*,' Ruy whispered, warm breath against her ear, his face very close. 'We were swept along by a powerful force that just kept intensifying. I felt it too. The ballroom was very hot. I thought you were going to faint. You just needed some air, so I brought you out here.'

As her mind staggered back to consciousness, Luna was suddenly aware of what had happened to her and now she dared not meet his gaze. A hot flush ran up her face and she stepped free of his arms. In all her life, there had never been a moment more deeply humiliating. She knew how she must look to him, still drowning in the wanton passion pulsing through her. Instinctively, she smoothed a hand through her hair as she tried to regain her composure.

Ruy's eyes were still fixed on her as he gestured towards the dining area inside the house. 'The buffet is open. Would you like to go in? We don't need to sit down; we can bring our food out here. Or maybe you would prefer to take a walk in the garden and then later we'll have something to eat.'

From her vantage point on the terrace, Luna had a good view of the grand dining room through the tall open windows. It was ablaze with light, which showed up the rich decoration of the room, the plastered and painted ceiling and the lavish gold leaf of the pillars. People were standing around in small groups, clutching glasses and talking while they sipped champagne; others drifted across to the long buffet laid with shining chased silver and polished cut glass in an exquisite perfection of detail. Placed at intervals along the narrow table were exotic blooming flowers in crystal vases and vermeil bowls piled high with luscious fruit.

Under the dazzling lights of the chandelier, the guests in their magnificent costumes looked like an exuberant flock of tropical birds. Noisy laughter and conversation filled the hot evening air. The effect was a strange buzzing of a million bees, a merry sound. There was no doubt that the El Pavón ball was a riotous success and its reputation as the event of the year was richly deserved.

A few couples were now trooping out on to the terrace.

'I'm not very hungry,' Luna said, her face still flushed, 'but don't let me stop you from …'

'Not hungry?' intoned a deep voice behind them. 'With all this delicious food laid out like a Roman banquet in there? Now that would be a shameful waste.'

Luna looked round to see a tall, middle-aged man detach himself from a group of guests and come towards them, smiling. Dressed as a pirate, with a wide sash around his waist, the man sported a swashbuckling beard and moustache of distinguished grey, and wore a red silk mask tied behind his head, behind which brilliant green eyes gleamed. Even with a disguise he was clearly very handsome.

'I see that new facial hair of yours has finally come into its own,' Ruy quipped, greeting him with a brief hug.

The other man shrugged. 'Your mother can't stand it. I only grew it for the party, so she says she's going to shave it off herself tomorrow morning in case there's a danger of my keeping it.' He smiled at Luna, who saw a sudden resemblance to Ruy in his expression. It made her stop short and stare at the two men.

'I rather think you may have given away your identity already. As that's the case, let me introduce my guest for the evening ... and this,' he said to Luna, gesturing to the older man, 'is my father, Andrés de Calderón.'

'It's a pleasure to meet you,' said Luna, shaking his outstretched hand almost with relief. She welcomed a disruption to the intense charge still humming in the air between herself and Ruy. It provided a chance to gather her senses.

'The pleasure is all mine,' replied Andrés de Calderón suavely with a slight nod of his head. 'I'm sure you'll find it unavoidable meeting most of our family before midnight, *senorita*. And I'm sure the rest of us will be as enchanted to meet you as I am.'

'She's already met *Abuelo*.' Ruy smiled at Luna. 'And has made her first conquest of the evening. Well, perhaps not her first,' he glanced at Luna, his mouth curving into a half-smile.

Luna searched for a response but every time she looked at Ruy, she couldn't help being distracted by that perfectly moulded mouth. Besides, she was still too disorientated by the memory of being in his arms to form coherent conversation.

Andrés didn't seem to notice her reticence. Instead, his bright eyes studied his son closely from behind his mask. 'You look well, *mi hijo*,' he said. 'It's good to see you bring a guest to the ball at long last. Your mother and I look forward to proper introductions after midnight.' There was a hint of amusement in his voice that Luna added to her list of similarities between father and son.

Ruy gave his father a pointed look. 'Enough *Papá*. There'll be plenty of time to get to know her. Tonight, please, introductions, not interrogations.' He took a step closer to Luna. 'Between the de Fallas and the de Ruedas, there's enough of a force to frighten her away for good.'

'Given my son's response, I'm glad to hear there'll be more opportunities to meet you again, *señorita*,' said Andrés.

Luna had also registered the meaning behind Ruy's remark and didn't know whether to feel happy or anxious at the thought. She watched the interaction between father and son, sensing a mutual respect and warmth. Yet there was something Ruy held back with his father; he was more restrained in his attitude than he had been with Salvador.

Andrés gave a debonair smile. 'Now I must leave the two of you to have fun. I only came out here for some air before getting more champagne for your mother, and she'll be wondering what happened to me. I left her with far too many men crowding round, and I mean to steal her away for another dance before one of them beats me to it. I'll see you both after midnight, no doubt.' He turned to Luna. 'Delighted to meet you, *señorita*.' With that, Andrés disappeared back into the ballroom.

Luna looked at Ruy and was aware of the atmosphere between them springing back to one of watchful intensity now that they were alone again, despite the other guests milling about on the terrace, talking and laughing buoyantly.

'I'll bring us some champagne, then show you around the grounds,' Ruy suggested. 'The moon is particularly bright tonight so the gardens will look stunning.' His voice was low and vibrant and there was a blatant sensuality in the gaze that held hers. The unmistakable message she read in them kindled a slow, warm glow that spread through her veins like quicksilver, causing any vestiges of the embarrassment she had felt a few minutes ago to flee. She stood still as a statue, her senses bemused before the passion in that look. Heady scents came from the garden below. It was a night to dream and love, and Luna felt herself surrendering to the magic of the evening, almost forgetting who she was.

Ruy did not need to go far. A waiter had just stepped on to the terrace offering flutes of iced champagne. Ruy gave Luna a glass and lifted his own, '*Días felices!* Happy days!' Then touching her elbow gently, he led her into the garden.

Here, El Pavón slumbered peacefully, set among flowers, all white now in diaphanous moonlight. Its pearly beams had turned the grounds into a poem of silver and dark velvet shadows, dappling the earth with patterns beneath the trees. The atmosphere was still warm and a little humid, thick with strange, exotic fragrances released by a late watering and the cooler night air. Only the crescendo in the sound of crickets and the sporadic soft croak of a frog chorus disturbed the tranquillity.

They walked through the darkness in silence without touching, aware of each other's nearness. Luna's mind, which had seemed in such a state of turmoil earlier, was calm again, except for those odd sweet moments of excitement that stirred her pulse, when occasionally Ruy's fingers accidentally brushed against hers.

It occurred to her to ask Ruy about his father but she sensed this was the wrong moment. Instead, as she surreptitiously stole a look at him, still wearing his mask over his princely turban, another thought made her break the silence.

'You promised to tell me the legend from *A Thousand and One Nights*.'

'Indeed, I did,' he said, smiling at her.

'Do you think now is a good time?'

'Yes, it's as good a time as ever.'

And so Ruy told her the tale of the handsome Prince Kamar and the beautiful Princess Budur, who lived on opposite sides of the world, refusing any match their respective fathers presented them for marriage. Brought together in their sleep on a magic carpet by Maimouna and Dahnash, two mischievous and meddling genies, they fell in love and consummated their passion in dreams, only to find when they awoke that they lived far apart, in distant cities and palaces.

'Each knew that the other existed because they had swapped rings,' Ruy explained. 'They pined away in dungeons, where they were to be kept prisoners until they listened to reason and married the family's choice.

'Taking pity on Princess Budur, Marzavan, her brother, decided to go on a journey around the world to find his sister's lover. By a stroke of *fate*,' Ruy said, quirking an eyebrow at Luna, who smiled back with amusement, 'there was a big storm and his ship ran aground next to Prince Kamar's palace. Having heard in the market about the lovesick prince, Marzavan presented himself at the palace, claiming he was a doctor and would be able to cure Prince Kamar from his ailment. As he laid eyes on the prince and saw his sister's ring, he knew this was the man he was looking for.

'When Kamar Al-Zaman learned who Marzavan was, his heart filled with joy and he decided to go back with him to the other end of the world. On the way, they met with many obstacles, fighting dragons and giants, until they reached their destination. So the shock of seeing him again would not be too great, Prince Kamar wrote a love letter to Princess Budur telling her of the adventures he'd had in the City of All Magicians and in the Ebony Islands in his quest to find her. He enclosed his ring in the envelope and asked the servants to deliver it to the dungeon where his beloved was kept prisoner.

'When Princess Budur read the letter and saw the ring, her heart filled with hope and she was allowed to receive him. As their eyes met, the lovers fell into each other's arms. There was a great celebration and all the sultans of the world were invited to their wedding. Naturally, Prince Kamar Al-Zaman and Princess Budur lived happily ever after.'

Luna frowned slightly. 'It seems slightly illogical that suddenly the lovers were allowed to marry when previously their fathers had insisted on making a match themselves.'

'Stop being so logical, Luna. It's a legend. The romance and symbolism is what's important.'

She looked sheepishly back at him. 'Fine. So what happened to the genies, Maimouna and Dahnash?' she asked.

'Oh, they were never heard of again but I'm sure they're still up to mischief, prowling around at night, meddling in people's lives and generally making things happen.' He winked at her and grinned, and it seemed to her that those mischievous little devils had taken up residence in his twinkling eyes, still expressive even behind his narrow mask, and she knew exactly to what he was alluding. 'The legend says that whoever dresses in Kamar Al-Zaman's or Princess Budur's costume will meet the love of their life the first time they wear it.

'Do you believe in legends, my beautiful Queen of the Night?' He was not looking at Luna now but straight ahead, his profile carved like a cameo in the shadows.

Unwillingly, her gaze glided to his powerful, masculine frame and slid away almost immediately. Blood pounded in her head; she felt dizzy with yearning, her soul exposed and vulnerable. She disliked the intoxicating effect he had on her. This eruption of novel sensations was alarming because she knew how easy it would be to succumb to their seductive temptation. He was playing a game, at which he was master and she was a novice.

'I try to keep my feet solidly fixed on the ground. Losing sight of reality can often come at a price.'

'Indulge me tonight ... just for one night. The legend may come true and we'll live happily ever after. Would that be so terrible?'

He looked at her with a boyish grin. 'Fate has a strange way of making things happen. Sometimes suddenly … unexpectedly.'

She looked at him sceptically. 'You know I don't believe in fate. Have you ever known legends to come true?'

'This one has already worked twice in our family. My grandfather was wearing the Sultan's costume on the night he met my grandmother, and my mother wore the Sultana's the night she met my father.'

They were walking in an orchard among lemon trees in bloom and fruit. The flowers were very like orange blossom and the fruit, hanging from glossy leaves, a mixture of large and small, ripe and unripe. Up ahead, the orange trees in the grove were in the process of being harvested. Tall ladders stood among the trees and handcarts were laden with oranges waiting to be moved. Behind the orchard, the moonlight skilfully climbed the big eucalyptus trees, giving their sage-coloured leaves a plated, lustrous look. Luna gazed at the scene, breathing in the beauty of it.

'What are you thinking?' Ruy asked.

'What a perfect night.'

'On such a night as this—' he began, and then broke off.

She looked up at him questioningly.

A moonbeam fell on his face. Behind his mask, his eyes appeared to sparkle with blue fire. '… Anything could happen.' His tone was teasing.

'Anything?' she echoed.

He lifted his gaze and pointed to the dark canopy above. 'Yes, the stars create the circumstances. It's for the individual to seize the opportunity. Sometimes the individual is blind, he lets the chance pass and his destiny is altered for ever.'

It was her turn now to flash him a teasing look. 'That's a little drastic, don't you think?'

'Maybe but, as you know, I'm a great believer in destiny.'

'But you're a scientist.'

'You think all scientists reject the possibility of mysterious forces in the universe? Tell that to Carl Sagan or Einstein. There are plenty more who attest to the incomprehensibility of the universe. God, fate, destiny ...'

'Yes,' nodded Luna, 'and their point was that it's all about uncertainty.'

'Precisely. There's no evidence to prove these things either way, so the possibility therefore exists that they are true.' He shrugged. 'I choose to believe. Perhaps it's the gypsy blood that runs in my veins, all those inherited beliefs. More often than not I feel I'm more *Caló* than *gajo*.'

'You mean that you actually feel more of an affinity with gypsies?'

'Yes,' he agreed quietly. 'It's a great mystery to my grandmother,' he laughed, a little derisively.

'Why is that? Because of the scandal you told me about in the car, involving your grandfather and the gypsies?'

'Yes. Grandmother has never really been comfortable with the *gitanos* as a result. The de Fallas and the de Ruedas have always been bound to them in some way, however. Our family has a long history with the gypsies. They live on this land, here at El Pavón; they're never very far away. So whether I'm in Cádiz or here, I'm bound to them too.'

'It explains why you were in the gypsy taverna in Barcelona and how you seem to have a foot in both worlds,' said Luna, her hand trailing along the top of a clump of soft-petalled carnations in the flowerbeds adjoining the path. 'One minute you're a gypsy in jeans and T-shirt playing the guitar in an offbeat nightclub, the next you're an eminent doctor appearing at a conference in a five-star hotel.'

Ruy chuckled. 'Yes, I suppose it is confusing. Most of my closest friends are gypsies, many of them knowledgeable herbalists and healers. They've helped me a lot in my work. A wonderful people, greatly misunderstood. They're the wild flowers of the world, blowing free in the wind with nothing to control or constrain them.' He smiled broadly. 'I'll introduce them to you one day. You'll like them, I'm sure.'

They had reached the summerhouse at the end of the garden. It looked like a fairy palace, surrounded by roses, creepers, nasturtiums and graceful convolvulus, falling around it in rich profusion.

In the dim light, Luna lost her footing and stumbled on the steps. Ruy caught her under the arm, strong fingers supporting her and, as he did so, the back of his hand brushed against the curve of her breast. She shivered at the intimate contact and felt them swelling from nothing more than the thought of his touch on them.

His eyes, alight with emotion, flickered to her face; he seemed transfixed by her nearness and his longing to express himself. He wanted her. She knew it, and she wanted him too.

Ruy made a sudden move towards her. She took a step back as the old feeling of panic abruptly invaded her. This time it had a different edge. Her own desire made it far more dangerous. She could not let herself give in to that terrifying lack of control again. Mid-stride, Ruy stopped, reading the hunted deer expression in her honey-brown eyes. She knew they were wide with fear, not as concealed as she would have liked by her mask.

He frowned. His whole body was tense with the strain of self-control. 'Why?' he murmured. 'You want this as much as I do. Every curve, every nerve in your body is crying out for me … You proved it tonight when you were in my arms. Have you forgotten the way you trembled against me, the eloquent way your body spoke to me? The memory of that dance will remain forever etched on my mind. I've never met someone as sensual as you are. I'm irresistibly drawn to you …' He hesitated. '… Bewitched.'

He took another step closer, his eyes dark pools of indigo blue. She had never seen them that colour before.

'You're attracted to me, too. Why don't you admit it? You can't help yourself when I'm near. I read it in your eyes … in your body.' He was standing just inches away now and his gaze dropped, hungrily taking her in. 'I don't even need to touch you, I can feel your urge to surrender to me.'

With alarm, Luna registered that he knew full well the power he had over her. Perhaps that was why she always had to try to resist him, she told herself. Because if she didn't …

She raised her chin defiantly. 'You don't know what you're talking about.'

'Oh yes, I do! You've been giving me the cold shoulder ever since we set eyes on each other because you're afraid of me, afraid that we're alike and that I'll discover underneath this calm, cool and aloof front you put up, there's a really hot-blooded, passionate seductress.'

Desperately, Luna hit back with the only weapon within her grasp. 'You seem very sure of yourself,' she said, forcing her voice to be steady. 'You must be so used to every female you meet wanting to fall into your arms that you can't accept it when a woman doesn't.'

It was a blatant lie and they both knew it.

Ruy's expression darkened and she could hardly blame him. He looked as if he were gritting his teeth and he had paled under his golden tan. Shaking his head, he gave a short, mirthless laugh.

'Don't worry, I'm not going to make you do something we both know you want. I know how to behave honourably with a woman.' A bitter smile twisted his sensitive mouth. 'You've got the most beautiful amber eyes, Luna, yet you seem to be blind. You've also a good brain, but it doesn't tell you everything.'

He was still only inches away from her, radiating frustrated desire. Seeing the look in his eyes, Luna's heart hammered uncontrollably in her chest.

'I don't know what you mean.'

'Don't you?' He caught her gaze and held it. 'When a man is hungry and thirsty, he needs food and drink, yet you don't seem to notice these human cravings. Or at least you pretend not to, though I wish I knew why. They're normal and natural. After all, this is the twenty-first century, not the Middle Ages.'

Luna stiffened. He had hit a raw nerve and she summoned as much self-control as she could muster. 'Who are you to judge me? You said it yourself. I've been discouraging you from the start but you've pursued me as if I'm just another of your easy conquests.'

Ruy arched an eyebrow. His eyes sparked with rough amusement but his voice was quiet with intensity. 'Believe me, Luna, there is nothing easy about anything where you're concerned.'

'Please don't stand so close,' she rasped, the danger of his proximity making her breathing more laboured by the second.

'Why, Luna? Because then I might kiss you and you want that so badly it's like a fire in your veins.'

'You know nothing about me, so don't presume to tell me what I want.'

'I don't presume, I know.' His gaze fell to her breasts, then her hips, right down to her feet, sliding back up to her mouth. 'Your body is as alive with hunger as mine is. Why do you keep denying it? Lie to anyone you like but don't lie to me.' He paused and his blue stare fixed on her beautiful face. 'Or perhaps it gives you a kick to arouse a man's appetite and then starve him,' he added scathingly.

Luna's eyes flamed. Suddenly the mortification of her wanton response to him on the dancefloor returned with renewed force. 'How dare you!' she hissed as she lifted a hand and slapped him across the face.

Ruy didn't flinch or blink an eyelid, only his eyes turned steel grey behind his mask.

Before she knew it, he had taken her in his arms, his mouth closing over hers with all the pent-up fire that had burnt them both since they had first met. Unable to resist, she responded with equal fever. He pushed his body against her until she was backed up against the wall of the summerhouse. Flames erupted between them as their lips, hands and bodies tried to satiate the craving that had tortured their days and nights. The hard pressure of his arousal pushed against the curve of her thigh and pleasure surged through her like white, liquid heat. His tongue found hers, plunging into her mouth and retreating over and over again in such a wildly suggestive rhythm that she thought she would go mad. In that moment, with the whole of the world shut out, only the two of them existed.

'Tell me you want me, Luna.' His mouth went to her ear. 'Tell me you're not a dream from which one day I'll wake up and you'll be gone.' His hand slid into the bodice of her dress, searching for the curvy softness of her breasts. The feel of his warm palms on her quivering skin was so sweet she cried out with pleasure.

The sound of it echoed in her head, bringing her down to earth with a bump. She gave a horrified gasp and, panic-stricken, wrenched herself from his embrace.

'Please, Ruy,' she whimpered. With a muffled sob she flung herself away.

'What is it?' he asked. He was breathing heavily, his eyes scanning her face, trying to understand.

Luna flushed under his dark and fathomless gaze and bit her lower lip hard. She looked at him through glittering eyes, willing herself not to cry.

'Nothing,' she whispered, evading his eyes so he could not read in them a different message. She was on fire; she wanted him inside her, that was the simple truth, and what he had said about her had been right, every word of it. Yet, paradoxically, a strong feeling of fear, almost repugnance, was urging her to reject him. She knew she was going to bitterly regret it, but she didn't have any choice. The shame inside her had won again. She was flawed, she admitted chillingly … It was the only explanation for her perverse behaviour. She was some sort of emotional freak.

Ruy stepped towards her and stood just inches away, leaning his hand against the wall of the summerhouse. 'What's stopping you from letting go, Luna? I don't care if we have a professional relationship, what does that matter?' Frustrated, he pulled off his turban, letting it fall to the ground along with his mask. He raked his fingers through his hair, which stood up wildly, making her want to reach out and touch it. But her hand remained by her side.

He leaned in towards her. 'Think about this in your bed out there on your deserted beach; I'll haunt your thoughts and I'll be in all your dreams just as you're in mine. Don't try to fight the wind and tide of your destiny. We're bound to each other by fate. Do you want to risk a life half-lived because you were too afraid?' His eyes were as dark as night now, the blue in them obliterated by his dilated pupils as they bored into her like hot pokers, scorching each part of her with the passion and desire they radiated.

Luna's eyes slid guiltily down his body as he spoke and she shuddered, knowing he was right, the pain of emptiness already filling her. 'I'm sorry, I can't,' she whispered in a choked voice.

Picking up on her distress, he stared down into her face and his features softened. He studied her with an expression of speculative tenderness. 'It's alright, *niña*. It's me who should be sorry.' He lifted a finger and traced the line of her cheek, smiling ruefully. His voice was barely a whisper. 'I'll be waiting for you … when you're ready for me.'

Ruy's words went straight to her suffering heart. She was grateful for his understanding, thankful that he was prepared to give her another chance … just until she sorted herself out. This powerful, unyielding man, who had endured her dishonesty in ways he didn't even realize, was trying to reach out to her and the only response she could feel at this moment was mute bewilderment. The tears she had tried to swallow back were now trickling down her cheeks silently. He produced a handkerchief from under his wide belt and touched her hand: a brief contact, instantly withdrawn.

'It'll soon be midnight. Shall we go back to the house?' His mouth twisted wryly as he bent down to retrieve his turban and mask, fixing them back on. A ghost of a smile crossed his face. 'They'll be giving out prizes for the best costume, and I've no doubt who the winner will be.'

There was a sort of eerie, melancholy air to the garden as they walked back to the ball in silence. The magic of the night had gone; the dream was over. Now the moon was sulking, and nothing was left in the sky but a few pallid stars that had stopped flashing their brightness. Shrouded by night, even the great hacienda's walls seemed to be frowning, rising grimly against the darker sky beyond. Luna sensed rather than perceived that Ruy had moved away from her. She had hurt him. Her rejection cut deeper than the hurt of a slapped face, and he was not a man to be rejected or slapped.

The bell of a neighbouring church chimed the first slow, sonorous stroke of midnight. As it rang out, rockets hissed and roared high into the sky and burst into a thousand coloured stars that fell like rain in the darkness, causing every sleeping bird at El Pavón to rise, startled, into the air. Then suddenly, as Ruy and Luna reached the steps leading up to the terrace, a girl appeared, luminous in the glare of the fireworks.

On the cusp of womanhood, she was small and slender with golden skin and a mass of unruly hair as flamboyant as the sky at sunset, a shining goddess dazzling and beautiful as the day – a sun child. The remnant of a torn, transparent golden kaftan barely covered her firm young breasts, and her shapely legs were naked below the knee. She danced in a wild and whimsical way to a tune only she could hear, seeming to respond to a fiery impulse within her. Above her, the sky, alight with exploding colour, formed a spectacular circle of orange, purple, blue, green and white.

Ruy spun round and caught his breath. At first he seemed confused and turned to Luna to say something, but then he turned back anxiously in a moment of indecision as the girl moved off into the trees.

'Sabrina ... Sabrina!' The words floated like a sigh into the night as he went after the luminous, fairylike silhouette and disappeared in the black, velvet shadows.

As the series of bangs, whizzes and crackles fizzled down in the midnight sky, masks fell and El Pavón began to throb again with squealing, riotous laughter and music under a motley rain of confetti.

The moon had reappeared; the hum of voices came to Luna like in a dream. There was a lot of laughing and clapping going on. They were giving out prizes for the costumes. The colour had drained from her face; everything she saw was blurred and unreal. The atmosphere was getting hotter, she thought, as the night advanced. How long had she been standing there? Luna felt choked. It was as if the balloon of ecstasy that had buoyed her up at the beginning of the evening had finally burst.

She put her hand to her throat and walked up the few steps to the terrace. Alone, at the edge of the archway, she gazed into the brightly lit ballroom. A dizzy frivolity had descended upon El Pavón at midnight, now that everyone was unmasked, and the feeling swept through the excited crowd packing the dancefloor.

Suddenly, Luna was caught up by a group of dancers who had linked hands and were moving around the room, scooping up everyone in their path. The place was a swiftly changing kaleidoscope of shouting, capering figures – now pulling this way, now that – falling, laughing, leaping and dancing. Round and round she was whirled, swept like a feather before the wild broom of excited revellers. El Pavón's guests had let themselves go, and were soon drunk with their own merriment. The pace grew faster ... Luna was exhausted; she thought that if she didn't get out of there soon, she would fall over.

Breathless, she pushed her way through the crowd towards the archway.

She could hardly believe her own gullibility. Lured by the prospect of a masked ball, filled with excitement and tantalizing romance, instead it had turned into a night of disastrous disappointment.

Staggering out of the throng into the hallway, Luna chastized herself bitterly, frustrated by her own chaotic emotions whenever he was near. One moment her body had melted with abandoned desire against Ruy's, the next she'd rejected him for responding to this electrifying heat between them.

Was that why he'd abandoned her in the garden and taken off after a wild, half-naked young woman? Was she his lover? She couldn't have been much more than eighteen or nineteen. Had Ruy caught up with this girl, who seemed to produce such a strong reaction in him? No doubt he had found someone to relieve his 'cravings', she thought, a faint nausea squeezing her stomach.

Luna spotted a couple of women coming out of a large downstairs powder room. Grateful to find somewhere to catch her breath and calm down, she hurried inside.

She found herself in a small antechamber with elegant marble-topped cabinetry lining one wall, part of which formed a dressing table. Above it, three mirrors with overhead lights had been hung, and a couple of bijoux silk-covered chairs stood empty in front. Beyond was a separate room, divided from this one by an archway that concealed a similar arrangement, but with a couple of marble-topped sinks instead. She closed the door behind her and went into the farthest room.

Determinedly, Luna fought to bring her indignant fury under control as she pulled off her mask. In her haste, she tangled the strings in her hair and tugged at it angrily, before throwing it on the marble counter. She stared blindly at her reflection in the mirror. Her eyes were still glazed with confusion. Taking a hand towel from the basket on the side, she dampened it under the tap and let the cool moisture soothe her hot brow.

What had happened to her judgement? Had she taken leave of her senses in accepting Ruy's invitation to the ball? It was always destined to end badly.

Destiny. Luna almost laughed hysterically.

She was angry now, angry and humiliated. Her self-esteem was bruised, her heart sore and she was unreasonably maddened with jealousy. How could Ruy treat her this way? Didn't he pride himself on knowing how to treat women 'honourably'? She felt such a fool for desiring him. Then again, he was probably an expert at making women do so.

Men! They were all alike – pretending to be nice to get what they wanted, but rotten at heart. She was finished with the lot of them.

Luna was still composing her features in preparation for going back out into the hallway when she heard the door open. Female voices floated through to her part of the room.

'He's driving himself far too hard at work,' a woman pronounced, 'but I've finally persuaded him to take a fortnight off. He never has any spare time these days.'

'Perhaps he would, if he spent less of it down at the camp. I think you've been a little soft on him,' came an older woman's gently sceptical voice.

'The past is the past, *Mamá*. Things are not as they were in your day. Besides, I rather like Ruy's friends.'

'Darling, you've always been far more accepting than me. I think that's where Ruy gets it from; you were always fascinated by gypsies when you were young. Perhaps they help him let off steam, it's true.'

'Yes, he gets terribly intense. I do worry about him. Now and then I see that look in his eye.' There was a pause. 'I think he's still haunted by that dreadful business in Boston ... He won't talk about it, of course. Proud, like his father: always thinking he can solve things on his own. But, like you so rightly say, his friends do seem to give him an outlet for all those pent-up emotions.'

The older woman's voice took on a reassuring tone. 'Ruy is a young man who dulls his pain with many things ... ambition, impulsiveness, that flippant façade of his. He'll find his way, Luz, don't you worry. He just needs the right woman to help him. He's not so different from Andrés in that respect,' she added with a chuckle.

Luna's ears had pricked up at the mention of Ruy's name. Taken aback, she realized with a sinking feeling that it must be Alexandra, Ruy's grandmother, and Luz, her daughter – Ruy's mother – having a private word, oblivious to her presence. How on earth was she going to extricate herself from the room without speaking to them? She was suddenly panic-stricken. All she wanted was to leave El Pavón as quickly as possible, by taxi if need be, and there she was, trapped – and by Ruy's closest family.

Luna heard Luz's voice again. 'I wish Ruy and his father would spend more time together.'

'Those two are as stubborn as each other.'

There was a smile in Luz's voice. 'The women in our family seem to like a stubborn man, wouldn't you say?'

Alexandra chuckled. 'Indeed we do.'

Unable to remain concealed any longer without it looking as though she were deliberately eavesdropping, Luna took a deep breath, reached for her mask, and walked out of the back room.

Both women turned to look at her, and she felt the flush rise in her cheeks.

'Oh, I'm sorry, I didn't realize there was anyone else in here,' said the older of the two, whom Luna knew must be Ruy's grandmother. Dressed in a long, purple evening gown, she appeared to be only in her late sixties, though she must be much older than that, Luna realized. Alexandra's hair was a delicate shade of silver and her still-sparkling green eyes held Luna's inquisitively.

'I was just on my way out,' Luna explained apologetically. 'I didn't mean to intrude. My mask got caught in my hair, I was trying to untangle it.' She managed a weak smile and endeavoured to take on the air of someone too preoccupied to have overheard the conversation.

'What a wonderful costume, *señorita*,' said Alexandra, clearly distracted by Luna's dress. 'You look perfectly ravishing.'

'Thank you.' Luna didn't want to offer an opening into more conversation but neither did she wish to appear rudely brusque. 'I was lucky to get it at the last minute,' she added.

Luna glanced at the beautiful woman next to Alexandra, whose jet-black hair was artfully piled on top of her head, ringlets cascading over her shoulders, one of which was bare, due to the cut of her elegantly simple Greek goddess robe. Her eyes were mesmerizing. The deepest sapphire blue, they gazed back at Luna with spirited curiosity. This had to be, without a doubt, Ruy's mother.

She smiled warmly at Luna, who noticed that her face carried the faint creases around her eyes that came from frequent laughter. 'We had so many people to meet when the masks came off just now but I don't believe we've had the pleasure of being introduced. I am Luz Rueda de Calderón and this is my mother, Alexandra de Rueda.' Her smile faded slightly as she studied Luna's face. 'Do I know you, *señorita*? Have we met before?'

'No, I don't think so,' answered Luna, politely. She stretched out her hand and shook hands with the two women. 'I'm Luna Ward.'

'It's just that your face seems familiar.' Luz continued to gaze at Luna oddly.

Luna was too numbed by surprise at being in this predicament to wonder at Luz's reaction. She cleared her throat. 'You have a beautiful home, Señora de Rueda.'

'Thank you, Señorita Ward.' Alexandra's gaze suddenly took on a kindly look of recognition and her green eyes seemed to twinkle even more. 'This must be the young woman I was telling you about, Luz!' She beamed at Luna. 'You've made quite an impression on the men in our family, I hear. I do hope you'll come and join us for a drink later?'

'Oh ... yes, thank you.' Luna's heart sank. Ruy's grandfather must have mentioned her to his wife. Were all his family lining up to meet her?

This is getting worse and worse, she thought.

'Well, we're delighted Ruy has finally brought a guest to our ball, aren't we, Luz?'

'Yes, this is a first,' said her daughter, her eyes still searching Luna's face in a strange way that made her uneasy.

'Actually, I'd love to stay longer,' said Luna, 'but unfortunately I have to be up early to get a few things done. Family business,' she added hastily, scrambling around for an excuse to leave. It was unthinkable that she should stay and be drawn into socializing with Ruy's family now. The way that his mother was quietly scrutinizing her made it an even less appealing prospect. 'Perhaps another time. It was lovely to meet you both.'

'I do hope we haven't scared you off with our talk of Ruy's bringing someone to the ball at last,' said Alexandra, in sudden alarm.

'Now you're only making it worse by rubbing it in, *Mamá*,' said Luz wryly. 'We should know better, you and I. There's nothing like this family when it comes to heaping on the pressure – not to mention the full Spanish inquisition, of course.' She took

Luna's hand with a sudden warm impulse. 'You mustn't mind us. Naturally, you must go home whenever you want.'

'Of course you must, Señorita Ward. Still, let's walk outside together,' suggested Alexandra. 'Guests are starting to leave and, as hostess, I really ought to say goodbye.'

Before Luna could react, Ruy's elegant grandmother had taken her arm and steered her towards the door.

When they returned to the hall, Luz paused, scanning the crowd near the front door.

'Was Ruy waiting for you out here?'

'No, he wasn't,' answered Luna quickly. How on earth was she going to explain that she was going home alone when they knew she had arrived with Ruy? She decided it was best not to even try. 'I think he's outside somewhere,' she added vaguely, forcing a smile, praying his mother in particular would not question her any further.

Luz's gaze fixed speculatively on Luna. 'Shall I come outside with you to find him? He shouldn't have disappeared if you need to leave, Señorita Ward, and we haven't seen him properly yet. I really don't know where he could have got to.'

He's running after a half-dressed wild siren in your garden.

Luna stifled the thought and breathed deeply. 'Please don't put yourself to any trouble, Señora Rueda de Calderón,' she said. 'I'm sure I'll find him, and you have your guests to attend to.' She noticed the major-domo, who was standing at the bottom of the huge staircase, handing a woman her bag and shawl with a polite nod.

Alexandra seemed to sense Luna's reticence and squeezed her hand. There was a whole world of understanding in that clasp, Luna sensed, not least that Luna wasn't used to a maternal touch. Alexandra followed her gaze towards the major-domo.

'Yes. Be sure to ask Alberto to sort you out a car home and I do hope we'll be seeing you again soon.' As Luna looked back at her with a weak smile of relief, she fancied she saw a wise gleam in her eye. 'Now, Luz, come and help me find my shawl before we join your father. I've no idea what I've done with it.'

'I think you left it in the ballroom when you were dancing with that besotted artist, *Mamá*,' said Luz, raising an amused eyebrow.

'Oh nonsense, darling,' answered Alexandra. 'He's eighty-five if he's a day, and at our age one isn't besotted, one is merely "charmed".'

Luz let out a light laugh and, as Luna observed the playful, loving repartee between mother and daughter as they moved off arm in arm, she experienced a fleeting pang of regret for the family life she herself had missed.

Luna sighed, then pulled herself up. Her mind now switched to the immediate difficulty of finding her way home on her own as quickly as possible. She didn't want to risk the chance of Ruy reappearing, and hoped at this hour she wouldn't have to wait long for a car to take her home.

She made a beeline for the major-domo.

'Excuse me, I'd like to get back to Cádiz. I understand you might be able to call me a taxi?'

The major-domo nodded and smiled. 'Of course. There are a number of taxis outside, *señorita*. I will go and hold one for you if you like?'

Luna almost sagged with relief. '*Gracias, señor*, that's most kind.'

She picked up her shawl and bag and joined the queue of guests at the front door waiting to say goodbye to their hosts. As Luna came up to Count Salvador de Rueda she held out her hand. He took it, and carried it to his lips in a chivalrous kiss. His steel-grey eyes fixed on her.

'We did not see you for the prize-giving, *señorita*. *Que lástima*, what a pity, I would have liked to make your acquaintance before you left,' he said in English. 'I hope we will be able to make up for this contretemps some other time. *Buenas noches*.'

A pink hue rushed to Luna's cheeks. '*Gracias por su amable hospitalidad, señor,* thank you for your kind hospitality, *señor,*' she whispered in Spanish, meeting the old man's perceptive gaze.

She should have known those alert, metallic eyes would not have missed a thing.

CHAPTER 7

S ome time later, in the early hours of the morning, the lights were still on in a small house at the top of a hill on the edge of Cádiz, which looked across the isthmus to the slumbering city. From the outside of the hacienda could be heard the sounds of sleepy cicadas mingling with the random notes of a lone mandolin.

Ruy stretched out in a hammock on the terrace of El Viento, staring up at the stars. A guitar lay abandoned on a chair a few feet away, next to some sheets of music. With a half-empty glass of brandy on the floor beside him and his mandolin resting on his chest, his fingers picked idly at the strings, occasionally stopping to strum a chord quietly. He loved the view of Cádiz at night, its ancient towers illuminating the city like a mysterious, beckoning lodestar, but tonight the city seemed to glitter forlornly: a remote jewel, out of reach against the inky sky. Over the past hour, he had been replaying the evening in his head; the same evening that he had looked forward to all day, sending every part of him stirring in anticipation, but which had turned into a fiasco. In a few hours it would be dawn but, for now, the heart of night still felt vast and solemn above.

When he returned to the ball, Luna had already left, 'alone in a taxi because you weren't anywhere to be found,' his grandfather had told him reproachfully. Ruy had stayed long enough to placate his family – and evade their questions about Luna – before heading for his car. If the circumstances had been otherwise, he would have gladly stayed and had a drink with them all, but this wasn't the way he'd envisaged the evening would end. Luna was meant to be with him and he would have taken great pleasure in presenting her to his family properly. Instead, she was gone and who could blame her? So he'd made his excuses and left.

The drive back to Cádiz had seemed long. He'd almost been tempted to head straight for La Gaviota to speak to Luna but knew that would have been a foolish mistake. Instead, his mind had picked over what had happened, trying to make sense of everything.

He was a logical man and Luna's attitude towards him was puzzling. She still evaded him, despite this silent hurricane of electricity between them. The edges of his self-control had been fraying dangerously thin ever since he met her, and tonight her stubborn denial of her feelings and attempts to cast him as the persistent womanizer had made him snap.

Now, watching a cloud drift across the doleful moon above, Ruy groaned inwardly, remembering his harsh words to Luna in the garden, brought on by physical and mental frustration. His hunger for her had been so strong that the lust-crazed beast within him had been exposed again and, as he had pushed her up against the wall of the summerhouse, it was all he could do not to rip that wisp of a dress from her body and give in to his primitive urges.

What was happening to him? He had never lost control, nor had he ever pursued a woman who hadn't been putty in his hands; he hadn't needed to: women chased *him*!

Ruy clenched his fist, the muscles of his forearm flexing with tension, and brought his fingers down harshly across the strings of the mandolin in a discordant sound.

Damn it, he must get a grip on himself.

He frowned. No, Luna was not a tease, Ruy knew that perfectly well – so why? Why did she persistently reject him? Why, when she obviously wanted the same thing as he did? What was it that scared her? There was a fixed look in her calm, quiet eyes that always made him wonder what was going through her head and a hint of some hidden fear, which inspired an urge from deep within him to protect her; but protect her from what he did not know.

Are you like this with all men, Luna – or is it just me? The thought made him slip further into pensiveness. He leaned over and picked up his glass, taking a gulp of brandy, enjoying the hit of fiery sensation in his throat.

An image of Luna drifted into his mind once more. When she had opened the door to him at La Gaviota, the sensual impact had hit him like a freight train. Had she been naked under those diaphanous shrouds of material? It certainly looked like it. The dress dipped low at the front and his eyes had lingered a little too long on the white snow of her delicate neck, her alluringly curved shoulders and the shadowy cleft between the soft swell of her breasts. The sight of her pearly complexion, her slender and elegant limbs that moved so gracefully, the brilliant mane of silk-like blonde hair, was almost more than he could handle. He was captive; a prisoner of the Queen of the Night, so ravishingly beautiful that whoever set eyes on her would not be able to turn away. How he had longed to touch her …

Desire, pure desire: this was why he couldn't think straight about her.

Not that Ruy was a stranger to desire where women were concerned. Women had always been drawn to him even when he wasn't interested. In his youth, his adolescent libido had found its release in the usual ways – though never with *gitanas* from the gypsy camp, who were far more provocative with their flashing smiles and earthy sexuality than *busno* girls. His father, as well as Chico, had schooled him in the unforgiving nature of gypsy law and so he was careful to channel his urges in other directions. When he was older, Ruy found that he didn't even have to try – women responded to him with very little encouragement and a few charming words. The more sophisticated and worldly they were, the more he enjoyed the chase. Yet, that heady rush of excitement had become increasingly hard to recapture as time went on.

Now Ruy's senses were under siege, like a banquet being presented to a starving man. Hot, forceful desire unlike anything he'd ever known, even in his panting adolescence, coursed like wildfire through his veins for one woman only.

Luna.

The irony was that now she must be thinking he'd run off into the woods after one of his many conquests, when the situation was anything but. He gave a groan of frustration. Why couldn't everything be simpler?

Ruy almost feared the power Luna had over him.

It was probably why he had not seen the obvious before. Why it was that she had rejected him when the look in her eyes reflected his own desperate longing. He had worked with patients before who had suffered trauma, and he cursed his own blindness with Luna. The reality was that he was much too overcome with his feelings for her to think straight. It was if his natural intuition had been skewed.

He strummed his mandolin gently while he turned the thoughts over in his mind. Yes, it all figured. She must have been scared somehow by a past experience and he'd been too blinded by his own hunger for her to register the reason. His jaw clenched, berating himself for his own insensitivity towards her at the summerhouse. He'd always known she was too direct and forthright to lead a man on yet, in the heat of the moment, when he was desperate to feel her body under his hands and her lips on his, he'd grasped at the ridiculous notion, used it to taunt her.

Was she still a virgin? Somehow Ruy thought so. The idea gave his masculine pride a guilty surge of satisfaction, to think that she hadn't been touched by another man; and yet the idea that another man might have been the reason for her vulnerability made that same male instinct in Ruy rise up fiercely in anger.

She was a beautiful sophisticated enigma who kept men at arms' length because someone had hurt her and, most probably, they'd had neither the intelligence nor the finesse to deal with someone like Luna, or to see through the elaborate barricades she'd built up as a defence.

Still, it was a force beyond desire that overwhelmed him. It was Luna herself.

He wanted her, and Luna wanted him. Ruy had been aware of her longing as they danced, knowing that he himself was feeling the same electrifying sensation when he took her soft palm in his. She had quivered under his touch like the strings of a Stradivarius under the bow of a virtuoso, echoing the notes of his desire. Her body had moved with his, alive and receptive, her long shapely legs against his hardening thighs, in a way that nearly drove him insane. The chemistry between them was like a primitive impulse, which their bodies, moulded against each other, were unable to fight. He had pretended not to notice or understand, but he knew all along that she had been fantasizing about him silently as he held her. Just as he was doing with her, imagining that glorious body naked against him as heat built intensely in his groin and spread wildly through the length of him. If he had not been so conscious of the people around him, his self-control would have snapped there and then. Just thinking about it now aroused him, and he pushed an unsteady hand through his hair.

Though Luna's rejection of him was galling, it was more the intensity of his desire for her that exasperated him. This woman had the ethereal looks that were as fresh and innocent as a spray of white jasmine, and a sensuality that haunted his every waking hour and assaulted his nights, rousing him repeatedly from his dreams panting, tortured by an aching need. This attraction was not just prompted by lust – though he longed to possess her as he had never longed for anything else before – but it was as if invisible external influences beyond his control were at work.

Were those invisible forces pushing Luna away from him tonight, just to test his resolve?

His thoughts turned to Sabrina. The young gypsy girl was hopelessly in love with him and yet his feelings for her had never been anything but those of a brother for a younger sister. On her deathbed, her mother, Leyla – or 'La Pharaona' as they called her in the neighbourhood – had entrusted her daughter to him. 'She's not one of the *Calés* of Cádiz, she's alone in the world. One day, like all good gypsies, she will fly by her own wings but, until then, guard her with your heart, Ruy. Remember the old saying: "God waits to win back his own flowers as gifts from man's hands."'

Ruy scowled, as dark phantoms from the past loomed closer in his mind's eye. La Pharaona had saved him. Her care and remedies had kept him sane when all he'd wanted was to shut the world away and let his own darkness consume him. The memories crowded in again, but he shook them aside. Yes, he owed La Pharaona big time, and the day had come when he must deliver.

Still, why did Sabrina have to appear at the ball and ruin the slim chance he had of gaining Luna's trust? Already their fragile relationship had been fractured by his outburst at the summerhouse. Running after Sabrina, as he had done, may well have given the kiss of death to any chance of his making amends to Luna.

Now she would put up more resistance than ever, but he knew that he'd already breached the defensive walls of her emotions and, if he handled her carefully but let her know in no uncertain terms how he felt, he might still have a chance of redeeming himself. It would mean giving her space, though, and for him that would be the hardest challenge of all. His need to be close to her was strong, compulsive and so visceral it made his blood pound and his body ache.

Ruy sighed in frustration and lifted himself up. Gitano-Negro jumped off the balustrade where he had been dozing and rubbed against Ruy's leg. He meowed twice and followed his master into the spacious living room. Ruy squatted down and scratched him under the chin, making the cat purr throatily. 'What d'you think, Gitano-Negro, *ey*? Should I go after her or just drop the whole idea?' Gitano-Negro gazed at him for a moment with knowing golden eyes before closing them to slits as his master stroked him gently behind the ears. 'You're right, no choice there. One thing's for sure: I have to find a way to apologize. I've got to somehow try to act professionally in the office too.' Ruy straightened and breathed out heavily. 'The devil's been in my body all evening and, if I don't calm down, there'll be no rest for me tonight,' he muttered as he pulled his T-shirt off restlessly and headed for the bathroom.

*   *   *

She had to get away; she must get away before he caught her again and ripped her nightdress off. Though she was running as fast as she could, her legs were heavy, so heavy, as if weighed down by lead. She thought she had been in bed but now she was in a wood, stumbling through rough brambles, trying to find the path out of the dense trees that leaned towards her with gnarled, twisting branches. Up ahead was some kind of light, glowing between the trees, and somehow she knew it was her salvation. She mustn't stumble before she reached it. If she tripped and fell, then he would be upon her. Branches scratched her face and arms as she tried to push towards that distant luminescence. She could hear his ragged breathing right behind her. He was getting closer ...

closer. Any moment now he would catch up with her. If only she could move faster ... If only she were not so afraid ...

He seized her nightdress, and the scream died in Luna's throat as she woke up choking; panting and gasping for air. Sick terror and a sense of helplessness invaded her, the very distinct memory of the nightmare hitting her again, leaving her with a panicked sense of impending doom.

The bedroom was bathed in moonlight, its pearly beams throwing monstrous shadows on the white walls. At first Luna did not know where she was. Wide-eyed, she stared blankly at the chandelier hanging from the beamed ceiling, trying to make out her surroundings. Was anyone lurking in the dark corners? Intense fear continued to envelop her as, still numb with sleep, her brain staggered to wakefulness, searching for landmarks that would indicate she was safe, miles away from the trauma that, like an insidious disease, had changed her life over ten years ago and marked her personality.

Trembling, Luna sat up on the edge of the bed, her face ashen, eyes glassy with fear; hideous flashbacks and images leaving her feeling bruised and soiled. A long shiver traversed her from head to toe. Her skin was icy and damp, and she was trembling fiercely. She was cold ... so cold. Now she closed her eyes and hugged herself, rocking to and fro. Minutes passed. Fully awake now, she realized that she had just emerged from another of her nightmares – the worst she'd ever had. She reflected desperately that even the earliest ones had not been so terrorizing.

The shivering had almost stopped. For a while she sat there staring at nothing then, putting out a hesitant hand, she felt for her bedside lamp and flicked the switch, but turned it off immediately with a wince of pain: the glare hurt her eyes. The fear had almost subsided, leaving her with a violent headache and a parched mouth. She slid out of bed with a groan and made her way unsteadily to the bathroom. Filling a glass from the tap, she drank it in one go, then stepped into the shower and spent a good twenty minutes letting the warm water wash away the anxiety and stress that had invaded her.

Why were these memories beginning to surface? Luna hadn't ever remembered being in a wood before. These terrifying nightmares always followed the same formula and took place inside a room, usually her bedroom. She wondered what this sudden change meant. Since she'd arrived in Spain, the order and control she'd always taken care to maintain in her life had been in utter turmoil; it was perhaps inevitable that all this would find its way into her subconscious.

Luna slipped into a clean nightdress and tried to throw off the uncomfortable conclusion that it had something to do with Ruy. The emotions she was afraid to feel for him tormented her enough in her waking hours, and now they were confusing her dreams.

Morena's words floated back into her head: *Someone close to you is dangerous, and you keep running, but run towards the dazzling light.*

Was Ruy something to do with the light – or the danger?

He had often appeared in her other dreams – dreams that were intense but achingly sensual and passionate. The only fear she ever felt was when she woke and began to analyze them. It was then that the initial fantasies about being with him were brushed aside, and the endless scrutiny of the risks to her heart would start, with her habitual logic and cautious instinct for self-preservation holding sway.

After what had happened tonight, Luna was inclined to think that she should have listened to her logic all along.

Back in bed, she tossed and turned but couldn't get back to sleep. No matter how she tried to put him from her mind, her thoughts returned inevitably to the ball and to Ruy, remembering the way they had danced and the warmth of his body radiating through the thin material of his silk shirt. It had felt good, so good!

She had never experienced anything so sensuously powerful: hard, masculine, virile muscle that had pressed against her, moulding itself to her own softer, feminine curves. Then there was that long, stormy kiss that had almost made her lose her mind – she could feel the need blossoming inside her at this very moment, just at the thought.

Luna sighed. Why was she remembering this now? It had all been thrown away in an instant, she thought unhappily, as she recalled the dazzling young siren with flaming red hair who had appeared out of nowhere – Sabrina, Ruy had called her. Yes, she'd been a siren all right; she had sung a tune only for his ears and, like those sailors in ancient legends, fascinated, he had gone to her without a second glance at Luna.

Ruy had run out on her. He had dumped her there, and then embarrassed her.

If this was his way of punishing her for rejecting him it was just as well that she had acted as she did at the summerhouse. Still, that was no reason for him to abandon her in the middle of the ball. After all, she was his guest. How did he think she would get back to Cádiz? What if there had been no cars left to take her?

Luna's mind raced on through all the other 'maybes' whipped up by her paranoia and discomfiture, not once considering that Ruy might have appeared soon afterwards, looking for her. Instead she told herself that she had been lucky to get a taxi, and that his family had been discreet enough not to ask why she was returning home alone. Still, that did not make it any less crushing for her.

Jealousy mixed with denial in Luna's feelings. The anger she had felt at the ball resurfaced. Was Ruy's idea of treating a woman honourably to switch affections when his advances were rejected? Perhaps this 'Sabrina' would be the one he'd be concentrating on now. Luna had thought he was different to other men, but he'd turned out to be just like all the rest.

She was better off alone.

A tremor raced through her as she became conscious of what such a thought actually meant: by running from any close relationship, at best she was condemning herself to a life half-lived, just as Ruy had told her; at worst, a desolate lifetime of loneliness. Was that what she really wanted?

She gave a sigh of utter weariness as she leant back against the bed's headboard and closed her eyes. What an evening! She could not remember a time when she had been so mentally exhausted.

Luna climbed out of bed and opened one side of the window. Having been cold before, now she was hot and restless. She breathed in the briny air blowing in from the sea and rested her forehead against the window frame.

If she was going to lie awake, Luna thought, she ought to be thinking about how she was going to handle working alongside Ruy, not about a kiss that should never have happened, however wild and passionate, from a man who was practised in seducing women and moved on as soon as he found something more enticing to chase.

Yes, she reasoned, perhaps it was for the best that Ruy had found a diversion in that young gypsy girl. At least it would make it less awkward working together if she wasn't constantly trying to avoid his attentions. It would be easier for her to focus on the job in hand, she reflected bleakly.

Her thoughts returned to her assignment. However he had treated her in private, so far, professionally, Ruy was not the man she'd anticipated from her initial research on him. Still, wasn't this partly what she was here to find out, an impartial investigation into his work and the practices of the Institute?

One thing was for sure: tomorrow she would have to harden her resolve to ignore Ruy's effect on her and concentrate on getting her hands on as many case files as she could. Ted would be expecting an update by the end of the week. Besides, the quicker she worked, the sooner she could return to New York.

Luna returned to bed. She would not think about Ruy any more, she promised herself; certainly not in a physical way. She pulled a pillow towards her and squeezed it hard against her chest. Her eyes, now finally heavy with exhaustion, slowly began to close.

She fell into a deep sleep and, with it, came more dreams. This time of sensuous masculine lips on hers in a hot, stormy kiss that seemed to go on forever.

*   *   *

On Monday evening, Luna sat in the laboratory at the Institute, working late. Huddled over a row of test tubes, she had finally wrestled her concentration back to a near-normal level today and, as always happened when she was troubled, had thrown herself even more intensely into her work.

With a determined effort to banish thoughts of Ruy, she had kept herself busy during the remainder of the weekend by driving into Cádiz and sitting with her laptop in a café in the Old Town, going over her notes. Still, that explosive kiss at the masked ball kept simmering in the back of her mind. The passion and fire of it spoke of pure lust, yet his whispered words of tenderness made it dangerously easy for her to imagine there was more than mere lust behind it ... until he had left her in the blink of an eye to run after another woman.

She'd expected Ruy to ring her on the Sunday to attempt an apology – it would have been easy enough for him to obtain her mobile number from the Institute's files – but her phone remained silent. Had he tried to call, she wouldn't have answered an unknown number just in case it was him, but perversely she was irritated that he hadn't made the slightest endeavour to do so.

When Luna had arrived at work that morning, Charo had informed her that Ruy was at a conference all day and would probably not be in until the next day. Glad to have another day's reprieve from the embarrassment of facing him again, not to mention the effort it would take to keep her anger in check, Luna had spent some useful time with Charo, getting to know the ropes a little more. They spent a while discussing some of the more interesting of the Institute's case studies which, on the face of it, she had to admit, reflected impressive results.

Finding out discreetly where the patient files were kept, Luna had then holed herself up in her office for a few more hours, poring over the documents, along with reports on the systematic testing of treatments and their findings, only to find that there was nothing damning in any of them. Far from it: the care and precision of the reports could not be faulted. The range of natural approaches, used alongside a careful selection of chemical treatments, including low-dosage chemo, had, seemingly, an encouraging success rate. In fact, the survival rate of the clinic's patients, at three times the national average, was compelling. Luna had thought, once she began digging through the files, that she would discover quite quickly that this extraordinary statistic had 'bogus' written all over it, but it didn't seem to be so at all.

She pulled out report after report, making copious notes on her laptop, before deciding to move to the laboratory to analyze some of the herbal preparations. Herbalism was an area about which she knew little at the moment, and which, to her mind, seemed potentially the most risky and unreliable element in the clinic's treatment programme.

Now the wall clock silently clicked its way closer to seven o'clock, and Luna was still leaning over her lab bench, doing one last test on an extract of holy thistle. If she were to find that the herb was used inadvisedly in any of the clinic's cases then it would be wholly right to blow the whistle. Tomorrow she would compare it with the properties of milk thistle, another in the *Asteraceae* family used in alternative anti-cancer treatments.

She wondered, not for the first time, if Ted really wanted a wholly impartial article from her. As things were going, her piece on the clinic and its work was likely to be pretty favourable – and 'favourable' wasn't particularly attractive in the world of hot news. No, she was quite sure he'd be expecting some newsworthy weaknesses in its approach.

Well, no matter. Ted had said he wanted an impartial, thorough investigation and Luna was determined to give him just that. Today, she had already made some important notes and this week would revise the outline of her article again, once she had more material.

It was funny, she mused, but she had set out on what she had to concede was a vengeful mission to right some of the wrongs to which her cousin Angelina had supposedly been victim. She'd expected a host of malfeasance and ineptitude on the part of the clinic; a discovery that would, in turn, fuel her righteous anger. In fact, she'd found none so far and the strange thing was she felt all the better for it. It was as if a soothing balm was slowly being applied to the painful wound of her grief.

Luna was so engrossed in her work that she didn't hear Ruy come in.

'How are you getting on?'

Luna nearly jumped out of her skin and her heart went into freefall. She let go of the glass flask she was holding, which crashed to the ground with a brittle splintering sound, and gave a startled cry. 'Damn it!' she hissed under her breath, mortified at his sudden, unexpected presence and her own resulting clumsiness. Keeping her back to him so he couldn't see her struggling to regain composure, she bent down to pick up the pieces of shattered glass.

'Hush, *niña*, leave it. I'll clear it up. You'll hurt …'

Too late.

'Ouch!' she cried out before he had even finished his phrase, as blood started to ooze from her hand.

Grabbing some surgical gauze pads that were on a trolley close to the door, he was at her side in a flash. 'You've cut yourself … Here, let me take a look.'

'I'm fine,' she protested, trying to move away from him.

Nevertheless, he took hold of her hand and, ignoring her objections, applied direct pressure to the wound with his long fingers. He then dragged her gently but firmly, as he would a child, to the anglepoise lamp standing next to the sink.

'I need to have a good look. There may be some tiny pieces of glass still in there. We need to flush them out so this doesn't get infected.'

He turned on the tap and let the water jet run freely over the gash in her palm before once more applying a gauze pad to stem the bleeding.

Now he was bandaging her hand, seated on a stool as she stood mutely in front of him. The masculine fingers that held the back of her palm felt strong, reassuring and thrillingly intimate. He worked quickly and silently, totally focused.

The quietude that settled around them was filled with a sensual tension. Luna was not thinking about the wound. How could she when his dark head was only inches away from her bosom and she could hear his husky breathing? Heat pooled between her breasts. She found herself wondering if those dextrous, capable hands were as confident when carrying out other functions. Blushing inwardly at those thoughts, she felt the first outline of a vivid fantasy creep treacherously into her mind. A shiver ran through her from head to toe.

Ruy must have felt it because his hands stilled. 'I'm sorry. Am I hurting you?' he asked, without looking up.

'No, no, not at all,' she murmured lamely, trying to push away the yearning assaulting her senses. His palms were warm, his hair was thick and shiny, his skin flawless and his profile that of a Roman god. Whiffs of delicious musky aftershave and his own male scent teased and tantalized her. She closed her eyes – it was so wonderful to give in to her dream; but then, like a diver suddenly rising from the bottom of the sea, she forced her eyelids open and took a deep breath to escape the images and tidal waves of emotion that were suddenly washing over her.

Luna's amber irises met Ruy's darkening gaze, and she almost flinched. He was looking up at her, direct and unguarded; the sight of the naked longing in his eyes caused her to give a tiny gasp. For a moment she was captive in the pools of his cobalt eyes and she leaned weakly against the worktop. He tightened his grip on her hand, moving to hold her wrist, as if he couldn't bear for her to draw away from him, out of his reach.

Ruy was only inches from her, his warm breath lightly fanning her throat. His gaze shifted to the shapely curve of her breasts. He closed his eyes and Luna could tell he was struggling to restrain himself. Her will to escape, to resist, was fading too. She longed for him to kiss her but didn't want to consent to it openly, for that would prove him right. Somehow, she preferred to be overpowered so she could then say afterwards: *I didn't want to.*

Ruy opened his eyes and looked up searchingly into hers again. Luna's heart sank shamefully, knowing he had read her all too well. He murmured something under his breath that sounded like an oath, though she didn't understand the words, before he swayed back. Giving his head a fractional shake and clearing his throat, he straightened up.

'There,' he said, trying for a tone of practical briskness. 'The wound is clean and tidy. You'll need to change the dressing in a couple of days. I can do it for you.' As he looked up at her, his blue eyes glinted with complex, animated warmth. 'That wasn't so bad, was it?'

Luna, whose knees had almost given way the moment before, managed what she hoped was a detached smile, and took a slow step backwards. She needed to cover her agitation over his close proximity, which was doing chaotic things to her senses.

Ruy's glance was now roguish. 'Don't look so alarmed. I'll be so gentle, you'll barely feel me touching you.'

He stood up so that their gaze was now level and she struggled to find words that would discourage him. Before she could do so, he said: 'I'll bring my car over from the car park. You can't drive in this state.' He rubbed his jaw, regarding her more seriously. 'Besides, we really need to talk, Luna.'

She finally found her voice. 'No, thank you,' she protested, a little too violently.

'You'll barely be able to hold the wheel with that thick bandage, and your face is white as a sheet.'

'Thank you, but I can call a taxi to pick me up. I'm used to doing that,' she said pointedly, her battered pride suddenly smarting once more. When she saw his surprise, Luna paused before adding: 'I didn't bring my car this morning. The air was so fresh, I walked.'

Ruy did not speak immediately. He took a deep breath; his shoulders hunched and then relaxed. 'Yes, of course. You must be angry with me about running out on you at the ball, and you've every right to be. I'm sorry, Luna, I can explain.'

'Oh, I'm sure you can,' she shot back. Walking over to the bench top where she had left her notes, she attempted to tidy them together with her good hand. 'I'm sure you've had a lot of experience with explanations.'

Ruy muttered an oath before following her over to the bench. 'Luna, listen, please let me do that for you,' he said as she struggled to push the papers into a neat pile.

She looked at him sharply. 'I can manage.'

Ruy gave up and watched her shove everything determinedly into her bag. He moved over to the door and out of the corner of her eye, Luna noticed him pick up something from the table beside it. She turned to see him lay a glorious bunch of flowers in front of her.

'These are for you, Luna. A peace offering from a rude Spaniard or just a gift from an adoring admirer, take it as you wish. I hope you'll forgive my callousness the other night.'

Oh, he was good with words … but it would take more than that to absolve him. She glanced at his gift, then fixed him with a dry look. 'Bravo, *señor*. As usual, you say all the right things, but I'm not impressed. You can keep your flowers.' There was no smile on her lips as she pushed them back at him.

Ruy looked at her sadly. 'I didn't think you would accept them, but it was worth a try.' He studied her closely. 'I knew it was unlikely you'd answer the phone yesterday so I came by your house twice to drop these off and apologize in person, but you weren't there.'

'No, I wasn't,' she replied simply. It hadn't occurred to Luna that he might have come straight over to La Gaviota to try to talk to her. Well, that was worth something, and more than a pretty bunch of flowers. Still, she was glad she'd been out and he'd been put to some inconvenience.

'Last night I did come looking for you as soon as I could to explain, but I must have just missed you.' He saw the disbelieving look in her eyes, yet carried on. 'Look, Luna, I can't apologize for kissing you because I'm not sorry for that.'

'As apologies go, that's an interesting start,' she remarked dryly, hitting a key on her laptop to save her work.

Ruy lifted an eyebrow, perplexed. 'You see, even when you're sniping at me I find it wildly attractive.' He took a step closer. 'I'm not sorry because I know you want me as badly as I want you but I *am* sorry for what I said to you in the summerhouse. I was frustrated, though that's no excuse. Then leaving you straight afterwards when Sabrina appeared … It was foolish, although at the time I felt I had no choice.'

Despite recognizing the sincerity in his eyes, and wanting his assurances to be enough, Luna couldn't help but guard herself. Turning back to her laptop, she pressed the key to logout.

'Who was she?' she asked without looking at him.

Ruy rubbed the back of his neck. 'Sabrina is one of the gypsies, but she lives on her own, up in the hills. Because of who her mother was, she has a special status among the *gitanos*, but she's not part of the gypsies of Cádiz. It's a long story but she shouldn't have been there in the gardens. The *gitanos* travel up from Cádiz to El Pavón for their own traditional fiesta, and Sabrina must have decided to join them. They all know to keep to the camp, beyond the main grounds. But Sabrina ...' he stared up at the ceiling, searching for the right words, '... she's a little unpredictable. I wanted to make sure she was all right and wasn't going to disrupt the party. My grandmother would have had a fit if she'd seen her.'

Luna wondered what this girl meant to him, and why her mother was so significant, but she was too proud to probe further. Before that night, she would have batted his apology away and not let him see how much he had hurt her, but everything had changed between them. In his arms at the ball she had allowed him a glimpse of her vulnerability – twice – and afterwards, as she had feared he might, Ruy had disappointed her. Now she wanted some space from him, time to think.

Ruy studied her as if trying to read her thoughts. 'Luna, let's have that dinner so we can talk properly. About us.'

She turned to him again. 'There is no "us".' Her tone was neutral; her eyes cool flints of amber.

His jaw clenched. 'Must you be so hard?' His gaze bore into her – a fiery, intense blue that burned with such pride and frustration, but also a flicker of barely concealed pain, that it almost made her relent. Almost ...

'Yes, I must – if it means you'll leave me alone. You need to understand that what happened was a big mistake, a gross lapse in judgement for both of us. On my first day I told you that this wouldn't work, and I was right. I should have listened to my instincts.'

Ruy made an exasperated gesture. '*Dios mío*, Luna, you're stubborn! Listen to me. I apologize for running out on you at the ball but let me explain and you'll understand.'

She shook her head, evading his stare. 'I'm not interested in your reasons.'

'Why are you wasting your time in denial when you know you want me?' His voice was soft and seductive, his lips curling into a provocative smile.

Luna looked up at him. Anger flashed in her eyes. 'Why are *you* wasting *your* time with someone who obviously doesn't agree with you?'

He leaned an elbow casually on the bench next to her, though the intensity in his gaze was unmistakable. 'Because I don't believe you. I want to make love to you, and I know that's what you want too.'

Heat shot through her at his words and her breathing quickened. Aware that she had never been a good liar, she decided to be direct. 'I admit there's something between us. A physical attraction, nothing more,' she said rapidly. Her heart gave a squeeze of regret and her spine stiffened. 'Whenever we meet, you delight in baiting me. Judging by our track record so far, we don't actually get along.'

He gave her that infuriating half-smile of his. 'Of course we do, Luna.'

She had to admit, they'd never had a *dull* conversation. That wasn't the point. She lifted her chin. 'I think you must be one of the most arrogant men I've ever had the misfortune to come across.'

'You love it.'

The nerve of the man!

'You're completely egotistical.'

'I'm exactly what you need. Someone who's strong enough to challenge you. Someone who can stop you being afraid and bring out all the passion you're so intent on hiding underneath that prim manner of yours.' He was still inches away and though he didn't move any closer, his blue gaze sparked with intensity. 'I could make love to you now, here, immediately.'

'You forget that it takes two to tango.'

'Oh, but *you* forget, I've seen how you tango, Luna.'

How could she forget? Still, she didn't allow herself to dwell on the thought. 'Trust me, doctor, there'll be no encore!' she snapped.

He sighed. 'Truly, Luna, the way between us has become such a stony path that I'm beginning to think fate has a warped sense of humour.'

'It's your doing, Ruy. It's entirely your fault that we can never be friends.' She pulled some sheets off the printer and slid them into her bag. 'When I first saw you, I liked you.'

'You don't like me now?'

She turned to him, her voice wavering. 'You do nothing to help me. All you care about is getting me into bed,' she exclaimed tremulously.

The smile on his face faded. He looked offended by her remark and she caught something dark and unfathomable in his indigo eyes.

Her tone softened. 'Thank you for the dressing.' She closed her bag and slowly exhaled. It cost her to reject him again but, if she did not assert herself now, the way ahead would be more than stony and she could not let herself go down that path unprotected. 'Is there anything you want me to prepare for tomorrow?'

'Tomorrow,' he echoed.

'Yes, I mean for work.'

For a long moment he stared at her. 'Very well, Luna. Tomorrow we'll talk about work, not now.' His expression had become unreadable again.

She glanced at her watch. 'It's late. I really must go. I need to get an early night.'

'Yes, you need to go home and rest that hand.'

She flashed him an impersonal smile and walked past him to the door without looking back. Maybe after this he would stop trying to break through her barriers, even if her heart ached at the thought.

'And Luna?'

Her hand paused on the door handle as she glanced at him. 'Yes, Ruy?'

'I promise not to pursue you any more.' His voice was firm but husky. 'However, there's nothing to stop you from changing your mind, whenever you want.' He gave her one last burning look. 'When you do, I'll be there.'

*   *   *

For the rest of the week Luna concentrated on familiarizing herself with the work at the Institute. The more case studies she read, the more her previous scepticism began to be replaced with interest and a grudging respect for much of Ruy's work. He combined clinical thoroughness with a holistic approach, encompassing the complex psychological impact of his patients' illnesses and managing each case with intelligent sensitivity.

Ruy breezed in and out of the office but, since their confrontation in the laboratory, he treated Luna with courteous professionalism: never an inappropriate word or an improper glance. In the end, she had gone to the *farmacia* in the centre of town to have her hand redressed. Ruy had done a good job, and the wound had healed well. If he noticed that she'd quietly managed this herself, he said nothing. Other than enquire how her hand was, now that she had a large plaster on her palm, he asked no personal questions.

She preferred it this way, Luna told herself. With any luck, they would both be so busy channelling their energies into their working partnership that the more they got to know each other, the more this annoyance of an attraction between them would fizzle out.

Whenever they did speak, Luna still found Ruy fascinating in the way he became animated by new ideas. So rather than Luna's personal interest in him waning, as she had hoped it would, her respect for him continued to grow. More and more, she regarded him with a new curiosity, realizing that he was a man driven by his passions in every way. She tried to pretend she didn't miss that fervour directed at her, but nonetheless often watched him for clues as to what he was thinking.

At one point, when she mentioned to him that she wanted to know more about herbs, he gave her a couple of journals on herbal remedies that the Institute had published.

'Read these,' he suggested. 'You can make notes and keep them if you want. We've got plenty of copies. When you know a little more about it, I'll take you into the hills so you can see the herbs growing and get to know the way they look, feel and smell. Touch and smell are very important in our business.'

Had she noticed a slight flicker of amusement at the corner of his mouth as he had said that? Did his words hide a more provocative meaning?

You're reading too much into it. Stop looking for signs that he's still interested, she told herself.

So Luna wrapped her pride tightly around herself and tried to ignore the distracting effect he still had on her.

Then there was Vaina, a name that often occurred in Luna's thoughts like an evil genie, causing her a pang of jealousy that always managed to annoy her and spoil the rest of her day. The managing director often visited Casa Vistaria, always elegant, not a hair out of place, not a flaw on her beautifully made-up face, leaving a trail of expensive exotic scent in her wake. Invariably, there was some excuse or other for her to enquire about '*El Medico*', as she always referred to him. When Ruy was around, they spent hours closeted in his office. On those days, despite her best efforts to shrug it off, an irritability would descend upon Luna like a thick cloud, which even Charo, Casa Vistaria's ray of sunshine, was unable to penetrate.

It was now Friday and Luna had spent the whole morning in her office, organizing the research files into a new system that she found more efficient and easier to access. It was also a good opportunity to select the best ones for her article.

A rapid knock sounded on the door and Charo's beaming face appeared.

'So, are you still coming this evening?' she said without preamble. 'What time shall I pick you up?'

Luna looked up from her desk with a confused look. 'This evening?'

'Yes, the Vargas exhibition. Remember?'

Luna had almost forgotten about her promise and would have preferred to stay late to finish what she was doing. Still, Charo had been so helpful in the past week it would be churlish to back out now.

'Oh yes, of course. Actually, would you mind if I met you there? I would really like to finish this before the weekend. I might need to stay for an extra hour.'

Charo gave her a mock-despairing look. 'Really, Luna, those files won't run away over the weekend.' She leaned on the doorframe, crossing her arms. 'You've been working hard all week. Let your hair down, it's Friday night.'

'It won't take long.' Luna smiled apologetically. 'I'll be there by eight, don't worry. I'll come and find you.'

Charo narrowed her eyes impishly. 'If you're not, I'll come looking for you.'

Luna burst into the first laugh she'd had in a long time. 'In that case, I'll be sure to work faster.'

Luna smiled fondly after her as Charo left the room and then closed the file in front of her. It was nearly midday so she thought she'd break for something quick to eat in the staff restaurant – she hadn't been down there yet. Grabbing some notes to read, she headed out of her office.

Ten minutes later, she was sitting at a wooden table in the corner of a bright and airy room in the main building, which looked out on to the central courtyard. With its terracotta flagstone floor, high-beamed ceiling and giant potted ferns, it was a cool refuge from the noonday sun that bore down on the courtyard garden outside.

The restaurant was already filling up with people. Surrounded by the rising chatter, Luna's head was down, distractedly eating a seafood salad while flicking through her pages of notes, when a familiar deep voice interrupted her.

'Do you ever take a break, Luna?'

Her head snapped up. Ruy stood there holding a tray, unfeasibly handsome in a simple white shirt tucked into jeans, having discarded his lab coat. Luna kept her eyes resolutely on his face.

'I am taking a break. I'm eating.' She lifted a fork to emphasize her point.

Ruy shook his head, amusement creasing the edges of his eyes as he took off his glasses and put them in the top pocket of his shirt. Little wonder she hadn't recognized him from the picture in her notes – he looked so different now and his hair was much longer. Luna's mind snapped back to the reason why she had a file on him, and she was aware of a shiver of guilt.

'You know, sometimes it's important to clear your head of work entirely. Do you mind if I join you briefly?'

'Not at all,' she lied, smiling politely. Now that he was here, she had little choice but to let him sit down. Luna was on her guard; particularly given her pulse was quickening, as it always did whenever Ruy appeared.

He set down his tray and slid his muscular frame into the chair opposite. Glancing at the heading of her notes, he opened his bottle of mineral water and took a swig. 'I'm glad you're looking at the intravenous Vit C therapy,' he said, nodding over to the paper. 'What do you think? I'd be interested to hear your views.'

Luna didn't have to feign interest. 'I have to say, it's fascinating with regard to melanomas and anything relatively chemo-resistant. The results I've been looking at suggest a fairly consistent level of tumour cells destroyed with the high-dosage infusions.'

'Good. Next week, I'd like to look at some additional statistical research on the probability of melanomas reacting favourably to a mixture of both Vit C and Vit K,' he said, tucking into his sandwich. He ate with such an obvious appetite that Luna's thoughts took an unwanted turn. Ruy raised his thumb to his lips and gave it a lick.

Unsettled, Luna quickly looked down at her food. 'Yes, of course,' she said.

Needing something to occupy her hands, she pushed her fork around her plate distractedly. He really did have the most attractive mouth she had ever seen.

Any woman would fall at his feet, and no doubt did – all the time.

Luna, stop torturing yourself.

She let out a silent exhalation and focused her thoughts. 'I've been through a substantial number of the case files this week,' she said, 'and I can see why the press is sitting up and taking notice of your results. Do you think it'll help get more funding for trials?'

'Yes, that's the aim,' he said. 'Double-blind trials, the full complement. It could well change the whole terrain for us. I don't think the medical establishment will change its tune, or the pharma moguls for that matter, but it'll be a start. Public opinion is always far more ready to shift direction than those tunnel-visioned monoliths.'

'I've heard they're nervous, though. That you might be redrawing the map.'

Ruy nodded in between bites. 'And so they should be.' He paused to take a gulp of water. 'Actually, I'm not sure they really are. They're so blinded by their own limited viewpoint: the gospel according to orthodoxy.'

Luna watched him speculatively. 'I've read quite a few of your articles. You really do have it in for the pharma industry.'

He shrugged. 'If I can stir up controversy about Big Pharma, then I'll take every opportunity to do so. Profit has become their religion, the shareholders more important than the public they should serve.' His eyes were flashing now. She had definitely touched a nerve. 'The research and development budgets they claim are obscenely higher than what they actually spend on new drugs. It's not just me. Every oncologist I know has been questioning drug pricing, saying the industry has lost its moral compass.' He paused and fixed Luna with a sudden quiet intensity, making her pulse dance again. 'So you've taken an interest in my articles, Luna?'

She blinked but hardly missed a beat. 'Of course. Wouldn't you expect any newcomer to do their homework?'

'I'm sure you've always been the kind of girl to do your homework, Luna.' He threw her a devilish grin and took another deep gulp from his water bottle. 'I bet you were top of your class at school.'

She deflected his gentle mockery with a smile of her own. 'Naturally.'

Luna speared a tiger prawn and popped it in her mouth, then caught him watching her lips, his gaze suddenly more intent. She swallowed quickly. Wanting to dispel the familiar charged atmosphere that had crept back between them, she groped for something to say.

'What inspired you to go into medicine?'

There was a subtle lift of his brow at her sudden change of subject.

'Well now, there's a question,' he replied, and took an orange from the fruit bowl on the table. He sat back and began peeling it with long, deft fingers. 'Luckily, my own family are fit and healthy and always have been,' he continued. 'But when I was a child, I saw many of the gypsies from the camp get sick and refuse outside help. Some were critically ill and could have been saved. Like my friend Chico's father, who died from a ruptured appendix and septicaemia. As a young boy, I knew that when I grew up, I wanted to stop people suffering unnecessarily. I wanted to make a difference in the world.' He grinned sheepishly, acknowledging how dewy-eyed it sounded. 'Yes, I know that sounds a bit like a Miss World acceptance speech but it's true. That, and curiosity.'

He discarded the orange peel and his eyes flicked up to hers. 'Isn't that what made you become a scientist, Luna, curiosity?'

Luna found herself drawn into Ruy's mesmerizing blue gaze. 'Yes, I suppose it was,' she admitted. 'Ever since I can remember, I've wanted to know how things work, and why.'

He smiled at her, rubbing his smoothly shaved jaw in contemplation. 'I imagine you were a rather serious schoolgirl.'

'Perhaps,' she agreed matter-of-factly. 'I was certainly more likely to be doing an experiment in my bedroom than playing with dolls.'

His mouth twitched. 'Somehow I have no trouble picturing that. Orange?' He held out half the peeled fruit to her.

'No, thank you.' She watched him bite into a segment and his eyes caught hers, sparkling with some secret amusement. 'I've been organizing the files into a more efficient system,' she added quickly.

'I'm sure you have, Luna.'

'There seems to be a lot that needs cross-referencing. It's a labyrinth of information, and frankly it's a wonder you can find your way around it.'

'Most of it is up here.' He tapped the side of his head.

'Which is no good to other people,' she said, giving him a wry look.

He shot her his slow, lazy smile. 'Then I'm relieved you're here to save me from my own inefficiency. It's impressive that you've found the time to do it in between the research projects you've started.'

'I'm very organized.'

'Again, I don't doubt it,' he said, grinning. 'Seriously, if the Institute is ever going to make a watertight case for the use of mind-body medicine alongside our nutritional supplements we do need all the data and I imagine you might well be our secret weapon there if your organizational skills are as good as they seem. By the way, you'll need to make mind-body medicine your study if you're to understand our holistic programme of treatment here. After all, even at a basic level, both positive and negative emotions produce a spectrum of physiological effects – chest pains, dizziness, sweating.'

He leaned back further in his chair and a sardonic glint came into his eye. 'Then of course there's increased heart rate and blood flow, the obvious arousal sensations, dilated pupils, blushing ...' His gaze held hers, unwavering. 'The list goes on.'

As if on cue, her cheeks began to warm, making her curse her predictability. There it was again, that crackling heat between them. Somewhere inside Luna, a warning voice whispered, while another part of her thrilled at the way he was looking at her.

She managed to keep her voice even. 'I've been reading plenty of critical articles about certain elements of mind-body medicine. Perfectly reputable scientists saying the science behind it is inconclusive,' she told him.

'Is that our devil's advocate speaking again?'

'It's something you need to consider if you're going to defend it,' she pointed out.

'True. Which is why we need to present the results we've been achieving at the clinic – and why, Queen Organizer, we need your exemplary filing skills!'

His smile melted into a more scrutinizing expression.

'It's quite extraordinary how you can direct a person's mental and spiritual energies towards physical healing. Some of the things I've witnessed have defied belief, Luna,' he said earnestly. 'It's equally strange how emotional problems can manifest in myriad unconnected symptoms.'

Something intense and searching flared in his eyes as if he were seeing into her soul. Luna stirred uneasily in her chair: was he perceiving something in her that she always strove to keep hidden? His stare was so probing and yet so gentle that Luna almost wanted to throw herself into his arms and bare all her pain and scars to him then and there; instead she looked away and poured herself another glass of water.

What he said next, without any preamble, was like an arrow meeting its mark. 'What made you want to come to the Institute, Luna?' She was almost caught off guard. There it was. His comment was perfectly straightforward and, although Luna had rehearsed what she would say if she were asked the question, it still managed to disconcert her.

She flushed, and took a gulp of water in an attempt to compose herself. 'I had a cousin who was very dear to me. Angelina loved Spain, and lived in Barcelona for a time. Her letters made me want to come over, revisit my roots, and so on.' She carefully chose not to mention that Angelina had died of cancer, or that she had been an advocate of alternative medicine, much good it had done her. Too much information would simply put her in greater danger of being found out.

Luckily, Ruy didn't have time to probe further, as he glanced at his watch, saying: 'Well, I, for one, am grateful to your cousin and happy you decided to explore your roots. I'm afraid, though, we'll have to carry on this conversation another time. I have a meeting in a few minutes, I'd better get back.' He stood up and gulped down the last of his water. 'I hope you're intending to take it easy this weekend?' he added nonchalantly.

Luna hesitated. She could tell that he was fishing to find out her plans and didn't want to let him know where she was going with Charo that evening in case he suggested joining them.

'I'm busy all weekend sorting a few things out with the house, but it's fine,' she answered vaguely.

'Well, if you'd like someone to show you around Cádiz at some point, I'd be happy to oblige. There are some wonderful restaurants down by the harbour.'

'Well, I …' Luna stumbled over the half-lie she was about to tell. 'I'm still not quite used to the time difference here so I should try and have a few more early nights.' She shifted in her chair. 'Perhaps another time.'

He looked down at her and smiled inscrutably. 'Another time then. Enjoy your weekend, Luna.'

She watched him walk away, knowing things weren't getting any easier between them after all.

*   *   *

Disappointment engulfed Ruy as he left the office that evening. He was not used to being rebuffed and did not accept defeat easily. No other woman had inspired such fierce emotions in him; he couldn't concentrate properly on anything. All week he'd been careful to play it strictly professional with Luna, even though being close to her drove him crazy. It had challenged his self-control to keep his distance and his frustration was mounting, along with his desire for her.

The two of them were like flint and steel, giving off sparks every time they came near each other. Just looking into her eyes, he could see her struggle: the core of explosive feeling that she tried so hard to contain. Why was she holding back? He was offering himself to her, body and soul. At the end of the day it was his fault. By deserting her at the ball, he had made it look as though he was pushing her away or playing games. What a fool he'd been. No wonder Luna was now wary of him. He should have known better, but somehow he hadn't.

How could he make her want him as much as he wanted her? How could he gently break down her resistance? He must not rush her, he must play it cool – be patient, let her come to him.

It was all about control with Luna.

At work she was sharp-minded, ordered and thorough. Emotionally, she kept everything reined in. From the outside, her personality seemed mirrored by those ice-cool blonde looks – it was even reflected in her name – but Ruy knew that inside, it was a different story. His mind went back to their dance at El Pavón and the way she had returned his kisses at the summerhouse. It was just a matter of time. She could not keep that passionate nature restrained forever.

The more they spoke, the more he wanted to know about her. At lunch, when he had talked about the Institute's psychological support techniques, the look Luna had given him wasn't one of interest or curiosity, it was almost beseeching. A fleeting expression and then it was gone.

He clenched his fists, wondering about the man who had hurt her. Whoever he was, and whatever had happened, those barricades with which she had fortified herself, against Ruy, were caused by some painful experience. For now, it was another enigma about Luna that drew him to her.

Likewise, there was something about her mode of questioning when they spoke about work. Something not quite right about her professional neutrality; something he couldn't put his finger on ...

As Ruy went across to the car park, he saw Vaina coming out of the main building. Reluctantly, he shelved his thoughts and braced himself for a conversation for which he was in no mood.

Vaina waved at him and quickened her step. He noticed that she had changed from her day clothes and looked glamorous in a shimmering black dress. It was a well known fact that all her clothes were unique, designed especially for her. She was undeniably chic, sophisticated and worldly. His usual type, in fact.

Why am I not chasing her instead? Life would be so much simpler, he thought to himself.

His parents would be delighted – his father had been friends with Francisco Jiménez Rivera since their school days. Vaina was beautiful, bright and rich. They had not only friends in common but also the Institute itself, of which Francisco was chairman and a patron too. If he wanted someone beautiful and sophisticated, why not her?

Ruy knew the answer perfectly well. He had tried that avenue a number of times but it had led nowhere: there was no chemistry. Vaina failed to stir him enough, physically or mentally. She was too perfect – a beautiful statue, like the ones his grandfather, Eduardo de Salazar, sculpted. Vaina could be fun but, whenever they had dated, they had quarrelled non-stop. Not because they stimulated each other, but because their characters were incompatible. She was jealous and possessive and Ruy needed space; she suffocated him. He had been honest with her – told her it would never work – but she refused to give up. Certainly he admired her persistence though soon he would have to find the opportunity once and for all to make things crystal clear without hurting her feelings. They had to work together, after all.

She caught up with him and flashed a perfect lipstick smile. 'Ruy, are you going to the opening of Ignacio Vargas's exhibition?'

'No, I'd completely forgotten about it.'

She fluttered her long black lashes at him. 'I've got two invitations. It's the hottest ticket in town. You're not going to let me go on my own, are you?' she purred, and gave a much-practised pout.

It was neither the lashes nor the pout that coaxed him into accepting her invitation. The fact was he had nothing better to do that night, so why not? He had longed to ask Luna to dinner, but as usual she had given him clear signals that such an invitation would not be welcome.

He smiled. 'Sounds like a good idea. I like Vargas's work. I've no plans tonight.'

Vaina beamed, clearly delighted. 'We can go out for dinner afterwards,' she added quickly, pushing her advantage. 'We haven't spoken much since your conference in Barcelona. I'd love to know how it went.'

Ruy paused and then nodded. 'There isn't much to say.' He was being unnecessarily curt, he knew, but all of a sudden he was feeling hemmed in. The plan had been to discourage her attentions, so how had he been roped into dinner with her? He'd already admitted to being free, so he couldn't see a way out of it now. He supposed he should use the opportunity to have a quiet word with Vaina, but he wasn't sure he had the heart for it that night. Oh well, there were bound to be people he knew at the gallery and it wouldn't be too difficult to snag some others to join them. The prospect of dining with a group felt better than that of sitting for hours across a candlelit table, with Vaina making eyes at him.

'I'll need to pass by the house to change,' he added. 'I suspect all Cádiz and a great deal of people from Seville and Jerez will be there tonight. Shall I meet you there or would you prefer me to pick you up in an hour?'

'I need to be at the exhibition a little earlier,' said Vaina. 'One of the organizers is a close friend of *Papá*'s, so I've promised to help hand out catalogues.'

'Fine. I'll meet you there at eight o'clock.'

CHAPTER 8

L una watched the buildings pass by as the taxi made its way through the streets of Cádiz, en route to the first night of Ignacio Vargas's exhibition. Hailed by critics as the next Pablo Picasso, the young contemporary painter of figurative art had been discovered fewer than five years back, and his paintings were already selling for astronomical prices. When Charo had told her about Vargas, Luna's interest had been piqued. In New York, one of her favourite ways to relax was by visiting art galleries and tonight, after hours poring over files at the Institute, she hoped she'd have a good time.

Luna had hurried home from work and, after a quick snack, put her mind to what she might wear. She chose a playful, floral mini dress in mocha, silk-blend chiffon. It had a light-as-air pleat detail, and a plunging V neck and back. The whip-thin belt encircling her slender waist, together with nude stiletto sandals, enhanced the willowy elegance of her figure. Stacked gold bracelets adorned her wrist and a pair of delicate, filigree leaf drop earrings in twenty-four-carat gold gave a bohemian, artisanal accent to her outfit. She let her hair fall long and loose around her shoulders, applied sheer lip gloss and mascara, and was ready just as her taxi arrived.

Now, Luna looked out of the taxi window at the narrow lanes and wide squares illuminated by ornate, bulbous streetlamps.

Buskers strummed flamenco songs on their guitars from street corners, while the tables outside the brightly lit restaurants were already filling up with tourists and locals out for an early drink and tapas. The night was only beginning and Cádiz was glowing with life. Luna watched it all pensively from the cocoon of the taxi, her thoughts floating back to Ruy.

She could tell that he had been trying to behave himself all week, and yet today the air had once more become charged between them, like an irrepressible force that had gathered for days and now couldn't help but show itself. Despite her efforts to push them down, the feelings he engendered in her had only intensified.

Luna had not known him for long yet she admitted to herself with a wave of misery that, underneath her panic, she still wanted him. No other man had challenged her as Ruy did. She also had no doubt that if she did surrender to him, he would then drop her like a stone.

Anyhow, his courting had been hasty and clumsy, and now he had justly paid the price. He had tried to storm her heart instead of laying siege to it. If he wanted to win her trust, there was still a long way to go.

The taxi drew to a halt, jolting Luna from her thoughts. She paid the driver and found herself on the pavement of a quiet square, with only a few street cafés on its cobbled side streets. The exhibition was taking place in a most curious and interesting twelfth-century church, hidden from the world in this small, inconspicuous corner of Cádiz's old town.

Luna passed through a pointed arch into an open courtyard, with balconies and windows bearing down on every side, and through the most beautiful wooden ecclesiastical doorway into a wonderful relic of the past. It was a long rectangular room with a Moorish nave and intricately worked horseshoed arches, supported by octagonal columns and topped with pine-cone capitals of worn stone. Lattice-paned windows overlooked a small, deserted enclosure.

Charmed beyond words, Luna stood at the entrance of the ancient building, transported to the days of the Moors. On every whitewashed wall hung Ignacio Vargas's work: reclining and dancing figures rendered in abstract, their complex splashes of colour and geometric forms creating a strangely romantic and anachronistic contrast to the surroundings.

The church was packed, the atmosphere heavy with the cloying scents of musty hymn books, incense and ancient wood, mixed with a lingering aroma of roses and white jasmine that cascaded from stone urns all along the walls. Overlaying the antique musk was the fragrance of expensive scents and aftershave from the mingling throng, whose chattering was like the buzz of a swarm of bees. Women were dressed in formal, exquisite clothes, some long but mostly short, and they wore sparkling jewellery. The men were all in tuxedos. Waiters circulated with trays of champagne and sangria, while waitresses carried large serving platters of appetizing tapas.

Luna spotted Vaina immediately, glamorous and glittering: her fingers, no less than her gown, sparkling with jewels. There were clips in her rich dark hair and diamonds dangling from her ears. She wondered if Ruy had given her those.

Her mind skidded to a halt. *If Vaina is here, will he be here too?*

Before she had completed the thought, her pulse leapt madly as Ruy appeared at the door. Her heart sank as he made his way towards Vaina. She watched him put a hand casually on the brunette's bare shoulder, his dark head bent towards hers to catch what she was saying. There was something intimate in the gesture, and Luna felt a hollowness in her gut. She knew that this jealousy was illogical since she had repeatedly kept him at arm's length. Still, she was puzzled by the growing tangle of her emotions. A few weeks earlier such extremes of feeling did not exist for her.

Now she was in the midst of an upheaval that was threatening the ordered safety of her world.

Ruy's eyes turned slowly towards her. The message she read in them told her he had been aware of her staring. Luna felt pinned to the spot by his intense blue gaze. A smile played on his lips, and she turned away self-consciously.

Oh, Luna, why did you have to give yourself away so obviously? she thought angrily.

Flustered, she looked around for a waiter.

'Here, Luna, you look like you need one of these,' came a voice behind her.

Luna gave a sigh of relief when she turned to see Charo, who was holding two flutes of champagne.

'Charo, I could kiss you,' said Luna, gratefully accepting a glass.

'By all means,' said Charo, obliging her with a kiss on both cheeks. 'I was wondering when you'd arrive. I'm glad I didn't have to go back to the office to march you down here. You look wonderful, by the way.'

Luna laughed. 'Thank you. Wonderful but clearly looking as if I'm in need of a drink. And you'd be right!'

'We all need to take time to relax. The clinic can be pretty intense at times.'

Luna raised her glass. 'Well, here I am and it's very impressive, I must say. The paintings look wonderful, though I've not had a chance to look at them properly yet.'

'They're fabulous, but it's not just the art that's eye-catching …' Charo looked around the room appraisingly and leaned in. 'There are some very attractive men here. Don't you think it's rather fun to combine culture with a little flirtation?' She batted her eyelashes comically and giggled. 'Nothing serious, of course. Well, not for me. *Ai, mi madre*, Miguel would have a fit if he were here. He's picking me up later so you can meet him.'

Luna laughed. 'I'd like that.'

Charo's vivacious chattering was a breath of fresh air and she did find herself relaxing as she sipped her champagne, letting the chilled bubbles cool her dry throat. Every now and again she couldn't help glancing over to Ruy, though. His sensual lips were caught in laughter at something another guest was saying to him and Vaina. From what she could see of him through the crowd, he looked breathtaking in his tuxedo, his broad shoulders filling out the suit in a sinfully masculine way. She remembered the solid heat of them under her hands when he had kissed her in the summerhouse.

Luna blinked the memory away and turned back to Charo, who was grinning at her.

'I wouldn't be surprised if *you* don't get the chance to flirt with many men this evening.'

'What do you mean?'

'I mean there's one man in particular in this room who'll be watching you, and may not be happy seeing you charmed by anyone else.' She smiled over the rim of her glass and followed Luna's line of vision conspicuously across to Ruy.

Luna shot her a pointed look. 'I've no idea what you're talking about.'

'Don't you?' Charo laughed. 'Come on, Luna. Are you saying you haven't noticed the sizzling chemistry between the two of you?'

'I'm sure the good doctor is rather adept at creating chemistry between himself and many women.'

'It's true, he has a noticeable effect on most women.' Charo's eyes became expressively mischievous. 'Look at The Virago, for instance. She's normally so spiky with us, but look at her now. All over him like a rash!'

Luna did not want to look at Vaina at all, but her eyes followed Charo's playful nod to see Ruy's companion throw back her head and laugh: mahogany curls, white teeth, lip gloss and diamonds all glittering in the light of the overhead halogens. As Vaina recovered from whatever little joke she was clearly sharing with Ruy, she put a hand on his forearm in an intimate gesture.

No, Luna absolutely did not want to look.

A waiter passed by, offering canapés. Both women accepted some chorizo from the tray.

'Mmm, these are delicious,' Charo enthused. She paused and glanced at Luna. 'I think you're a little hard on Ruy. I've got to know him quite well and, as far as I can see, it's women who throw themselves at him, not the other way round. Particularly Doña Vaina, of course. That woman needs to have a little pride and give up.'

Luna raised a disbelieving eyebrow. 'You mean he's really not interested? Perhaps they've just got one of those tempestuous relationships.'

'Well, yes, but that's mainly on her side. Ruy merely tolerates her melodramatic outbursts and somehow manages to remain outside her grasp. They do work together so I suppose it's not easy, but I've told him he's just too nice and should cut her loose once and for all.'

'You've discussed it with him?'

'Of course.' Charo shrugged matter-of-factly at Luna's look of surprise. 'If I like someone, then I can't help but wheedle interesting things out of them.' Her face broke into a broad grin. 'At first they resist, but eventually they give in and we become friends.'

'Yes, I can see how that might happen,' said Luna with a wry smile.

Charo grinned. 'He always jokes that I'm the annoying little sister he never had. Though he's more inscrutable than most, I must say.'

'What makes you say that?'

'He may seem like a smooth charmer on the outside but, deep down, he's anything but superficial.'

'Well, I've noticed that he's passionate and thoughtful about his work,' said Luna. His passion was something she knew rather a lot about and it still made her shiver with awareness, just as she was doing now, conscious that he was just across the room.

'Yes, but there's something deeper that I can't put my finger on,' continued Charo. 'A look that comes over him every now and again.' She leaned in closer and whispered theatrically. 'Perhaps he has a dark and thrilling secret, and just needs the right woman to discover it.'

Dark and thrilling certainly described him well, Luna admitted to herself. Secrets? Yes, a man like that with gypsy blood in his veins would very possibly have those too.

'If he does, then I'm sure you would be the first to get to the bottom of it, Charo. He wouldn't stand a chance against your interrogation skills. You know everything about everyone,' she smiled.

Charo chuckled. 'You make me sound dreadful! But, yes, it's true. Miguel is always telling me it'll get me into trouble one day. Curiosity killed the cat, and all that.'

'Don't worry, Charo. It's what we all love about you. Don't change a thing,' laughed Luna. Then, as an afterthought: 'And I'm sure the good doctor needs a friend like you.'

'Like a hole in the head,' Charo said wryly. 'Actually, I didn't realize he'd be here tonight. Mind you, Vaina never misses an opportunity to cling to him like a leech to make everyone think they're a couple.' She nudged Luna's arm. 'Ah, but look, he appears to have escaped her again.'

Ruy had left Vaina's side and was now making his way towards them. He strode purposefully across the room, his gaze focused only on Luna. It moved up and down her, slow and unhurried, as if he was unaware of doing it. Excitement coursed through Luna. She ran her fingers jerkily through her hair and glanced around the room, wanting to find a place where she would be safe from his dark and broodingly handsome figure.

'I've never seen him that way before,' murmured Charo, thoughtfully.

'Like what?'

'The way he keeps looking at you.'

Luna turned her gaze back to Ruy, who was cutting through the crowd in an unwavering line. She wondered if it was too late to slip away to the cloakroom, but he knew she had seen him.

Charo leaned over and whispered in Luna's ear. 'Something tells me, this is going to be an interesting evening.'

He came to a halt in front of them. '*Buenas noches, señoritas,* I didn't know you'd be here tonight.' His gaze settled on Luna.

'*Hola,* Ruy,' Charo said brightly. 'I was just saying the same about you. I can't believe I forgot to mention it, we could have all come together.' She gave them both an innocent look, though the twinkle in her eyes was lit with laughter.

Ruy flashed a grin. 'I can't believe it either, Charo. You must be slipping!'

Charo was unperturbed by his teasing. 'We were just saying how many attractive men there were in the room, Ruy.'

'Were you now?' His gaze flicked back to Luna.

'I think it was you who made that observation, Charo,' she said, sipping her champagne a little too quickly as her cheeks warmed.

The young woman sighed dramatically and smiled up at Ruy. 'She's no fun.'

He gave a short laugh. 'Charo, did I ever tell you that you're a bad influence?'

'All the time,' she grinned. 'And now I'm going to take my influence elsewhere. Particularly as I've just spotted someone I should go and say hello to.' She beamed. 'See you both later.'

With that, looking very pleased with herself, she swanned off into the crowd, leaving the two of them standing together.

'So you decided not to have an early night after all?' Ruy plucked a mini chorizo off the tray of a passing waiter and nodded his thanks.

Luna stared at him, grappling for an excuse. 'I'd forgotten Charo had asked me here tonight.'

'Must be the jet lag,' he said mildly. 'It can confuse a person. Though I just assumed you'd found out I was coming after we had lunch and decided you couldn't bear to miss an evening in my company.' He waved the chorizo vaguely and popped it in his mouth, the corner of his lips quirking into a grin as he munched cheerfully.

Luna was caught between laughter and embarrassment. Gazing up at the devilishly handsome man before her, she was relieved to see that rather than being annoyed by her evasiveness, he was amused. Now that he was here, she no longer wanted to avoid him but felt that familiar excitement tingling up her spine as she was drawn to his charismatic presence.

'Charo threatened to drag me here herself if I didn't turn up,' said Luna truthfully.

'Dear Charo, subtle as ever. She was right to get you out for the evening after you've been working so hard, though. Especially to an exhibition of this quality.'

Luna watched him lick his thumb and flicked her gaze back up. 'Have you seen the paintings? I've not had a chance yet.'

'Yes, they're wonderful. Bold, exciting, surprising ...' His blue eyes sparkled as he stared at her. 'Beautiful ... You should have a look round.'

Luna read the mischief in his eyes and her pulse skittered. She glanced across to one of the paintings, of a naked couple embracing, each part of their bodies fractured into an exploding schema of geometric shapes, yet it was clearly visible that they were wrapped around each other. 'Yes, they manage to be deconstructed but sensual at the same time. Surprising, as you say.'

'It's the complexity beneath the picture that reveals its sensuality.'

She turned back to him to see his dark blue irises gleam with intensity.

'Ruy, there you are,' came a familiar voice behind, making them both turn round.

Vaina had appeared, her white teeth making a contrast with her figure-hugging black dress. She was smiling at Ruy, and making a point of not including Luna in that smile. Finally, she deigned to cast a brief, condescending glance at her.

'Dr Ward, I had no idea you had an interest in art.'

'Why would you, Doña Vaina?' said Luna mildly, draining the last of her champagne. She watched with mounting annoyance as Vaina proceeded to ignore her and turned to Ruy again, smiling up at him in an alluring manner.

'You disappeared as I was about to introduce you to an interesting art collector I've just met.' Her dark eyes darted between Ruy and Luna edgily. 'No doubt you have plenty of time to talk about work in the office, so I'm sure that Dr Ward can spare you for a while.'

'Actually Luna and I were just discussing Vargas's work, not our own,' Ruy replied.

Vaina laid a possessive, perfectly manicured hand on his arm. 'Well, I really must steal you away. Truly, this collector is someone you should meet. Knowing you as I do,' she said, a little too pointedly for Luna's liking, 'I'm sure you'll find him fascinating.'

'Perhaps you ought to go then, Ruy, if you're being summoned,' said Luna, enjoying the effect of her little swipe on Vaina's self-satisfied expression.

Ruy was inscrutable, though Luna was pretty sure he was enjoying watching her pointed interaction with Vaina. 'Oh, I think he can wait a few more minutes, don't you? I promise I'll come in a moment. In the meantime, he can enjoy a few more minutes of your charming company.'

Vaina hesitated, then smiled tightly and stalked back the way she had come.

Ruy observed Luna's cool features with a glint of knowing amusement. 'Something tells me you're not Vaina's biggest fan,' he remarked.

'She hasn't been the most welcoming person since I arrived.'

'I expect she feels threatened by you.'

Luna fixed her interrogative, amber gaze on him. 'Threatened?' It would give her great satisfaction, she realized, to have him confess the nature of his relationship with Doña Vaina.

'You mean Charo hasn't taken great pains to enlighten you about my past relationships?' he said, watching carefully for her reaction.

'Your past relationships are really none of my concern.'

At this he grinned shamelessly and took the empty glass she was still holding. 'Let me get you a drink and I can show you round some of the paintings.'

She was about to tell him that she could manage quite well on her own, but he had already turned away and was heading for the bar.

Perhaps this was her chance to escape. She didn't know how long she could put up with seeing Vaina drape herself around Ruy for the entire evening. Worse still, he didn't seem to discourage it, even if he had sent her back to her cronies for a while. Maybe he was playing the two of them off against each other. Was that something that amused him? The thought made her simmer with anger.

She began to move as swiftly as the crush permitted towards the cloakroom, the only place she could think of to get away for a few minutes and master those intense feelings he always aroused in her.

Luna had nearly reached it when she felt a hand on her arm. She turned sharply.

Diego Montez greeted her with a wide smile. 'When I woke up this morning I knew it was going to be a great day, but I didn't realize how great,' he said smoothly.

'Señor Montez!' she said, startled.

'Diego, please. It's delightful to see you again, Luna. May I call you Luna?'

She stared at him. 'Yes, of course, please do.'

'I saw you from across the room and had to come and say hello. What a happy coincidence that we should bump into each other again,' he said, a brilliant smile lighting his face.

'Yes, it is,' said Luna, caught off guard. She looked over to the bar and saw Ruy collecting two glasses of wine. He glanced up and their eyes locked. An obscure emotion flitted across his face before he caught sight of Diego, and then a frown creased his brow.

Good, she thought, and though it was petty, inside she felt a surge of satisfaction to know that, for a moment, the tables were turned. He wasn't the only one with admirers.

'How is the house? Are you comfortable at La Gaviota? Do you need anything?'

'Mmm?' Luna tore her gaze from Ruy and smiled politely back at Diego, her focus returning. 'Yes, La Gaviota is wonderful, thank you. I've never slept so well. The sea air suits me, as does the solitude. It's a wonderful place.' She smiled flirtatiously, knowing that it would only inflame Ruy further if his eyes were still on them. 'I found the covered market. I've been doing most of my food shopping there,' she added.

'I'm glad you did. It's by far the best place to shop in Cádiz and the oyster stall sells glasses of *Albariño* that can make you lose a whole afternoon. I'll take you there one day, if you like.'

'I might well take you up on that, when I'm not so busy,' she said with an impish smile. Luna knew she shouldn't offer any encouragement but the desire to see Ruy piqued overcame any qualms.

He inclined his head in a debonair gesture. 'I'm glad you've settled in. If any of the furnishings are not to your taste, I'm sure I can persuade the owner, Señor Alvarez, to change them to something more acceptable.'

She noticed how his eyes creased attractively at the corners when he smiled, and also how little effect they had on her. 'No, everything is perfect, thank you. It's all very tasteful.'

'Anyhow, you've got my telephone number,' Montez carried on. 'Please don't hesitate to ring me if you need anything … really, anything at all.' He looked pointedly at Luna, whose gaze slid past him to Ruy, who was now heading their way, his expression dark.

She nodded, distracted. 'Thank you, Diego. I promise to let you know.'

Montez hesitated as though he wanted to say something and then smiled suavely. 'I hope I didn't offend you the other day by asking you to dinner.' His green eyes glittered with quiet admiration, and Luna noted with surprise and detached curiosity that she found him not in the least bit threatening, as she might have done only a few weeks ago.

'You must trust me when I tell you I meant no disrespect,' he continued. 'I was just paying homage to a very beautiful woman, and the invitation is still open if you change your mind.'

Luna smiled vaguely. 'That's very kind.'

'Ah, good evening, Dr Rueda de Calderón. A pleasure to see you again.' Diego held out a hand as Ruy approached them.

'Señor Montez,' came Ruy's icy-polite reply. He ignored Diego's hand, and gave Luna her drink, immediately putting his hand in the small of her back, subtly implying that they were together. 'If you'll excuse us, I promised to show Luna the paintings before I have to go. Luna?'

Before she could object, Luna felt his hand slip to the side of her waist, giving it a gentle pull, and she almost gasped.

'It was nice to see you again, Diego.'

Luna had no time to wait for the estate agent's reply before finding herself gently, but firmly, propelled back through the crowds by Ruy's strong fingers. His touch sent an involuntary rush of heat between her thighs.

'Charming, if a little obvious,' he murmured, as he guided her down one of the side aisles of the church, past a series of small alcoves constructed temporarily for the exhibition from large white screens.

'What are you doing?' she demanded, ignoring his remark. 'I was in the middle of a conversation.'

'I thought you needed rescuing.'

'Well, I didn't.'

'Too late.' His voice was almost curt.

In each alcove were housed different selections of paintings. Ruy took her to the one furthest from the crowds, behind a row of stone pillars in the transept. The hubbub was fainter here, and only a handful of people were milling around, peering at the colourful artworks adorning each screen.

'These are Vargas's earliest works, I believe.' He was still standing close behind her, his voice dangerously quiet. Luna knew that he was simmering with jealous fury, but his heavy-handed possessiveness was stoking her own anger now.

She was still holding her glass of champagne and took a large sip to steady her nerves, before putting it down on a nearby table spread with leaflets and postcards. She'd already drunk one glass rather rapidly and this was no time to lose control.

They were at the edge of the space near the row of eroded sandstone pillars. Her gaze moved along the paintings. There were four or five of them, each rendered in contrasting luminous cool blues, coppery oranges and fiery reds and yellows, less abstract than the painting of the couple Luna had glimpsed earlier but still a series of broken, overlapping shapes and lines that formed the central image.

She paused in front of a nude reclining on a couch, her blazing yellow hair cascading down to the floor. The model's face was upturned, one arm held languidly and provocatively above her head. One knee was open, brazenly.

'Complex yet arousing, wouldn't you say?' Ruy's voice was low, every word carefully enunciated.

He had moved behind Luna and a hot, sensual awareness of him gushed over her. She could feel his warm breath on her hair. An ache grew in her breasts and her nipples tightened against her chiffon dress. As her heart beat faster, a corresponding pulse throbbed at the apex of her thighs.

A couple of people left, heading back down the side corridor towards the main reception.

'I know what you're doing,' she whispered, lifting her chin. 'You're trying to intimidate me.'

'Is it working?' His voice had an intense, brooding quality.

Luna turned and saw the burning heat in his eyes. Ruy was standing so close that his mouth was only inches away. He dropped his gaze, raking it up and down her body.

'So you would have preferred that I left you with that lightweight, Montez?' he murmured, his mouth curling into an accusing smile.

Luna glared at him angrily. 'Since when is it up to you who I talk to?' she hissed, glancing around, fearful of causing a scene.

The remaining few people walked on.

Ruy glanced around to check they really were alone, then suddenly swept Luna into the corner. She felt the cold stone of the pillar against her shoulders as his hand went behind her head.

'You need a good ravaging, do you know that?'

He stared at her lips.

'You,' she said hoarsely, 'need to learn some manners.'

Then he held her still while his mouth swooped down on hers hungrily. He kissed her almost savagely, his tongue pushing into her mouth in angry thrusts.

Desire exploded in Luna. She could have made him stop but she didn't – she wanted it too. Whatever contest this was for supremacy, she was not going to let him win. She kissed him back, matching his aggression with a fervour that she didn't know she possessed. The hot friction of their bodies through the gauzy fabric of her dress made her feel his hard arousal against her easily, and a liquid heat coursed down to her centre.

His hand travelled over her body and found her breast, sliding his fingers into the flimsy fabric of her dress. His thumb grazed her nipple, the hard peak now straining against her bra, and circled around it. She gasped against his mouth, feeling his own hot breath against her lips as he groaned deep in his throat.

All the frustration and heartache between them poured into their kiss, crashing down like an angry, relentless tidal wave. Luna felt his helplessness the way she felt her own.

He broke off, panting, his gaze blazing hot with desire, and stepped away from her as if the heat of it was too much.

'*Dios mio*, Luna! What are you doing to me?' Ruy leaned both his hands on the adjacent column and looked down as if recovering from a ten-kilometre run. Still breathing heavily, he glanced sideways at her. 'That's a very short dress you're wearing. I'm not sure it should be allowed in public.'

Luna tilted her head back against the stone, her chest rising and falling rapidly too. She glanced around her, afraid someone might have seen them. After swiftly adjusting her clothing she smoothed her hair, trying to control the riotous responses of her emotions as well as her body.

'I need to go.' She started towards the side corridor, picking up her glass as she passed the table. Another drink suddenly seemed like a very good idea after all. She stopped abruptly.

'Luna, *mi querida*, is that you? I didn't know you were in Cádiz! How long have you been in Spain? Why didn't you let me know you were coming?' Isabel Herrera, Marquesa de Aguila, fixed a pair of blue, reproachful eyes on her great-niece.

It took Luna a second to realize who this perfectly coiffed woman was, then her face froze in shock. She touched her fingers to her lips, still swollen from Ruy's kiss, and her discomfiture was acute.

'Aunt Isabel!' she gasped.

She hadn't seen her great-aunt in over a decade, not since the *Marquesa* had stayed a night with Luna and her father en route to see her son Lorenzo. From what Luna remembered of the visit, Isabel Herrera had spent most of the time reminiscing about Luna's mother. Then, whenever Luna's father was out of the room, making things even more uncomfortable by insinuating how tragic it was that Adalia had married Montgomery Ward, whom she blamed entirely for Adalia's decline into drink.

Luna's shock gave way to dismay as she stared at her aunt and, for a moment, words failed her. She had wanted to avoid getting embroiled with the Herreras for as long as possible while in Spain. Ideally, she had hoped to avoid them altogether.

The *Marquesa* kissed her great-niece on both cheeks. 'Did Lorenzo know you were coming? You'd have thought he might have mentioned it to me. I get so few family visits. Then again you know how he is, so busy and important these days …' Doña Isabel's loud cascading laugh, which in her day had made many a man's heart beat faster, cut through the awkward silence, almost making Luna wince.

Her fingers holding her glass began to shake slightly, so that she had to hold them steady with the other hand. 'No, I didn't tell him I was travelling to Spain.'

Doña Isabel's faded blue eyes then noticed Ruy, who, having recovered his composure, had emerged from the alcove and was now standing silently behind Luna. Isabel's tone, though polite, became noticeably cooler.

'Dr Rueda de Calderón.' Her lips formed the words almost stiffly as she held out her hand to him.

'*Marquesa.*' Ruy was regarding Isabel Herrera silently, his features impassive. As politeness dictated, he took the *Marquesa*'s outstretched hand and kissed it, though the gesture was perfunctory; then he stared hard into Luna's agitated eyes.

'You know my aunt?' Luna searched his expression, noticing he had become pale, his blue eyes darkening.

'Our families are connected,' answered the *Marquesa* instead. She raised her chin and assumed a dignified air. Despite her advanced years she was still handsome, fortunate to have the type of skin that reacted favourably to face lifting. Over the years she had submitted herself to numerous operations to fight the signs of time and safeguard her beauty. Although the effect on her features was one of stillness, Luna thought, a lack of animation on a surface as smooth and brittle as bone china. Unconsciously, her mind recalled the gentle laughter lines of Ruy's mother, Luz.

'How is your grandfather, Salvador?' Doña Isabel asked, without a shred of warmth. 'I haven't seen him in years, but then it's been a while since I've been able to attend the El Pavón balls.'

'He's very well, thank you, *Marquesa*.' Ruy scooped up his own glass and took a gulp of champagne. 'You'll have to excuse me, but apparently someone has been waiting to speak to me.' He barely looked at Luna before turning and striding away towards the main reception.

Luna stared after him, a frown marring her smooth forehead. She was still quivering from his explosive touch. On the one hand, she was hugely relieved to see him go but, then again, she imagined him hurrying back to Vaina's side and jealousy pricked at her even more sharply than before. Now here she was, stuck talking to her great-aunt alone.

'Good, now we can talk properly,' murmured Doña Isabel beside her. She eyed her niece closely. 'Do you know that man?'

Luna blinked back at her, marshalling her thoughts. 'We've been introduced,' she said vaguely. Wanting to change the subject, she added quickly: 'I haven't seen you since I was a teenager, Aunt Isabel. I'm surprised you still recognize me.'

The *Marquesa* gazed at her affectionately. '*Madre de Dios*, you look so much like your poor mother! I would recognize you anywhere.'

Luna smiled thinly. 'Yes, that's what I'm told. I find I can't really remember what *Mamá* looked like and only have a few photos of her. She didn't figure very strongly in my childhood, to be honest. I was very young when she left.'

'Your mother was a passionate woman, used to being pampered and adored. Your father was too busy amassing his fortune to give her the attention and love she needed, but let's not go there,' she said, waving her hand gracefully. She sighed and shook her head as if gently scolding a child. 'Luna, darling, why didn't you tell me that you were in town?'

'I've only been here a week or so.'

'Tell me, where are you staying? There's plenty of space at my house in Jerez.'

'Thank you, but I've rented a house quite close to the clinic where I work.'

The *Marquesa* looked warmly over her great-niece. 'Well, my dear, my home is always open to you if you get bored living on your own. I must say, you look so like Adalia, it nearly takes my breath away.' Her blue eyes misted. 'Of course, you were always nothing like her, or your poor dear sister for that matter. You were so quiet and serious …' She shook her head. 'I never agreed with the idea of your father keeping you in America. We could have brought you out of yourself here in Spain.'

'I'm sure *Mamá* could have kept me here with Juliet if she'd really wanted to,' replied Luna more tersely than she intended. Not that she would have wanted to stay with her mother, but Adalia's rejection still left a rawness in Luna to which she had never entirely become reconciled.

Doña Isabel caught the edge in her voice and suddenly looked awkward. 'Yes, well, Adalia didn't always make the best decisions. Your father wanted you with him and she agreed it was for the best, though I did try to talk some sense into her. She didn't listen to anyone else when she got an idea in her head, though. Proud and stubborn. She and poor Juliet were very alike in that respect.' Her face brightened. 'Let me invite you to dinner. We have so much to catch up on.'

Luna smiled apologetically. 'I'm afraid I came with a friend tonight.'

'Not that de Calderón fellow?'

'No, not him,' she was quick to clarify. 'My friend Charo, who's around here somewhere.' She scanned the room and saw Charo laughing animatedly with a group of people.

Doña Isabel looked visibly relieved. 'Well, I don't want to keep you from your friends, but it's been such a long time since I've seen you, my dear. You're all grown up now. It would make me so happy to hear all about what you've been doing with your life.' She felt free to push, as old people do. 'Why don't you let me take you to a new place I know? Come on, humour your old aunt.'

'Well, I …'

The *Marquesa* ploughed on. 'There's a small nightclub I've heard of where the food is apparently first-rate, run by a young Croatian and his father. There's a band too, and I've been told the singer is a most talented musician.' Her alert blue eyes softened. 'Go on. Surely you can keep a lonely old lady company for one evening?'

Put that way, Luna could hardly refuse the invitation. At least if she had supper now, she could justify not seeing her great-aunt again for a while. In the back of her mind, she also welcomed an excuse not to witness any more of Vaina's proprietorial behaviour with Ruy.

'Of course, Aunt Isabel. I'm sure I can change my plans,' she acquiesced as graciously as possible.

Isabel Herrera grasped her arm with delight. 'Wonderful! Cadencia Tzigane is not far from here, we can walk to it.'

Luna left her aunt briefly to find Charo and explain her predicament, apologizing for leaving without meeting the famous Miguel.

'You will be missed, and not just by me and Miguel,' noted Charo with a raised eyebrow and an impish grin. 'But go, do your duty with your aunt.'

At Cadencia Tzigane, the owner, Radić Senior, welcomed them at the door. When Doña Isabel complimented him on his establishment's excellent reputation, he gave a satisfied nod. 'People who understand food and music usually find their way to my club. No need to spend money on advertising,' he told them with a wave of his hand as he steered them towards their table, overlooking Plaza San Antonio.

Luna was aware that the people dining there had taken great pains to dress up and that she and her aunt were very much on view, being scrutinized with interest by the other diners as they walked through the bar, passing under high archways to get to the more secluded dining room. Obviously one came here to see and to be seen. No wonder the *Marquesa* had been so keen for them to dine here. Luna's father always said that Adalia's family were shocking snobs – it was one of the main reasons Luna did not like mixing with them.

Different from the usual nightclubs, the décor here was bright and breezy; a big, soaring space with blown-glass chandeliers and mirrored walls. Floor-to-ceiling glass windows framed the view of the street and the square outside with its magnificent Isabelline Gothic architecture. Above the trees, the twin spires of the San Antonio church could be seen. Luna watched as waiters in their crisp black-and-white uniforms rushed steaming plates loaded with architecturally arranged food to the tables. This was restaurant theatre, serving drama on a plate.

Luna was just starting on an iced tomato and cognac soup, a sort of gazpacho with a twist, when she stopped, her spoon in mid-air. She stared across the restaurant at a couple seated at a small round table halfway across the room.

Isabel Herrera followed the young woman's gaze. 'Dr Ruy Rueda de Calderón,' she huffed. 'I didn't realize he would be here too.' Her eyes narrowed. 'How did you say you knew him?'

'Professionally,' Luna said noncommittally, trying to keep hold of her fury.

'He's having supper with Doña Vaina Jiménez Rivera.'

'Yes, she's the managing director at the Institute where I work.'

'I've heard of the place. I'm surprised a proper scientist like you would have anything to do with somewhere like that.'

Luna didn't comment. It would only end up in a conversation she could do without. Mind you, the alternative wasn't much better. Before she could change the subject entirely, Isabel continued, her eyes narrowly watching the pair at the other table.

'I thought they'd broken off their engagement.'

Luna stiffened but continued with her soup. 'I'm not sure if they ever were engaged or not.' She made a herculean effort not to look over to where Ruy was sitting with Vaina. Less than two hours ago he had been kissing her wildly, his hands all over her. How dare he appear at the same restaurant with another woman, rubbing her nose in it.

'Well, she's a good catch, I'll say that. He couldn't do better for a wife.' Doña Isabel lowered her voice unnecessarily. 'But he's confused, a tortured soul. You see he's one-quarter gypsy. The mixed *gajo* and *Calés* blood that courses through his veins pulls him in different directions. Can't make up his mind who he is, or what he wants.'

Luna beckoned to the waiter to ask for some bread, in an attempt to call a halt to the conversation, but her aunt continued without pause: 'He graduated as a *mèdico de cabecera* but gave up a proper career to open that so-called clinic of his. If you ask me, it's full of quacks and a whole lot of nonsense.' Doña Isabel's gaze swung sharply to her great-niece as her mind evidently put the pieces together. 'I really hope your having a job there doesn't put a blot on your career, *querida*. It does seem a strange choice. I suppose, over in New York, you weren't to know what sort of an outfit it is, though.'

A flush of irritation spread across Luna's cheeks. She took a gulp of wine, waiting for her aunt to take a breath, or move on to another topic. Still, she went on relentlessly: 'He dates the most beautiful women in Andalucía but, no, he can't be satisfied with that. Torn every which way. It's in his blood, you see. Keeps a gypsy mistress up there in the hills too.' She waved her hand dismissively. 'All this herbal nonsense is the gypsy influence in him. Then there's more, but I wouldn't even know where to start!'

Carefully, Luna made her face blank. 'Why are you telling me all this?' she enquired guardedly.

'I thought I'd give you the whole picture since you've already met him.' Doña Isabel eyed her great-niece closely. 'Just mind you don't get brainwashed by all the nonsense at that so-called Institute. I wouldn't put anything past that man. I've heard he hypnotizes patients. It feels very dubious indeed to me.'

Isabel's gaze softened for a brief moment as she regarded her great-niece and, as if suddenly remembering her familial duties, she took a new tack: 'A little word of advice from one who knows about these things. You're a very beautiful woman, my dear. I have no doubt he must be drawn to you like a bee to the honeypot. Be careful, Luna. I hear he never stays with one woman for long. We all know the type, all charm and good looks, but never the decency to put a ring on a girl's finger. For all his respectable appearance,' Isabel huffed, her eyes like flint, 'I'm sure he gets that ne'er-do-well streak from his father's side. At least the de Ruedas come from civilized stock.'

Luna ignored her aunt's appalling snootiness, but her remarks about Ruy managed to put a knife into a very fresh wound. It might have been old-fashioned to assume marriage was the natural destination for all relationships, but hearing the *Marquesa*'s account of Ruy's female conquests and womanizing behaviour made her chest constrict painfully. Not that any of this information came as a surprise, of course. She'd known about his reputation before she had even met him. Hurt battled with the anger already simmering inside her.

'If what you say is true, why does Doña Vaina put up with it? As you say, she apparently has so much to offer a man. She must have plenty of admirers.'

'If she has a sensible head on her, she won't want to jeopardize her chances with Ruy. If she dates someone else, then she's sure to lose him.'

It occurred to Luna that her aunt was an old hand at strategies for ensnaring men and getting exactly what she wanted. Typical of the Herreras, she thought grimly.

'Perhaps they're just friends.'

Doña Isabel gave a husky laugh. 'My dear, when you're my age you'll realize there's no such thing as friendship between a man and a woman. No such thing as love either. It's all about hormones and chemistry. Money and status too, let's not forget that.'

Luna frowned. 'That's a bit bleak, Aunt Isabel.'

'On the contrary, *querida*. That way you always know where you stand.'

'Well, since he apparently dates other people, she must be a fool not to do the same.'

Doña Isabel smiled indulgently at her niece's naïvety. 'If you are to spend time in Spain, Luna, you must appreciate our men have one set of rules for women and quite another for themselves.'

'That macho hypocrisy is the one side of Spanish culture that I dislike intensely.'

'Well, then you'd be wise to steer clear of Don Ruy. He's as male as they come and commitment is not on offer,' the *Marquesa* said pointedly.

Luna briefly closed her eyes, not wanting to hear any more. She felt slightly sick, feeling that between them, her aunt, Ruy and Vaina had somehow managed to sully her. There was something sordid in their little games and she wanted no part in it. Oh, for the clean white space of her beach house. She longed to lock herself in and take to her bed, close her eyes, and hope that when she opened them again all this would have gone away.

When she opened her eyes, however, she could not stop herself from glancing over at Ruy. She found him staring right at her and her mind was instantly thrown into turmoil once more. The look on his face was completely unfamiliar to her, unreadable.

They had finished their main course and while waiting for dessert, Doña Isabel lit a long, thin cigarette.

'I should also warn you against him for another reason,' her aunt went on. 'I don't know how much you've been told, but there's been bad blood between our family and the de Ruedas for many years.'

Luna had been about to ask the *Marquesa* if they could possibly talk about something else but this remark stopped her in her tracks. 'What kind of bad blood?'

'The kind that is not easily forgiven,' answered Doña Isabel, her mouth pinched into a thin line as she blew out a plume of smoke. 'The women in their family developed an unfortunate habit of stealing men from their rivals, shamelessly and ruthlessly.' Doña Isabel gave an indignant sniff. 'I myself was once engaged to Count Salvador de Rueda.'

Luna's eyes widened, remembering the suave old gentleman who had been such a charming host at the El Pavón ball. The last thing she wanted was to admit to her aunt that she'd been invited there by Ruy, or that she'd met his grandfather, so she kept quiet.

'Yes, I'm sure you didn't know that,' the *Marquesa* nodded self-righteously. 'But as soon as she arrived from England, Alexandra de Falla, that was her maiden name, managed to ingratiate herself with her Spanish family and proceeded to manipulate Count Salvador until I was quite forgotten. She even promised herself to my brother, Felipe, at the same time, and was caught with Don Salvador on the very night Felipe was to announce their engagement.'

Isabel Herrera's faded blue eyes flashed with a look of disdain, which Luna thought something more akin to hatred. 'It was truly scandalous and, I can tell you, for months our family was the subject of humiliating stories in aristocratic Spanish circles. To add insult to injury, history repeated itself a generation later when Luz de Rueda did the same thing to poor Adalia. Everyone knew that Adalia was virtually engaged to Andrés de Calderón. They were inseparable, but it didn't stop Doña Luz.'

She inhaled on her cigarette and her eyes narrowed through the smoke. 'They look so innocent from the outside, those women, but scheming and deception is in their blood. It's the English streak in them, I always said. Is it any wonder your mother was driven to drown her sorrows in drink?'

Doña Isabel's expression became pained as if she had told this story many times before with an equal sense of injury with each telling and, though taken aback by her great-aunt's account of the past, Luna couldn't help reading between the lines and wondered how much of it was true. She knew enough about the Spanish side of her family to see that none of *them* were strangers to deception. Remembering her brief encounters with Ruy's family, and their instinctive kindness, she wasn't prepared to credit Isabel's words as having a great deal of truth to them.

Luna's brow creased. 'So you think that somehow Rueda de Calderón is tainted by this so-called bad blood?'

'How could he not be, my dear? The same blood runs in his veins. Three generations on, and we're still feuding with the de Ruedas and the de Calderóns. The Herreras have been hurt enough by them, that's all I'm saying.'

She stubbed out the cigarette impatiently as their dessert arrived: tiny *tocinos de cielo*, a rich crème caramel typical of Andalucía.

Was Ruy aware that he was the centre of their conversation? He lifted his head and caught Luna's eye once more. His hooded gaze smouldered over her face with an expression that appeared confused, intense and almost reproachful. Vaina, meanwhile, was smiling languorously, her velvet black eyes turned up to his as she spoke, gesticulating to emphasize some point she was making; but Luna could see he wasn't listening to her, that his thoughts were elsewhere. Was he, likewise, condemning her now for being related to the Herreras? Her glance fell away from his glowing eyes, and she found herself looking into the enormous, flashing dark orbs of Vaina as she suddenly caught sight of Luna across the room. She then said something to Ruy, who finally tore his gaze from Luna and began whispering a response, which clearly his companion didn't like.

While they ate, the band played. It was gypsy *Tzigane* music played by an orchestra of violins and led by Goran Radić, the owner's son, a tall, handsome, sultry-looking man in his thirties who, judging by the admiring glances from the women in the audience, had his fair share of fans. However, Luna was not paying much attention; her mind was on the *Marquesa*'s words and the new thoughts they had sent whirling around in her head.

A queer pain tugged at her heart. There were times when Ruy's eyes had given her a deeper message than just a man's admiration for a pretty girl, a passing flirtation. Often she had sensed his turbulent emotions running riot, out of the bounds of his willpower. Then there were his kisses that haunted her … Twice now, he had thrown her senses into chaos with that mouth of his; on the first occasion literally making her lose control.

She sighed inwardly. It humiliated her to think how she had allowed him to kiss her … and how she had clung to him. The devastating physical hunger she felt every time she thought of him … the same hunger that made her respond to his violent passion earlier that night. Why was he here with Vaina? As a pang of jealousy stabbed at her again, she tried to stir up resentment against him and, although her mind rebelled at the thought of his arrogance, her body had a mind of its own and only one desire: to be possessed by him.

Her aunt's voice pierced the haze of her distraction. 'You know, I'm surprised your Uncle Lorenzo didn't tell you about these unfortunate chapters in the Herrera family history. He was the only one of us to see you for all those years while you were growing up in California …'

Luna steadied her hand as she raised her glass to her lips and drank her wine. She would not be drawn into conversation about her childhood with her aunt. However, Doña Isabel was now too preoccupied with watching the dark-eyed, flamboyant figure of Goran Radić wooing his audience to notice Luna's discomfort. She seemed content to keep up a steady monologue.

'Of course, I don't expect your father was interested in the slightest about our family's background after he married Adalia and they were living in America …' Doña Isabel paused and fixed her pale blue eyes on Luna. 'So I suppose he never told you much about Juliet's death. You were a child when it happened, after all.'

'Juliet died in a car accident.'

'Yes, of course. What else do you know about the accident, though? Did Lorenzo ever talk to you about it?'

Luna put a hand to her head, which was beginning to ache slightly. She felt as if everything was closing in on her and she badly wanted the evening to end. Having Aunt Isabel dredge up the past, while only a few feet away Ruy was glowering in her direction, was becoming more than she could take.

Now, Goran Radić came down from the platform, playing his violin and threading his way slowly among the tables towards the twosome. He paused in front of Luna and bending towards her, looking soulfully into her eyes, he continued playing while serenading her with a most poignant love song in his own language. Everyone's heads turned to look at her, especially those of the jealous women in the room.

She smiled uncertainly at the musician and though she wanted to look anywhere but at Ruy, her eyes strayed across the restaurant to him as if programmed to do so.

His jaw had stiffened, dark brows furrowing, and his pale blue eyes had turned steel grey, splintering with cool shards of light, capturing her with their hypnotic gaze. She had never seen them like that before. The explicit stare of anger she read in them brought a flush of warmth to her cheeks. She remembered Charo's comment at the gallery earlier about Ruy not wanting her to be charmed by other men. He had clearly been angry at her merely talking to Diego Montez. Was he upset at the overtly romantic attention the musician was giving her? Maybe even remembering the night, not so long ago, when he himself had so passionately sung to her?

Yet there he was with Vaina.

This power he had over her was tearing her apart, and at that moment she wanted none of it.

Why was he scowling at her? Was he sorry that he had kissed her again? Did he regret getting caught up with her, now that he knew she was a Herrera? Could Luna help it if she'd been born into a family for which she had no respect, let alone affection? Is that why he was flaunting his relationship with Vaina under her nose, to punish her?

For some irrational reason, Luna wanted to make him angrier still. As the violinist knelt on one knee while serenading her, she bestowed another smile on him, this time brighter, all the while trying to look less self-conscious, as if she welcomed his attentions.

She couldn't help but dart a glance at Ruy and what she saw gave her some bitter satisfaction. His eyes narrowed and the muscles in his jaw jerked as if something had snapped inside him.

As he stood up, tension radiated from him in waves. He clicked his fingers at the waiter, who hastened over and gave him his credit card. People were watching now. Vaina had also risen from her chair; she looked shocked, a little haggard even. Ruy paid the bill. He glared at Luna once more, his lips pressed together, and then, slipping one hand into his pocket, he took Vaina's arm with the other and strode quickly out of the club.

Like everybody else in the room, Doña Isabel had witnessed the whole scene. Luna knew that the *Marquesa*'s sharp eyes had not missed any of the goings-on, neither had her alert mind failed to summarize in one word the silent, electrifying message Ruy's eyes had conveyed to her great-niece. Luna heard her whisper almost imperceptibly, as though to herself: 'Passion, the man is devoured by passion.'

She turned her sharp gaze on Luna. 'I wasn't going to say anything, *querida*, as idle gossip really doesn't sit well with someone of our social standing, but I think I should warn you … That man did a very great wrong to our—'

But Luna had had enough and she stood abruptly, pleading a headache. The *Marquesa* never had the chance to finish her sentence in the hurried departure her great-niece had instigated, and very soon they were back at Doña Isabel's chauffeur-driven car, now parked nearby, where Luna said her goodbyes. She was desperate to get home but refused a lift from the *Marquesa*, hailing a taxi instead before her aunt could protest.

Doña Isabel drew Luna to her and kissed her on both cheeks. 'Well, *mi querida*, I'm delighted you're in Spain. I feel we've only just begun to catch up.' Her pale blue eyes fixed on her niece. 'Do you have my telephone number?'

'Yes, I think I do somewhere. With the new job, I've been rushed off my feet and I just haven't had time to breathe.'

'*Bueno*, I'll wait for you to get in touch with me, when you have a space in your diary. I know how irritating pushy old aunts can be. But don't forget to call me.'

Luna gave a wan smile and watched as Isabel Herrera's car pulled away into the stream of night-time traffic. Her aunt would have a long wait, she thought wryly, climbing into the welcome solitude of the taxi.

*   *   *

Ruy turned off the water and stepped out of the shower. His head spun with a million questions, none of which made sense. Rubbing a towel roughly over his face and hair, he tied another around his waist, just above the scar that crested his right hip, and went to the kitchen to make himself a large cup of black coffee. He needed to get his mind into gear to work out this confusion – it was as though a dark web were closing around him.

It had been over a decade ago, but he remembered that night as clearly as if it were yesterday. The lights, Carlos's shout, the screams and then the awful silence. The pain and the waiting, paralyzed. The bitter taste of bile filled his mouth. There was a strange, haunted look in his blue eyes, as if those eyes saw something they wanted to forget. He dressed and went outside into the starry night.

Deep lay the indigo shadows as he sat on his veranda fixing a blank spot on the dark horizon, memories rushing forward, crowding his head with images that unrolled pell-mell in front of his eyes. That night had left him with more than physical scars. A terrible anguish had enveloped him, until he had met Leyla, La Pharaona the gypsy healer, who had saved him from himself and helped him live again.

He had thought the nightmare was behind him, even though he still fought feelings of guilt and self-recrimination, which everyone had long agreed shouldn't have been his to shoulder. Of course he hadn't bargained for it to rear its nasty head again, but today the past had come back to haunt him.

He shook his head. It was a small world indeed; he huffed derisively at the cliché. He had never made the connection between Luna and the Herrera family – why should he? It was only after he had heard the *Marquesa* at the exhibition telling Luna how much she looked like her mother, Adalia, that he made the terrible connection.

It was bad enough that she was half Herrera – that would be a hard one for his family to accept – especially as Lorenzo Herrera was loudly critical of the Institute. But Luna wasn't like the rest of the Herreras, he told himself. It had been this certainty that had caused him to stop ricocheting between shock, anger and disappointment, as the realization dawned that his feelings ran far too deep for him to care to whom she was related. His thoughts poured into a mass of truths that coursed downhill in a torrent – of her wit and intelligence, her beauty and indefinable allure, what life would be like if he didn't have her – all rushing and crashing down to their inevitable end point, making him reel with the force of it.

He loved her.

The knowledge came swift and profound, and changed everything. He loved Luna, and that meant that he would do anything – accept anything – to be with her.

So she was a Herrera. Everything was clear now. Luna had known his identity all along and that was why she had been fighting the attraction between them.

Ruy walked over to the veranda's balustrade, which overlooked the gentle slope of trees, down the hill towards the isthmus. He crossed his arms over his chest and leaned against the pillar, gazing across the water to Cádiz, while he considered how much Luna must know. Why had she never brought it up if his family background was no secret to her?

Perhaps she doesn't know.

For him to keep this from her was unthinkable. It was a secret that would only fester, and she was bound to find out eventually. Still, what would she say if she knew? Would she understand? Would she forgive him?

He let out a gruff laugh. Was he 'fortune's fool'? Fate had brought them together and now it was throwing more obstacles in their path. Playing the Montague to her Capulet was not how he had envisaged their love affair unravelling, but he wanted Luna more than any woman he had ever known, and he'd be damned if he lost her now. How ironic that the discovery she was a Herrera, rather than discourage his feelings for her, instead served to clarify them entirely.

Ruy knew he loved her; the sight of her being fawned over by that slick estate agent Diego Montez and then serenaded by a restaurant violinist had made his passionate gypsy blood boil. Unfamiliar and senseless jealousy rose and fell in his heart like flames in a brazier, devouring and scorching, and threatening to unleash a primitive, unreasoned ardour, the strength of which was alarming. His wild, impulsive nature was his enemy but nevertheless was so out of character, even for him. Ruy could never recall having to pursue a woman. They were always willing and eager to run after him; and in the past he had habitually taken advantage of this by dulling the torment of his inner demons with a constant stream of women.

With Luna, that had changed. She was an unknowing temptress – provocative, elusive, alluring – who made him want to kiss the rebellious, resistant words from her sensual, inviting lips and discover all the secrets of her heart, which she defended so fiercely. Whenever he was in her presence, he had to fight the wild urge to pull her to him and take her wildly, there and then. In the gallery, in a frenzy of lust and something much deeper, he had come close to doing just that.

Ruy sighed and went inside. Timing was everything. He would watch and wait for the moment to speak to her. First, he needed to win her over and then she could be the judge. After that he would let fate do what it might.

Falling down on his bed, he closed his eyes and thought of Luna's body, rare in its loveliness, ethereal like a moonbeam, and he fell asleep to dream of endless lovemaking in her arms.

*   *   *

It was a hot night. The moon shone its ghostly white light through the windows and cast sharp shadows in the room. Luna thrashed in bed, unable to sleep, tormented. Half-awake she lay, thoughts churning, stomach in knots and her feelings in tatters. Her great-aunt's words simmered, and by now were slowly fermenting and poisoning her mind. This should have made things easier for her since she had repeatedly told herself she ought not to have anything to do with Ruy; but the mental and physical turmoil she was in was enough to prove the power he had over her. Try as she might, she couldn't forget the way he had kissed her that evening, so dangerously public and yet the erotic wildness of his mouth on hers, the delicious feel of his hands on her breasts ... Just the thought of him made her ache and burn, and that was the hardest part to admit to herself.

She must stop thinking about him – but how, when they were thrown together daily at work?

Her situation was impossible. Not for the first time, Luna inwardly winced. She was falling for a man who was not just her new employer, he was also the focus of her secret investigation.

This was insane!

Soon, she would have to submit her article and Ruy would discover the truth. Still, no one had ever been able to lead her where she did not wish to go. She was here on a job, she repeated to herself for the umpteenth time. Undercover. It was the reason she had come to Cádiz; she must never forget that.

Luna kicked off the sheet and flung an arm over her face, covering her eyes.

Her own deceit in all of this weighed a hundred times heavier, knowing what she had already allowed to happen between them. She was being sucked deeper and deeper into the mire with nothing in sight to pull herself out.

Why had she ever let him pursue her? How could she have lost control of her feelings in this way?

Luna knew why. She had always regarded herself as strong, and so the awareness that Ruy had reached inside her and made her mindlessly weak with yearning and desire frightened her. She had also never been prone to jealousy, but the thought that he might be tangled up with a wild young gypsy girl with a curious hold on him, added to the fact that one of his old flames was constantly hovering around, now sent an unfamiliar stab of pain to her heart.

Luna's thoughts returned to her great-aunt's sudden appearance: something that had been worrying the frayed edges of her mind. She was feeling distinctly uneasy about having met Isabel. However, it was not the curious revelation that Ruy's family had always been enemies of her own that actually bothered her. After all, her feelings for her Spanish family were not exactly warm; in fact, they were bound up with memories that she had tried to bury for so long.

What bothered her more was what might be going through Ruy's mind at this moment. It was obvious that he hadn't known of the connection between Luna and the Herreras until this evening when the *Marquesa* had suddenly made an appearance.

Now Ruy's reaction at the restaurant made sense. Perhaps after all it wasn't jealousy of the serenading violinist that she had seen in his thunderous gaze.

What would his next move be? Would he still pursue her, knowing she was part of a family with whom his own had been feuding for generations? Not just that. She had to admit that her Spanish family weren't the most savoury of characters. Would she be tarred with the same brush in Ruy's eyes?

Luna shifted again and stared up at the ceiling. *Why are you curious about his next move if you know this is all wrong in so many ways?* Oh, the agony of uncertainty: half hoping he would chase her, despite being who she was, and half wanting to run away.

How long are you going to deceive yourself? Face reality: once you reveal your identity and the article is out, he'll hate you for that alone and you'll never see him again anyway, she argued cynically.

It was clear she was swimming way out of her depth.

Out of the corner of her eye she thought she saw something move past the window. She had left the sliding doors of her bedroom open.

Luna slipped out of bed and went out on to the terrace. Moving to the railing she looked out into the still night. Shrouded in moon-shadowed darkness, the beach and the bay formed an awesome and infinite picture of mysterious beauty, with the sea smacking long and slow and hissing up the shore.

'Is anybody there?'

Only the gentle swish of the sea answered her.

It must be my imagination. Her body was on fire, so she lingered a few moments longer outside, letting the breeze cool her burning skin.

She was tired and sleepy. Her head still ached. She wondered whether or not to take a painkiller, but decided against it. She'd had quite a bit to drink and analgesics did not mix well with alcohol. She smiled wryly at herself: always so sensible, but look what a mess she'd got herself in.

Luna went back inside and locked the doors. She must be cautious; an intruder could be lurking in the dark. After climbing into bed she closed her eyes.

When she opened them again, she was staring straight into his pale blue gaze. A dizziness engulfed her.

In the moonlight, his face seemed to swim in front of her. Luna dragged her arms up, branching them out towards him, slowly raising her fingers to touch his lips, those strongly etched, beautiful lips she'd craved ever since she had set eyes on them; but he was out of reach. She breathed his name and, trembling, lifted herself up to bridge the gulf between them. The silky material of her nightdress was hugging her hips in a sweet caress and clinging to the smooth swell of her breasts and the taut peaks of her nipples.

'Ruy,' she whispered again as the need for him blossomed inside her.

Then suddenly he was gliding towards her: a magnificent prowler moving stealthily towards his prey. Heart thundering, head thrown back, arms outstretched, eyes pleading, she watched as he came forward, his long limbs moving in slow motion. In the phosphorescent light of the room he was all in shadow, but she was aware of his broad shoulders and muscled chest, and she could see he was naked. Her eyes were drawn to his narrow hips, to his lean thighs and … to that part of him which proudly flaunted his virility. She felt her loins contract as her ache for him deepened and she arched her back, inviting him to explore the secret place between her thighs, where desire pooled with a liquid heat.

It felt as though he was taking an aeon to get to her, fanning the flames of her desire, so that when his mouth finally touched her burning lips, her body seemed to turn molten, every sense raw and quivering with anticipation.

A sob died in her throat as he took her into the sanctuary of his arms and, peeling off her nightdress, set out on a heated exploration of her sensitized flesh. Tongue, lips and palms travelled down her silken skin, subtly discovering hidden places, fondling and stroking, conquering it inch by inch, leaving behind a fiery trail; and she cried out her pleasure, luxuriating, without inhibitions or guilt, in his masterly lovemaking.

Now she was begging him to stop teasing, pushing her hips upwards, parting her legs, seeking relief from the unrelenting need that had been torturing her for so long. Though she had never made love before, she didn't care. She yearned for his touch and wanted him to take her now … to feel him moving and vital inside her … To be one with him.

Silently and lovingly his body inched closer to hers and, opening her thighs still further, he slid down between them and guided himself to the place where she ached for him. Whispering tender words in her ear, he parted the soft petals covering the heart of her desire and gently began to rub and caress the moist centre of her.

Luna purred sensually and moved in rhythm with every stroke, delicious heat spreading through her. Urgency was building and she rocked from side to side in a frantic quest for fulfilment, her lips parted in gasping breaths. Release when it came was fierce. One convulsion after another shook her body, drawing moans from her more like cries of pain than of pleasure, until she was catapulted into delirious bliss. She remained languid a while, a delicious lethargy sweeping over her.

'Ruy,' she murmured, her voice thick with sleep. She stretched out an arm to feel for him in the space next to her, searching for the man who had brought her body to life and shown her what paradise could be. 'Ruy, where are you?' she called out again.

Luna opened her eyes heavily. Dawn had gilded the room with a special but fleeting light. The shadows were dying out as the first blush of a new day took over and the brightest star waltzed out of the night into a fulgent, coloured sky. Flaming swords, purple and orange, marked the east. There was no one in the room except her – she must have dozed off.

Hot and sticky, she sat up. Her nightdress clung to her body, her hair to her scalp. She distinctly remembered Ruy sliding the garment off her but she did not recall herself putting it back on again.

Ruy! Her body still throbbed with wonderment at his lovemaking. The shock of her own wantonness made her blush inwardly, though there was no other witness to judge her for it. With careless disregard for consequence she had abandoned herself. What must he have thought? She shrugged, still groggy with sleep and confusion. Yet she felt liberated … free. She slipped out of bed – she needed a shower.

As the cold water slid down her body, awakening it from its numbness, so it aroused her brain from its stupor. Sensibility supplanted numbness, and consciousness succeeded stupor. Gradually reality dawned.

Luna stepped out of the shower and staggered back to the bedroom. She gazed about her vaguely, looking for the familiar to restore her sanity. Though the sheets were tangled, it was obvious that she had slept in the bed alone. She sat down on the untidy heap and stared incredulously ahead of her. It had all been a fantasy … a beautiful dream. She shook her head. It had felt so *real*. Within minutes, her morale had sunk from the dizzy heights of ecstasy to a bottomless pit of despair.

For a long time she sat there, hot tears of disappointment and frustration running uncontrollably down her cheeks.

CHAPTER 9

Luna walked aimlessly in a straight line along the beach. After her shower, she had spent a bleak hour ruminating on the vivid dream that had so graphically invaded her night and had decided she needed some early-morning fresh sea air to clear her head.

At this hour the beach was peaceful and still. The only sounds were the gentle ripples of water frilling in small waves along the shore and the rumble of trapped surf out on the rocks. A five-storey liner floated in the distance like a swan on the sea's glassy surface. The sun had risen in dazzling radiance, the sky and the Atlantic Ocean were touched with turquoise, and the white line of foam along the coast gleamed cream.

Comic little crabs drifted in and out of their holes in the sand. Gulls and storm petrels flew and dipped in the wide blue yonder. Wild shrubs and sparse green tufts of grass appeared like emeralds in the dazzling platinum dunes and among the rocks, and the drooping fronds of the palm trees rustled faintly with every puff of air.

Luna felt lost and lonely; but there was no one to whom she could go, no one she could trust. She sat on top of a dune, tears blurring her sight. In this peaceful place, she should be able to think calmly and rationally about the dangerous turn her life was taking. She was going mad!

Pictures of people and places passed rapidly through her mind like the pattern of a tapestry: Ruy at the tavern in Barcelona; Ruy challenging her at the lecture and appearing on the plane; the Institute, Vaina and Charo, and discovering Ruy was her boss; going with Ruy to the masked ball and him kissing her in the summerhouse. Ruy bandaging her hand after the frisson of sexual tension in the lab; his jealousy when Diego Montez appeared at the exhibition and the flames rekindling, passionately and out of control, before the shock of meeting Aunt Isabel; Ruy bending his dark head intimately towards Vaina. Ruy with Vaina at Cadencia Tzigane, the Croatian singer serenading her, then Ruy again, this time with anger in his eyes.

Ruy, always Ruy. Ruy's arms ... Ruy's kisses ... Ruy's burning touch that she could not erase from her mind.

The dream haunted her; the passion she had felt was so potent that the fantasy had seemed real. Certainly the climax she'd experienced had been no figment of her imagination; it had actually happened.

Where had such ferocious yearning emanated? She wanted to turn away from it, so that she could hide this terrible, naked fear that crouched in its shadow. Shame and desire warred in her like dark adversaries on the shifting plateau of her tormented mind. Luna repressed a shudder.

Over the years, she had met handsome, intelligent and powerful men, none of whom had ignited anything in her. They had all left her cold. She had not given it much thought, taking for granted that she was one of those people who had never really been interested in sex.

Yet the instant Luna laid eyes on Ruy, the rush of desire that had surged through her like the swift beat of wings had been all-consuming. It consumed her still; an almost barbaric impulse neither mind nor will could control, it was like nothing she had ever known before. Whether she liked it or not, Ruy had a powerful hold on her, physically and emotionally. The self-possession, which she had so carefully pieced together as a shield against hurt, was cracking under the strain of these unfamiliar sensations and those needs that he provoked in her.

Time stood still as Luna wept once more, arms clasped about her shins, head on her knee, feeling empty, hollow; powerless.

A pat on her arm broke into her sorrow.

'*Por qué llora, señorita?* Why are you crying? *Madre de Dios!* What is the matter?'

Luna raised her head, her face bathed in tears, and looked up into the concerned eyes of Señora Sanchez, the woman with the black spaniel she had spoken to on the beach when she first arrived. Their paths had crossed a few times after that, invariably during her evening walks on the seashore, although since that afternoon they had only exchanged polite greetings and smiles.

Luna pressed her fists into her eyes, struggling to master the flood of tears that coursed down her cheeks and regain some self-control. 'I'll be all right in a moment. I'm so very sorry to make a spectacle of myself like this, but … it's such a relief to let it out for a change,' she whispered as her face flamed with embarrassment.

There was a short silence while Señora Sanchez watched her with dark, steady eyes. 'Is someone ill? Is it your poor cousin that you're still grieving for?' She paused and looked alarmed. 'Please tell me no one else has died,' she exclaimed, wide-eyed, as she crossed herself.

Despite her distress, Luna couldn't help but smile inwardly at this Spanish sense of drama. 'I miss Angelina, it's true, but no, no, nothing so tragic.'

'*Gracias a Dios!* Ah! It must be an affair of the heart, yes?'

Luna nodded dejectedly.

'You can talk to me. It is often better to talk about these things to a stranger, who can look at the problem objectively,' Señora Sanchez said with maternal solicitude as she settled down on the sand next to Luna, the black spaniel at her feet. 'We have a proverb in Spain. *El ciego se entera major de las cosas del mundo, los ojas son unos ilusionados embusteros*, a blind man actually knows more about the ways of the world because the eyes are only hopeful deceivers.' Her steady gaze was eager but kind. There was no morbid curiosity there, only genuine concern.

Luna gave a little broken laugh as her tears flowed uncontrollably again. 'I'm so confused, I wouldn't know where to start,' she admitted miserably. 'It's all happened so suddenly. One day I was in control of my feelings, the next it was as if I were enslaved to them. I've always thought of myself as an intelligent woman, but this man makes me positively stupid whenever I'm around him. It doesn't make any reasonable sense.'

The Spanish woman gave her a knowing smile. 'You cannot reason love away, my child. Nor can you ever know when it will claim you. *El amor coge al corazón desprevenido, nunca llega a la hora de la cita*, love catches the heart unaware, it never arrives at the appointed time.' She looked across to the sea wistfully. 'That is what creates passion and makes love such a wonderful thing.' Head tilted now on one side, she peered at Luna, who was gazing dejectedly at the sand. '*Este principe azul*, this Prince Charming, he loves you?'

Luna forced a laugh. 'This Prince Charming, as you call him, unfortunately has a very big heart. He loves all women.'

'Ah, but there is only one woman for each man! When the time is right, it is for the woman to reel in her catch slowly and carefully like a skilful fisherman. It's she who must be the clever one.'

'Love? I've barely known him a couple of weeks and all he wants is to get me into bed.'

'Ah, men!' Señora Sanchez sighed and shook her head sadly. '*Ay*! Alas, some men only think with that part of their anatomy. The times have passed when a man waited patiently for the day he could proudly deflower the woman he loved. You do not desire this man then?'

That was her problem. She wanted him more than any man she'd ever known, but a fear of so many things stopped her in her tracks. Something she could not possibly admit, even to this warm and straightforward woman.

It was Luna's turn to sigh heavily. 'Yes, I do, but I'm not the type of woman to leap into bed with the first stranger that tries to woo me. Anyhow …' she waved her hand vaguely.

'Anyhow?' Señora Sanchez probed.

Luna shrugged. 'Oh, it's all too complicated.'

The Spanish woman looked at Luna uncertainly, knitting her brows. 'You are a virgin, yes?'

Luna blinked at her and nodded.

'A rare pearl! Girls today don't care about their virginity. You must be proud of it. This man, does he know you are still pure?'

Luna gave a self-deprecating laugh. 'But you see, I'm not *that* pure, *señora*, and he knows it.'

She began talking in a flat monotone, unburdening herself of all the confusion that had weighed her down since meeting Ruy in the tavern in Barcelona. Without revealing more details she explained that she was now working for him. She told the older woman how much she longed for Ruy – still withholding his name – and how, when he touched her, she lost her self-control and had great difficulty resisting him. Naturally she did not mention her dreams and fantasies – or the nightmares that left her paralyzed. How could she, when all she wanted was to forget them? To forget, too, the shame that dogged her heels.

'It's not clear to me that this man is *not* in love with you. So far, nothing you have told me proves that his only intention is to get you into his bed.'

'He took me to a party, then deserted me to run after some girl, and spends hours locked away in his office with a woman to whom he was almost engaged. Isn't that enough proof?' Spoken aloud, it sounded pretty damning to Luna.

'Ah, *señorita*, you must believe the wisdom of my years when I tell you that appearances are often deceptive. *La verdad es hija del tiempo*, truth is time's daughter. Things today may be confused because you do not have all the information, but time will tell.'

'I can't afford to get hurt.'

'But can you afford to lose your chance of happiness?'

'How do I know that he's my one chance of happiness?'

'If you don't try, you'll never know.'

Luna looked at her and shook her head. There was still the matter of how she had lied to Ruy about her work at the Institute. 'I may never get the chance for that.'

Señora Sanchez mistook her answer for despondency of another variety. '*Niña, pacienca, pacienca. En una hora no se ganó Zamora*, Patience, child, patience. Zamora wasn't taken in an hour.'

Part of Luna couldn't help but grasp at the fringes of hope. 'After everything I've told you, you still think I should give him a chance?'

'*Sí*, unless you are prepared to live your whole life without knowing.'

'Without knowing?'

'Whether you let real happiness pass under your nose.'

Luna gazed off into the distance, watching a seagull glide down on to the beach and begin pecking at the soft, wet sand. The dog stirred from its place at their feet and took after it.

'I'll think about it. Probably best to wait and see.'

'Just so long as you know the difference between patience, which can be a good thing, and procrastination. In Spain we say while the grass grows, the horse starves.' Señora Sanchez tapped Luna's knee gently. 'Sometimes it is better to act than think. When we are born, we do not choose our country and we do not choose our family, but once we are here, we do have the power to mould our life.'

A familiar sadness pricked at Luna. She agreed with Señora Sanchez on this at least. Her own family would certainly never have been hers by choice, and it was exactly for this reason that she had striven to forge her own life and never sought out her Spanish relatives. She'd had to make her way with minimal guidance from her father, who'd never been around much. Luna had always been her own guide; she had found her own strength – strength now challenged for the first time.

'What about pride? Isn't that important too?' she said in a low voice.

Señora Sanchez regarded Luna with just a hint of amusement. 'Yours or his? The way things stand, I think he's the one whose pride has been bruised.'

'But if I give myself to him, he'll have won.'

The Spanish woman's eyes twinkled mischievously, making her look years younger. 'Sex is not the only way to entice a man, *señorita*. My mother used to say the torch of love was lit by the kitchen stove; she was right. I am neither a great beauty, nor am I a genius, but I'm an excellent cook. My dear Pedro, God rest his soul, always said I was the best. He could never resist my *magdalenas* straight from the oven.' She chuckled. '*Pche!* But I'm getting carried away again. There are so many other ways to a man's heart, you just need to apply a little ingenuity.'

She levelled her benevolent gaze at Luna, wagging a plump finger in the air. 'My child, you already stand out from the crowd. If he's an experienced man, and a man of honour, he'll appreciate that. Trust me, no matter how much they deny it, no man can resist the purity and innocence of a woman like you. Your virginity is the reward after the wait. You must come to my house one day. I will cook you my special paella and tell you a very beautiful love story, which I witnessed thirty years ago.'

Luna laughed, feeling cheerful for the first time in what seemed ages. 'Thank you, Señora Sanchez, I'd love that.' She laid a hand on the Spanish woman's arm and her eyes met her serene gaze. 'It was kind of you to listen to me and share your wisdom. I'm afraid I got somewhat overwhelmed by everything,' she whispered. 'I feel quite relieved now.'

Señora Sanchez beamed. 'I'm very happy to have been of use. It is bad to bottle up such things. Rest assured, my lips are sealed.' She crossed herself again. '*Que Santa Maria y los santos son testigos de mis palabras*, may the Virgin Mary and all the saints be witness to my words, your secret will be buried at the bottom of a well.'

Luna helped her get up and once Señora Sanchez had whistled for the spaniel, who came bounding back from the water's edge, she watched her move away until the older woman and her dog were two black specks in the distance.

She started back to the beach house feeling calmer, as though a great weight had been lifted from her shoulders. Señora Sanchez's words made a lot of sense; perhaps she should act upon them. If only she could get rid of this crack in her personality that seemed to divide her thinking into two contradictory aspects, life would be so much simpler. It wasn't only Ruy she was torn about. The article she had to write was dividing her loyalties too. If only she could find some clarity.

It was just past noon when she got home. She made herself a cup of coffee and a sandwich, turned on her computer and stared at her notes.

The more she thought about Ruy and what she'd seen at the Institute, the more the morality of his work took on a different aspect in her mind. Her mission to expose him as a quack seemed ridiculous now, after everything she'd seen and researched. His passion and dedication, not to mention his innate skill, were obvious, and Luna's previous commitment to the god of orthodoxy now seemed not only misplaced but downright pigheaded too. She stood up from her desk and walked out on to the terrace, where she paced back and forth. Could her conscience allow her to continue with the article or with the deception? None of it felt right. Her mind struggled to formulate a plan – anything to extricate herself from the tangle in which she found herself.

Ruy. His compassion moved her, and his passion terrified her.

Her conversation with Señora Sanchez circled around in her head, alternating with the unwelcome images of her dream.

Restless, she picked up the phone, dialled a number and listened to it ringing.

Almost immediately, Charo answered. She sounded delighted to hear Luna's voice. 'Of course I'd love to have coffee. I was just about to leave for the Plaza de las Flores to go shopping. Why don't you come along and meet me there?'

Luna grabbed her bag and headed out of the door. Company was what she needed, and Charo was the perfect choice.

*   *   *

Less than an hour later, Luna was sitting outside a lively street café with Charo, sipping an ice-cold *granizado de limón* and watching the crowds of people browsing the colourful market stalls of Plaza de las Flores.

'You know, Spanish families are full of dramatic feuds and secrets,' Charo shrugged, as she added milk to her coffee. 'But I must admit, that's a pretty fascinating story,' she added with a grin.

She had told Charo about her aunt's disdainful revelations, hoping to sound her out discreetly about what she knew of Ruy's family, if anything. Charo had listened attentively to Luna's brief account of her conversation with the *Marquesa*, her large blue eyes widening at the part about Ruy storming out, dragging Vaina with him.

'Luna,' Charo's voice was now hesitant, 'given Isabel Herrera's reputation, I'm not surprised that she would try and tarnish Ruy's integrity by telling you all that.'

'Reputation?' Luna asked casually, interested to have someone else's take on her great-aunt.

'Well, I don't wish to speak ill of your family …'

Luna waved a hand as she took another sip of her drink. 'Feel free. There's little you can say that I don't already know. There really is no love lost between us.'

Charo looked relieved. 'I think there were stories going around years ago about the Herreras, all sorts of scandals and intrigues. Ruy would never talk about his family's past, he's too private, and of course that's his business. Do you believe everything your aunt told you?'

'No, of course not. I'm sure elements of her story are true, but I took it all with a large pinch of salt. I don't believe for a minute that the Herrera women were the innocent party in any of it.'

Charo nodded and raised her eyebrows. 'Yes, even at her age the *Marquesa* still has a reputation for being somewhat ruthless in getting what she wants, either for her or for her family.' She leaned forward, propping an elbow on the table, her eyes sparkling with curiosity. 'Is it true that she got her title by marrying a *marqués* three times older than herself, who keeled over from a heart attack as soon she married him?'

'Something like that,' Luna admitted ruefully. She knew little more herself but remembered her father had chuckled over it on a few occasions, admiring Isabel Herrera's astuteness, if nothing else. 'I think Ruy's grandfather, Salvador, had a narrow escape not marrying her, to be honest. I'm under no illusions about my aunt's character.'

Charo peered at her. 'Yet there's something bothering you?'

Luna shifted in her chair. It was true, something *was* bothering her but pride prevented her from voicing it. *Spanish men are a rule unto themselves … you'd be wise to steer clear of Don Ruy … commitment is not on offer.* Doña Isabel's words still echoed harshly in her head.

'No, nothing's bothering me,' Luna lied, then added truthfully, 'except the fact that I'm not particularly proud to be a member of the Herrera family, nor do I wish to see any more of them while I'm here.'

Charo held her gaze steadily. 'Well, I can't see why it would make any difference to Ruy whether you were a Herrera or not, despite all this bad blood between your families.'

'He didn't look too pleased after he met my great-aunt.'

'Look, Luna, I must admit when you told me at the gallery that the *Marquesa* was your aunt, I was surprised too for a minute but anyone who knows you can clearly see you're nothing like the Herreras.'

Luna looked warmly at the young woman who was fast becoming a true friend. 'Thanks, Charo, I'm relieved to hear it.'

'As for Ruy's reaction in the restaurant,' Charo eyed Luna with a wicked smile, 'didn't you say the owner's son was serenading you at the time? Everyone says he's quite a dish.' She adopted a dramatic swooning expression. 'I hear all the *señoritas* would kill to have him turn up at their table – or their door.' She giggled. 'I told you Ruy wouldn't like another man paying you attention.'

Luna rolled her eyes. 'Oh, Charo!'

Yet the idea of Ruy being jealous still gave her a secret thrill, just as it had when the flirtatious attentions of Diego Montez had provoked him in a way she was unlikely to forget.

'Well, if you're in no hurry to see your relatives, at least you'll have more time to come out with me. I think you could do with a friend in Cádiz, someone to loosen you up a bit and stop you becoming one of those hopeless workaholics.'

Luna smiled at Charo's teasing. 'You may be too late for that.'

'*Ay Dios!* In which case, I have my work cut out for me. Listen, as you were ambushed by the scary *Marquesa* last night at the exhibition and we couldn't go out, why don't you come to a concert with me this evening? It's at the cathedral. I have a spare ticket and Miguel can't come.' A gleam appeared in Charo's eye. 'There's a very special soloist playing.'

'Oh yes? Who's that?'

'Rodrigo Rueda de Calderón. I hear he's a very gifted guitarist.' She laughed, seeing the look on Luna's face. 'It's a fund-raising concert for a cancer charity that Ruy is very involved with. Did you know he was a musician too?'

Luna's mind flew back to the tavern in Barcelona: Ruy's long fingers speeding over the strings of his mandolin, the fiery vigour of the music invading her, body and soul. 'No, I didn't,' she lied. The idea of listening to him play again made her spine tingle.

'So you'll come?'

Luna hesitated. 'I'm not sure.'

'Come on, Luna. It'll be fun.' Charo's shoulders slumped in mock despair. 'Otherwise, you'll be making me go on my own.' She made puppy-dog eyes at Luna and pouted. 'And I'll be lonely.'

Luna still wasn't convinced, but Charo's face made her burst out laughing.

'Yes, all right, enough, enough! I'll come. Besides, I haven't been to a concert in a long time and I'd love to see the cathedral. I've walked around St Patrick's in Manhattan, which is stunning, but listening to music somewhere like that must be something else.'

Charo leaned her chin on her hand and sighed. '*Ay*, Manhattan. It must be so exciting.' She paused, her gaze refocusing on Luna's face. 'So, *amiga*, why did you decide to come to Spain and apply for this job when you could have found a research position somewhere in New York?'

Luna stared at Charo for a moment. She had instantly taken to the young woman's sisterly warmth and she was so easy to talk to; besides, she was becoming tired of carrying so many secrets around. Perhaps it wouldn't give too much away to tell her some of the truth.

She hesitated, lowering her gaze, then said: 'I had a cousin who loved Spain. I lost her to cancer. It made me interested in finding a cure, I suppose.'

'Poor you ... poor her.' She gave a sad little shrug. 'Cancer is often so unpredictable. You were right to come here, though. Ruy has a natural gift for predicting which way it's going to go, and how best to fight it. You've seen for yourself the number of success stories resulting from his approach.' Her expression became sombre. 'He does a lot of work in the San Servando hospice. I know it gets to him, particularly when the person dying is young. It must be truly heartbreaking when it's someone you love. I do feel for you.'

Her words prodded a raw place inside Luna. She had studied science in the quest for knowledge – partly because it fascinated her, but also to make a difference to people's lives. Still, it seemed such a second-hand gesture. She was a loner, and poring over test tubes in labs had allowed her to keep some distance from the world. Here was Ruy, doing frontline work, helping to save lives and also giving comfort to the dying. Yet again Luna was seeing a whole other aspect to the man reveal itself.

Charo continued. 'The gift that Ruy has is quite extraordinary. His very fingers seem to heal, and somehow he has a spiritual ability to make things better, and ease the person's fears and grief, like no one else. I've always thought it must be something in his gypsy DNA.'

Something in Luna's mind was beginning to shift, lit by a new understanding, like someone rounding the corner of a maze and knowing they will soon be at the heart of it. How could she have been so wrong, so set in her narrow tramlines, that she had actually set out to ruin something that she was coming to see was quite precious – the work of Ruy and his clinic.

Luna's head finally lifted, meeting her friend's concerned gaze. 'Are you all right, Luna?'

'Yes, Charo.' Her smile was luminous. 'I'm fine.'

As Charo waved to the waiter for another coffee, Luna sat perfectly still, trying to assimilate this new information, to steady herself in the rush of feelings that beset her following her friend's revelations. So much about Ruy conflicted with the image her great-aunt, and his general reputation, would have her believe: that he was a shallow philanderer and some sort of flaky medic.

At that moment, a renewed compulsion took her over: she wanted to find out more about the complicated, enigmatic man who had turned her life upside down. It was now not only the foundations of her assignment that were teetering precariously, but so much of what she had held as dependable truth about herself was crumbling into dust.

*   *   *

A lilac dusk descended over Cádiz Cathedral. Inside those soaring, floodlit walls, the echoing hum of conversation and movement swelled as the nave filled up with people. From a pew near the front, Luna watched the city's great and good arrive for the gala concert, dressed to impress, enjoying the ceremonious feel of the occasion.

The cathedral's vaulted ceiling rose above them in a tessellation of rounded arches, reaching up to the famous dome itself, which was suspended like the pale insides of some magnificent giant sea urchin. Below it, wall lights and tall candles offered a warm, sacred glow; the air smelt of cool marble, roses and incense. Luna's gaze travelled over the heads of the audience finding their seats, and around the vast stone hull of the interior. History and piety, suffering and bliss were etched into every piece of wood and stone that surrounded them, and it was hard not to feel awed by it all. Yet, added to this, an unexpected feeling of comfort struck her; she was not immune to the profound spiritual atmosphere here.

Beside Luna, Charo was talking to a stranger in her usual ebullient manner. Content to rest with her own thoughts, Luna picked up the programme and glanced through it. Ruy was playing the Adagio from Rodrigo's famous *Aranjuez Concierto* for solo guitar. Of course she knew the piece but had never heard this arrangement before and hadn't realized, until Charo had invited her here, that Ruy also played the guitar. She thought back to the wild magic of Ruy's mandolin playing, how its gypsy fire had mesmerized – how intriguing it would be to hear something so utterly different from him tonight.

Her gaze was drawn to the empty chair and music stand that stood on one side of the dais, at a respectful distance from the altar. Knowing he would soon be performing just a few feet away made her excited and nervous – for him, but also for herself. That savage, wonderful kiss at the exhibition had stayed with her all day. It had turned her inside out. Her pulse skipped again at the thought and at the prospect of seeing him again: they were bound to meet once the concert was over. After the drama of the previous evening, how would he respond to her?

A nudge from Charo jolted her out of these thoughts. 'So, have you spotted your great-aunt yet?'

Luna looked at her sharply and then relaxed, seeing her friend's mouth twitch with amusement.

'That's not funny, Charo.'

'Well, after all, this is the kind of event where all the powerful, rich and influential people of Cádiz want to be seen. Then again, given the *Marquesa*'s antipathy to the de Calderóns, I think you'll be safe tonight.'

Luna followed her friend's gaze to the opposite side of the nave, where Count Salvador sat at the front with his wife, Alexandra. Next to them was Luz de Rueda, dressed in pearl-grey chiffon, her dark hair drawn into an elegant chignon. She too was scanning the audience, and her sapphire-blue eyes eventually fell on Luna.

For a moment a curious expression flashed in them before she smiled and nodded a silent greeting, then turned to resume her conversation with the Countess.

Luna's awkward smile of response faded on her lips. Of course Ruy's family would be here. Foolish of her not to have thought of it. Now that she knew the history between them and the Herreras she felt tense but she couldn't help craving their approval somehow. If only she could let them know that she viewed her Spanish relations with just as much distaste as they did.

She had seen that same speculative look cross Luz de Rueda's face before, when they had met at the El Pavón ball. With dismay, Luna now understood what it meant. Ruy's mother must have recognized her as Adalia's daughter, or at least suspected as much. Would Ruy confirm his mother's fears? If they knew Luna was a Herrera, would the de Ruedas be as welcoming as before?

Her eyes still lingering on the de Ruedas, she murmured to Charo: 'I don't think even Aunt Isabel would dare to appear here tonight.' Then she transferred her gaze to her friend. 'Did you tell Ruy you were bringing me as a guest instead of Miguel?'

Charo looked guilty. 'Not exactly. I thought it would be better to surprise him at the end. We don't want his concentration ruined, do we?' she added with an impish grin.

Luna gave her a long-suffering look and was about to retort when the crowd hushed. A man dressed in an elegantly tailored, dark evening suit had emerged from the left-hand aisle to stand at the front of the nave. Luna recognized him instantly as Andrés de Calderón, Ruy's father.

'Ladies and gentlemen,' he began, in a strong, deep voice that was clearly accustomed to addressing an audience, 'thank you for joining us on this very special evening. As you know, tonight is part of the Fiesta de las Rosas, a series of charity concerts and social events in aid of cancer research. As the foundation's chairman, I'm delighted to see so many familiar faces supporting us again this year.'

He went on to speak briefly about the charity's work and thanked the audience for their generosity. 'Now, I have great personal pleasure in introducing our first artist, who will be performing a classic piece, courtesy of his namesake … Rodrigo Rueda de Calderón.'

The audience clapped warmly as Ruy appeared on the platform, guitar in hand. He bowed and took his seat.

Luna inhaled sharply. There he was, looking stunning in a plain black shirt and trousers, one knee raised by his foot stand, his guitar resting on his lap. He looked so different to the unkempt, tousle-haired gypsy who had met her eyes across the bar in Barcelona, yet he had the same relaxed air, as if he were in his element. Luna wondered if he would look up and see her now, as he had before. The light from the column behind him lit up his face as he briefly gazed out at the crowd, tuning his strings, yet his eyes never paused to rest on her this time. He began to play.

Ruy's rendition of the music was stunning. His strong, sensitive fingers moved from a slow rhythmic strum to picking out the mournful tune over the top; then as the music progressed, his hands became fast and furious, executing a series of intricate chord progressions and complicated strumming patterns using his thumb. Luna watched, hardly breathing, as his hand glided from the sound hole to the base of the strings, caressing the instrument like a living, breathing creature in a fluid, sensual movement that made the pit of her stomach quiver. One moment his head hung down in concentration, the next he raised his face up, eyes closed, as if the music were rising within him, transporting him to another place.

Luna knew Ruy was a talented gypsy guitarist from their first sizzling encounter, but this was an entirely different side to him. She sat, transfixed, as his playing sent a new, dizzying array of emotions through her. The music spoke to her deepest self and, because it was Ruy creating this sublime sound, something else indescribable and profound conjured a sensual yearning within her, making her heart swell almost unbearably.

No doubt there were many women in the audience lost in admiration for the handsome young guitarist – or their own private fantasies – while the music filled the cathedral, but Luna's flights of imagination were connected to something real and remembered.

Those strong arms of Ruy's had held her close at the masked ball; and only last night, those same dextrous hands had moved over her body with hungry desire. More than once, that sensual mouth, now twitching slightly in concentration as he played, had taken hers in mind-blowing, passionate kisses and had whispered her name, hot and urgent: '*Tell me you want me, Luna ... I'll be waiting for you ... when you're ready for me.*'

Would he still be waiting for her now?

Yet it wasn't just a physical awareness of Ruy that was growing inside her now. Her lunchtime conversation with Charo had nudged a tender place within.

If only Angelina had been treated by someone like Ruy in her last days.

Now, listening to him play, her emotions were undergoing a strange transformation, a process gathering its own momentum. As the music was rising in a fierce crescendo, her defences were falling away, leaving her raw and completely overwhelmed like never before.

The last tremulous notes from Ruy's guitar sounded, making her heart almost stop in her chest. Now the music was over, and Luna clamped her eyes shut. The audience errupted into thunderous applause. She realized her face was wet with tears.

Ruy stood, breathed deeply, and took a bow, gripping the neck of his guitar with both hands. Straightening up, his eyes finally caught

Luna's. Visibily taken aback, his bright blue gaze burned into hers for just a moment or two, searching her face with quiet intensity. He quickly regained his composure and smiled at the audience. Then, as the applause died down, rather than leaving the dais at the side, he walked straight down the front steps into the nave.

Luna's mouth went dry: he was heading directly for her.

She swallowed as he slipped into the pew to sit beside her. The tension between them was palpable. Wordlessly, he produced a handkerchief from his pocket. Keeping his arm low, he offered it to her, and his hand grazed the side of her thigh as he did so. Their eyes met and her heart and stomach swapped places with a leap. He looked sombre but something else glimmered in his gaze, some emotion she couldn't read. Was it tenderness or confusion? She took the handkerchief from him and discreetly dabbed her cheeks.

The dramatic, sweeping sound of Barber's *Agnus Dei* started up from the choir stalls and Luna's every nerve ending was aware of Ruy as they sat together listening to the exquisite voices climbing and falling. Whatever he was thinking, she was close enough to feel the warmth of him. She thought back to those torrid few minutes alone with him at the exhibition. The memory of his bruising kiss, his heated stare, overcame her once more; her body reacted instantly, making her breasts ache and a warmth flood her thighs. The awareness they had of each other was electrifying, though she sensed they shared an unease as well as a desire.

For the next half an hour, the choral music continued through a series of short, stirring pieces that resounded through the cathedral, every note mirroring the intensity between the two of them, and the heavy anticipation that hung in the air. Every now and then, Luna moved her head slightly so that she could see more of Ruy's profile, but his expression was difficult to discern. Whenever she turned her head back to the front, she felt him, in turn, look at her, and her whole body tingled in response.

The final applause broke out and as the wall lights brightened again for the interval, the cathedral filled with the echoing noise and chatter of the audience. Before Luna had a chance to think of something to say, Charo leaned over. 'Ruy, your performance was absolutely amazing.' Her bright eyes moved from one to the other, watching them both closely. 'What did you think Luna? Aren't you impressed that our good doctor has so many hidden talents?'

Luna glanced at Ruy nervously, wondering if she would be met with mockery or reproach. His blue gaze lingered on her speculatively, but otherwise it was unreadable.

'Yes,' she answered, 'I was more than impressed.'

And I seem to be learning more about him every day, she thought.

'Well,' Charo whispered quickly, 'I've been sitting next to the loveliest woman, who it turns out knows my cousin in Seville, so I'll leave you two alone while we queue up for a drink, if that's okay?'

'Of course it is, Charo,' replied Ruy. He gave her a fondly sardonic look. 'I'm sure Luna and I can find something to talk about without you.'

Charo beamed. 'I'll see you later then,' she said brightly, and moved off to join her friend in the aisle.

Ruy half turned to Luna, resting his arm on the back of the dark, polished wood of the pew. 'Charo didn't tell me you were coming this evening.'

'She didn't?' Luna wondered if he was annoyed.

'No. You know how incorrigible and scheming she is, but I'm glad you came.' He smiled suddenly – a languid, dazzling white smile that filled her with relief. Things between them hadn't changed after all. 'The music seemed to move you very much,' he added softly.

'It did. Your playing was incredible.' She gazed around the cathedral's interior. 'Perhaps it's the setting of this place and the emotion of the music, but I couldn't help thinking about someone close to me who died.'

The words were out before Luna could think. The thrill at his proximity was heightened even more since his stirring performance, and something new had replaced her feelings of caution and resistance.

A dark expression, almost like shock, passed across Ruy's features as his mind seemed to grapple with some unknown thought. 'I'm sorry, Luna,' was all he said, and a silence fell between them.

Luna wondered what that strange look had meant. Unease prickled at her, though she wasn't able to give it form. Trying to move the conversation away lightly, she asked: 'Is this the first time you've played at one of this charity's events?'

'No, I've played at quite a few. As my father is the chairman, it seems natural for me to contribute what I can.'

'Yes, of course.' Luna remembered Charo's mention of his hospice work. Her opinion of him had undergone such a transformation in the past few hours that she felt an odd kind of nervousness. 'I've never been to a concert in a cathedral before,' she continued. 'The atmosphere is so powerful.'

He nodded, still looking sombre. 'As it's intended to be. The acoustics are perfect for music, of course, but then worship and music go hand in hand. The reverberation is beautiful.'

His cobalt-blue eyes were so still on her that her pulse fluttered frantically.

'A ship of souls,' she said, slanting her gaze past him to the pillars of the domed ciborium overshadowing the altar, and then across to the pews on the other side of the patterned central walkway. Sensing he was still watching her intently, she started to babble, as was her wont when she felt awkward.

'Did you know that "nave" comes from the Latin word "*navis*", meaning ship? Symbolically speaking, the cathedral is the ship bearing God's people through the stormy seas of life, buoyed up by their faith and worship, I suppose.'

Ruy stared at her before breaking into a broad smile. He was about to respond when a group of people approached to congratulate him on his performance. Among them was an attractive redhead, who kept casting looks of admiration his way. As he thanked the group graciously, Luna felt a pang of irritation at the woman's openly flirtatious body language, although Ruy seemed oblivious to it. Then, just as the group was moving away, the woman suddenly noticed Luna and flung her a look of barely concealed envy.

After they had gone, Luna hesitated and looked at him wryly, deciding to test the waters: 'I'm surprised to see that Vaina isn't here tonight.'

'I didn't invite her.' Ruy leaned against the back of the pew, resting one ankle on his other knee. He regarded her pensively. 'Listen, Luna, I'm sorry for the way I behaved last night. It was ungentlemanly in every way.' He ran a hand through his hair, groping for the right words. 'I didn't expect to see you there, and then you showed up … and things between Vaina and me are a little …'

'Complicated?' she offered.

'Yes … well, no.' There was no arrogance or teasing in his manner now. His eyes were unguarded and earnest. 'It's not complicated as far as I'm concerned. I told her as much in the restaurant. I'm afraid it was difficult for me to come over and speak to you and your aunt, for a number of reasons.'

A brooding expression crossed his face but he said no more.

Luna knew exactly what those reasons were. Leaving aside their explosive kiss just moments before her aunt had appeared, Ruy would have found it awkward to approach her in the restaurant with Aunt Isabel sitting there and Vaina in tow. In fact, had he done so, it would have been highly embarrassing for all concerned. If the *Marquesa* hadn't found a way to behave in a rude and obnoxious manner, Vaina would have succeeded in making a scene instead.

Still, she felt like pushing him for more and asked carefully: 'So you and Vaina have broken up?'

His gaze settled on hers. 'If we had, would that make a difference to you?'

'I'm sure it's none of my business.' Luna couldn't help the prickles surface in her tone.

He smiled. 'We were never together really. I made that clear to her at the restaurant.'

Luna's heart relaxed and gave a small, triumphant cheer. 'She certainly didn't look happy. Then again neither did you when you left.'

'Do you blame me?'

'What do you mean?' She tensed a little, knowing she might be drawing out something that it would be uncomfortable to talk about; an admission of the bad blood between their families. Still, she wanted to hear it.

His eyes flashed suddenly with blue fire. 'Were you trying to make me jealous?'

'Jealous?' She almost laughed with relief.

'First with Montez, then with the violinist.'

'Are you serious? You really left that restaurant because a man at the gallery spoke to me and a violinist at the restaurant was serenading me as part of his act?'

He sighed. 'I'm not the jealous type, but with you, Luna, I feel things that are completely new to me.' His ardent gaze traced her features, then settled on her mouth. 'I lose my self-control. Don't you see that?'

She stared at him, her heart beating in her chest like the wings of a bird struggling to fly free. 'The lights are going down. It looks like the performance is about to start.'

He held her gaze and then looked away as Charo slipped back into her seat. 'I hope you two haven't been bored while I was away.'

'Far from it,' murmured Ruy as the music started up again.

*   *   *

The powerful Ducati sped through the night, its beam lighting the dark highway that stretched to the mainland. Through his helmet, Ruy could hear the dull hiss and crash of the waves on both sides and leaned into the wind as it whipped up from the sea. He deftly manoeuvred the bike between a string of cars and twisted the throttle to surge ahead of them, needing the rush of speed to release the ache of tension from his mind and body.

Thoughts of Luna filled his head like a beautiful, taunting dream.

Twice in two days she had appeared unexpectedly. Charo's matchmaking efforts were working overtime, he mused fondly. Still, her ministrations had only partially worked. As he'd anticipated, Luna made her excuses and hurried away after the concert, before his family had even made their way over to hug him and exclaim at the virtuosity of his performance. For the rest of the evening, Ruy had enjoyed being wrapped up in their warmth, as they sat with a group of friends over a late dinner, but he couldn't help wishing with all his heart that Luna was beside him, a loved and accepted part of their group. The thought of her, and his pressing desire to be with her, distracted him to the point where he couldn't follow the thread of the conversation at the table.

While he'd been playing, it was images of Luna that inspired him as the melodies sang through him, almost out of his control. He had never got so lost in his music before. Then afterwards, when he had looked up, there she was, as if, by some mysterious force, he had conjured her into being with the plucking of his strings.

He thought he would read indignation in her eyes. After all, he had jumped on her at the exhibition like a lust-crazed beast; no matter that she had responded to his voracity with equal force.

She had wanted to get away from him as quickly as possible, that much he could tell.

Yet tonight there had been nothing cool or aloof in the the the way she'd looked at him as they sat together in the cathedral. Curiosity mixed with shyness flickered in her gaze, as well as something darker. He had felt it too. Desire had enveloped them both and every time he had looked into her eyes, alive with intelligence, and let his own drop to that soft, luscious mouth, slightly parted in surprise at what was happening to them both, it was as much as he could do not to take her in his arms again.

What was this power she had to make him take leave of his senses?

The memory of that kiss still made his body react with instant, relentless arousal. He had never lost control like that.

'*All you care about is getting me into bed.*'

He remembered her judgemental riposte; he deserved it for he could see what it must have seemed like to her. He was a man, and Luna's enticing womanly allure undid him every time.

Being in her presence was becoming a waking torment. He could still taste her lips, feel the contours of her body under his hands; that scent of her skin like honey and apple blossom. This hunger for her was uncontrollable, raging in his blood like pure, sweet madness. Every time they were together he wanted to take her then and there, to know how it felt to be inside her.

And he'd known her less than a fortnight.

Ruy's gloved hands clenched on the handlebars. He slowed the Ducati and turned it sharply off the road, heading towards the beach. His house was still a few miles off but he needed to breathe the sea air and pull himself together.

He brought the bike to a halt on a scrubby clearing edged by boulders. Below, dark waves churned and swirled into rock formations that looked like a craggy giant had lain down in the sea to sleep on its side. The clear midnight sky held pinpricks of gleaming stars and a mysterious half moon threw its pale glaze over the inky ocean.

It had been on a night like this when Juliet and Carlos had died.

Ruy wrenched off his helmet and gloves, taking a deep breath and letting the salty air fill his lungs. Sea spray dotted the heated skin of his face and he sank down on to a boulder.

His mind flashed back to his university days in Boston. The years peeled away and suddenly he was back in that car, trapped and powerless to do anything, with his two friends slumped bleeding, twisted and lifeless beside him.

How could he tell Luna that he'd been the driver of the car in which her sister Juliet had lost her life, the accident that had caused their mother to drink herself to death?

Even though he had been absolved of all responsibility, he had not for one moment let himself off the hook. Had he been firmer with Juliet, no one need have died. Nothing would ever change the fact that he had been driving the car. Maybe if his reactions had been one split-second quicker … Perhaps he might have had more time to break or swerve …

It still plagued him after all these years.

His love for Luna came at a cost, he understood. He knew that when he looked at her, at any moment those dreaded phantoms of the past would rise up to torment him. Yet one part of him almost willed them to come. For so long his own feelings had been frozen, too, and now the floodgates had burst and he found himself impelled to open up to the horror of past memories, as well as the feelings of ecstasy that Luna herself had unleashed in him. Somewhere deep and raw inside of him had ached for her when he saw those tears run down her beautiful face in the cathedral.

'*I couldn't help thinking about someone close to me who died.*'

Her words had then struck him like a knife in the stomach.

Juliet.

Ruy tossed his helmet on to the ground and put his hands to his head, pushing his hair back from his face. He exhaled with a heavy breath.

How would Luna react if she knew his part in Juliet's death? How could she ever forgive him?

CHAPTER 10

I n the week that followed the concert, Luna saw nothing of Ruy. The next morning, Charo informed her that he would be away from the Institute on business all week. Luna didn't ask where or why, as she was conscious of the bright and enquiring gaze of her friend and had no wish to reveal any hint of the sea change in her feelings for the doctor.

Something had shifted irrevocably for her in the last twenty-four hours, she knew. The barrier between her and Ruy, which she had maintained assiduously over the past two weeks, had almost – but not quite – disintegrated. Before, she had always kept him at bay with rebuffs and retorts, turning down his invitations to dinner and generally making herself unavailable to him … but all that had changed. There was a palpable closeness between them now; she could feel it in the relative lack of sparring, and a new honesty in their conversation.

Ever since her lunchtime talk with Charo and the concert later that evening, Luna had felt as tender and vulnerable as a clam whose shell had been prised open. For the first time in her life, her head had let her defenceless and throbbing heart lead the way, and now she was terrified.

Luna's feelings of agitation only intensified as the week passed. She could barely concentrate on her work, though she tried valiantly to do so in the hope of putting Ruy from her mind for just a few hours each day. There was almost no respite: he pulsed through her thoughts during her waking hours, and ravished her body in her dreams at night.

For once, self-possession failed her. She couldn't help but glance repeatedly at her mobile phone checking for messages or emails then immediately berated herself for doing so. If only he had called the day after the concert! He could have taken her out to dinner or for a walk along the beach and she wouldn't have had to go through a week of this insecure fretfulness.

Yet there was nothing from Ruy. Absolute silence: no texts, no calls, not even an impersonal work email.

Luna had never considered herself to be a neurotic person but she had to concede, wryly, that she had been wrong about her own weaknesses in all sorts of ways. Every single day over these past weeks had brought with it some sharp new realization about her personality, and she found it more than a little disturbing. Then, these few days since the concert, alone at the beach house in the evenings when she was trying to concentrate on her article, she would gnaw at her thumb, restlessly turning over tormenting questions in her mind. Had Ruy chosen to absent himself from the office in an effort to avoid her? Perhaps he felt the heightened intensity between them and decided to run for cover? Or maybe he'd found that now she was open to his advances, there was little thrill in the chase? Perhaps his parents had rounded on him after the concert, advising him to leave the Herrera girl alone; saying she would be nothing but trouble, like the rest of her reprehensible, scheming family?

She simply couldn't get Ruy out of her head.

Luna felt unnerved, but also on fire. She had always been such a rational and logical person, utterly in control of her feelings; so how was it that her whole being seemed invaded by an emotionally charged, capricious sprite – an alter ego designed to upturn her very existence? It was as though some dual personality had taken hold, forcing her behaviour to swing wildly between passionately headstrong and defensively fearful.

There was no respite from her enervating and unpredictable emotions – everything she did led her relentlessly to thoughts of Ruy. Her research at the clinic, the article she was working on … all of it concerned him so closely. She had always said only a madwoman would get involved with someone she worked with, and only a simpleton would allow herself to become drawn into an affair with her boss, and now she was having to eat her words. Yet in her heart of hearts, if the same choices had been thrown at her now, she knew she would do it all again.

The more research she did on the work of her gypsy-doctor, the more her respect for the man grew. The files she'd been asked by Ruy to go through were adding up to a remarkable series of statistics. He was certainly an extraordinary healer; and the figures – as well as endless glowing testimonials from patients – seemed to prove it. As a result, Luna had started to write quite a different piece to the one she'd planned.

She found she had the greatest clarity late at night, working at the beach house, where she came to her studies with a new open-mindedness that kept surprising her. Determined the piece about the clinic be completely unbiased, just as Ted had stipulated, she also knew that he would be surprised, and quite possibly irked, to see her championing some of the Institute's more cutting-edge practices. Charo had commented on Luna's quiet mood and the shadows under her eyes, but she had brushed her friend's concerns aside, promising to get more rest at the weekend.

She found herself almost dreading the weekend, as there wouldn't be any clinical work to take her mind off Ruy. After she had driven away from the Institute on the Friday, she went home to her desk and worked into the small hours. She was so mentally exhausted by the time she collapsed into bed that she fell into a deep sleep, lulled by the ever present sound of the sea, and did not wake until mid-morning the next day.

For the first time in a week she felt refreshed and relaxed. The sun was high in the sky; gulls were wheeling and calling, seeming to beckon her outside. She raced to get dressed, full of a sudden joy to be alive.

After a bracing swim in the sea, Luna came back to the beach house ravenous and wishing she had been shopping earlier. As if a kindly genie had read her mind, there was a casserole dish sitting on the table of the veranda. Next to it was a plate of *magdalenas* and a note beside them: '… *porque es necesario engorde!*, because you need fattening up!' It was signed by Señora Sanchez.

Delighted, Luna laughed out loud and lifted the casserole lid, which revealed a delicious-looking paella *de marisco*, still warm and fragrant with brightly coloured orange prawns, red peppers and pink *calamares* nestling like edible jewels in the creamy rice. Her new neighbour had taken to stopping by with little gastronomic offerings on her way to walk her dog or visit the town, and Luna had basked in the older woman's breezy presence and welcome banter. With the endless parade of thoughts about Ruy marching through her head and plaguing her body, Luna found that Señora Sanchez's solid matronly wisdom was about the only thing that had kept her sane.

As Luna tucked into the mouthwatering food she made a mental note to buy her friend some delicacy from the covered market the next time she was there. She would pay a visit to the *señora*'s cottage and return the compliment. Food and friendship, those time-honoured partners, were so prevalent here in Cádiz and Luna loved that about the city.

Rejuvenated by her lunch, she decided to go exploring parts of Cádiz that she had not yet visited, away from the walled city. Apparently there were interesting Moorish ruins to be seen inland. It would make a nice change from the beach and the bay.

Equipped with a bottle of water, a compass and a map, she drove to the outskirts of Cádiz and across the isthmus, parking at a small harbour. The sun beat down on her as she stepped out of the car, and Luna was thankful she'd exchanged her jeans and shirt for a mini-skirt, spaghetti-strap top and hat before going out.

The streets of the town that nestled around the bay climbed steeply towards the hills. Soon the rise was gentler, eventually plateauing out at the top. She paused to catch her breath and take a drink from her water bottle, looking out to sea and down on the glittering bay as she did so. In the other direction stretched a fertile plain with cornfields, rich green vineyards and olive groves. She put away her water and set out along the track that bordered the fields, while skylarks fluttered high above, trilling their liquid waterfall of song. Now she was passing a large hacienda with its enormous orchard of laden orange trees, making a striking contrast of colour against the prevailing olives. At the end of the stone wall that bounded the property she finally came to a small hamlet of cottages, their gardens filled with brightly hued bougainvillea that fringed the walls or hung in long trails from little flat rooftops.

As Luna walked further from the coast and its luxuriant vegetation, pretty whitewashed cottages and lobster-pink haciendas, the countryside grew parched in a uniform umber. There was little sign of life now, other than the odd lizard that skittered away into a crack in the dry stone wall. Occasional patches of wild shrubs dotted the parched earth, with a few scattered fig trees and carobs with their long green pods. There was precious little shade and Luna was glad she had brought her hat.

The afternoon sun was still beating down hard, and she paused to sit under an olive tree and drink some water. She had reached a crossroads of sorts, with several paths, all of which climbed upwards again; she took out her map to get her bearings. One of the rutted tracks must lead to the ruins of the Moorish mosque – but which one? After a while, she resumed her walk. This time her path climbed steeply, with a low bank on either side, clad with various kinds of native laurel.

Luna was so absorbed in her expedition that she had successfully avoided all thoughts of Ruy since she left home. Besides, thinking straight under such a baking sun was a challenge in itself. It was lovely to look back at the valley lying below, filled with a shimmering light haze, and see how far she had walked. She could just make out the white villages bathed in the afternoon light, tinting them rose and brown in the distance. Above, the clear sky blazed like a furnace.

Then suddenly, after having climbed steadily for some time, the path narrowed for a few yards before plunging towards what seemed like a vast quarry of sharp grey rocks and brown earth. It was not the ruin Luna had hoped for but – to her, at least – it was just as interesting. This apparently useless piece of terrain had been made habitable.

Luna took in the unexpected, vivid picture of the gypsy camp, excitement coursing through her veins. The asymmetrical ground harmonized into a mass of large inhabited barren knolls. A few caves had been cut from the side of the quarry to make irregular dwellings; some had shacks appended, made from wood and corrugated iron. A small number of garish-looking barrel-topped wagons, the odd car or motorcycle, and a handful of horses populated the area, which was otherwise dotted with junk. Here and there, clothes were hanging from windows and branches to dry, adding a splash of colour to the scene.

On one side of the quarry, evergreen beeches marched up brown slopes. Further away, a tidier corner of the camp had been planted out with plane trees, many decades ago, under the precious shade of which men were dozing, their mouths wide open, while mangy dogs sniffed the dust around their feet for morsels of food. Half-naked brown urchins swarmed in the area outside the wagons, shrieking at the top of their lungs. *Gitanas* sat at their doors chatting in groups: some plaiting baskets, others sweeping the earth in front of their dwellings, keeping a vigilant eye on the group of young girls playing hopscotch and blind man's buff under a gnarled fig tree.

Despite the heat, a number of old-fashioned braziers were smoking at the entrance to most of the dens, with huge black pots hanging above them. At the centre of this hidden community was a flat area of old tiles and stones pressed into the earth, which formed a kind of courtyard, where a large covered well had pride of place. Around it, chickens pecked the dusty earth and a few goats rummaged in the small heaps of rubbish nearby.

Greatly entertained, Luna stood fascinated, her eyes fixed on this amazing sight. She was so engrossed that she failed to hear a gypsy woman approach her from behind.

'*Buenas tardes, señorita. Encontrastes la cañada de los gitanos, ey?* So you've found the gypsies' glen, hey?'

Luna spun round to stare straight into the laughing black eyes of Morena, the *gitana* who had sold her the beautiful costume for the masked ball. She felt all at once guilty and ashamed at being caught like a gawping tourist, an interloper on territory that was private and should have been kept sequestered from prying eyes.

'I didn't mean to be intrusive. I was actually looking for the ruin of an ancient mosque which is supposed to be somewhere around here,' she said with an embarrassed smile.

Far from looking offended, Morena smiled broadly. 'It is a good omen, Señorita Luna, that you have come here this afternoon. Yes, I remember you from Mascaradas. The lovely but guarded Queen of the Night.'

Her eyes seemed to take in everything about Luna with a hawk-like sharpness that she found somewhat unnerving but then the smile split her face in two again, and Luna was charmed.

'You've arrived just as my sister is having her baby. Any moment now, the first child of Carmencita and her husband Juan will come into this world and then he'll be baptized.'

'What? Right now, this afternoon?'

'*Sí, sí*. I have read in the stars that it will be a boy. Then we'll celebrate with a *zambra*, a revelry. There will be food and wine – *una fiesta maravillosa*, a wonderful feast. Come, you must join us too. Your timing is perfect!'

Luna was admittedly curious and, anyhow, she could hardly refuse an invitation that was clearly regarded as an honour. 'I'd be delighted to join your celebration, thank you,' she told her.

They picked their way down an awkward bumpy footpath, paved with chunky cobbles, and Luna felt she had entered a strange new world, so remote from anything she had known. There were many more caves than she had at first thought; they were grotesquely shaped and eroded by the years, in stark contrast to the more modern gear stationed beside them. She smiled to herself. Primitive versus contemporary: even in a place like this – seemingly forgotten by time – one could not get away from the modern world.

No sooner had they descended to the camp than the gang of children running wild gathered from the four corners of the site and clustered around them, shouting all at once, jostling and nudging each other to get to the front. Morena gently pushed them back, swearing at them in a language that sounded to Luna like Spanish, yet was indecipherable. The men who had been lying out on the slopes were now sitting up, scratching their heads, their sharp dark eyes alert and instinctively distrustful. Meanwhile the women had stopped chatting and, motionless, maintained their position in front of their dwellings like the Vestal Virgins of the hearth, guarding the safety and wellbeing of their homes and eyeing the newcomer suspiciously. The silence was ominous.

Heading towards one of the larger caves, Morena shouted something in *Caló*. A tall old man with a long wispy beard and a beaten-up flat cap nodded and grinned, shouting something back. The very next moment the atmosphere lightened and the whole camp relaxed again. Many of the gypsies leapt up in a single bound to welcome Luna, and Morena turned to her with a chuckle. '*Les dije que usted es una vija amiga*, I told our chief you're an old friend.'

While the men stood in a semicircle, a little apart, gaping at Luna speculatively, the women stood at a distance, whispering among themselves, while the children surrounded her, half giggling and half begging impudently. A little dazed – appalled by their poverty, though amused by their cheek – Luna spontaneously opened her bag and distributed the few euros and the bar of chocolate she had with her.

Suddenly a great deal of noise was emitted from one of the caves and a matronly woman appeared on the threshold. '*Es un niño*, it's a boy,' she cried out. '*Un oscuro muchacho como la noche con los ojos azules como el cielo de Andalucía*, a boy dark as the night, with eyes blue as the sky of Andalucía.'

Luna stared in disbelief, the smile frozen on her face. Behind the matron, a man in jeans and T-shirt had appeared, holding the naked newborn. In her shock, Luna's mind refused to function at first; then it started careering between questions.

What in God's name is Ruy doing here? Surely he can't be the father?

Morena had told her the baby was her brother-in-law's. How was it that she kept bumping into Ruy like this?

She flushed indignantly, amber eyes sparking fire. This man had the affront of the devil. First, the wild passion that had seized him at the gallery, with no thought of her feelings or how the public nature of it might embarrass her, followed by the jealousy that overtook him at the merest hint of a rival. To then be incommunicado for the past few days, making her life an utter misery, was outrageous.

Now, here he was, holding a baby, as if he had no other care in the world – as if he had quite forgotten her and moved on to pastures new.

The anxiety and frustration of the past week finally caught up with Luna, fuelling the righteous anger steadily building in her breast. She prickled with resentment: he hadn't had the simple courtesy to get in touch, if only to put her mind at ease, so she didn't feel like a fool for letting her own passions run riot. Yet her anger was tinged with embarrassment. She feared it could look as though she was following him, haunting his footsteps like a plaintive spirit – and the idea that Ruy might think so irritated her even more.

'*El Mèdico* is going to be *el padrino*, the godfather of our little Luis,' Morena whispered proudly to Luna. 'He's a *gajo* who is not only one of us by birth, but also *el hermano de sangre*, the blood brother of Chico, Juan's brother. *Luis es un niño muy afortunado*, Luis is a very lucky boy.'

But Luna was not listening. She had just caught Ruy's eye. Dark brows knitted together, and she saw his jaw tense as he stared at her. In that look, she read the attitude of a man who liked his private life to remain private. Maybe he was the kind of man who preferred to keep his girlfriend apart from his friends. She felt herself colour under his gaze then, quick as a flash, she saw him regain his composure and his mouth twisted quizzically before he turned away again to look down at the indignantly squalling child as he followed the *gitana* out of the dwelling.

There was a large hollow in the ground next to the cave and a small fire had been lit alongside it. The matron poured water into it and Ruy immersed the child twice in the hole. He then held little Luis over the flame while enunciating a few words in *Caló* before giving him to his mother.

'He is bestowing upon him the gift of immortality,' Morena whispered, 'an old tradition that some of us follow and that will bring much luck to the child.'

Bestowing the gift of disease, more like, thought Luna. *For God's sake, Ruy! You're a doctor, you should know better.*

She could understand superstitious gypsies abiding by such archaic customs, but a qualified medic? What was he thinking? She recalled her Aunt Isabel's words: 'The mixed *gajo* and *Caló* blood that runs in Ruy's veins pulls him in different directions.'

A cradle made of bamboo was brought out. The matron handed Ruy three sprigs of garlic and three pieces of bread, which he placed underneath the mattress. Then, dipping his finger in the hot cinders, he marked the child's forehead with a semi-circular sign illustrating the moon.

As Luna watched, it was as if a stranger was performing these alien gestures. She felt so far removed from this culture of arcane symbolism and superstition … and separated from Ruy too. Could she ever feel a part of this? There she was, fretting about hygiene and birthing practices, while Ruy casually daubed dirt on the newborn. Yet she sensed an odd stirring inside too, as though some inner part of her was reaching out to it all, like a hungry sapling seeking the sun.

Morena was still explaining these rituals to her and she struggled to focus on the gypsy's words. 'The garlic and the bread are for the three goddesses of fate. *El Mèdico* has explained to us that this tradition we have comes from the ancient legends of Greece. The first goddess spins the thread of life for each person with her spindle, the second measures it with her rod, and the third determines when and how it should be cut. *El Mèdico* is very knowledgeable. *El es un hombre sabio y un curandero,* he is a wise man and a healer.'

Morena's jet-black eyes were shining bright as jewels as she spoke of Ruy. He seemed to inspire hero-worship, if not infatuation, in every woman Luna came across. She wondered how the gypsy men felt about that and if he was as popular with them as he was with the *gitanas.*

'He's been here most evenings this week, when he's not been at Sabrina's helping her out.' Morena smiled. 'He's a wonderful man, a true friend.'

Away on business? Luna recalled Charo's words and seethed inwardly to think that Ruy had been here, at the gypsy camp, carousing with his friends or – worse still – alone with that ravishing minx Sabrina, 'helping' her.

If Morena noticed the tightening of Luna's lips she didn't let on, but continued to explain matters. 'He has chosen for my nephew the name of Luis. That is the name he will be known by, but his parents have given him another, which will remain a secret so the devil will be deceived and will never know who the child is.'

Luna couldn't help smiling. The naïvety of these people beggared belief, yet she found their ways charming.

There was a short pause and then Morena, all of a sudden, took a new tack. '*El Mèdico* often comes here when he is troubled. Always running away from something,' she mused. 'It does his soul good to be among his gypsy brethren, as it does when he tends his herb garden.'

Luna couldn't help but wince at the thought that Ruy might be running away from her, from their growing intimacy. Intrigued, she asked: 'Where is it, this herb garden?'

Morena gave her a keen glance. 'It's about a mile up that way.' She pointed to a narrow path that Luna could just make out, snaking its way up into the wooded hills. 'You see? There.'

Luna nodded. 'Does he use the herbs to treat people in the camp?'

'Sometimes. Though we do have aspirin and antibiotics, you know.' Morena gave a throaty laugh. 'But yes, there are recipes for salves and poultices which La Pharaona passed on to Ruy, ones that have been used for generations. He's perfected her art and knows more about plant lore than anyone now, living or dead.'

Then as an afterthought: 'Sabrina knows some, but her mother realized that Ruy was the true apprentice, the one she'd been waiting for. Every healer, every shaman, seeks the one to whom they will pass their secrets, their power before they depart this world for the next. Like my mother Paquita passing her mantle to me. For La Pharaona, her natural successor was Ruy.'

As if by voicing his name Morena had managed somehow to summon Ruy, he now walked over to join them. Not once during the ceremony had he looked in Luna's direction, which in some ways had been a blessing because it had given her a chance to vaguely soothe her fractured feelings. She gave him a tight smile, while he greeted Morena with a hug. 'So the little chap has joined us at last!'

'He was a long time coming. Didn't want to leave Carmelita's belly, the lazy little *gitano*!'

Morena chuckled, then winked. 'I'd better leave you to it. They'll need my help preparing the food. You know each other, I see.'

Luna detected a world of knowledge in Morena's gaze. She wouldn't have been at all surprised had the gypsy fortune teller known exactly what was going on between her and Ruy, right from the time they'd first met at the costume shop – and not because Ruy himself had breathed a word about it. The *gitana* would not have needed him to. No, nothing would surprise Luna about this strange, earthy but ethereal woman.

For a moment she and Ruy stood silent while they watched Morena walk away to join the others, her colourful underskirt kicking out in a flash of red as she strode along.

'Luna, what a surprise! I didn't know you were also a friend of the gypsies.' If Ruy detected Luna's pique, he didn't show it. Instead, he leaned his head towards her. 'Just another thing we have in common,' he whispered in her ear.

'I don't think so.' Her voice was clipped. 'I'm beginning to think there's very little we have in common.' She kept her attention focused on Morena, who was spooning something from a great big cooking pot into a gaudy earthenware bowl. Luna hardly dared look into his eyes again, fearing he would see the hurt and longing she was feeling just being near him again.

Ruy's tone changed, all pretence at humour now gone. 'I'm sorry I've been elusive,' he murmured. 'I know how it must look to you. A stronger man would have called you, sent you a message this week. But I'm not a strong man at the moment, Luna. The truth is I had to stay away from you.'

She looked up at him sharply. 'Really? Why is that? Did you have better things to do, other than being away on business, of course?' Wasn't that what men said when they were carrying on an affair? Luna tried not to think about the young gypsy siren again. She was acting like a jealous wife and the intensity of her feelings alarmed her.

Ruy dragged a hand through his hair. 'It's only the evenings I've been here at the camp, Luna. My days have been filled with meetings outside Cádiz. I did arrange them on purpose so that I wouldn't be in the office and see you every day, though. What I said to you at the concert was true, I can't control how I feel around you.' The blueness of his eyes was like bright lasers, and she couldn't speak, couldn't think. 'I had to get my head together before I got in touch again. I didn't want to say the wrong thing, do the wrong thing.'

Luna took a breath and bit back a sarcastic comment. What he'd said, and the earnest manner in which he said it, gave her pause. 'I ... I think I understand what you're saying ...' She found herself stammering a little; she always felt uncomfortable talking about her feelings. 'Let's not dwell on it. Apology accepted.'

Ruy smiled and exhaled with obvious relief. He gestured towards his surroundings. 'Being here has made me see things clearly,' he said, and she could sense him relax again. 'And, for a moment at least, with little Luis coming into the world, all other concerns seemed to melt away.'

'Except the medical ones, clearly.' She couldn't help the acerbic remark. 'Ritual is one thing, but where were the standard birthing hygiene measures for that baby? You're supposed to be a doctor, for heaven's sake, not a voodoo sorcerer!'

'Don't be angry with me, *chica.*' He tweaked her cheek, and laughed. 'What I did couldn't harm the child.'

Luna huffed. 'Dunking him in muddy water? You're joking!'

Half irritated and half bemused by her antics, he gave her a quizzical smile. 'Have you looked at the hole?'

She threw back her head defiantly. 'No, why?'

Was it anger that darkened his face?

'I wouldn't judge before you have the facts, Luna. If you had, you'd see that the hole is tiled and the water was clean and warm.'

She felt the wind taken out of her sails somewhat, but her chin was still set at a stubborn angle.

'You should be trying to educate them, not encouraging these weird superstitions dating from the Middle Ages,' she retorted provocatively.

'I'm afraid tunnel vision is not my forte.'

Luna glared at him. 'Are you accusing me of being narrow-minded?'

He returned her glare with a wicked smile. 'Yes,' he said softly. 'I believe I am.'

She caught that glimmer of laughter in his eyes. Miffed, her lips compressed, she gave him a furious look. Just who did he think he was?

He smiled sardonically, obviously reading her mind. 'One day we'll have to sit down and seriously discuss our differences like adults.'

Just then Morena interrupted their tête-à-tête and he was spared Luna's crushing answer. 'You must taste one of our gypsy delicacies,' the *gitana* said, addressing Luna as she held out a large tray of round cakes topped with sugar. 'They are called *jalluyo* and are made of flour, sesame seed, sugar and olive oil. The wine is homemade.'

Luna politely took one of the cakes, but refused the glass of bluish-black wine with dark glints of vermillion. Just as she was gingerly biting into the rock of brown dough, she met Ruy's mocking gaze.

'I promise it won't harm you. Well, maybe you'll break a tooth or two, but that's about it!'

His sarcastic comment was just what she didn't need. At every turn he seemed to accuse her of being uptight, strait-laced or narrow-minded and she'd had enough. She was worn out; it had been a long day. Here she was, among a group of gypsies all talking at the top of their voices in a strange language that she couldn't fathom, with a man who insisted on following her every move with ironical eyes, scrutinizing her, judging her. Where was the closeness she thought they had shared at the concert now? She felt torn between the sudden need to cry, and wanting to stomp off.

Just then a giant of a man with tousled long black hair ambled over and slung a muscled arm around Ruy's shoulders. His garish T-shirt barely contained his massive torso and Luna couldn't help thinking of a fairy-tale giant, making her even more acutely conscious of the strange otherness of the camp, a place and a people completely out of her ken.

He gave a slight nod of greeting. 'You must be the lovely Luna that Ruy's told me about.' His eyes weren't overly warm as he surveyed her.

Luna didn't know what to say, other than to make a retort that she might regret, so she remained silent. One part of her was quietly glad that Ruy hadn't after all been keeping her presence in his life secret from his gypsy friends.

'Luna, this is my best friend, Chico,' Ruy broke in quickly, throwing a warning glance at the huge man.

'Well, enjoy,' said Chico, raising the gourd he was carrying in his left hand to his mouth and taking a swig. 'There's a feast being prepared, and it mustn't go to waste.'

With a last speculative look at Luna, he walked off, and she almost fancied she could feel the ground shake beneath her feet as he did so.

Luna turned to Ruy, glancing at her watch. 'It's time for me to go,' she said in a decisive tone. 'I must get back before dark.'

'You can't leave now, Luna. The *zambra*, the party to honour the newborn child, has barely started. They'll take it as an insult if you go.'

'Well, I'll just have to live with that. I've parked my car in town and it's a long walk. I'll never find my way if I don't leave now.'

'I'll give you a lift.'

'No, thank you. I …'

The rest of the phrase died on her lips as toasts were raised and the frenzied thrumming of guitars started up, punctuated by *olés* and *andes*. While Ruy and Luna had been talking, mats, chairs and cushions had been placed outside the cave for the audience, with the *quadro flamenco* in one corner.

Ruy's fingers closed on her arm in a grip that brooked no argument. 'Come, let's sit down. Don't worry, I'll give you a lift back to your car tonight. You really can't go now.'

'But I must …'

'Don't be so argumentative.'

Argumentative? *Her?* The cheek of the man! She wasn't going to have a fight here. Anyhow, she was tired; all this bickering was wearing her out.

They moved towards the gathering of *gitanos* and, silently, she let herself be led, his very nearness causing her every nerve to quiver with discomfort. God, he was much too close! Her breasts tingled, her stomach churned, her heart knocked against her ribs. A fragrance floated towards her, making her head swoon – a combination of spice, musk and mint that characterized him so well. It was his scent; she would recognize it anywhere. Her throat felt parched and she swallowed hard, praying for this uneasiness to subside. She didn't want to give herself away. He must never guess how vulnerable she was with him, how much she had needed him – wanted him – this past week when he had clearly decided to make himself scarce.

Night was beginning to fall. Luna watched as the sky became a greenish-blue with a few purple puffy clouds shot with golden tints. Gradually the camp became shrouded in darkness, wrapped up in the veil of night against the clear sky. The moon and stars became visible and more braziers were lit. In the glowing light of the flames, there was something unearthly about these people, these gypsies with their long unkempt hair, coarse swarthy features and magnificent dark and deep-set woeful eyes. Clinging desperately to their primitive ways, they sang and danced to forget their misery. It all combined to give an overpowering sense of unreality and Luna felt as though she was in an epic dream. She decided to give in to it; give herself to the power of this strange and time-honoured revelry, to let Ruy guide her through whatever arcane rites she might be witness to or, indeed, be required to face.

As the night progressed and the wine kept flowing, so the fiesta became noisier. Men and women capered and jumped in the air like mythical fauns, or tapped their feet with eyes half closed, while others performed the *toque de palmas* – the famous hand clapping – or snapped castanets. All the while, there was the eternal stamping, stamping, stamping of feet, which made the already disorientated Luna feel positively giddy.

Now, gypsy girls with rouged lips and cheeks, in brightly coloured dresses that hugged their waists and hips, took their place in the middle of the stage, one after another. They danced with arms raised above their heads, before moving spiralling hands down their quivering bodies in graceful undulating movements. The audience was growing raucous, everyone drinking, dancing and laughing, loudly joining in the choruses as if they had not a care in the world.

Luna's mind and body felt inexorably drawn into the whirling noisy maelstrom, wholly sensitized, as if her nerve-ends were electric somehow. She was also painfully aware of the man sitting beside her. He was close, so agonizingly close. From the corner of her eye she noticed his tanned bronze face turning every now and then in her direction, his blue gaze scrutinizing her thoughtfully.

He was going to give her a lift back to where she'd parked. The mere thought of being trapped alone in a car with him filled her with panic. What if he tried to kiss her? A sudden warmth flooded her body. Wouldn't it be exactly what she needed, everything she had been aching for? No, it wouldn't, a voice at the back of her mind castigated. How could she untangle the snarl of different emotions she was feeling? There was no logical reasoning or explanation she could whip up against a force so powerful that her whole being trembled with the intensity of it. She sighed.

Immediately she felt his hand on her arm.

'Tired?' he whispered softly in her ear.

She shook her head without looking at him.

'Next, it will be my turn to sing. We can't leave yet.'

Her heart fluttered like a captive butterfly. 'You're going to sing?' she uttered, breathless, as memories of another time when he had sung rushed back. She looked up at him with wide amber eyes that were unable to hide her feelings.

'Yes, I'm going to sing a ballad for you, just for you, beautiful Luna.' His bedroom eyes beckoned and the seductive whispered words were full of promise. When he left his seat to take his place in the middle of the *quadro flamenco*, Morena came and sat next to Luna.

As Ruy's powerful sultry voice rose into the night, the atmosphere around him trembled and stirred. Time stood still while Luna was caught up in the magical quality of the tender melody. The melancholy notes floated towards her, making every nerve-end vibrate, releasing her mind from the anxiety and stress that had beset her these past few days, stealing it away to a dreamland where their souls were one. Every note seemed to be a pure expression of love and passion, one that the singer wanted to remain forever engraved in the heart of his intended. Every girl's eyes in the camp were feasting on the handsome singer, no doubt imagining what it would feel like to be the object of such adoration. How could Luna ever feel secure in his regard – whatever that was – when Ruy was such a magnet for every other hot-blooded woman around?

When the song ended, she met his gaze and although he was surrounded by gypsies hailing him cheerfully, she was aware of the tension flowing from him to her, a kind of wild expectancy that was almost tangible. Her pulse quickened and her gaze tried to skitter away from his, but he held her suspended, anticipating and captive. Once more, her doubts melted away in the fire of his stare. In the midst of a crowd they were alone in the world, each knowing what the other was thinking; each lost in the fierce emotion between them.

Morena flashed a friendly smile at Luna. '*El Mèdico* has eyes only for you, *señorita*, and you, you tremble when he looks at you,' she murmured.

Then she took hold of Luna's arm, and her features darkened. In the glowing light of the fire Luna saw the usually vivacious eyes glaze over in a glassy stare. She had witnessed this once before, at Mascaradas, and apprehension filled her as she tried to gently prise herself away from the gypsy's grip. Morena's fingers clutched her tightly, digging into her like a bird's claws. 'The electricity between you hovers in the air. It is suspended above your heads, menacing, and charged with foreboding.'

Once again, her voice had become cavernous and hoarse. 'Such a powerful passion is dangerous. It can cause the earth to tremble and volcanoes to erupt.' She paused for a moment and then, closing her eyes, raised her voice in a chant and recited an incantation, before ending gloomily: 'There is a full moon tonight and the moon is a jealous goddess. Sooner or later, she will claim her share and you will pay for it with your tears.'

Morena blinked as if shaking something off, then rummaged in her pocket. 'Do not despair,' she said, taking Luna's hand and slipping into it what felt like a warm smooth pebble. 'This charm will guard you from the evil spirits. It will induce calm and peace within your troubled heart. It has mystic powers, but must stay buried in your heart. Wear it against your breast, but never tell anybody of its origin. No permanent harm will come to you as long as this magic jewel is with you.'

Luna smiled awkwardly, noting this was the second time that the gypsy had warned her, but she refused to dwell on the thought. 'Thank you, Morena, I will take good care of it,' she promised. She did not really believe in this hocus-pocus nonsense, she told herself, but she was sensitive to the gypsy's kindness and hospitality. After all, she had been included in a family celebration without any reticence or prejudice. In return, why not give the benefit of the doubt to these people?

They embraced and Morena moved away just as Ruy, having freed himself from his effusive fans, walked towards them.

'I didn't know you had friends among the gypsies.'

'Morena sold me the Moon Queen costume.'

'Ah yes, at Mascaradas,' he said, the glimmer of a memory lighting his eyes. 'She's engaged to Chico, you know. I'll introduce you properly to him after the dancing has finished. He's not the growling giant he seems, I promise.'

They paused to watch as the music started up again and dancing couples began to twirl once more in a flurry of clapping and singing.

Ruy nodded towards them. 'One thing about gypsies, they know how to celebrate. Have you enjoyed your evening?' he asked courteously.

'Very much. I think people were a little suspicious of me at first but Morena was very kind.'

'You know what they say about gypsies? They make wonderful friends and formidable enemies.'

Luna said nothing, although for an instant her mind flicked to the memory of Chico's glowering face.

'Have you ever tried it before?' Ruy smiled at her quizzically.

She gave him a blank look. 'Tried what?'

'Dancing flamenco.'

Luna let out a nervous laugh. 'Sadly, no, but it's fascinating to watch. I can't boast any experience of that side of my Spanish heritage.'

'We'll have to remedy that then,' Ruy murmured.

She looked suddenly taken aback. 'I would have to drink quite a bit of sangria for that ever to happen, and even then, your feet wouldn't be safe from my lack of rhythm.'

He looked at her through a wayward lock of dark hair. 'I think you have very good rhythm, Luna.'

She swallowed lightly at the look in his eye.

'Come, Luna, let's dance.'

'What now? I've never danced flamenco before. Please, Ruy, I can't. Not in front of all these people!' Luna protested.

His hand was outstretched and she paused a moment, meeting his spirited gaze.

'I promise you can even step on my toes if you want to.'

She reluctantly took his hand and Ruy pulled her with him in one swift movement to where the gypsies were standing in a loose circle, in the middle of which dancers spun around each other. The velvet canopy of night hung above them, but all around was the orange haze of firelight and braziers. Spicy smells of

woodsmoke, tobacco and grilled chorizo wafted in the air, borne
by the faintest of warm breezes now that the heavy heat of the
day had eased. Two guitarists were now strumming fast chord
progressions alongside the percussive beat of tambourines, and
the syncopated rhythm of hand clapping and fingers snapping.
There were various couples, young and old, all stalking and
twirling around each other with abandon, hands weaving above
their heads. The tassels on the women's shoulders and bodices
flew around in colourful arcs as their dresses shimmered in the
firelight. Dancers held on to each other and turned this way and
that to the loud chorus of voices wailing in unison around them,
goading them on with whoops and cries of '*Olé*!'

As she watched the vivid spectacle, Luna could feel the enticing
beat of the music seeping into her, despite her reluctance to join
in. This was better than any live show of flamenco she had seen
back home in California. She sensed Ruy standing close behind her.

'Shall we?' he murmured.

Her stomach gave a little jump and she spoke without turning
round. 'I'm not sure if I can do this. I need to see how to count
out the steps first.'

The smile was audible in his voice. 'You don't need to count
anything, Luna. My father taught my mother to dance flamenco.
I will do the same for you. Just relax and trust me.'

Luna almost laughed. *Wasn't she always trying to do that?*

His breath was warm in her ear and he stood so close to her
that she almost leaned into him though, for some reason, it was
hard to look at his face.

Ruy placed his hands on her shoulders and turned her round
towards him, forcing her to meet his eyes. 'Don't be nervous
with me, Luna.' His gaze was as tangible as the heat from the fire.
'Open your heart and let out your passion. This is Spain, these
are your people. Just let go.' The music pulsated around them as
he lifted her hand and gently closed her delicate fingers into a

fist, wrapping his own, strong and dexterous, gently around it. His eyes were like liquid blue fire as he held her clenched hand between her breasts. 'Feel it here.'

Luna's heart was thumping so hard beneath his fingers she thought it would burst. Ruy led her into the throng of dancers and immediately sent her into a spin with just a flick of his wrist. She had no time to think; she could only react, following his lead. For a moment she almost collided with his broad chest, but his steadying hand caught her effortlessly at the waist and held her tight.

'Just follow where I take you,' he murmured, lifting one arm into the air, his mouth just inches from hers.

He moved around her in a circle while his hand held her waist, his other arm bent behind his back, then turned her in a figure of eight. She was painfully aware of his lithe, muscular frame as it brushed against her. He stepped back, spreading his arms wide and high, then bringing his hands down to his waist. Then he nodded at her to do the same and she obeyed, echoing his gestures, transfixed by the electricity between them.

Luna found that she had remembered some of the movements she had seen the other women make, and started to move instinctively, gyrating her hips gently and raising her arms more expressively than before. Ruy's eyes widened in appreciation, his gaze sliding fervently down her body, and Luna found herself basking in the hunger she could feel emanating from him. All embarrassment melted away and a liberating wave of emotion carried her higher and higher as the music and clapping crescendoed.

Ruy now moved one foot in front of the other, proudly stamping out the steps with the heel of his boots, each arm coming down to his waist as he moved, one jet-black lock of hair falling moodily in front of his brow as he did so. He was pure gypsy, Luna thought. It was the most sexual, mesmerizing thing she had ever seen.

Ruy took both her arms now, lifting them above her head and holding them in place as he let his hands glide down the sides of her body. Luna's breath caught in her throat and heat fired in her core. For a moment her eyelids fluttered closed as her head tipped back. She was in Ruy's arms again, as she had been at the masked ball, and nothing felt more natural. His masculine power overwhelmed her.

While they danced, Ruy's eyes never left her face, often sliding down to her mouth and remaining there while his hand held her waist, his body moving against hers to the insistent rhythm of the music. His gaze was intoxicating, searing her like blue lightning and her head span with the delicious pleasure of it. There was nothing but the music and the fierce longing she saw in his eyes and the heat of their desire.

As the music came to a triumphant conclusion, Ruy sent Luna into one last spin and then drew her against his muscled body, crushing her breasts to him. Her breathing was laboured against his chest, which was rising and falling rapidly in tandem with hers. His eyes left her mouth and, without speaking, they were locked in an intense gaze as if all the words of passion and emotion they had for one another were struggling to express themselves in that moment and could not.

Luna tried to steady her deep, trembling breath. She brought herself to her senses, and pushed gently at Ruy's chest, taking a step back from him, though in helpless thrall to those riveting blue eyes. Exhilarated and disorientated by the wash of fire still sweeping her body after their dance, her mind was stupefied.

Ruy led her to a log that had been fashioned into a rudimentary bench. They sat a moment in silence, each recovering from the dance. It took a while for Luna's heart to slow its thunderous beating; her emotions were in such disarray.

Finally she managed to speak. 'Thank you for the dance,' she whispered, letting the polite words cover the confusion mixed with naked longing that was still assailing her.

Just then, Morena and Chico emerged from the onlookers, arms around one another. Chico looked altogether softer, no longer the boorish ogre of before. When he spoke to Luna now, his voice was warm, if a little slurred. 'You two dance as if you were made for each other,' he said. 'There's no Herrera can dance like that, I'm certain. You must be a changeling after all.'

Luna blanched at the mention of her family. Ruy was quick to intervene.

'No talk of Herreras,' he said, leaning over to cuff his friend, before turning to Luna, his eyes glittering softly. 'Let me get us some water. You stay here and get to know my blood brother.'

'You know, Luna,' said Chico when Ruy had walked off, arm in arm with Morena, 'I owe you an apology.' He sat down heavily beside her with a gourd of wine and his great craggy face was a picture of regret, enhanced no doubt by the quantity of alcohol he'd imbibed.

'You don't have to say that,' said Luna, flushing slightly.

'Thing is, I thought you'd be just another of those no-good Herreras,' he said. 'And that was wrong of me, *muy equivocada*. When Ruy told me who you were, I thought you might be *mala suerte*, bad luck for him. We have a saying: the seed never falls far from the tree – but that's rubbish. We can all escape the cards we're dealt at birth.'

'You were just trying to protect your friend,' said Luna. 'That's only natural. He's a lucky man to have you looking out for him.'

'No, it's me who should be grateful. I know Ruy would risk his life for me without a second thought. That's the kind of man he is,' Chico replied fervently. 'That's what it is to be blood brothers.'

Luna was instantly curious. 'I heard Morena and Ruy both call you that. What does it mean exactly?'

'He hasn't told you? It happened when I was sixteen, Ruy was ten.' Chico took a gulp of wine from the gourd and settled into his story. 'I used to do some work for his family at El Pavón, a bit of this and that, mostly in the gardens. Anyway, one day he saw me pinch his mother's Cartier watch. She'd left it by the swimming pool.' He waved his hand dismissively. 'It was a stupid dare from one of the other kids at the camp, who was jealous I'd got the job. Next thing I knew, Ruy was riding his bike like a crazy devil into our camp. He told me the police had come, that his mother had said I'd been the only person in the garden that morning.'

'What happened next?'

'He said I'd better give him the watch as the police would come searching. Then he took it and rode off. I found out later that he'd taken it back to his house and put it in the cupboard under the sink in his parents' bathroom.'

'And the blood brothers' thing?' asked Luna.

'After that I went looking for Ruy. I needed to show my thanks. He saved me from screwing up my life. I found him in his garden and we performed the rite. It's a time-honoured ritual that us *gitanos* would defend with our lives. I cut both our palms with my *navaja*, my knife, then pressed them together to let the blood mix.'

At this Luna just managed to stop herself from mentioning that they could have caught hepatitis or any number of infections. In her mind's eye she could imagine Ruy intuiting her thoughts with his customary knack, and regarding her with his gently mocking twinkle.

Once on the subject of Ruy there was no stopping Chico. 'Ruy may be only a quarter *gitano* but he's as much a gypsy as any of us, *pueden pulgas comer mis ojos,* and may fleas eat my eyes if I'm wrong. As a kid he was like a sponge, absorbing our ways, all our lore. Every spare moment he had, he'd be tearing off to our camp. Exploring the sea caves.' He gave a booming laugh. 'That boy never did care what the *gajo* world thought of him.'

'I can see that,' said Luna reflectively. 'Otherwise he wouldn't have chosen to pursue his line of work.'

'That's right.' Chico gave a hiccup and tapped his chest with a massive fist. 'He's always followed his star. When I was a youngster I just wanted to have a laugh, bit of work here and there … partying whenever it suited me. Ruy's not like that. He wanted to make a difference, see.'

'Yes, I suppose I do.' And she did, she realized. Ruy, whom she had found so devilish at times, was still a man full of compassion, loyalty and integrity. A man who was laying siege to her heart, though if she allowed herself to fall in love with him she could well regret it bitterly.

'I hope Chico hasn't been divulging all my secrets,' came a deep voice behind them. Ruy was back. 'He's got a loose tongue when he's had a bit of manzanilla.' He grinned at Luna, who took the glass of water he offered her and drank it straight down gratefully.

Chico rested the gourd clumsily on his knee, peering up at his friend. '*Hermanito*, you know what they say. *Para todo mal, manzanilla, para toda bien, tambien.* For every ill, drink manzanilla. For everything good, as well. *Salut!*'

Luna stood up. 'I really think we should be going,' she said.

'Come on, my friends,' said Chico, pulling his great weight off the bench. 'The night is still young! There's plenty left in the barrel. Stay and see the sun rise. It's not every day a babe's head is wetted.'

Luna was grateful that Ruy didn't join his friend in insisting she stay. Instead he agreed that it was time to leave, and was smilingly firm with Chico, who staggered to his feet and raised his gourd to them both. 'All right then. In that case, I'm going to see what Morena is up to. I want a dance with my woman.'

As Chico bade them farewell and went back to join the revellers, Ruy crossed his arms. 'Did Chico give you a hard time about being a Herrera?' he asked, the casualness of his tone belied by the slight shifting of his weight from one foot to the other.

'He apologized, actually,' said Luna. 'In not so many words, he said I wasn't, as far as he could tell, a chip off the old block.'

'He didn't say anything else?' There was still a tautness about Ruy, Luna could sense it. What was it that he was hiding? Something that Chico was aware of, evidently. Once more, disquiet curled its tendrils around her heart, squeezing it uncomfortably.

'Nothing you should be worried about.' Luna gave a short laugh that was somewhat forced, uneasy. 'Look, I realize my being a Herrera must be difficult for you. Maybe your family's not best pleased … but you must know that my mother was nothing to me, and I was nothing to her. I don't like a single one of the Herreras, and that's that.'

A look of surprise, relief even, crossed Ruy's face. 'Luna, is that what you're dwelling on? Listen, I don't care who your family is.' His gaze was intense. 'You mustn't think we're judging you in any way. For God's sake, we're hardly ones to talk. There's never been a lack of feuding in our family. My grandmother, Marujita, the gypsy queen, fought tooth and nail to bring down Salvador and Luz. I've got the blood of bitter rivals coursing through my veins already.'

It was the first time that the subject of her family had been raised, and Luna felt as if a burden had been lifted from her shoulders. She smiled, relieved. 'You don't mind that I'm half Herrera then?'

'Luna, I wouldn't mind if you were half Martian.' He gave her a raffish grin, then suddenly changed the subject. 'Have you ever ridden a motorcycle?' he asked.

Luna frowned. 'No, why?'

They were walking now towards a low shed at the far end of the camp. 'Well, you're about to have your first ride.' He held open the rickety door for her as they stepped inside, and there it was: the latest model of a Ducati GT 1000 SportClassic in flaming red. Appalled, Luna's eyes widened in disbelief.

'Even though it's quite powerful, it handles confidently. You'll find it exciting to ride.'

She gave a little cry of alarm. 'I could never get on one of those things. Anyhow, I'm wearing a skirt.'

'Don't say "Fountain, I'll never drink from your water." It may be your only resort to quench your thirst.' His eyes moved over her in mischievous appreciation, his teeth flashing white as he grinned at her. 'Your skirt is short enough, you'll be able to straddle the bike without needing to lift it an inch.'

Colour flooded her face. 'Are you always this irritating?'

'And are you always this negative? Here, put on this helmet.'

'What about you?'

'I've got mine. This is a spare. I always keep an extra one just in case. You never know what might crop up … like tonight, for instance.'

Oh yes, she was convinced that he found countless occasions for women to wrap themselves around him. *Wrap themselves around him? Was that what she was going to have to do?*

Luna stiffened and drew away from Ruy as he tried to help her with the helmet. 'I'm quite capable of doing this for myself,' she said quickly. She liked feeling in control, and being on the back of someone's motorbike represented the complete opposite. Then, just as suddenly, she was contrite, hating her snappish tone. 'Sorry, I'm just a little nervous.'

'Trust me, it's built primarily for security. It's really very comfortable.'

Trust *him*? She wasn't sure she was quite ready for that. Momentarily paralyzed, she stood helplessly gazing down at the machine.

Ruy sighed and rolled his eyes upwards. 'Come on, Luna, we can't stand here all night. Do you really want to spend it in a gypsy camp?'

When she didn't move, and without giving her time to protest, he suddenly lifted her up and sat her on the back seat of the motorcycle. Then he straddled it himself.

'Hold me tightly around the waist,' he commanded. 'The tighter you hold, the less chance you have of falling off.' He had put on his doctor's tone and sounded brisk and authoritative. She had heard him speak like that whenever a junior argued with him. At this point, she knew better than to cross swords and meekly fell into line.

Her pulse seemed to race out of control when she put her arms around him, her heart pounding as she pressed herself against his muscled back. Her hands rested at the base of his stomach, heralding the first swirling of physical arousal that could be heading in only one direction. She dared not move her fingers in case they slipped unintentionally over that part of him that had intrigued and fascinated her ever since the day on the beach when she had seen it outlined against his tight compression shorts, which, incidentally, had not compressed anything – the reverse if anything: the imprint had been quite flagrant. He was a potent, virile man, whom she was sure had found no difficulty in satisfying the hunger of the army of starving women that had graced his bed.

Her body was getting tenser by the minute. The cool night air caressed her burning skin, creeping under her cotton top and caressing her bare thighs. A shiver of excitement slid through her.

With only the moon to guide them, the motorbike roared through the darkness. The jealous moon, Luna thought, recalling the gypsy's words. At one point the bike bounced over a bump in the road, jerking her forward against him and making her linked hands slide down, almost skimming the top of his crotch. The powerful shudder that ran through him sent a current up her body; he stiffened as the tips of her fingers brushed his throbbing bulk, and through his jeans she could feel him hard with desire. The awareness of his need sent her senses wild, stimulating her imagination and provoking the inevitable.

She closed her eyes. The seat she was straddling was hard; it rubbed against her, the vibrations of the engine shooting through her middle, stimulating the core of her desire. Despite herself, she tightened her embrace and pressed herself against him. Luna could feel his longing for her growing, pushing hard against his denims. She envisaged herself unzipping his jeans to relieve his agony, holding his hot virility and placing it just there …

The machine ground to a halt, jerking her back down to earth, and she opened her eyes, smothering a throaty sob as she realized once more she had been the victim of her fantasy. She was trembling; the coil deep in her loins was painful, her thoughts were jumbled.

Ruy turned a fraction. 'Where are you parked? he asked, without taking off his helmet.

'In a little side street, off Calle Ancha in the old town,' she whispered, almost inaudibly. Had he been aware of what had happened to her? She knew he wanted her just as much; that, at least, had not been an illusion: bodies didn't lie. Maybe he had been dreaming too of … The need for him was still pulsing dangerously under her skin; she swallowed back her agony. She could see her car; they had arrived.

'We're here,' she said, trying to sound normal, but wishing they still had a long way to go.

He parked the motorcycle on the side of the deserted narrow street. Not a soul in sight. Shutters were closed. The moon threw silvery beams on to the whitewashed walls of the buildings, creating an eerie atmosphere of light and shadow.

The engine stopped and Ruy got down from the motorcycle before helping Luna off. He removed his helmet. 'Was it so bad?' he asked, searching her face, his gaze running over it, judging her mood.

She shook her head, unfastened her helmet and gave it to him, evading his brooding stare.

He clenched his hands into fists against his sides as though to stop himself from reaching out and pulling her against him.

Their gazes clashed. Her eyes were bright and provocative as she felt a faint shiver run through her, completely intoxicated by his closeness. He looked at her with such passion that her own desire leapt up to meet his. They moved closer as if in a dream. Something tripped inside her; more confusion flooded her mind. She faltered and he was quick, so quick he did not give her a chance to rebuff him.

He drew her against him, squeezing her so close it left her breathless. Then he tilted his head towards her, running his thumb over her sensitive lips and, as he felt them quiver under his touch, he very gently took her mouth with his.

'You taste so sweet, so good,' he whispered as he moved to her eyelids, down to her cheekbones and to her throat. Her curves, soft and yielding, were moulding into his hardness.

They were swept along by a force stronger than themselves and could not help it. Stirred by the hunger that had consumed them for days, a hunger increased by delay and the romance of the moon in the velvety sky, passion was finding a way out. They became a part of the beautiful silver night – aware only of themselves, loving and kissing, wrapped in each other's arms in a world of their own.

He slipped his hands under her blouse. The searing heat of his palms when they found her breasts made her cry out his name, begging for release. 'Make love to me, Ruy,' she pleaded, blood burning like fire in her veins.

Her words made him groan low in his throat. His head dipped further down, and using his hands, his lips and his tongue he massaged and licked and nibbled at the pink aureoles around her nipples, until the twin peaks were hard as little rocks and she was moaning her pleasure aloud, urging him on, yearning for the fulfilment he could bring her.

Then he hesitated. Looking swiftly around him, making sure there was no one about, he dropped to his knees, pulled up her skirt, and in one swift gesture peeled off her panties.

Luna knew she should pull away, stop him in his tracks, but longing, passion and need alienated her will and all rationality was thrown to the wind. She leaned fractionally against the motorcycle and spontaneously parted her legs a little to allow him in. Her eyes closed and she gasped as his fingers went in search of her desire. They were cool against the burning brand of her soft, moist inner flesh.

He dropped his head and she felt him press his face against the quivering triangle of hair between her thighs, delighting in the warmth of his skin against her own most sensitive part. Showering feverish kisses first on her lower belly and then moving down between her legs, his marauding mouth and fingers roamed mercilessly, making every nerve in her body throb, creating a rapturous feeling that made her moan softly.

'You make me lose my mind …' he whispered, his voice ragged with the thick ache of his desire. 'Luna, my beautiful Queen of the Night … you taste so sweet, you're so soft, so wet and inviting … I want to kiss you, stroke you … love you until you forget your own name.'

He delved deeper, fuelling the flames within her and, finding her throbbing impatient core, he brushed his lips gently against it, drawing from her a sob of rapture as he taunted her need, his tongue trailing teasingly around her swollen lips.

She was only vaguely conscious of what he was doing to her and too absorbed in the erotic molten pleasure that was flooding her to be embarrassed.

'Faster, yes, Ruy, don't stop,' she moaned deliriously while she buried her hand in his black mane, curling her fingers around the silky strands, tugging at them mercilessly in rhythm with every probe of his tongue. The more she cried out her pleasure the quicker he stroked, fondled and licked. It was not long before she shuddered and convulsed as the explosion of her climax ripped a cry from the depths of her that resounded through the silent night. Cupping the soft round cheeks of her bottom, he gathered her closer to him, supporting her trembling frame while the powerful spasms raked through her body.

CHAPTER 11

For a long while Ruy held her tenderly in his embrace, encircling her hips and bottom with his powerful arms and caressing her back, whispering loving words against the soft curve of her belly. Breathless, Luna trembled from head to toe, her knees barely supporting her as the waves of bliss pulsating through her body faded. Her fingers were still twisted in his hair and now she let her hand drop to her side.

In the aftermath of their intimacy, once he released her, neither spoke; they just studied each other solemnly for a few seconds in the moonlight: Luna ill at ease and Ruy a little subdued. He walked her silently to her car and followed on his motorcycle until he saw she was safely home.

They were both too overwhelmed to say much but, as they stood at the door to La Gaviota, Ruy lifted her chin with a single finger, his eyes shining in the silvery shadows of the night. 'One day soon, Luna,' was all he said.

'Ruy, I …' How could she put into words the melange of sweetness and shame that suffused her, making what had felt fluent and natural – loving even – suddenly seem awkward?

He silenced her gently by a sweep of his thumb against her bottom lip. 'Let's talk again when you've slept.'

After he'd gone, Luna shut the door and leaned back against it. She was dazed, embarrassed and amazed at herself. He had taken her by storm and she had enjoyed every moment of it. There had been no fear, no revulsion; no panic attack. She flushed bright red as she admitted to herself not only had she enjoyed it, she had bared herself to him wantonly. He had given lavishly and selflessly and she had taken with avidity, totally abandoning herself to the sensuous magic of his hands. Not just his hands – that beautiful mouth had done wicked things to her lustful body too.

Exhilaration mixed with guilt and confusion. There was no going back now. How could she ever reject him after what she'd just allowed to happen? Then again how could she not, without becoming just another number in the legions of women he'd conquered?

Most of all, how could she ever look at him in the eye again? No man had done that to her before; she had neither indulged in heavy petting with her boyfriends, nor had she ever touched herself intimately. The thought of it always filled her with shame and guilt.

She was acting like a bitch in heat. Luna flinched; the comparison struck her like a slap in the face. Though what else would you call someone who had behaved the way she had? Barely able to believe what she had let Ruy do to her, she recoiled with revulsion at her conduct. In hindsight, there was something degrading about the whole scene as it came back to her in all its vividness. Yet, at the time, all she had felt was unbelievable pleasure and nothing but wild desire for the man who had made her sob with ecstasy.

Luna closed her eyes and breathed deeply. This was a first for her, and would be the last – at least with him.

After he found out she had lied to him, Ruy would never want to see her again. Whatever the outcome of her article, whatever their family backgrounds, that much was true. The tangled web was growing tighter around her.

None of this was supposed to happen.

In the meantime, she would have to face him at work. Surely she was compromising her undercover role now? Maybe she could ask to be assigned to a different researcher; somehow find her way out of this job. Perhaps she could pack it all in and go back to the States and live quietly for a while; but that meant running away, not completing the job, and letting Ted down. Luna had always been a finisher – she had been brought up to see things through. Until she had completed the assignment, her future was not her own. Once she had delivered the article, she could go somewhere else and start a new life for herself. The irony was, she *had* finished the piece – she just couldn't yet bring herself to email it to Ted; perhaps because then her cover would be blown – there would be no going back. Her laptop was still open on the table where she had left it that afternoon, a reminder that her task was not yet completed. Luna pushed away from the door and moved across the room. She dropped her bag on the table and closed the lid of her computer thoughtfully.

Deep down she knew that after tonight, Ruy had only to snap his fingers for her to yield to him. She would be his until he chose to release her.

Luna stared out to sea, watching the dark waves hurl themselves on to the rocks edging the bay. Above the vast ocean, the full moon shone luminous and bewitching, primitive in its magic, as if reminding her of its power to bring out passion, savagery and love in all those who fell under its spell.

Her heart gave a lurch.

Was it love?

How could it be? She hardly knew the man. No, she argued, it wasn't love, simply hormones. Her senses were enslaved even though part of her had fought it ever since they'd met.

Like all the women who came into contact with him, she was intoxicated by the magnetism of his charming smile and the intensity of his vivid blue eyes. Yet, she admitted ruefully, something deeper drew her to Ruy. There was an aura about him, a certain way he had, that instilled admiration in Luna, despite herself; coupled with a faint vulnerability she could detect every now and again that touched her deeply, stirring a tender, wholesome feeling towards him, perhaps akin to love. Maybe that was it. It was as though love was constantly waiting around the corner, but something always stood in the way.

How would she have responded to Ruy's advances if the dark shadow of her past hadn't dogged her heels all these years, shaping her caution until it shut down a part of her? Like an insect caught up in a spider's web, struggling to survive, she was trapped in her own confused emotions – where lust and love, disgust and fear fought for supremacy. And if she gave in to this unprecedented feeling of desire, lost control of her heart, and risked loving and being loved …?

The price seemed too high.

She winced inwardly. What chance did she have? The more involved they became, the more he would hate her eventually when her time at the Institute was over. Ever since she had landed in Spain, she'd had the weird feeling of being in a dream. If only she could break through these romantic illusions and see clearly.

Luna's thoughts wandered back to the gypsies and to Morena's words. She remembered the stone the *gitana* had given her.

Going back into the house, she emptied her bag on the table. The amulet drew her eyes hypnotically. Strangely shaped, it was a golden-yellow rock crystal of sorts with a hole pierced through the middle. It was so bright and clear that it could almost be mistaken for a cognac diamond. The static charge Luna felt as she took it in her hand made her jump. She examined it under the light; it seemed to have a life of its own, as if some sort of energy was pulsing through it. The fragmented shades of colour seemed to shift as she stared into its depths, changing shape before her eyes. Was it her imagination or was that Ruy's face reflected there?

She shuddered. On impulse, she was tempted to throw the charm away, but something stopped her. Was she seriously entertaining the thought that it might bring her bad luck? Superstition is contagious, she mused, as she carefully tidied it away in her bag. Then, on second thoughts, and remembering the words of the *gitana*, she took it out of her bag again and hung it on the delicate gold chain that she had always worn around her neck since her sister Juliet had bought it for her in Italy many years ago.

For a moment she stared at it, remembering her half-sister with a sudden lurch of feeling. They had never been close as children, but a part of Luna wondered what kind of relationship they might have salvaged as adults. She had to acknowledge that Juliet had often been kind to her in her own capricious, sporadic way. It hadn't been her fault that their mother had chosen her over Luna. Didn't the fact that Luna had kept the gold chain close to her all these years mean something too? She held the chain with the pendant in her palm and closed her fingers over it.

Maybe Juliet's chain, together with the talisman, would help change her luck. Anything was possible.

A foolish thought perhaps, but Luna was past caring about what made logical sense. Ruy had upended her fragile existence – one she had always thought so steady, well ordered and invincible. Now look at her. Adrift, lost to the madness of love, or whatever this insane feeling was that had her in its grip.

Luna went to the bathroom, tore off her clothes and stepped into the shower. She let the warm water flow over her body, hoping against hope that it would lend her some clarity of thought. A clear conscience was another matter entirely.

*   *   *

Ruy drove back to the gypsy camp filled with turmoil at what had just happened. His head was full of Luna – her scent, her mouth, her breasts under his hands, the taste of her …

Once again, he'd completely lost control. No woman had done that to him before, though at least he had exercised some restraint. He could happily have gone a step further in the worked-up, carnal state he'd been in. It would have been so easy to take her home and make love to her; he doubted she would have resisted, given how overcome by passion she too had been. He could feel the pent-up craving within them both. It was as much as he could do not to take her there and then, up against his motorcycle.

But he had no doubt she was a virgin and he needed to talk to her, tell her everything, before he snatched her innocence. Perhaps it was the craziness of the full moon that carried them away, but he didn't want her to regret her impulsiveness in the morning. What was it about this woman that aroused in him these chivalrous feelings?

Ruy remembered his hesitation in that alleyway, asking himself if what he had in mind was too risky. Yet at that moment, with Luna hot and needy against him, he'd been compelled to have more of her. He hadn't cared about his own pleasure; instead, he wanted to make her climax, to feel her lose control again – the way she was making him take leave of his senses every time he touched her.

This was a first for him. Even as a randy adolescent he hadn't indulged in such out-in-the-open games – there had always been somewhere private to go. Still, it had been so easy; her skirt was short. Just the thought of what he could do to her had caused him momentarily to lose a sense of reality while he went down on his knees before her in the street, his own aching arousal pushing mercilessly against his clothing.

She had felt wonderful: soft, wet and burning hot.

He'd drunk in the warmth she radiated and inhaled the intoxicating scent of her arousal that mingled with the vague suggestion of fragrant soap. The feel of her fingers in his hair, the sound of her moans and her voice calling out his name had almost been his undoing. When she had cried out at the moment of her orgasm, the surge of happiness that had run through him was all he had cared about.

Luna was a passionate, sensual woman, only just beginning to discover the wonders of lovemaking. Despite her virginal innocence he suspected she would be wild in bed: unbridled and audacious. Being buried inside her would be paradise. One day soon he would possess her, he promised himself. He would be the first – and the last – man to thrill her. Luna was the one: the kindred spirit for whom he had been waiting, and she would be his forever.

Ruy exhaled heavily. A cold shower would rid him of this hot frustration. He didn't know what Luna was thinking now, and that merely increased his restlessness.

He slowed the bike at the edge of the *gitanos'* camp. The place was quieter now. Dotted about the scrubby quarry, dying fires glowed softly in the dark, half illuminating the shambolic aftermath of the night's revelry. Tethered goats butted pieces of rubbish with their horns, as well as the passing legs of a few *gitanos* only now staggering to their beds. Other men and women slept where they had fallen, empty bottles and gourds littering the ground around them; dogs lay motionless nearby, ears twitching. Faint sounds of babies squealing carried on the air, alongside the constant rasping of cicadas and the occasional bleat or bark of an animal.

Leaving his helmet and leather jacket on the bike, Ruy made his way along the main trail leading into the camp. He went straight over to the makeshift courtyard where Morena and Chico were sitting together around a low fire, sharing a pipe. Chico looked up at his approach. 'So, *hermanito*, you're back already.

Didn't expect to see you again until tomorrow.' He gave a crooked smile, his black eyes shining with amusement.

'Let's not go there.' Ruy dropped down on to an empty camping chair beside them.

Morena handed the pipe back to Chico and stirred the fire with a long stick, allowing the small flames to elongate. 'She's very beautiful, Ruy,' she said, eyeing him closely. 'Very troubled, too.'

Ruy sighed. 'Yes, I know, Morena.'

'She's a mystery to you, isn't she?'

He nodded, leaning forward to throw a piece of wood on the fire, watching as it caught. 'I don't know what's happening with me ... with us. She won't let me get close to her and yet there's something pulling us together.'

Chico snorted. 'Never thought I'd hear you say that about a woman, certainly not a Herrera! I can see for myself that this one's different, though.' He dragged on his pipe, letting the smoke blow out through his nostrils.

Ruy nodded. 'Yes, Luna's no Herrera. At least, she's nothing like the rest of them.'

A lizard skittered across the ground and Chico kicked it with his booted foot, cursing. '*La bicha*, the lizard. Not a good omen.' He looked up and met the eyes of his friend. 'When are you going to tell her about the accident?'

Morena dropped her stick. '*Ave María Purísima*,' she muttered under her breath. At the same time, she cast around for some iron to ward off the evil spirits the small creature might have brought with it, and touched a cold cooking pot beside her, containing the remnants of rabbit stew. 'Yes, Ruy, you must tell Luna.'

Ruy pushed a hand through his hair. 'I need to pick the right moment,' he said. 'I have to get closer to her first, otherwise she'll hate me when I tell her the truth.'

'Well, be careful not to leave it too late,' warned Morena. 'Your attraction to each other is destined, and fate will do its work, but you must play your part too if you're to come through the darkness together and avoid all hell breaking loose first. Destiny sometimes comes at a price.'

Chico joined in. 'Never mind destiny, *amigo*. Fact is you need to get on with it, sort it out. I can tell that this Luna, Herrera or not, has got you good. I've never seen you so worked up about a woman before. Just be careful.' He surveyed Ruy thoughtfully.

'Careful of what?' Ruy replied.

His friend drew heavily on his pipe and then spoke over the smoke. 'Her family, that's what.' He shrugged his massive shoulders. 'Luna might be different but nothing happens around a Herrera without trouble showing its face somehow.' The *gitano* stretched over to pick up a gourd, shook it, and found it was empty. He spat on the ground. 'But you might as well go for it – I know you will anyway. Just stop waiting for every last *cicada* to chirp. Worst case, you'll have a wound to lick, but that never killed anyone. Although, knowing the Herreras …'

'Hush, Chico,' Morena gave him a reproving shove. 'You think the path of love is easy? True love grows strongest where the path is stony and full of obstacles.' She arched an eyebrow. 'You should know better, *mi amor*.'

Ruy shot his friend a wry look. '*Sí, hermano*. If it was that simple, Morena here would never have let your sorry carcass near her in the first place. As it is, love is patient, as well as blind.'

Chico picked up a pine cone from the ground and flung it at Ruy, who dodged it, chuckling. 'You see, sometimes I'm right, too,' Ruy said.

The *gitano* emptied his pipe on the ground. 'I'm just saying, watch yourself. Her family is poison and you don't want them sticking their noses in your business. I admit, Luna doesn't seem like the rest of them.' He gave a lopsided grin. 'She certainly keeps you on your toes, and after the dull, forgettable women who've trailed after you and stroked your ego, I'm all for that.'

Ruy stretched out his long legs in front of him, crossing them at the ankles. 'Luna is more challenging than any other woman I've ever known. She's fiery, unpredictable … magnificent.' He smiled to himself. 'One minute, she's passionate and responsive and looks at me in a way that makes me think all my prayers have been answered. The next, she's angry, stubborn and defensive, as though she wouldn't throw water on me if I were on fire.'

Chico let out a deep, gravelly laugh. 'Like I said, she keeps you on your toes.'

'She doesn't know what she wants, that's all,' said Morena. 'You need to treat her gently, Ruy. Be honest with her, though, no matter how hard that is.'

Her knowing glance was enough to make Ruy gaze silently back at the fire.

Be honest.

More easily said than done. He had no idea what his next step should be, or when the right moment would come.

*　　*　　*

Luna woke late the next morning. The room was flooded with hot sunshine. Contrary to what she'd feared, she had slept heavily and soundly. She stretched her arms languidly and glanced at the alarm clock on her bedside table. Already twelve o'clock! She slid out of bed, pulled back the glass doors and walked on to the terrace. A summer mist blanketed the sea, which was as still and unsubstantial as a desert mirage.

In the sunshine, the confused and tortuous thoughts of the night had almost evaporated. She was feeling calmer and in better spirits; refreshed in the knowledge that this was a new day. Those problems that had seemed unsolvable last night seemed more in proportion in the bright, clear light of morning. She wondered what would happen now, but she wasn't agitated about it. Instead, she decided not to dwell on whether Ruy would call today, not to obsess about him and what he was thinking. Part of her wanted reassurance from him, to know that he hadn't thought her a wanton hussy, and yet she also wanted to be alone, to let things settle. If only she could feel like herself again rather than this fractured, impulsive version of Luna that gave her such disquiet.

She had to acknowledge that keeping secrets – ones in her past and in her present – had only made her feel worse, as if she were trying to walk on dangerous ground, fearful she might step into quicksand at any moment. Ruy had said they should have a serious talk one day; perhaps it was time to straighten things out between them.

As Luna turned back to the house, something caught her eye on the terrace table. Had Señora Sanchez left a little something for her? That immediate thought was dismissed when she saw what it was: a single white rose tucked into a sheaf of paper, weighted down by a rock from the beach. The gentle breeze was lifting one edge of the note in tiny flutters.

Luna's pulse lurched with tentative excitement. Moving over to the table, she took the note and unfolded it to read the contents.

Dear Luna

I'm sorry if things went too fast for you last night, but I'd be lying if I said I regretted any part of it. All my reason seems to evaporate when I'm with you. There's something between us that neither of us can deny. Whatever it is that is troubling you about being with me, we can fix.

Hard as it will be to stay away from you today, I suspect you need your space. Just know that you are never far from my thoughts.

Ruy

Luna's heart raced as fast as her mind. Picking up the rose and breathing in its strong, heady scent, she gazed thoughtfully at the vast blue ocean, glittering with infinite possibility under the bright sun.

Her stomach gave a little somersault at the thought of Ruy's eyes burning into hers, sometimes with tender warmth, other times with a fierce passion that ignited an answering blaze in her, scorching and uncontrollable.

Thoughts of his herb garden, that Morena had mentioned, drifted into her head. He had talked about taking Luna up into the hills himself one day. *I learned a lot from my wise gypsy friend and her herb garden*, he had said. Apparently it meant a great deal to him.

Why not go this afternoon?

She was suddenly filled with energy. First, she needed something to eat – after such a long sleep she was starving. Then she had planned to pick up some food at the market. After that she could have her walk, catching the rays of the late afternoon sun. *That's what I'll do*, she thought. *I'll find his garden.*

She chose a simple linen dress that came just above the knee and covered her shoulders. It was a pale mint colour that suited her delicate complexion and sheath of champagne-blonde hair, which she deftly tied in a ponytail ready for the hike ahead. She rustled up a quick meal made from the last of the chorizo and peppers in the fridge. As she washed her face, she noticed in the bathroom mirror how her skin glowed from the sun and how much healthier it seemed. It made her look younger somehow – less the efficient scientific researcher. This, together with her ponytail, gave her the air of a schoolgirl about to engage in a game of hopscotch or French skipping. Something indefinable in her expression had relaxed and opened and, for a moment, she blinked at her own reflection.

Luna had an instinct that once she had seen his herb garden, she might begin to understand Ruy better. His role as gypsy healer was integral to him, sparked by an inheritance, an almost sacred bloodline, which had shaped the man he was. Unless she appreciated the particularities of his healing role and its significance – the mantle his former gypsy mentor had bequeathed to him – she would never wholly get to the heart and soul of the man. The garden was as good a place as any to start.

While she was there she could gather some herbs and identify them later, with the help of the reference books Ruy had lent her. She might even analyze the more interesting ones at the lab. He wouldn't mind her showing some initiative, would he?

She sighed. Who was she fooling?

If Ruy was so attached to this place, his private sanctuary, she was also curious to see it for reasons that were wholly personal. It was a way of getting closer to him, even though she knew that doing so might be pure folly, but she didn't care. Now she was giving in to a spontaneous urge that took her by surprise but was liberating.

Walking past the table her laptop caught her eye again. She stopped and flipped the lid open. Taking a deep breath, she hit 'send'. The article had gone to Ted, it was in the lap of the gods now. 'Let's see what happens after this,' she murmured to herself.

A couple of hours later she set out, having been to the market and stocked up on some supplies, which she took home to her almost-empty fridge. She drove across to the mainland, past the small harbour and beyond, then parked under the shade of some olive trees and took the path Morena had pointed out. It snaked inland, away from the bay and towards the wooded part of the hills. She recalled exactly which path it was, remembering it zigzagging like a vivid silver scar over the hillsides. Before she set off, Luna clipped her small pack around her waist: it contained a bottle of water, a slim plant identification guide, her camera and a torch.

She took in the quiet beauty of the scene, spread like a feast in front of her eyes, and lifted her face to the sun, letting its

warm beams permeate her skin. Whatever was said about the
dangers of ultra-violet rays, it felt good. The air was soft but
warm. She climbed up the winding path through the wildest and
most stunning scenery, with little white cottages strewn here and
there like glistening pearls in the afternoon sun. Although from a
distance the hills presented an appearance of bare rock, she found
that trees, shrubs and wild flowers were in abundance there, and
she stopped several times to examine one plant or another. Some
she knew, others were unfamiliar and not even referenced in her
book of plants and herbs.

Cork oaks grew far and wide, offering shelter to a colony of
magpies, which flitted from tree to tree. Evergreens, with their
dark foliage and gnarled and stunted trunks, looked almost
as ancient as the huge boulders of grey granite and sandstone
that lay scattered along the way, which Luna guessed must
offer convenient hideaways for a host of insects, birds and wild
animals. She looked out for a white vulture or black eagle, both
of which her guidebook had indicated might be seen here,
having ventured from the sierra to make this place their habitat,
but she was out of luck. From time to time she came across
large patches of sweet-smelling wild flowers: pink mallows,
red and purple poppies, yellow spiny broom, white daisies.
Bees and butterflies in ephemeral colours she never dreamt
existed fluttered in the gold light of early evening. In the placid
countryside with its lengthening shadows, there was an almost
unearthly stillness.

Already low in the sky, the sun was gilding the stunted olive
groves. The solitude and the sound of the wind whispering among
the trees in the fading light of dusk caught at the strings of Luna's
heart and tears welled up in her eyes. The melancholy beauty of
her surroundings was breathtaking. Suddenly a wave of longing
washed over her: a desire to be loved and cared for that was almost
an ache, the sort of love only a man could satisfy. All at once she

found herself wishing that Ruy were there to share the magic and serenity of the place.

She glanced at her watch. It was almost eight and she hadn't yet found the herb garden. She ought to think of starting back, maybe save it for another day. It would not be a good idea to be wandering alone in these wooded hills after dark. Already she had been walking for a couple of hours so it would take her a good while to retrace her steps, even though much of her route would be downhill.

Nevertheless, it didn't turn out to be as simple as she had predicted. At some point Luna realized that she must have taken a left fork, when she should have chosen a right, and now her route was looking wholly unfamiliar. At first, though irritated that she hadn't done the sensible thing and brought a map, this didn't overly concern her as she could tell by the position of the rapidly sinking sun that she was walking in roughly the right direction. So long as the sun and the sea were to the right of her she couldn't go far wrong, could she? But now the path bore her sharply to the left, into a stretch of pine woods that she hadn't come through earlier, and she was finding it increasingly difficult to keep a safe footing on the carpet of pine needles, criss-crossed by snaking roots. She berated herself for coming out here on a mere whim and not planning the route more meticulously with her usual sense of caution.

Darkness was gathering about her, a gloom that was felt rather than seen, and a distant rumble echoed through the hills. There was a sudden chill in the air and she lifted her head to the sky. An ominous black confusion of thunderclouds was moving in swiftly in a rolling formation directly above her. As she advanced through the wood, the solitude she had appreciated earlier now made her shiver with trepidation, and she found the sound of the wind whispering among the pines positively eerie. The density of the foliage and the cloud cover was such that she could no longer get her bearings at all. Where was the path of cork oaks she had come through on the way up?

Luna was so busy looking around her, trying to gauge where she was but not paying attention to where she was placing her feet, that she stumbled and fell. She found herself skidding on her heels down a steep slope that lay to one side of her path. Coming to rest at the bottom, and about to pull herself upright, her ears picked up a sound. She paused a moment, listening.

Above the soughing of the wind in the pines, she could definitely hear a voice: the crystalline notes of a woman singing. The limpid tremolo echoed like a love call in the night. Then another voice – a man's, this time – answered with soft warm notes to the accompaniment of a guitar. Luna almost laughed with relief. The sounds came from nearby; her troubles would soon be over. Without a doubt, the owners of those beautiful voices would help her find her way. She took out the torch from the pack she had around her waist, turned it on, and carefully made her way towards the sound.

Luna picked her way through brush and undergrowth to a small path that wound its way through the trees. Now she could see a clearing ahead of her, surrounded by pines. A moment later, her eyes widening in surprise, she stopped dead in her tracks.

Shock, disbelief and finally chagrin flashed across her face.

Outside a shabby wooden hut, in the middle of the glade, the young gypsy girl danced like a diaphanous barefoot nymph, oblivious to the ominous skies. It was Sabrina, clothed in a knee-length sleeveless muslin dress that hung loosely on her nubile form yet was so flimsy that the contours of her body were clearly visible beneath. She seemed lost in her dreamy dance, improvising, flooded by emotion, her alabaster skin almost translucent in the dramatic half-light. Her movements were sinuous and erotic, arms writhing and circling sensually. The fire burning in the glade reflected on her fine features and her large pale eyes looked like deep pools as they lifted now and then heavenwards, telling of the insatiable passion that burnt inside her.

She was not only baring much of her slender body to the man, who sat leaning with his guitar against the trunk of a tree in front of her, she was also baring her soul. The style of her movements was simple but eloquent, her song ardent, yet light and whimsical, which intensified the impression of despair. A primitive summon to the man she loved, to fulfil a basic need. She was a mass of contradictions, an enchantress at one with nature and the encroaching night.

Sabrina.

It was as if the wind whispered her name.

And Ruy sang. It was a song of extreme tenderness, poignant and halting; a song of loneliness and unrequited love with guttural mournful cries that burst into the bruised sky of the Andalucían twilight like a wailing prayer. His fingers skimmed over the strings of his guitar, barely brushing them, and the instrument vibrated with such a deep sadness that Luna felt a lump form in her throat. His voice was husky, deep and strong, losing itself in the repeated cascading sounds and in the modulation of the drawn-out cadences. In the purple twilight, his eyes were silver with a sad, faraway look. Like Sabrina, there was something of the supernatural about him – a fallen angel in despair.

It was all wrong. The song was drawing Luna in, speaking to her very soul. It should have been meant for her alone – it was *her* song! So, why then Sabrina? Why was he singing it to the gypsy seductress?

Luna watched, unable to pull away, breathless, jealousy twisting her heart. Ruy had painted the gypsy siren as someone 'unpredictable' as if he were some kind of protector, but perhaps the simple truth was that he was obsessed by her – with her free spirit, her beauty. After all, Sabrina was a *gitana*, and their shared heritage could speak to Ruy's restless gypsy soul in a way that Luna couldn't compete with.

Every note he played, every sound emitted, wrenched a painful chord in Luna's heart. None of this made sense. Singing to Sabrina now did not fit with the ardour of Ruy's lovemaking whenever he had touched her, kissed her; made her bare herself to him. Luna could recall the trembling, thrilling note in his voice as he had whispered so many wonderful words to her. How could he sing to another woman like this after the intimate things he had done to her? Yet the evidence was there, before her eyes.

Was this the secret that Ruy was hiding from her?

The man was a monster!

She smothered a sob. Humiliated and mortified, Luna finally turned on her heels and scrambled back up the slope, uncaring of the brambles and twigs that scratched at her bare arms and legs. Compared with her hurt pride and wounded heart they were nothing. Hurt, confusion and anger blistered her mind, almost blinding her as she fought her way up through slippery pine needles and fallen branches, scraping her hands on tree roots protruding from the slanting earth like long, malicious fingers.

It was only when she reached the top that she remembered she was lost. She became aware of the thunder now, cannonading and rolling across the hilltops and echoing along the plains. Every pine needle in the wood seemed to be shivering in the electric stillness. There was an air of waiting, as if the trees around her presaged some doom-laden event. The heaviness in the atmosphere was like a weight reflecting the overwhelming load in Luna's heart.

A vivid streak of lightning flashed down to earth from the sky, followed immediately by an ear-splitting crash that seemed to shatter the ground about her, a deafening roar of mighty thunder that rolled and reverberated angrily from directly above, grumbling as it travelled away into nothingness. That tiny part of Luna that still clung to a modicum of reason registered that the storm was passing over. Then again there came more blinding flashes of light that shone through the trunks of the trees like the sharp flickering of old cine film. In fact, the storm was edging closer.

Luna's misery was eclipsed by growing alarm but she soldiered on, using her torch to guide her way through the woods. The air was oppressively close. She fancied she could see in the distance pin lights flickering in the darkness. *Please let it be houses or the headlights of cars on a road.* Her heart thudded madly. *It can't last, the storm has to blow over soon!* she thought wildly. She trembled now, not with cold but with stark fear. Once again, reason took over for a moment: *Don't panic*, she told herself, trying to steady her nerves. *It'll be all right.*

With the next blinding flash of lightning came the longest, deepest peal of thunder. It shook the hills wrathfully, followed by rain that sheeted down with a hissing noise, stabbing the ground like so many tiny spears. She began moving faster against the deluge, trying to shield her eyes from the lashing wet; her dress clung to her, sodden and heavy. The dark forms of the trees reared up like menacing sentinels around her, and in Luna's mind it was as though she was back in the terrifying wood of her nightmare, helpless and fighting her way through the trees, running towards the light. Her heart was pounding and her throat contracted as wave upon wave of panic started to flood her. She glanced behind her but all she could see through the driving rain were shadowy, indistinct shapes in the murky tangle of the forest.

Now the ground was uneven and Luna cried out as she stumbled, but her voice was drowned by the noise of the storm. Losing her balance, her foot slipped in the mud and she fell, entangling herself in a heap of branches and wet leaves. In doing so, she dropped the torch and lost a shoe. *You're awake, no one's after you*, she told herself over and over again, trying to control her growing hysteria. Sobbing, she groped for them on hands and knees in the darkness to no avail. Logic struggled to get a grip on her fear: *It's no use. Try and find shelter until the storm subsides.*

Luna moved forward, tears and rain blurring her vision, thrashing her way through the maze of trees, arms striking out as if fighting invisible dragons, branches whipping and scratching her face and ripping her clothes. It wasn't easy clambering, one foot shoeless, over roots and stumps in the dark, her toes sinking into wet leaf mould. The gusts of wind through the trees numbed her limbs, and the sole of her foot felt raw, making it increasingly painful to walk. She was exhausted. Violent shudders raked through her and panic took hold again. What if she never found her way out; what if no one came looking for her? Then a rational voice would break in with a mantra she repeated fiercely over and over again as her feet kept on stumbling forward: *Don't be ridiculous, breathe slowly, the storm will pass soon.*

She was suddenly aware that the thunder and lightning had stopped. The rain was still falling in a light drizzle, but nothing like the torrential sheets of earlier on. Her eyes, accustomed to the darkness at this point, could see a pale patch of light not too far off … possibly the end of the wood, she imagined, hope flaring at the thought. Or maybe another clearing with a house; perhaps she would be able to find help. She hurried ahead, moving almost like an automaton now, ignoring her painful foot and the biting cold penetrating her bones.

Finally she came to the end of the wood. Luna gasped with relief and would have jumped for joy, had she not been so tired and in pain. She had come out on to a main road. There was no traffic at this hour but she figured if she sat on the side of the road, someone was bound to come along, even if she had to wait until morning. She was too exhausted to walk further anyhow. The storm had subsided and the moon, now emerging from a bank of cloud, looked upon her with a smiling face. The evening had quietened. It was still cold but she didn't care any more; she was safe. She lay down on the grass verge and huddled up to keep warm; all she had to do was lie there until someone found her.

She had not been there long when she heard the sound of an engine. Was it her imagination? She sat up stiffly, peering into the night. Yes, a car was approaching. She scrambled jerkily to her feet and waved her arms frantically. The headlights swept the road, strong yellow beams shining like two enormous wild cat's eyes in the dark, bearing down on her as the driver slowed, indicator flashing, and then jammed on the brakes.

The vintage Austin came to a halt by the kerb.

A frisson of recognition fluttered through Luna even before the door of the car sprang open and the tall, handsome figure of the man who haunted her thoughts appeared, silhouetted against the night.

In two strides Ruy was looming over Luna like a fierce demigod. His eyes were a different kind of silvery-blue than the liquid softness they had exhibited while singing to Sabrina. Now they were as hard and cutting as a diamond.

'Luna, what in God's name are you doing up here?' he growled, his long, lean fingers biting into her shoulders through the torn slits in her dress. 'Only a fool would venture into these hills alone.'

She turned away from his piercing gaze, her eyes pricking with tears again, suddenly aware of the shabby state she presented. Her clothes were torn and filthy, smudged with earth and blood. Her wet hair, which had come loose from its earlier neat ponytail, was plastered against her head; her feet were muddy. And her face – she didn't want to think about the state of her face. How did she compare with the ethereal nymph he had just left? She felt speechless with humiliation and wounded pride.

Still grasping her shoulders, Ruy's gaze raked over her, quickly taking in the blood on her dress and her missing shoe. His steely expression changed instantly to one of concern. 'How did you get up here? Where's your car? Did you have an accident?' The questions came thick and fast.

She shook her head without looking at him. 'I left the car at the bottom of the hills and walked up,' she said in a choked voice. Something in her was closing down against the torrent of emotions threatening to carry her away.

He said nothing more, but trailed one warm finger down her cheek and gently turned her face towards him. 'It's all right now, *querida*. You're safe now. I'm here and I'll look after you. Come, let me take you home. You're hurt and those cuts need to be seen to. I'll sort out the car tomorrow.'

Luna pushed back her tears. She didn't care about the cuts on her body, it was her aching heart she needed him to heal, futile as that seemed. As she tilted her chin up to him, she struggled to control the chaos of conflicting emotions he engendered in her. The moonlight fell directly on his face. Now the look in his eyes had softened – patient, tender and loving. The man was like quicksilver, and it was impossible to guess his mood – or whom he might next be wooing, she thought bleakly.

'Let's get you to the car.'

Ignoring her small sound of protest, in one strong movement he scooped her up, one arm under her legs and the other around her shoulders, holding her tightly against him. Treacherous feelings flooded her. Oh, the warmth and tautness of his wonderful body! Despite her fatigue and confusion, Luna couldn't help but enjoy those ephemeral few seconds of contact. His breath on the side of her face heated her cold, wet skin and her heart was pounding as she fought a compulsive urge to touch those generous chiselled lips, just inches from hers.

With one hand he opened the door of the Austin and gently lowered Luna into the passenger seat. Seconds later she heard the boot click and he returned with a cashmere blanket. He moved her seat back to create more leg room.

'Stretch out your legs. Make yourself comfortable and cover yourself with this,' he ordered, handing her the blanket. 'You're still in shock. You're trembling.' Then, as she hesitated to take it from him, he unfolded the rug and helped her wrap it round herself as if she were a small child.

'I'm covered in mud and dirt,' she whispered apologetically. 'I'll ruin it, and your seat.'

'Don't think of anything now, *niña*. Just try to relax.'

Luna leaned back in her seat, shivering and weary, her wet body wrapped in Ruy's beautiful soft blanket that smelt of wild lavender. She rested her throbbing head against the padded headrest. Her drowsy gaze flickered over the man who had just eased himself into the driver's seat beside her, giving her a look she was unable to read; then she closed her eyes and went to sleep.

*   *   *

Ruy switched on the ignition and reached for his seatbelt. He put his foot down and they sped off into the night. His eyes flitted towards his passenger: she was a deathly pale but sleeping soundly and breathing evenly, her lashes long and soft against her cheeks. Huddled in the corner of her seat, her arms crossed over her chest, she looked so vulnerable. However strong and capable Luna might appear, she had a fragile side and there was still a mystery behind that aspect of her that he couldn't fathom. He felt a surge of protectiveness and almost put out his hand to touch her, but didn't want to disturb her peace.

In profile, sleeping, she suddenly had the look of her half-sister Juliet; something about the curve of her cheek and her mouth, which turned up slightly at the corners. In colouring they were nothing alike, but it was apparent nonetheless. He was amazed that he'd never seen the resemblance before.

She was so different to Juliet, who at times used to behave in such a spoilt and self-centred way, often causing misery to his best friend Carlos, whom she had led on a merry dance – one that had ultimately contributed to his death. But what use were recriminations? The poor girl had paid for her capriciousness with her life. Ruy had paid dearly too, inwardly bearing a huge weight of guilt and self-loathing. Of course he did – what man wouldn't? The court hadn't held him responsible for the accident, nor had Carlos's family – although the Herreras had done their best to dig in the knife, of course – but he'd shouldered the burden anyway.

Ruy sighed and looked down at the sleeping Luna beside him. When she came into his life, he reflected, he couldn't help but feel an insane hope that everything in his world would change for the better. But then he found out she was Juliet's half-sister, and the knife of guilt was twisted agonizingly in his gut once more. Frowning, he pushed a hand through his hair, pensively. He knew he needed to clarify things with Luna – and as soon as possible. To go on like this, hiding the truth from her, was unthinkable.

He looked down into her sleeping face and reflected on the evening's strange turn of events. What had Luna been doing all alone up in the hills tonight? She certainly wasn't the reckless type, though why she had ended up in the gypsies' camp the day before was another mystery he hadn't yet worked out. His gaze softened with an almost liquid tenderness. Despite her sorry state she still looked beautiful, so innocent and pure. The urge to enfold her in his arms and hold her tight was so strong that he could scarcely restrain it. In the past he had never welcomed the idea of a woman being dependent on him but, with Luna, all he wanted was to look after her, protect her.

After their earth-shattering intimacy the previous night, he knew beyond doubt that he deeply and truly loved Luna. She was his destiny. Nothing – no secret or shame – could come between them. They were fated to one another.

Suddenly an image came into his head unbidden, a memory of a summer's day at the beach with his father. He must have been no more than ten years of age at the time. They were sitting on the sand and Ruy remembered looking up into the glare of the sun and seeing the shape of an old woman looming over him. She seemed ancient to him then: a gypsy, old and bowed by age, her skin wrinkled and shrivelled like an apple that had seen better days. The *gitana* and his father were speaking together in *Caló*, he remembered; it seemed they were old friends.

Before going on her way she had looked at Ruy with strange hooded eyes, which he met without flinching. She chuckled at the budding arrogance of his stare and ruffled his hair. 'You're a cocky one, *ey*?' Then she had taken his small palm in her gnarled hand. 'The moon will sail up into your sky one day, my boy, and will take hold of your soul. Fate has a strange way of playing tricks on its chosen ones. Go with the tide. If you fight your fate, you will be punished. She is a capricious mistress.'

She turned to go but before she left she looked back at him one last time, with a gaze that glittered with hidden fires. 'Don't forget, my boy: go with the tide and listen to your heart.'

The old gypsy had made such an impression on him that day that although he hadn't understood her words at the time, they were forever branded on his memory. His father had clearly thought the *gitana*'s predictions were worth taking heed of, for he had paled, and the young Ruy gathered from his curiously watchful expression that there must be something of significance to them. It was then that Andrés had told him how the gypsies had shared a long history with their family; it was if their destinies were intertwined.

'Many gypsies profess to know the future, Ruy, but usually it's just a trick to take money from gullible *busnos*. That woman, Paquita, is different. To my knowledge she has never been wrong. Today, her words may appear no more than a riddle, but the day will come when you will understand their meaning and I hope you'll be wise enough to act upon it.'

Now he understood.

*   *   *

Ruy carried Luna into the house and up the stairs to her bedroom, where he lowered her gently on to the bed. Luna hadn't had the strength to argue when he'd woken her and helped her from the car. The storm had moved on and here on the coast the rain had started up again and he'd made his way to the house in a heavy downpour, once more lifting Luna up against his powerful chest to shield her from the elements.

As Ruy laid her carefully down, Luna noticed that he'd placed some towels over her bedlinen so that it wouldn't be soiled. If she hadn't felt so miserable and exhausted, she would have thanked him but she didn't have the strength to remark on his thoughtfulness and simply remained mute.

'Now, just relax,' he said, with a flicker of a smile, 'and let Dr Calderón examine you.' The familiar faint aroma of him made her shiver as he bent forward to study the cuts and bruises on her arms and legs, the scratches on her face and neck. 'You have a few cuts. Nothing major, you'll be glad to hear.' He carefully felt her left ankle. 'It's a little swollen. Just a mild sprain, thankfully. Nothing a good night's sleep won't cure.'

Luna pulled away from his touch, managing a taut response. 'Yes, I'm fine, really. Just tired.' She drew her legs up and leaned back against the pillow, turning her face to the wall. 'You can go now.'

There was a moment of silence. 'Look, Luna,' he said gently, carrying a chair to her bedside and sitting down. 'I know you've had a scare, but you can trust me. You know you can.'

Trust him? How could she trust a man who played his women as skilfully as he played his guitar?

'Give me a chance to take care of you, Luna. I want to look after you. It's all I've ever wanted … to make you happy.'

Luna closed her eyes. She could imagine the poignant look on Ruy's face, the longing in his eyes. A sour taste surged in her throat. She turned to face him, eyes flashing. 'Make me happy? Please me, as you would a whore?' she cried out impulsively before she could stop herself.

His eyes clouded as he stared back at her. 'Is that how you see our relationship?' The concern painted on his features was the very picture of sincerity, moving something deep inside her, but she wasn't about to give way to it.

She fought for self-control and her expression hardened. 'Don't give me that act, Ruy. You should have received your doctorate in theatre studies – oh, and womanizing. That too.'

His look changed to a puzzled frown. 'Are we really back to all that again, Luna? What on earth are you talking about?'

However Luna couldn't see beyond her own angry contempt now. 'I mean, all this time you've been carrying on with Sabrina, that gypsy harlot you spend your spare time "nurturing". The one you were serenading tonight in your little love nest.'

Ruy paled, his blue eyes now a steely grey. 'What do you know about Sabrina that you can judge her? She's anything but a harlot, and I won't have you say that about her.' he declared.

Her jaw set stubbornly. 'I've got eyes! I saw the way you ran off after her at the ball and I watched you singing to her while she cavorted about almost naked tonight. For goodness sake, what do you take me for?' she retorted hotly.

Ruy leaned forward in his chair and braced both elbows on his knees. When he spoke next, his words were careful, measured. Luna could tell from his eyes that he had softened, the way they had changed colour again as he fixed her with a steady look.

'Sabrina has never been with a man, so let's get that part straight. She's a free spirit, a girl from the wild. She lives alone in the hills and is known among the gypsies as La Selvage, the wild child. What you saw tonight was just one of her ways of communing with nature. I'm not in love with her and when she has met the man to whom she is destined, she'll grow out of any infatuation for – or reliance on – me. She's only eighteen, virtually a child, and tomorrow, when you're not so upset and overwrought, I'll tell you her story. Then you'll understand why I nurture her, as you so rightly say.'

Luna listened in confused silence. Now she spoke up, in a quiet whisper this time, which had a little catch in it. 'Your voice was so full of emotion when you sang to her.'

'What makes you think the words … the feelings … were for her? Do you have a gift of divination, can you read other people's minds?'

'I had the impression your song was about an impossible love. A man's passion for a young gypsy girl, a man who should know better, it seemed exactly to fit the bill. An unstoppable, inappropriate hidden love.'

The intensity in Ruy's gaze remained but it had transformed into something new and there was a fire that blazed in its blue depths. 'Ah, woman of little faith, couldn't I have been singing about someone I fell in love with the moment I set eyes on her in a little nightclub in Barcelona? A woman I've been chasing ever since because I know we are fated to be with each other? A woman who haunts my days and nights … whom I love more than life itself? Ah, Luna, how much more do you want me to beg … and for how long?' he asked, his voice thick with emotion, deep and intoxicating, more potent than wine.

A mixture of joy and disbelief surged in Luna for the briefest snap of a finger before it was smothered. She half turned so he wouldn't notice the quiver of her mouth, unconsciously pressing a nervous hand to her throat. She would be a fool to believe him. Tears were welling in her eyes and she was trying hard to keep them from falling.

'Let's leave this conversation for when you're feeling better, but please let me take care of you tonight. You've had a nasty shock,' Ruy said quietly, standing up. 'I'm not leaving you on your own. Anyhow, I need to bathe and dress those cuts.'

Luna nodded wordlessly in consent. Though exhausted and bewildered, she was glad he was there: grateful for his strength, his reassuring presence.

He pushed back his damp ebony hair that was flopping down on to his forehead.

'Do you mind?' he asked, starting to unbutton his wet shirt.

Luna's eyes widened in alarm. 'What are you doing?'

His smooth lips quirked, mischievous devils dancing in the leaping blue flames of his eyes. 'I'm not about to ravish you, if that's what concerns you.' She was too tired to think of a clever retort, and he went on without waiting for her answer. 'It's soaking wet and I won't be much of a help to you if I catch pneumonia.'

Luna swallowed hard; she could hardly refuse. 'Yes, that's fine. There's a hot rail in the bathroom if you'd like to dry it off there.'

He grinned, the little devils still watching her intently. 'Thank you, *señorita*, that's most magnanimous of you,' he said, easing the shirt off his broad shoulders and down his strong arms, biceps flexing as he did so.

Luna's eyes fastened on his muscled chest and the silky jet-black pelt that arrowed so provocatively down to his navel. The maleness of him was primitively beautiful. He was magnificent. Despite herself, her eyes darted to where his hand was poised on the belt-buckle over his jeans. His gaze flicked up; caught her watching. He smiled, a little embarrassed, but only slightly. 'I can't help that,' he murmured tautly. 'That's what you do to me.' He looked at her calmly. 'But I promise you, Luna, I know how to control myself.'

He pulled off his belt and hung it over the chair. 'I'll run you a bath,' he said, heading for the bathroom with his wet shirt. 'There's nothing better to soothe aching limbs and relax the nerves.'

A few minutes later, he returned to find Luna easing herself off the bed with a wince. 'What is it? Does that hurt?' he asked, coming to stand over her.

'Just a twinge,' she said, sitting on the side of the bed and giving her lower back a rub.

'You must have pulled a muscle climbing those wretched hills, you silly girl,' he growled.

'I had no difficulty climbing, I assure you. I regularly run six miles,' she shot back, miffed that he might think her unfit or wishy-washy. 'If you must know, I stumbled in the dark and fell. I'll be fine tomorrow.'

'Let me help you to the bathroom.'

'I'll manage, thank you.'

He stood a few feet away from her, watching her doubtfully.

Luna gave a gasp of pain as she tried to stand up, before collapsing back on to the bed again.

'Now will you let me?' he queried sardonically. 'Unless, of course, you want to be doing this sort of exercise all night. In the meantime, your bath is getting cold.'

She met his quiet gaze. Emotionally drained, she gave the barest nod.

It seemed he'd had the last word again.

CHAPTER 12

Ruy returned to the bathroom to add more hot water to the bath.

'I'm afraid I used all the towels to cover your bed. Do you have any spare? I couldn't see a bathrobe anywhere.'

'It's in the wash. Towels are in the top of the wardrobe.' Ruy seemed so at ease in her house, Luna thought, as she watched him move about with an efficiency she had to admire. He was organized and systematic, unlike most of her friends' husbands or boyfriends.

He took the towels to the bathroom and came back to the bed, using a small one to dry his still-wet hair. She watched his biceps flex as he vigorously dried his thick dark locks before throwing the towel on to the chair. He bent over Luna to say something, his face so near that she thought he wanted to kiss her. Instinctively she drew back, shrinking away from him.

His eyes when she met them were unfathomable. 'Luna, *déjate llevar*, let yourself go. Forget it's me, the man who loves you, and leave it all to the doctor.' His voice was warm, tender and loving but that only increased her fear of him – and more precisely, the fear of her own feelings. His earlier declaration had destabilized her. She didn't know what to think any more, but she really didn't like being reliant on this man, doctor or not.

'First, let's get you out of those wet clothes.'

'There's really no need for you to help me. Please go away and let me cope on my own. I've been doing it for twenty-five years and I'm very good at it.'

'Oh, I can see that,' he responded to her forceful assertion, fighting to keep a straight face.

Luna's amber eyes blazed up at him in annoyance at this obvious sarcasm, though she said nothing.

'Luna, be reasonable. You're hurt. I haven't examined you properly yet so I can't assess the extent of the damage. There's no point in being childish about this. For the moment you need to do what I say. I'm a trained doctor, for goodness sake.'

There was a tinge of exasperation in his tone and Luna finally capitulated.

Ruy had his faults, but deep down he was a gentleman and he was proud. He would never take advantage of her in this state, she knew.

He sat opposite her on the bed. Luna tried to lift her arms to take off the dress that clung to her wet body, but dropped them with a yelp of pain. 'I can't do it!' Her eyes filled with tears of frustration.

Silently he reached out, slipping his hands under the dress and brought it up her thighs, then carefully slid it out from underneath her bottom. Luna held her breath while his hands went to the buttons at the front of her dress, and silently she watched his long dexterous fingers at work, her senses captive to his touch.

Trailing his palms up the side of her torn dress, his wrists brushed against her flesh, warm and firm, as he gently eased it off one arm, then the other, and finally over her head. His touch was warm and featherlike, barely brushing against her cold skin, energizing her senses. She heard him suck in his breath as the garment fell to the bed and she was left sitting there naked in front of him except for her panties. Her breasts were tight, the pink halo around her nipples darkening as they became taut. She tried to cross her arms in front of her chest, but only managed to bring one up.

Luna finally managed to meet Ruy's gaze and she saw his jaw clench. 'You've hurt your collarbone,' he said. 'I can see the shadow of a bruise already, but it doesn't look broken. Even if it's fractured, there's nothing one can do about it apart from prescribing painkillers.'

Ruy was speaking quickly, his voice a little husky. She could see he was making an insurmountable effort to keep his eyes averted from her nakedness, but she could not keep her own from trailing down his bare, muscled chest to the telltale bulk outlined against his jeans, and she knew he was throbbing for her.

The shivering had started up again. Every inch of her body clamoured for the sensations that only he knew how to arouse, her insides quivering with anticipation.

'You're cold. I'm sorry I'm taking so much time over this, but I'm loath to hurt you.' He met no resistance when his fingers went to the top of her panties and she swallowed hard as he peeled them off in one smooth movement. With a sick pang Luna wondered just how many women he had relieved of their underwear in exactly the same skilful manner, and she couldn't meet his eyes.

'It's all right, Luna,' he whispered, sensing her unease as he scooped her up in his arms to take her into the bathroom. 'You're safe with me.'

His intimate tone tugged at strings inside her, strings connected to her confused and conflicting emotions, which secretly revelled in his barely concealed desire for her, even though she did not wholly trust his intentions and was unwilling to yield to him. Until now, Luna had never been carried in such a way by any man but the feeling of being held so effortlessly and protectively against the smooth skin of his arms and chest was unlike anything she'd ever known. Unable to lift her arms around Ruy's neck, she let herself rest limply against him, fighting the urge to lean her head on the curve of his shoulder. There were scratches on her arms and legs, and a wound on her left thigh where her dress had been ripped, the blood of which had dried in brownish streaks.

'You've really made a good job of this, haven't you?' he murmured as he lowered her into the warm water and knelt beside the bath, leaning his forearms on the edge.

Luna slid into the scented foamy liquid and rested her head against the side of the bath. She closed her eyes, letting the heat penetrate her aching limbs. It was strange how, after a while, her inhibitions around Ruy always seemed to evaporate. Despite her tiredness, at this precise moment she would welcome anything he wanted to do to her, and she waited in anticipation.

He concentrated first on her hands, which were painful and full of small cuts and grazes from the thorny bushes, then her elbow, which was sticky with blood. He washed away the dirt from her face. 'It's only mud and a few scratches,' he murmured softly, letting his thumb roll sensuously over her cheeks, too close to her parted lips for comfort. 'Nothing too serious, it'll all be gone by tomorrow.' The smile he gave her sent tremors down Luna's spine, making her stomach flip with an urgent need.

Soon she felt the wet bar of soap glide first down her neck, then around her shoulders and along her arms. The sensation was one of liquid heat. He lifted an arm to wash beneath it, and very slowly did the same to the other on her injured side. Silently, she willed him to move to her breasts – they were hard as rocks and the twin peaks were begging for his touch – but he had taken hold of one of her legs now, letting the soap trail over it gently before moving to the other. It was both agony and bliss.

The sole of her foot accidentally brushed against the bath and she uttered a small cry. Ruy immediately gave it his attention.

The twigs and sharp rocks had cut into her delicate skin like so many viciously sharp knives.

'I lost my shoe,' she explained as she saw the dark brows gather in concern.

'I know.' He shook his head and replaced her foot gently in the water.

The soap in his hand was now rolling over her waist and flat stomach, arousing new and unexpected twinges of pleasure. She inhaled sharply.

Ruy's hands stopped moving. 'Am I hurting you?' he asked, his voice low and husky.

Luna passed her tongue over her lips, her eyes full of misty sensuality as she silently met his molten gaze. She said nothing, and her lashes lowered once more.

And then his hands moved again, smoothly over her thighs, soaping them first on the outside, then the inside, so close to where she was intimately throbbing that she could scream. The warm water was caressing the core of her, but that wasn't enough to soothe the urgent ache, the heat that was building up inside, driving upwards inexorably towards the junction of her thighs; she wanted to feel the touch of his strong fingers stroking and kneading her as they had done before. Every inch of her flesh was tingling, crying out for the drug he had served up to her, and to which she now knew she was addicted.

'Right,' he said, as he abruptly stood up. 'I think I've attended to everything. Let me lift you out.'

Luna fell from paradise with a bump. A strange twist of disappointment squeezed her heart as she realized this longing within her would be left unfulfilled. She opened her passionate, glittering eyes and met his smoky blue gaze. If the eyes are the mirror of the soul, those dark irises staring back at her offered no reflection of his feelings.

'Feeling better?' he asked.

Damn the man, surely he knew the havoc he had provoked. She managed to look up at him, meeting his indigo gaze without flinching. 'I feel just great, thank you. The warm water seems to have done the trick. You were right – it *is* the best remedy for aches and pains. More than anything.'

He shook his head slowly, his golden-brown hand moving gently over his jawline as he regarded her with a thoughtful expression that didn't conceal his amusement. Then, pulling a towel off the hot rail, he lifted her up and out of the bath, standing her on the mat and supporting her against him, wet and dripping. After that, he wrapped the towel around her body before scooping her up again and laying her on the bed. The entire motion was achieved so swiftly she had barely time to blink.

He seized the medical kit and once more sat himself down on the bed beside her. 'Now that the fun bit is over,' he smiled, 'I'll have a good look at those cuts. Some need more attention than others, like that gash on your thigh. It looks quite fierce.'

'You don't waste time, do you?' Luna said, piqued by his haste. 'I think you quite enjoy playing doctors and nurses.'

He winked at her. 'In this instance, doctors and patients,' he corrected as he took out what he needed to cleanse, dress and tape a wound. There were all sorts of arcane things in his case: weird-looking plants and twigs, bundles of herbs, small dark bottles of liquid, tiny capsules and transparent little boxes filled with different-coloured powders. A real Aladdin's cave of unconventional oddities, Luna thought, a little disparagingly, then immediately checked herself, blushing inwardly at her unkind thoughts. What was happening to her? All her reactions were so out of character; what was she becoming? It was as if there were two Lunas and she really disliked this stranger inhabiting her.

And then paradise was in reach again, clouding her mind. Ruy was lifting the towel up to her thigh and trailing his lean fingers over the scratches. Predictably, his touch aroused her at once, in an almost Pavlovian response, as flames of sensuality chased through her body, blood thundering in her ears. Her eyes trained on his dark bent head, his neck and bare shoulders, his chest. She was so tempted to brush her fingertips over his golden smooth skin, wondering if it was all as silken and warm as she imagined.

He must think I'm accident prone, she thought, remembering it was only recently that he had dressed her hand.

There was a rhythm in his movements as Ruy examined, probed and swabbed. He was concentrating on the gash on her thigh now. Luna winced as he daubed it with antiseptic. 'You have quite a collection of cuts and bruises. Anyway, what *were* you doing up there in the hills?'

'Looking for plants.'

He lifted his head, eyes narrowing. 'Looking for plants or playing detective?'

Luna's gaze shot to his. 'What are you insinuating?'

'I find it rather a coincidence that you should come across Sabrina's glade just like that, don't you think? And the gypsies' camp ...' he left the end of his phrase trailing expectantly.

'So you think I was snooping around just to spy on you, is that it?' Her stare became defiant. 'What I do and where I go is none of your business. I don't need to justify myself to you.'

'Oh yes, you do, when it has to do with my private life. What makes you think you've the right to invade my privacy?'

She could see he was now getting angry too, but it didn't matter.

'What private life? What privacy?' she rasped. 'Your so-called private life is the talk of Andalucía.' Then, appalled at the unpleasantness in her tone, she blushed again, letting her head drop back against the pillow. 'I'm sorry,' she murmured. 'You've been very kind to me and all I've given you is grief. I don't know what's got into me ... I'm tired. Forgive me.'

He had finished applying strips to close the gash on her thigh, covering it now with a gauze dressing. Slowly he lifted his gaze to meet her contrite look.

'Sexual frustration, I suppose. Don't you think?'

She sucked in her breath and felt her cheeks burning crimson at his directness. Her eyes evaded his intent blue stare.

'Don't look so shocked, Luna. You may not want to give in to this chemistry between us, but you really can't deny that it's there.'

Of course she couldn't. She bit her lip and closed her eyes.

'What you need now is a good night's sleep. You're exhausted. Let me help you with your nightclothes. Are they in this cupboard?'

She nodded lamely. He was right, why fight what was so obviously there, and which felt so good?

Why fight? Because this man could hurt her – hurt her so badly that she might never recover from the wounds.

He had come back to the bed. 'How's the back now?'

'Much better, thank you. The hot bath really helped.'

He lifted one faintly quizzical eyebrow. 'More than anything, *ey*?'

So he had understood her earlier jibe. Luna shook her head. 'No, not more than anything,' she heard herself admit in a hollow voice. She wanted to beg him to touch her, but instead mutely lifted her amber eyes to his, unable to conceal the longing and pent-up desire that burned inside. He held her gaze for a lengthy moment.

'Can you stand up?'

'I'll try.' Luna slipped her legs gently off the bed and he helped her to her feet. She winced, but managed to stand up unsteadily, letting the towel slide to the floor. His strong supporting hand settled at the base of her spine and when he handed the nightdress with the other, she noticed it was trembling slightly. She had no doubt the wild desire that was setting her on fire was scorching him too.

'I'll make you a hot drink and bring it to you,' he said a little brusquely. His gaze flew away from hers as he turned down the bed and helped her back into it.

I could get used to being fussed over like this, Luna thought, as she settled herself between the cool sheets. Laying her head back on the pillow, she let herself sink into the softness of the mattress and closed her eyes.

She listened to the wind whistling eerily between the window slats like a wandering lost soul and the sea howling and pounding relentlessly against the rocky shore. Nature unleashed, she thought, not unlike the way her senses and emotions ran riot whenever Ruy was near, and as dangerous and unpredictable as the passion simmering in her blood. She knew it would soon boil over if he were to remain around her for much longer.

Luna heard him come into the room; he was very quiet but her hearing was sharp. At first she kept her eyes shut, aware that he was very close to the bed, looking down on her. Then, after a brief moment, she opened her eyes and felt herself melting under his burning gaze. Silently, she stared up at him, lost in unexpressed emotion.

'I was so afraid,' she murmured.

Ruy was holding a tray, which he put down on the bedside table, and he sat on the edge of the bed. 'I'm here now. Drink this. It's a mixture of poppy seed, chamomile and passion flower. It'll relax you … help you sleep.'

She noticed he was wearing a clean shirt, and had washed his face and smoothed back his hair, which was still a little damp. He must keep spare clothes in his car, she thought – more the organized doctor now than the gypsy. The pain in her back had returned and she struggled to sit up. He put his arm under her waist and gently lifted her, piling cushions behind her against the headboard, before passing her the tea.

The liquid was warm, sweet and strangely aromatic. It felt good and she sipped it slowly, wanting to prolong the feeling. Gradually, as the hot brew soothed her body, it melted away the stress that kept the tears frozen behind her eyelids. All she wanted now was to throw her arms around Ruy's neck, bury her head in his strong shoulder and feel his heat radiate through her. 'I'm a mess. My life's a mess,' she murmured, tears streaming uncontrollably down her cheeks.

'Shush, *querida, no llores*, don't cry, darling. You're tired and you need a good night's sleep.' Gently he took her in his arms and hugged her close to his powerful chest, stroking her long silky hair, whispering loving words against her ear while Luna sobbed quietly against him. 'I'm not leaving you tonight,' he told her when she finally stopped, thankfully echoing what she had been silently wishing for. 'I'll bring up my sleeping bag.'

'You can't spend the night in a sleeping bag!' she exclaimed, aghast.

He laughed at the shocked look in her eyes. 'I'm used to it. I often sleep on the beach under the stars. Waking up with the sun, watching it rise gradually above the hills, listening to the birds and to nature as it rises from slumber. It's the most wonderful feeling of freedom and oneness with the world. You should try it.'

His eyes, now the colour of a bright cerulean sky, glittered with a different sort of passion, lighting up his face with a radiance she had never seen before. Aunt Isabel was right: the voice of Ruy's gypsy blood sang much louder than his other genes. She reached out a hand and pushed back a strand of raven-black hair that had slipped across his forehead.

She felt the tremor run through him, but he visibly checked himself, breathing in deeply. Taking her hand, he turned it palm up and brought it to his warm lips, then closed her slender fingers over his kiss.

'*Buenas noches, querida, y duerme bien*, goodnight, my darling, and sleep well.'

*   *   *

Ruy helped Luna snuggle down into the bed and tucked her in. Before leaving the room, he stood there a while and watched her fall asleep. Then he went down to the car and returned with his sleeping bag, smiling to himself. He never thought the day would come when he would have to keep a check on his sexual urge because he had such a passionate need for a woman who rejected him, and for whom he felt so much love. Usually, women were never happier than when he undressed them – but not Luna. She was still resisting him, even now.

The realization of it made him frown. The fear in her eyes each time he had come too near was palpable. She needed help; that much was clear. He had guessed for a while now that she had likely been the victim of a traumatic experience and, although he didn't know the nature of it, he wanted to find out. How long she had been living with its memory and how deep the damage had gone were still mysteries, and he needed to be careful how he approached the subject without upsetting her. All he knew was that she had appeared unexpectedly in his life like a shimmering moonbeam on a dark night, and that he loved her.

He sat on his sleeping bag in Luna's moonlit bedroom, his back against the cupboard, watching her sleep. She was so beautiful, with her long pale hair spread over the pillow, thick lashes fanning her cheeks – an angel in repose, so vulnerable.

At some point she pushed back the sheet; her nightshirt had ridden up, so that it revealed her wounded thigh. Her leg looked shapely and smooth in the moonlight. The thought struck him that he had actually felt and kissed the inside of those thighs. He grew hard just at the idea of her wrapping them around him.

'So much for self-control,' he thought guiltily, with a sigh of self-derision, as he tried to control the erotic images running through his excited mind.

Ruy turned his brilliant, restless eyes away from the bed and looked out into the night. The storm had subsided now; the black, furious Atlantic was calmer and the wind had dropped, reducing the frothy white horses that had galloped over the ocean all evening to harmless waves, barely rippling the surface of the water. Out there the sky was mellow, powdered with twinkling stars, and the moon smiled enigmatically at him.

His gaze drifted back to the bed. Luna had shifted a little, her arm spread out along her body, her delicate hand resting on her mound of Venus. In one fluid movement he got up and went to stand quietly next to the bed. Her pink lips were parted as though inviting his kiss. The strap of her thin nightgown had slipped on to her shoulder, offering a tantalizing glimpse of breast. She had beautiful, firm breasts, high and rounded. It had been sweet torture while he soaped her body. He'd never been a voyeur, but this woman awakened the most basic and primitive instincts in him. And now, gazing down on Luna, he felt like baring her skin to his mouth and hands, inch by inch, smelling and tasting her; feeling her shudder with abandon beneath his touch. How was a man to resist such temptation? Still, he was a doctor and she was worn out and needing careful treatment.

So he turned away and went back to his sleeping bag. Heaven only knows how he'd get any sleep tonight with images of Luna racing through his head: Luna in his arms; Luna so passionate and eager, her softness leaning into his hardness, crying out her pleasure and her need for him as she had done the night before. He was there to look after her, not to indulge his fantasies, though. Tomorrow they would talk more, and perhaps he would try to unravel the mystery that was Luna Ward.

*   *   *

Luna was awakened by her own cry as the first light of dawn broke with a gossamer mist over the Atlantic like a delicate white finger pointing across the sky in the east. As she jerked upright, shaking convulsively, blood pounding in her head, teeth chattering, the nightmare still pursued her. She had been running endlessly in the woods, breathless, desperate to escape the menacing shadow tearing behind her, close on her heels, so close that she could almost feel the heat of his breath on her skin. Then there had been a light ahead, marking the edge of the forest, and she could just make out the silhouette of a figure outlined against it. Ruy … and he had his arms held out to her. She sprinted, stretching her legs as far as she could, running faster and faster; she needed to reach him before the shadow man grabbed her.

And then she fell against him, sobbing his name as his embrace closed around her. She looked up, but it wasn't Ruy's eyes she met … it was *him* … and his gaze held nothing but cruelty … and triumph. She had cried out in fear, a strident, piercing, primal sound that seemed to have been torn from the core of her being as she thrashed about, striking out like a wild cat, struggling to free herself from the shadow man's icy, powerful grip.

'Hush, *querida*, hush. *Es solo una pesadilla*, it's only a bad dream.'

Luna emerged from her nightmare, disorientated for a few seconds; then she hiccupped a sob of relief. Ruy was sitting on the side of her bed, holding her to him, stroking her head gently, pushing her hair away from her clammy forehead and whispering reassuring words.

In the early morning glow her tearful eyes settled on his concerned face.

'Ruy,' she murmured. 'Oh, Ruy! … You were there … trying to save me …' She was pale, shaking uncontrollably, and she shrank closer, clinging to him in a bid to calm her breathing and quieten her heartbeat.

'It's all right, I'm here. There's nothing to fear, *querida*,' he said tenderly. 'I'll fetch you a drink, I won't be a second.'

But her grip tightened on his shirt. 'Don't go,' she pleaded. 'Please don't leave me.'

'I'll just bring you a little hot milk. It will help calm your nerves.' Reluctantly she let go of him and he helped her lie back against the pillows. 'I won't be long, I promise.'

Luna gave him a pale smile. 'Thanks. Thank you for everything.' Her voice was unsteady and he winked at her before heading for the stairs.

Lying back against the pillows, she stared out of the window over the sparkling blue sea that stretched as far as the limitless horizon. Ideas fought for clarity in her head. She was so used to these nightmares, but this time there had been a light at the end of the tunnel, and she knew all she had wanted … needed … was to gravitate towards the sanctuary of Ruy's arms.

He came back carrying a glass of hot milk on a tray with some grapes. 'Here, drink this, *querida*. I've added some honey and a little brandy to give you a boost,' he grinned. 'My father's remedy for everything. The grapes will refresh you too.'

'Thank you. I'll have a sip of the milk, but I'll pass on the grapes.'

'You haven't eaten since yesterday. Besides, the sugar is good for you. It'll restore your energy.'

She ate a couple of grapes and smiled wanly. 'I'll cook us some breakfast before getting off to work.'

'You're not going anywhere today and neither am I. I'm on holiday this week, and you're certainly not going into the clinic. Doctor's orders.'

'I really should catch up on things at the Institute,' she persisted. 'Thanks to you, I feel much better now.'

'The only way you can thank me is to do as I say and take a break for the next few days to recover.'

'Sorry about last night …' Luna gave him a timid smile.

He looked at her uncertainly. 'Sorry about what? You had a very traumatic experience. I wouldn't like to be caught up in a storm in those woods.'

'Still, I behaved like a spoilt child,' she whispered, sipping her milk and avoiding his eyes. When she lifted her head, his gaze was on her, intent and thoughtful.

'Anyway, I tried to ask you last night, and I'm sorry if I was a bit aggressive … The thing is … what were you doing out there in the storm?'

'I went to see if I could find your herb garden. Then I got lost … and heard voices … and it was you and Sabrina …' Her voice tailed off miserably.

'I'm happy that you went to look for my garden,' he said with a wry smile. 'Even happier that you failed to find it, but now I can show it to you myself one day … and you won't be able to trample all over the seedlings.' Ruy smiled, and then his expression became more serious. 'But your nightmare …' His eyes were kind, unwavering. 'It isn't the first time you've had this sort of thing happen to you, is it?'

She shook her head silently.

'Is it a recurrent dream? The same each time?'

Her mouth trembled. 'Sort of,' she whispered.

'Would it help to talk about it?'

Ruy wasn't rushing her. By now Luna had enough clarity to realize that he was beginning to heal and reawaken her, but she found it hard to bare her soul to anyone, let alone the man whose contempt she most feared. Still, he was a doctor and it was becoming starkly obvious to her that she needed help if she was going to find the real Luna again … or earn a modicum of peace or happiness. She needed to feel safe enough with a man to be able to lower her guard if she wanted to lead a normal and healthy life in the future. Of that, she was sure.

'It's all about trust, isn't it?' she said at length. She meant it more as a statement than a question, and Ruy nodded silently. There was another lapse of time while she pondered on the issue before she spoke again. 'I think I'm beginning to trust you,' she said slowly, looking into his glowing eyes. Something in the way their fire lovingly caressed her features made her feel the last vestiges of ice around her heart begin to melt away.

His hand moved to cover hers, a warm strong hand, gentle and reassuring. He gazed into her eyes and she knew what it was to feel safe and secure.

'He was a member of the family ...' she said at length, slowly, as though the words were dragged from her. She had never told a single person her shameful secret, and she shook with the effort of voicing it.

'Go on, take your time.' Ruy's voice was soothing, tender, as if quieting a troubled child.

'He used to come over now and again while I was growing up, just flying visits in the holidays. I had so few people in my life, apart from Grandma Ward and Aunt Bea ... It was nice to feel connected to more of my family somehow.' A lump in her throat prevented her from continuing for a long moment.

She was looking at Ruy now without seeing him, locked into the memory, reliving her nightmare.

'Don't be afraid,' he whispered encouragingly. 'Go on.'

Luna took a breath. 'My father wasn't around enough of the time. He was grateful that someone was there to take care of me, I suppose.' Her bottom lip quivered and her eyes filled with tears. 'This man ... he took me places ... to the zoo, the cinema ... an art gallery ...' She swiped a hand across her eyes. 'I trusted him, you see. I was still only twelve. Of course I was naïve. I was just a child, for God's sake. But he made me feel responsible ...'

Ruy's hand was still covering hers. He squeezed her fingers gently. 'You're doing very well,' he whispered encouragingly. 'You'll feel much, much better when this is out.'

Luna heard his words, but couldn't yet feel the truth in them, so nauseated and fearful was she. She just knew she needed to cling on to that life raft of trust she had instinctively in Ruy.

'He came to my room to say goodnight. My father wasn't at home, away at some conference or other,' she said bleakly. 'The thing is, I knew it didn't feel right. There was something uncomfortable about it. He just kept staring. His eyes ... All I could do was pretend I needed to go to sleep ... pulled my covers up to my chin. It was as if he didn't notice, though.

'Then his hand reached under my bedclothes ... I felt it on me ... everywhere. I was so scared, I went completely rigid. At first I couldn't speak at all ... then I asked him to stop ... but his face was suddenly against mine, his tongue pushing in my mouth. I couldn't breathe. I felt so dirty, so ashamed ... I struggled and pushed him away.' She gave a strangled sob, her hand covering her eyes. 'He didn't go any further, told me it was our little secret.'

Ruy clenched his jaw. His face struggled with emotion before he regained his self-control. 'There was no need to feel ashamed, Luna. This is what abusers do,' he said softly, his hand going to her head and stroking her hair slowly, as if calming a frightened horse. 'They prey on the innocence of children, making them feel like it's all their fault.'

Luna realized her secret was now told, it was shared at last, and it was like a balm to her soul. It was as if she had poured her heart out to someone she had known for a very long time. Someone who understood her and was on her side; someone who listened attentively without interrupting, and without judging her. The shivering was subsiding now. She felt strangely purged; almost like a young child again.

'There, *querida*, that feels better, doesn't it?' Ruy's voice was so soothing it made every muscle in her body sigh with relief.

She blinked away a tear. 'Yes, it does. It really does,' she said with a smile that wobbled a little. 'I wonder if this means the nightmares will stop.'

'Quite possibly,' he said reassuringly. 'Some traumas continue to surface but, with a little of the right treatment, they should fade entirely. But, *mi amor*, you've taken the first step, and that's crucial to your healing. If a secret has been damped down for so long, of course it will surface in other ways, trying to push away the lid confining it.'

'And now I've taken the lid off …' Luna said thoughtfully.

'You have, and that took real bravery,' he said. 'Nothing less than I'd expect of you, of course. Truth is second nature to you, I know that.'

For a brief second, Luna's mind darted to the other secret she was keeping from Ruy. Then she discarded the thought. She was feeling so heartened, so positive by what had just happened that nothing could dislodge the idea that everything was going to be all right.

She'd deal with it very soon … when the time was right. Of course she would.

*   *   *

Luna took her time showering and dressing while Ruy was downstairs making breakfast. She wanted to feel attractive again, and looked in the mirror appraisingly. The scratches on her face weren't that deep or obvious, she could disguise them with concealer. Though her cheeks were a little hollow, making her cheekbones stand out, she marvelled at how her luminous eyes were shining.

Anticipation was pumping adrenaline into her veins, making her pulse race, and already she was light-headed with excitement just knowing he was downstairs. She chose a tan shrug in thin, almost transparent cotton, which she slipped over a fitted vest that provided a tantalizing glimpse of the rounded curves of her breasts. She teamed these with some beige jeans, which clung to her sensuously, showing off to advantage every contour of her trim body, while hiding the cuts and scratches on her legs. Her hair was silky, lush and shining, and she let it hang loosely down her back. Her feet were still tender; for the moment she was better off leaving them bare. She glanced one last time in the mirror.

Yes, much better, she told herself with a satisfied smile. Not bad at all, given the circumstances.

When she went down to the kitchen, she found Ruy had set out breakfast in a shaded place on the terrace.

'I thought it would be nice to eat outside,' he announced as he placed the cafetière of steaming coffee on the table. He straightened and looked at her, riveted. His magnificent eyes, so intensely blue this morning, raked over her slowly. '*Querida*, you look good enough to eat,' he murmured in a rusty-sounding voice. He dragged his gaze away from her. 'First, *you* need some food, though. We've got coffee and *churros*. They're nice and warm, I've just taken them out of the oven.'

Luna would have preferred him to take her in his arms and kiss her, but he had gone to a lot of trouble to cook breakfast and the least she could do was show some appreciation of his efforts. Besides, her appetite was stirring at the smell of the freshly warmed pastries.

'Yes, I am really hungry,' she admitted, sitting down where he had pulled out the chair for her.

'How d'you take your coffee? Black, milk, sugar?'

She laughed. 'The works! One lump of sugar, please, and a *soupçon* of milk.'

Smiling, he poured them both a cup and passed her a *churro*.

'These little doughnuts bring back memories of my early childhood, when my sister Juliet and I spent our holidays at Aunt Isabel's house in Granada.' Luna smiled at the memory. 'Juliet could be so funny sometimes. She used to cut up the *churros* to make a moustache. I would laugh until I fell off my chair.'

Luna glanced up at Ruy. Had he stiffened, his eyes clouding? If he had, he recovered himself immediately and the moment was gone.

'For me, it's memories of my mother's housekeeper, who taught me how to make them,' Ruy said. 'She's retired now. Quite a character, Mela, full of life. She's had a hard time lately since her husband died, though.'

'You're quite domesticated,' she remarked. 'A dab hand at cooking. She did a fine job.'

He gave a shrug. 'I've lived on my own since the age of eighteen. First at university, then here in Cádiz.' He chuckled. 'Despite my mother's protests, my father has always insisted I have my own apartment. *Lejos de las faldas de su madre*, away from your mother's apron strings.'

'So you're not a mummy's boy,' she said with an amused grin. She hadn't thought he was.

'No, but she's very protective. Especially since she lost the child she was carrying – a girl – before she had me.'

Luna's face fell. 'I'm sorry. That must have been so hard on your mother. And to think ... you would have had a sister ...' She paused for a moment before continuing. 'I lost a sister too. Juliet, whom I just mentioned ... I was twelve. It was around the same time as ...' Luna looked down. Such a difficult time in her life ... Exhaling deeply, she went on. 'She died in a car accident. My mother went downhill after that. Aunt Isabel likes to say she died of a broken heart, but she drank herself to death, to be more precise. It was not long afterwards.'

Her words provoked a sudden change in Ruy's deep blue eyes, an expression Luna could neither read nor understand, but he stiffened and turned his gaze towards the sea, his eyes travelling the far horizon from east to west. Below the terrace there was a curve of sable sand, with a fringe of lace-like foam at the water's edge. Seaweed was everywhere, whipped up from the deep and carried inland by the storm. A few fishing boats were coming in slowly, and scavenging birds swooped and quarrelled over the scraps floating on the oily-looking water. For a few moments they sat in silence. Luna felt her heart swell with emotion at the wonderful, serene sight of nature after the storm. She laid a hand on Ruy's arm and breathed his name.

He turned back towards her.

'Ruy, I don't want to have secrets any more,' she said tentatively, searching his face. Her eyes fixed on his, trustingly. 'I want to tell you everything.'

He was impelled to speak. 'I know, Luna. I don't want anything to come between us either. There's something I need—'

'First,' said Luna, interrupting with a steadfast need to have her say while she had the courage to do so. 'I must tell you the whole story, about my nightmare, about the man who, you know … betrayed my trust.'

Ruy's look of edgy impatience was replaced with one of wary curiosity. 'Of course, *querida*. What is it?'

Luna paused. 'I said he was a member of my family. What I didn't tell you is that it was my uncle, Lorenzo Herrera.'

At this Ruy's eyes blazed, and he shot up in his chair. 'That bastard!' he cried. 'I knew he was an untrustworthy, greedy, self-seeking wretch, but I didn't know he was a child-molester too.'

He fell back in his seat, clenching and unclenching his fists.

'I never told my father what had happened with him,' said Luna. 'I don't know what I would have done if it had continued, but Dad didn't much care for any of the Herreras, so in the end I didn't have to worry. My father always took a dim view of sharp practice in business, and shortly after the incident he berated Lorenzo for some dubious piece of wheeling and dealing. It was the last we saw of my uncle, thank heavens. Little by little I seemed to forget … although I didn't, did I?'

Ruy shook his head. 'No, my poor Luna, you didn't forget. You just buried it all safely underground, where much of it lay in your subconscious.'

'Anyhow, after that I just found that I couldn't relax with boys,'

Luna added. 'If they came on too strong, I would simply freeze so I became used to being standoffish, aloof. I grew up not trusting any man. Then you came along …'

She gave a shaky laugh.

Ruy reached for her hand, squeezing it gently, though his expression was still intense. 'Yes, I came along, and I'm never going to let you suffer on your own ever again,' he said, then followed his vow with another, grimmer one.

'I'm going to bring that *canalla* down if it's the last thing I do, Luna. Your uncle was already my nemesis before you told me any of this.' He released her hand, and stared out to sea again, looking thunderous. 'He's done his best to destroy the Institute, commissioning articles for the medical press using bogus statistics to discredit us. In the meantime, he pumps his ill-gotten gains into offshore accounts, those overpriced drugs he withholds from desperate developing nations, while lining his own pockets.'

Ruy's gaze held hers fervently.

'And now I find that he's hurt the one person closest to my heart …'

'But what can you do?' asked Luna, warming inside at his admission.

'I don't know right now,' said Ruy grimly. 'But I assure you, one day that man will pay dearly for what he's done.'

CHAPTER 13

Luna hugged her arms to her body and stared out to sea. Unburdening herself to Ruy had given her a new kind of peace but she knew this was just the start of her healing.

'I'm not sure what to do next,' she whispered almost inaudibly. She turned her face towards him. 'Can I ask you something?'

'Yes, *querida*?'

He was studying her intently. His eyes were definitely his most stunning feature, vibrant with intelligence and simmering with a depth of feeling that took her breath away, she thought distractedly.

'You mentioned treatment … to help with the nightmares. Do you think you can help me, Ruy?'

Before, she would have been too proud and too fixed in her ways to ask such a thing of anyone, but now it seemed natural to put herself in someone's care – in *his* care.

'Of course I can, *querida*, of course,' he said softly, lifting his hand to her face and tenderly brushing a stray hair away from her temple. 'The important thing is that Lorenzo did not hurt you physically. Given time, everything else can be remedied. I know a colleague to whom I can refer you for therapy, if you'll let me.'

He was leaning in close towards her and Luna became aware of his familiar masculine scent again.

'Yes, of course,' she murmured.

His trailing fingertip left a heated sensation on her silken skin as it moved down to caress the side of her cheek. At that moment, it dawned on her how easy it would be for Ruy to kiss her. How she wanted to feel the touch of his mouth on hers again, to have him hold her.

The realization made her senses alert and inflamed. Her sudden stillness caused a flicker in the depths of Ruy's gaze. Taking in her expression, his breath caught and the tension gathered between them, neither one of them moving. A tiny pulse was beating at the corner of his mouth. He said nothing, just stared at her. Luna moved an inch towards him, but Ruy pulled back and dropped his hand.

'If I touch you now, Luna, there'll be no escape.'

Her gaze fell to his mouth. 'Who wants to escape?'

He exhaled heavily. 'I don't want you to rush into anything.'

She looked into his eyes that cloaked her in their azure blueness. 'Ruy, I've been blind.'

His voice was softly abrasive. '*Querida*, believe me, you can't know how tempted I am, but you're exhausted and vulnerable, and my self-control is already at breaking point.'

'But Ruy, I'm fine, I just need—'

'You're not fine, Luna. Not yet. I've always told you that I will be waiting when you're ready, but now is not the time.'

'Do you always have to have the last word?'

'Yes, I do.' His face broke into a wide smile. He stood up and held out his hand. 'Come, it's a beautiful day. Let's not waste it. Besides, I could do with going for a swim and working off all this excess energy,' he added with a mischievous raise of his eyebrow.

'An excess of bossiness more like,' she quipped.

A deep laugh rumbled in his chest. 'Now who has to have the last word?'

Luna grinned at him as she took his hand to stand up, pleased at least there was an easy mood between them now.

They spent the rest of the day swimming and chatting casually, with Luna occasionally napping on the sand next to Ruy as he read quietly. She was surprised to find that he was right: she was still tired; the events of the last twenty-four hours had drained her.

Despite her sleepiness, however, Luna was feeling better. Most of her aches and pains had subsided, including the stiffness in her back; her collarbone was only bruised, and whatever medicine Ruy had used to treat the wound on her thigh had been so effective that she only felt a slight discomfort now. The salt water had stung at first when they swam together in the refreshing cool of the sea, but Ruy had told her the iodine and salt could only do her good, and he was right. Luna was beginning to be converted to his earthy commonsense way of healing.

She noticed how careful he was around her. All day she had longed for him to touch her and, infuriatingly, he had kept clear of any tactile contact. Every now and then he caught her watching him and, as his amused blue eyes searched her intent amber gaze, she was unable to stem the pink hue that coloured her face.

So many times, while they talked and strolled along the beach or sat and ate beneath the clear blue skies, he would turn and, for a moment, it seemed that time stood still as they looked at each other in silence, her eyes bright and feverish, his dark and unfathomable.

That night, as Ruy slept just a few feet away and Luna lay in her bed alone and restless, her body on fire, still crying out for his, she realized that she no longer had a sense of which of the two of them was waiting to be ready.

*   *   *

It was still early but the sun was already brilliant in a cloudless sky when Luna woke the next morning. Surprisingly, despite her disturbed awareness of Ruy's presence so near to her, she had eventually given in to exhaustion and had slept soundly through the night. Now, stretching her arms, she yawned and lay in bed for a while, savouring the feeling of wellbeing that filled her heart and her body. Her spirits were high and she felt charged up with vitality, physically invigorated.

She sat up and saw Ruy fast asleep on the floor next to the open window. In repose his face looked so young. His raven-black hair fell across the side of his forehead, almost covering one eye. Her gaze settled on his taut, beautifully moulded lips. They had kissed hers a bare three times, but she would never forget the fire of their passionate touch and the sensual impact those kisses had had on her senses.

Her eyes moved down to his chest. He was naked to the waist, the bottom half of his body covered by his sleeping bag; her fingers itched to touch his copper-gold skin, so smooth and satiny. The blood heated in her veins as she wondered if his lower half was naked too. Her desire for him had never been so strong and she felt neither guilt nor shame about it.

Her mind drifted back to the day before, when he had bathed her naked body, soaping every part of her with such exquisite tenderness and torturous erotic awareness. She remembered every single thing he had done to her and the memory of his touch was intoxicating, causing sharp ripples of excitement to quiver down her spine and across every inch of the skin his fingers had run over. She didn't try to subdue it: on the contrary, she welcomed the sweet yearning that possessed her and made her feel dizzy.

She knew he was fighting his desire for her – he had admitted it outright. Luna smiled to herself, a sudden touch of mischief kissing her eyes. Today, if he lost the battle, she would not attempt to escape him. The jealousy she had felt over Sabrina – and Vaina for that matter – had evaporated now that he had explained about them, and she wanted to give him the benefit of the doubt. He had proved that she mattered to him and for now that was all that counted.

I'll wash and then I'll wake him, she thought, her loins throbbing with anticipation, and she hurried to the bathroom to shower. She didn't linger, as was her custom. Ten minutes later, scrubbed and scented, she came back into the bedroom with a towel wrapped around her middle; her eyes alight with a wicked glint.

Luna lay down beside Ruy, her head propped on her elbow. She looked at him wonderingly, her eyes following the contours of his features, the sweep of his brows, his dark lashes, the strong, masculine jaw. Bending her head, she touched her lips to his mouth. He was warm with sleep and she inhaled his male fragrance. He moaned and she ran her fingers lightly over the silky dark down of his chest, feeling his muscles flex gently beneath her touch. Shivering, he moaned again. She liked it when he did that, so she lowered her mouth to his chest and closed it over his brown nipple, sucking it softly and then nibbling at it with her teeth. He gasped and opened sensuous, drowsy eyes; she saw his pupils enlarge and softly glaze over with a mixture of desire and pleasure.

'Luna,' he whispered, his voice thick, and then he closed his eyes again. No, Ruy was not asleep, no part of him was asleep; she could feel his heart beating under her palm as rapidly as hers, every part of him responding to the thrill she was creating. She smiled inwardly as she slipped her hand into the sleeping bag, looking for his arousal – she had never done this, never dreamt that she would do anything so daring. He was naked underneath the cover and she heard his loud intake of breath as she found him and cupped him tentatively.

His hand joined hers, pulling it away.

'Luna, you don't need to do this,' he said, his breathing fast and shallow.

'Do you like it?' she whispered huskily.

'*Do I like it?* You don't know what you're doing to me.'

'And you don't know what it does to me to feel you like this. You're so magnificent,' she murmured as she revelled in the heat and strength of his arousal pulsing under her touch. She fondled him with one hand, her fingers lightly exploring and massaging, while the other unzipped the sleeping bag to uncover his manhood. An overflow of desire suffused her body as he lay in glorious nakedness in front of her, and she heard him groan and whisper her name as she dipped her head to take him between her lips. But before she reached him, he laced his fingers in her blonde mane and pulled her up gently, sweeping his arms around her and lifting her on top of him.

Then his mouth was on hers, hot and demanding, his tongue exploring and tasting and stealing her breath away; a hungry mouth that took possession of hers with a wild, almost barbaric passion. His warm palms cupped her breasts, kneading them sensually in a circular fashion, making her whole body shiver and press into him instinctively, her softness moulding into his hardness. She moved sinuously on top of him, stroking him with her body, brushing against his arousal and fuelling her own need as she felt him throb underneath her.

Her exuberant delight was a compelling aphrodisiac, urging him to push further into their lovemaking. His hands slid down to her bottom, caressing it, moving up and down her thighs. Totally attuned to his body language, she parted them and straddled him. She cried out his name as his burning need touched her sensitive pulsing core and the warmth flooded her loins. He made her lean backwards, arms straight, with her palms behind her, resting on his lower thighs, while he cupped her breasts that swelled and ached as his fingers stimulated the little pink peaks that visibly darkened with every tease. She arched her back, pushing against him, her aroused body completely exposed to him, uninhibited, as she cried out, urging him to please her more and more. One hand slid from her flushed breast down to her flat stomach, covering it and, raising his torso, he ran his hot lips over her quivering flesh, kissing and licking, her tormented moans urging him to provide her with ever greater enjoyment.

'I want to feel you inside me,' she sobbed. 'I can't take it any more. Please, Ruy, I want you, I want to be yours,' she begged, her breath coming quickly as she writhed above him, luxuriating in the satiny feel of his hardness throbbing against her swollen damp core.

Then with one swift movement, he flipped her over, pinning her down with the hard length of his body. '*Dios*, Luna, you have no idea what it was like to sleep near you all night and not be able to touch you,' he muttered deep in his throat as he moved over her. 'I've been thinking about nothing else,' he whispered in her ear, his voice soft and seductive as velvet.

His words triggered a rush of desire so fierce that she almost came. Luna's breath caught audibly. She arched her back, pressing up against him, every part of her crying out to be possessed by him, but it seemed he was still obstinately holding back, struggling against a basic instinct. She couldn't understand his hesitation.

'Why,' she asked breathlessly, 'why are you still fighting me? Don't you want me?'

His hand came round her head to fist in her hair, stopping her words with his mouth and their gasps mingled in an urgent kiss. Breathing heavily, he rested his head against her forehead.

'Of course I want you, *querida*. You can't imagine how much I want you. I just need to know that you're sure about this before it's too late.'

'I've never been more sure of anything. I want you now,' she moaned impatiently, wanting to experience all that Ruy's magnificent body promised, and her hand slid down between them in search of his hard strength, her whole body trembling as she did so. 'Let me touch you, I …'

The rest of her phrase disappeared into the burning inferno of his mouth as he claimed her lips, crushing them hungrily. He inhaled sharply, then gave a strangled cry of pleasure as her fingers found him.

'Luna, you're playing with fire.'

He gripped her shoulders tightly and closed his eyes, relishing her touch, and she could tell how eager he was for her, how he was struggling to keep in check the surging of his body that was threatening to overwhelm him.

'I don't care. Tell me how much you want me.' She fondled him with long strokes of her fingers, pushing mercilessly at his self-control, and he gave a deep growl in the back of his throat.

'Let me show you, *mi amor*.'

In one easy movement he rolled off her and suddenly she was in his arms again as he carried her swiftly to the bed. Her heart sang and she sank into the softness of the mattress, voluptuously enjoying the weight of him against her. She lifted her arms and clasped them around his neck as he took her parted lips into his mouth, his hands possessing her aching breasts with desperate passion. His kiss was wild and hungry, his tongue plundering and pushing forward, and she revelled in the erotic power of him deliberately using his male strength to subdue her, inexorably miming the act of love he had abstained from for so long.

Then she gasped in disappointment as he wrenched his mouth from hers, panting, and she tried to pull his head towards her again.

'*Poco a poco me amor, poco a poco*,' he murmured tenderly against her mouth. 'I want to savour every second. We've waited so long for this, *querida*.'

'There'll be no holding back?' She looked deep into his fascinating eyes, which were so close to hers that she could discern the midnight-blue dots in the pale-blue sea of his irises.

He smiled at her. 'No holding back, I promise,' he answered, stroking her hair before running the back of his hand down the side of her face.

His fingers then reached down into her dampness. He fondled her with circular strokes, wickedly spreading the slick moisture of her swollen heat, applying more and more pressure as he did so. She parted her legs and placed him where she was crying out for him, and he moved, hot, hard and silky against her wetness with almost uncontrolled fever. She moaned with pleasure, completely melting under his delicious strokes, aware of the violent blood-beat at the core of her, knowing that soon, very soon, it would explode into a thousand shattering rainbows.

When he began kissing his way down between her breasts to her navel, Luna held her breath. His head settled between her thighs and as he parted the slick petals of her secret flesh, and his warm mouth took into it the swollen, pulsing blossom of her passion, she sobbed, pleading for him to end her exquisite misery. She felt the strength of his own desire being held in check, and his powerful shoulders tensed for a moment before he slipped one finger inside her. She stilled and he stopped, then once more he kissed her rosy bud and as more heat flooded her, this time he slipped in two fingers. She moaned a low sort of whimper, and again he withdrew. A few seconds passed before he inserted three fingers, gently stroking and kissing her, whispering reassuring words, telling her how much he loved and needed her.

Suddenly her flesh was generously opening for him, her body telling him how much she wanted him inside her. Then he was on top of her, positioning himself between her legs and stroking them slightly more apart. His arm tightened around her, bringing her body level with his and, tenderly, he took her lips with his own. As he pushed his tongue into her mouth, he gently eased himself inside her tight, moist, silken warmth in lingering degrees until he filled her.

She emitted one sharp intake of breath and he paused.

'*Querida* ...' he murmured hoarsely, 'am I hurting you?'

'No.' She shook her head in surprise, then her body yielded and welcomed him with minimal resistance as slowly she began to move with him, digging her nails into his back as momentum built between them.

He teased her, thrusting in and out, watching the pleasure-pain his potent hardness was building inside her painted ecstatically on her face. Fire roared through her veins. Her legs cinctured his waist, pulling him closer to her, drawing him deeper, further and faster, enveloping him in her honeyed warmth. She sensed his mounting need vibrating in her middle like waves of molten flames flooding her with heat and a building momentum of urgency.

With a sense of exultation, their limbs entwined; they savoured each other with epicurean delight. They were in total harmony, in sensuous movements as old as time, dancing to the melody of their mindless passion, guiding each other towards fulfilment in the awareness that nothing would ever obliterate the memory of the first fusion of their love.

Release came in a shattering storm as the earth and sky shuddered, and the flood bore them away. Wave upon wave of rapturous pleasure rippled over their convulsing bodies again and again until, finally, the world gently quietened around them and they lay panting and clinging to one another.

Luna's heart trembled. She could scarcely believe what had happened to her. Now she could admit it: every heartbeat, every breath, every thought proclaimed it; and she could finally say it out loud.

'I love you, Ruy. I will always love you.'

'And I, *mi amor, mi tierno amor*, will never let you go.'

They slept and woke up, and made love again and again, mutual hunger for each other acting like a powerful aphrodisiac on their senses.

It was late afternoon when Ruy finally left her. 'I'll be only a couple of hours, *querida*,' he promised. 'I need to get a change of clothes. I haven't been home for almost two days.'

'I'll miss you,' she murmured, putting her arms around his neck and he pulled her tight against him again.

'I won't be long. Tonight, I'll take you to dinner at a small restaurant I know and then we'll come back home and I'll love you over and over until you've had enough of me.'

'I'll never have enough of you,' she breathed, her amber eyes glowing like pools of fire.

Ruy groaned deep in his throat. 'Don't look at me like that.' His kiss parted her lips, which opened eagerly and hungrily to receive his tongue, and she closed her eyes. This time he explored and teased gently and tenderly, then slowly withdrew. She opened her eyes; his thumb caressed the side of her cheek.

'*Hasta luego, querida.* The sooner I go, the sooner I'll be back.'

*   *   *

From the outside, the restaurant Océano looked like an upturned boat with a transparent hull as a roof. The elegant domed dining room, equally adventurous in design and encircled by floor-to-ceiling windows, seemed to float like a bubble, flooded with the pinkish hue of the evening sun and the reflected lights of the harbour across the water.

Luna had already travelled extensively for her age and had been wined and dined in some of the most expensive and elegant restaurants across the globe but this was a whole new experience. As with La Gaviota, she sensed the genius of a fanciful architect at work, the mischievousness of a whimsical mind.

'It's fabulous,' she whispered, looking around her as they walked through the wide French-window-style front door.

Ruy chuckled. 'Wait till you see the rest.'

The main floor had a spacious, pillar-free open layout that gave on to a central atrium. The lights were dim with a bluish cast to give the impression of being outdoors, while the views through the glass all around were breathtaking. Luna felt a little disappointed when the white-jacketed head waiter directed them to the centre of the room and down a modern spiral staircase to the lower-ground floor of the restaurant – she would have preferred to have this first tête-à-tête dinner with Ruy surrounded by the sea. But then, as the downstairs decor came into view, she gasped. It was a sensory explosion. This room was also dimly lit, though here the walls were alive with exotic fish of all types and colours, darting between the plants, swirling together and nosing the glass of the aquarium that encircled the room.

Luna had the impression of truly being underwater. 'It's like stepping into a fishbowl.'

'If you find this place claustrophobic and prefer to have dinner upstairs I'm sure it can be arranged,' Ruy told her.

'No, this is glorious and it's surprisingly peaceful too. It's the silence, I love it.'

He slipped an arm about her waist and nuzzled her neck, drawing her close to him for a moment.

They were shown to their table and given beautiful menus written in calligraphy and hand-painted with creatures of the sea. Fascinated by the living picture surrounding her, Luna watched the fish dine while Ruy studied the wine list. They ordered baby octopus in a saffron sauce as a starter and tuna Basquaise to follow.

'This place is amazing. Each floor has its own charm. Who's the architect? Is he contemporary?'

At this Ruy smiled. 'My grandfather, Eduardo de Salazar. More than thirty years ago he came up with the concept of this place before anyone had even thought of aquarium restaurants. Anyhow, it was too avant-garde for Spain at the time and was never constructed. My father finally had it built a couple of years ago.'

Luna blinked, remembering something that Diego Montez had said to her. 'I've just realized, my beach house is apparently inspired by your Eduardo de Salazar's architecture. I knew the name rang a bell.' She decided it best not to mention that the flirtatious estate agent had imparted the information.

Ruy nodded. 'I'm not surprised. I thought as much when I first saw La Gaviota.'

'I love the house so much, you know. I'd really like to buy it.'

'Once we're married, perhaps we could have it as our special hideaway.'

Stunned, Luna shot upright, scarcely able to believe her ears. She gave a gulp. 'Are you asking me to marry you?'

Watching her, Ruy's eyes were as deep and blue as the evening sky; hers were bright when they met them.

He slanted her a grin. 'I'm not asking you, *querida*, I'm *telling* you.'

She could hear her heart thudding at such a pace she thought it would break her ribs. Suddenly she couldn't think straight. 'I'm not sure I understand. Isn't it a bit premature? How can you be so sure?'

'Any two people who created the magic we made today must be compatible ... and we've only just started.' His eyes gleamed with mischief.

Confused, she stared into his face, trying to read what was in his mind and then gave him a tremulous smile.

'I hope you're not basing your entire judgement on sex, Ruy. Life is long and I'm told passion ebbs away as the years go by.'

A familiar whisper of warning crept into her mind. She felt a wisp of the old Luna – the cautious, pragmatic Luna – surface, unable to get carried away entirely in the joyous tumult of emotion that Ruy's proposal had unleashed.

'*No, no, no!*' Ruy shook his head violently. 'We are made for each other, *querida*. I know it deep down in here.' His eyes blazed as he made a fist and placed it on his heart as if he had to make her understand. 'When you're with me, Luna, I feel complete. As soon as we separate there's a hollow in my gut. I know it's a void only you can fill.'

They were interrupted by the waiter bringing the first course, which he delivered with a flourish before gliding discreetly away.

Luna gazed at Ruy, relishing the glorious sight of him and the love she could see shining in his eyes, yet still she hesitated.

'But there's so much we don't know about each other,' she breathed, panicked for a moment about the secret still unshared, the secret that might very well detonate like a hand grenade should she be unable to persuade Ruy of her earnest intention to put things right.

He reached over and placed a finger on her lips, his eyes imploring her not to spoil the evening.

'Shush, *querida*. Trust me, all will go well. You're the one for me and I'm the one for you. That's all there is to say.'

The promise gleaming in his deep-blue irises and the ardent fire in his voice caused any doubts to flee in the face of a most wonderful liquid feeling of love and contentment. She smiled at him. Did she need to know anything more? Luna didn't have to tell him her answer; she could see that he knew – he could read it in the glow of her cheeks. Tenderness swept over his face. He lifted her hand to his lips and closed his eyes.

'*Gracias, mi bello y tierno amor.*'

She gazed adoringly at him. 'I can't quite believe it,' she whispered, looking around the other diners, wondering at how they hadn't sensed the amazing and cataclysmic event that had just overturned the lives of herself and Ruy. She turned back to him. 'Can we just keep it as our secret for a little longer?'

'*Ciertamente*, we'll take as long as you like. Remember, *querida*, I would never pressure you but I will always be here for you.'

A little later, over the next course, Luna managed to guide the conversation to Sabrina, reminding Ruy that he had promised to tell her the girl's story. She no longer held any vestiges of the fear and jealousy that had overcome her the previous evening. It felt like a distant memory now and she was simply keen to fill in the missing piece of jigsaw in Ruy's own story.

'Sabrina's mother originated from the *Tziganes* of central Transylvania,' Ruy explained. 'Leyla, or La Pharaona as they called her, had been tried and found guilty of adultery by a gypsy tribunal. Her life as she knew it was over. She was banished from her people, with no hope of ever returning. Pregnant, she fled to Spain, where, for a few years, she led a hard life on the streets of Seville with her child, Sabrina.'

'How did you get to know her?' Luna asked.

'She finally ended up in Puerto de Santa María. La Pharaona had already been making her name as a healer among the gypsies in Triana, the poor quarter of Seville. She had brought with her such a wealth of herbal knowledge from the hills of her homeland. It was such a gift.' Ruy paused to take a gulp of wine, a half-smile playing on his face. 'Anyway, as fortune would have it, she heard about the many plants that grow in Alcalá de los Gazules and, when she'd gathered enough clients, she went into the hills and built herself a hut in the glade where you found Sabrina and me yesterday evening.

'La Pharaona would always carry the stigma of being ostracized by her own people, and so the *Calés* were happy to keep her at arm's length. Still, people came to her from all over Andalucía and she made a good living.'

'How did *you* get to know her, though?'

He studied her face and then cast his eyes down, turning his napkin over in his hand. 'My father, being half-gypsy, came across La Pharaona when I was having a difficult time at university. She showed me her plant remedies and we became friends.' He looked up, his eyes warming. 'She taught me such a lot, especially about healing being a matter of treating the mind, body and spirit – a truly holistic undertaking. If it wasn't for her, I wouldn't be the man, or the doctor, I am now.'

Luna could see a mist cloud Ruy's eyes as he paused and took a gulp of wine.

'Anyway, sometimes, when La Pharaona had to go down to Puerto de Santa María to visit a client, I kept an eye on Sabrina up in the hills. As the child grew older she became infatuated with me, but on my side there's never been anything but a brotherly feeling towards her. On her deathbed, La Pharaona effectively passed me her healer's mantle, together with the responsibility of recording her remedies for posterity and tending her beloved herb garden. She also gave me something infinitely more precious to her to keep safe. The guardianship of Sabrina, until the time should come when the girl could fly with her own wings.'

Luna swallowed. 'That's a lot to ask.'

'It has been more of a pleasure than a duty, thankfully. La Pharaona would never have asked if she hadn't recognized that we'd established a close, almost familial bond already. Not only that, she was generous enough to teach me the herbal lore she'd inherited from her forebears.'

He paused to reflect a moment.

'I owed her a great deal. No, it wasn't really a lot to ask.'

There was something in his expression that puzzled Luna but she decided to leave it until another time when they were completely alone. Instead she told him: 'You did the right thing. Sabrina is so lucky to have you.'

Ruy smiled. 'Anyhow, the time has come for Sabrina to spread those wings. She's leaving Andalucía and joining a family of gypsy healers in Murcia. They heard about her skills and sought her out. They've just lost their daughter so it seems right. I'm happy for Sabrina. Hopefully, she's finally found people who will understand and appreciate her. She's very good at what she does too. Her mother taught her well. The other night when you saw her dancing in the moonlight, that was her way of saying goodbye.'

'I hope she finds happiness.' Slowly, Luna traced a line in the tablecloth with her fingertip. 'I know what it is to feel motherless and adrift. I had my cousin to support me through difficult times, we all need someone …' She glanced up at him earnestly. 'I hope that one day, when she's over her crush, Sabrina will be able to count me as a friend too.'

Ruy's eyes glowed with love and approbation. 'I feel the happiest man alive,'

It was all he said, and all he needed to say on the matter. He tucked into his tuna with relish. 'This is delicious. Try yours.'

Luna took a mouthful. 'Wow, that's amazing!'

'It's fished locally on the Costa de la Luz. If you're interested I'll take you to watch the *Almadraba*. It's an ancient Andalucían way of fishing the red tuna.'

Luna's eyes lit up. 'I'd love that.'

'I'll call Chico in the morning to have the yacht made ready for us. He spends as much time on her as I do and often takes her out. He'll be glad to help out. The boat's moored in Conil de la Frontera. We can drive down tomorrow and spend a couple of days there. It'll be in the midst of the Feria de Primavera de El Colorado, when they celebrate the change from spring to summer. It's a good time to go.'

The gentle glow of the exotic aquarium around them created an intimate bubble that made Luna keenly aware of the charismatic force of the man sitting across the table from her. Indeed, if charisma and a dominating personality were the measure of masculinity then Ruy was a giant among men. In the past, this would have brought on a feeling of irritation or belligerence in her, she realized, but now it made her feel feminine and safe. Deep down she knew it was precisely her own femininity that could – if she chose to use it – reduce this powerful man to a meek lamb.

'Let's go home,' she whispered, the sudden desire for his arms around her eclipsing any rational thought. 'Let's not have coffee here. I'll make some for you at La Gaviota – or a hot chocolate if you like?'

His lips quirked. 'I read somewhere that love is like swallowing hot chocolate before it's cooled off. At first it takes you by surprise, but keeps you warm for a long time.' His eyes turned a rich, vibrant blue as he gazed at her face. 'Have I told you how ravishingly beautiful you are tonight?'

Luna blushed. 'You make me feel beautiful all the time.'

This was the beginning of the most deliriously happy few days of Luna's life.

CHAPTER 14

Ruy left La Gaviota shortly before midnight, after Luna had spent a blissful couple of hours in his arms. She had wanted him to stay but he told her to get some sleep as they'd be off bright and early. However, rather than go to bed straight away, she decided to call Ted Vandenberg, her editor in New York. On the East Coast it would still be working hours and, if she was going to sort out the mess into which she had plunged herself, she wanted the conversation with him to be over and done with as soon as possible.

As she had already summoned the courage to email her final article to Ted, now she was preparing herself to give her verbal resignation. What did it matter if she was without a job? The situation as it stood was utterly untenable and, after dwelling so much on issues of trust and honesty these past few days, she had begun to realize that the world of investigative journalism was not for her in any case.

Ted's voice when he answered the phone was cautious, less ebullient than usual. Luna asked him what he had thought of her feature.

'To tell you the honest truth, I was a bit taken aback,' he admitted in his familiar smoky drawl. 'I thought you were going to give us a juicy exposé, even though I cautioned you against bias in your investigation. Instead, I received something rather astonishingly different.'

Luna's heart sank. 'But did you like it? I promise you that I never lost sight of the need for integrity, careful fact-finding and respectable research. I can see it isn't what you'd term a "juicy story", though.'

'I knew you weren't the type to have the wool pulled over your eyes, Luna, and would see through every bit of flakiness.' Ted still sounded tentative, choosing his words carefully. 'But I wasn't expecting this would be the result. You've given me a hymn of praise for the Institute, that's for sure. I just need to get my head around it. Maybe our readers will find it newsworthy simply *because* they'd expect us to dish the dirt on the place.'

'Which it in no way deserves,' said Luna shortly. 'I've investigated the clinic thoroughly. Is it my fault if what I found there was exceptional, even laudable?'

Ted paused, then sighed. 'So long as you weren't led down the garden path by a charismatic boss with a renowned eye for the ladies.'

'If you're saying what I think you're saying,' said Luna, apparently forgetting for a moment that she had indeed come under the doctor's spell, 'you don't know me very well. If you think that I could ever let personal issues skew my editorial integrity ...' Her temper was rising and she was about to put down the phone, when Ted cut in quickly.

'Now then, Luna, wait a minute—'

But Luna didn't give him the chance to apologize; she needed to say her piece. 'Ted, I've enjoyed working with you until now but I think it's best if I hand in my notice,' she said quickly. 'I won't be coming back to New York. Let me know if you do decide to run the article. I worked hard on it and the Institute deserves its findings to be featured.'

At this Ted was assiduous in trying to persuade Luna to stay on, saying her potential was such that he really didn't want to lose her. He didn't exactly promise to publish her feature, but she was pretty certain that he would do so. Mollified, she softened her tone but she was still quietly firm on the fact of her leaving. When she finally put down the phone, Luna heaved a sigh of relief. If she were to have a hope of redeeming herself in Ruy's eyes after she'd told him the truth about her work at the Institute, then her feature appearing in the next issue of *Scientific US* was essential, she told herself. Until it was in print, she reasoned, she might as well remain quiet on the matter.

*   *   *

It was a usual Spanish early morning of blue skies and lemon-yellow sunshine when they set out for Conil de la Frontera in Ruy's vintage Austin. A slight pale haze in the atmosphere floated over the rooftops, conveying a dreamlike impression that enveloped the travellers in a languorous mood. For Luna, since Ruy had asked her to marry him the previous evening, it was like entering a new world, where it seemed the sun must always shine if only for the reason that she was in love with the most wonderful man and would soon have the right to share his life.

The two of them spoke little during the journey, dwelling tenderly on love and enjoying the beauty of the coastal road and the wildness of the scenery about them, which was gently mountainous with baked brown earth and scrubby green bushes and plants that made it look almost desert-like. From time to time Ruy smiled softly at Luna and she melted, floating on air, her heart and soul going out to him.

A few miles before they arrived at Conil de la Frontera, Ruy turned down a rough track that looked as though it was leading nowhere.

'Are we not going to Conil?'

'Yes, but you get to it down here. Conil is built on a cliff. It's one of the *Pueblos Blancos* of the Costa de la Luz. Historically, it's always been a strategic location because it's at the southern tip of Spain and so close to Africa,' he told her. 'After Guzmán el Bueno heroically defended Tarifa against the Moors at the end of the thirteenth century, King Fernando IV of Castile awarded him Conil, along with a handful of other neighbouring towns. El Bueno went on to fortify and repopulate Conil, building a harbour three miles out of town in a spot that gave the best anchorage.'

As they approached the port, Luna revelled in the scenery, which was now transformed. Backed by towering cliffs covered in lush vegetation, endless white beaches seemed to stretch to infinity, fringing water so clear it reflected the beautiful undersea world. The profusion of plants, shrubs and wild flowers on either side of the road took Luna's breath away. 'Wow!' she cried out spontaneously. 'Have you ever seen anything more beautiful? I can see now why you keep your boat here.'

Ruy smiled at her enthusiasm, devouring her with his gaze. 'There's a pretty walk along the clifftop of Conil harbour, leading to lots of nice coves. We'll do that one day.'

Suddenly, as they rounded the corner, the fishing harbour of Conil appeared like a miniature enclave with polychromatic toy boats bobbing in a variegated turquoise bay. Some were arranged in an orderly fashion along the narrow quay; others were leaving the harbour, looking to Luna like ducks swimming hurriedly on the placid water. A pleasure paddle steamer on a trip from Tarifa was making its way towards Cádiz, leaving in her wake a wide expanse of white froth.

Vela Gitana, *Sailing Gypsy* awaited them at one end of the busy harbour. It was a thirty-five-foot motor yacht built of mahogany planking over teak frames with a shoal draft keel. The dark-blue hull was painted to a high-gloss finish, with a thin red streaking line from bow to stern, interrupted by a row of small portholes. Her sheer was elegant and higher than the ones Luna had seen on more modern yachts but, despite her years, *Vela Gitana* was a handsome and romantic lady.

Chico was waiting for them, a broad welcoming grin beaming on his leathered face. This time his massive torso was without a shirt, and running diagonally across it, from shoulder to waist, Luna noticed a scar, white against his tanned, muscled chest.

'*Buenas días*, Ruy,' he called as they approached the boat. 'You're earlier than I expected. Was there no traffic on the roads this morning?'

'*Hola*, Chico. We left very early.'

'Luna.' Chico gave a comical half bow. 'Good to see you again.'

'You too, Chico,' Luna replied almost shyly. She was aware that things had changed between her and Ruy since the christening at the gypsy camp and suddenly felt self-conscious in front of his old friend. 'I didn't know you liked sailing.'

'I'm a sea-gypsy. In other words, half man, half shark.' He grinned and winked at Ruy.

Ruy laughed, then looked up at the sky and sniffed appreciatively at the keen air. 'What's the weather forecast? Is there going to be much wind?'

'The sea's calm and the wind is good. About seven knots per hour,' replied Chico. 'You'll reach hull speed, and you won't need to worry about large waves and accidental jibes. It should be a pleasant sail.' He turned to Luna and chuckled. 'Unless of course *la señorita* would prefer a more adventurous sail, in which case you should motor to Tarifa. The wind there this afternoon will reach about ten knots and *la señorita* will be able to whomp through the waves and let the wind and spray cool her down.'

Luna laughed wholeheartedly. 'No, no, this *señorita* is very happy to go for a gentle sail and swim.'

Chico extended a hand to her and she climbed aboard the boat, which was rocking slightly against the jetty on the breeze-ruffled water. Ruy followed.

'There are a couple of bottles of champagne and some other provisions in the fridge,' Chico told them as he stepped off the yacht. 'I also filled up the tender this morning, checked the aqualung cylinders, and left you the oilskins and diving equipment. Everything is ready if you fancy diving.'

'*Mucho gracias, hermano.* I don't think we'll dive today, maybe tomorrow,' said Ruy. '*Hasta luego,* see you later. We're booked at a hotel, so we probably won't spend the night on board.'

'But if the night is romantic, who knows, *ey*? *La luna, las estrellas y el amor.*' Chico sighed and winked at Ruy, the expression on his face full of innuendo.

'I've told you before, Chico, romance is in the heart, everything else is theatre.'

Ruy helped Luna to the striped blue-and-white side seats, where she sat while he cast off. In no time, *Vela Gitana* was elegantly moving away from her mooring. Chico stood on the quay watching them, a gap-toothed smile broadening his rugged face. 'Watch out for the tunny nets. This year they've extended them to two miles offshore!' he shouted.

'He's such a character, Chico,' remarked Luna as they waved at the receding figure of the giant *gitano*. 'Where on earth did he get that huge scar?'

'Chico's a crazy daredevil sometimes,' said Ruy with a wry smile. 'That scar was given to him by a shark. He's quite proud of it.'

'Why do I think that the shark didn't come out of it so well?' laughed Luna.

'Quite right. He fought it to the death. God knows how, as it was a mighty brute apparently. Chico knows just about everything about sailing. He takes good care of this treasure, scrubbing decks, polishing wood and mending sails when I don't have time to do it myself. He keeps it fully stocked with provisions too. We often go sailing together.'

Luna looked at his face in half profile. In his faraway gaze she read the wildness of his gypsy soul and his craving for freedom. Would he ever be able to settle down or would she ever be able to find the courage to be the adventurer at his side?

Anything, so long as they were together.

Standing behind the chromed wheel, Ruy manoeuvred the boat through Conil's small harbour, staying on the motor until they were clear of other craft.

Gradually Luna lost awareness of the scene, staring at the sea, her mind on other things. She tried to analyze the thrill of happiness that had been surging with ever-increasing power in her heart since the night of the storm. There was no need to wonder why the sky was such a heavenly blue, or the sea so turquoise, or that the sun seemed to shine with more golden warmth than ever before. Her spirit was light; life appeared roseate, and all because of this new rich emotion flooding her, making her long for Ruy with a strength that surprised her. Yet a shadow of doubt still played on the periphery of her happiness – but she was quick to shake it off. She was here with him and they loved each other. Nothing was insurmountable, was it?

'Why so silent?' Ruy's voice intruded on her reverie.

The water was like a table of oil. He had put the ship on autopilot and was coming towards her, bare-chested, his eyes shining. He looked like a primitive Roman god and the sexual stir she felt in her belly was instant, confusing her thoughts. Dark brows knitted together.

'What's wrong?'

She looked up into his eyes through the strands of hair that the breeze had swept across her face. 'Isn't it rather dangerous, putting her on autopilot?' Luna didn't really mind, but it was the first thing that popped into her head.

His devilish gaze seared her with its intensity. 'A little recklessness has never hurt anybody. Now and then it's good to test your fears so you can appreciate calmer times.' He bent slowly over her and, pushing her hair away from her face, put his warm mouth to her lips, brushing them with a feather kiss. 'Don't worry,' he added, drawing back, 'the deck winches are hydraulically powered and *Vela Gitana* is equipped with state-of-the-art electronics. Everything is automatic. I only need to touch a button for the boat to respond immediately.'

Luna's wide amber eyes held the amused sparkling blue ones, melting under his captivating stare. His lips quirked.

'And now, shall we go down so you can change into something more comfortable?'

Below deck, the finish was partly teak, partly mahogany. Luna was surprised by the unexpected sense of space, but more so by the embracing comfort of the design with its seductive elegance of chrome fixtures and broad blue-and-white striped soft furnishings.

'What a dream,' she breathed.

Ruy stood close behind her. 'My father bought her shortly after my parents were married. She'd been built in 1953 and only had one owner before him. She's been refurbished twice: once when my father acquired her and again before my thirtieth birthday, when my parents gave her to me. We've had a lot of use out of her and, in spite of her years, she is still very fast and seaworthy.

'Last year she entered the regatta of Les Voiles de St-Tropez, which used to be known as La Nioulargue, and she more than held her own among all the modern yachts, as well as some really beautiful traditional ones. She has a very competitive handicap, you know.'

Luna gazed around. 'She's a beauty. I like that she's built of wood. It's so much more romantic than fibreglass. I've always loved boats. My grandfather kept one in California. Much smaller than this but it was great fun. We used to sail to various beaches and picnic in little coves.' Her eyes sparkled at the memory. 'But I haven't sailed for a while. My skills are a little rusty, I fear.'

'You don't need to worry. *Vela Gitana* can be sailed single-handed, even in bad weather. Chico tends to skipper her when I go diving, though.'

He went over to the large top-loading fridge with a chart table above. 'What have we here? Let's see … champagne and a selection of crustaceans fresh from the market today. I can see Morena's hand in this!' He glanced at his wristwatch. 'Not yet eleven o'clock, it's still quite early. Would you like to have a swim before lunch or wait until this afternoon? There's a sheltered cove not too far from here where we could anchor and snorkel if you like. Then we could either have lunch on board or picnic on the beach.'

They decided to do exactly that, and so they made for the little island accordingly. Luna was quite happy for Ruy to take the decisions. Since her arrival in Spain, she hadn't had much time to relax. His protectiveness bordered on possessiveness, but again she didn't mind: it made her feel good.

The bathroom was stunning, like everywhere else, with a wet-room shower equipped with a body jet. Images of Ruy's magnificent tanned body enjoying this liberating experience under cascading flowing water crowded her mind and she lingered a little longer in front of the floor-to-ceiling mirror, critically scrutinizing her own body to regain control of her senses before joining him.

He was at the wheel on deck and his eyes grew dark as she appeared – a fluffy beige towel was swinging from her hand and she was clad in a brown leopard-print bikini that seductively set off her sun-kissed skin. His gaze moved deliberately and slowly up her figure. Starting with her slender ankles, it climbed the length of her long legs, accentuated by the cut of her bikini, lingered on her flat stomach and slim waist and then rose all the way to her full, firm breasts that were already beginning to tingle under his intense scrutiny.

Luna returned his stare. The sight of his magnificent male beauty, *his* near-nakedness, barely covered by a moulding black brief, threatened to send her senses on a wild merry-go-round as her thoughts floated back to the shower. Electricity between them sizzled in the breeze and the dazzling sun.

The yacht had picked up speed and was making good progress. There was a bit of a swell.

'Come and have a go,' Ruy said, stretching his arm out towards her. She hesitated. 'Come here,' he repeated. 'I'll show you. It's not rocket science, especially nowadays with all these modern devices. Just try to hold on to the wheel gently, as though you were driving a car, and don't let it spin out of your hand. A gentle but firm touch, I know you can do that.' His blue eyes glittered mischievously, engulfing her in their tidal wave. 'I'm right here, anyhow.'

Ruy positioned her in front of the wheel and stood behind her. 'Keep your eyes on the horizon. Even if it is a little choppy and everything else is rising and falling, that's one thing that will always remain steady.'

Nothing was steady! Though they were not quite touching, she could feel the heat of his body scorching her naked back. The familiar combination of mint, soap and the masculine fragrance emanating from him, mingling in the air with the salt and other sea smells, tormented her and she filled her lungs with the heady smell. She tried to stay still. If she leaned back just barely, she would feel the bulge of his virility and then they would be lost. Not yet. A time and a place, she kept telling herself, her imagination running riot and the need inside her building up. This was neither the time nor the place.

A rope was flapping against a mast, and there was the incessant swish of water as the ship's bows cleaved through the sea. They sailed in silence, their bodies almost touching but aware of each other in an aura of pent-up passion fuelled by delay and the anticipation of an afternoon in paradise.

Soon the little island they were heading for appeared like a lone green-and-gold jewel in a blue setting of sea and sky. They anchored a few yards away from the shore of the small half-moon bay, with its sheltered aqua-blue cove and private sandy beach backed by a great cliff topped with pine trees, and sparse emerald tufts of grass that grew on the side of the rocks.

While Luna packed the snorkelling gear, sun-cream, a couple of bottles of water and towels, Ruy sorted out the tender, an inflatable dinghy with rigid sides, lowering it into the water by means of a hydraulic winch.

'You're very well organized,' Luna remarked as they set out.

'I used to do a lot of diving. Now my work takes up most of my time.'

Five minutes later, he was pulling the tender on to the beach and helping Luna out. She stood on the sand, glancing at the cool clear sea that seemed to be dancing in the morning sunshine, watching dreamily each rhythmic heave of water break, white and foaming, over the jagged rocks that skirted the cove.

'What a beautiful, lonely place,' she murmured as she turned to look at Ruy. His eyes on her were dark and amazingly intense.

'The sun is scorching hot. Your skin is so delicate I'm afraid you'll burn.'

'My tan is well on its way, don't you think?'

Before she could protest he had pulled out the sun-cream from the beach bag and was unscrewing the cap. 'Lie down and let me rub some of this stuff on to you,' he said, handing her a large towel and helping her spread it on the sand.

She heard the impatience in his voice and put her hand to her forehead, laughing, though she shivered with giddy nervousness. 'Yes, sir!' she saluted as she lowered herself down on to the towel and stretched out on her stomach, her senses already acutely aware and attuned to the man beside her.

He knelt down and straddled her, his warm bare thighs only just squeezing her hips and, with the tip of his finger, flicked the fastening of her bikini top, which dropped on to the towel.

'This time it's not the doctor who will be treating you, *querida*, but the lover,' he whispered thickly against her ear as he bent over and gently lifted her hair out of the way, revealing the swanlike curve of her rounded neck.

She let out a short, sharp moan of pleasure as she felt his cool hands slip over her nape, smoothing and rubbing in the fragrant sun-cream. An expanding sensation of heat washed over her as his palms gently slid down on to her back, massaging it with outward strokes, brushing against the sides of her breasts. She closed her eyes, wanting his lips against her flesh, taking their taut peaks into his mouth. The excitement coursing through her was deliciously unbearable.

The occasional contact of his hardness as he moved on top of her made Luna want to drive his desire further so it would match hers, and she lifted her arms backwards to find it. She heard the hiss of his breath and, when she cupped him, his groan as he called out her name was almost a savage growl. As she traced her fingers over the outline of his manhood, the strength of the pulsing she could feel proved to her more than words the power of his passion.

He gasped. 'Not yet, *querida*, no, I will lose control.' It was a deep guttural plea and she felt his fingers clench slightly on her bare shoulders as he fought to contain his need.

Before he knew it she had turned beneath him and, lifting herself on her forearms, she touched her lips to his throbbing bulk.

'I want you to lose control,' she murmured huskily as she reached into his briefs, pushing them aside, and started to caress him with her lips, her fingers and her hands. 'I want you inside me, I *need* you inside me. Please, Ruy, love me.'

Her amber eyes glowed like burnt-orange flames and the fire of her gaze and her improvised yet bold caresses made him groan loudly. She sensed that he was close to the edge and the thought that she was making this passionate hunk of a man, who'd had so many women, moan with uncontrollable pleasure under her inexperienced touch, heated her desire even further. She knew he would not be able to last much longer.

Sure enough, Ruy's hand grasped Luna's wrist gently as his other hand stroked her face so near to his raging arousal, his eyes blazing with primitive hunger as he looked down at her. He bent his head towards her and gently tasted her lips, his hands running over her, shaping the curves of her body. Peeling off her bikini top, which was still cleaving to her breasts, his tongue darted forward, exploring and savouring the inside of her mouth, possessing it with long, languid strokes of his tongue.

He then rid her of her bikini briefs, for a moment just taking in her nakedness exposed to him under the sun, in all its vulnerability. The heat of his gaze seared her and her breath quickened imperceptibly as she waited, eager for him to give her some release.

Luna's senses were already sharpened, her nerve ends quivering with the need that had been niggling at her all day. Her flesh burned with the flames of her passion. When Ruy kissed her again, her trembling lips parted instinctively to drink in the sweetness of his kiss. Her breasts were hard and aching when he cupped them and his mouth felt good against the dark aureoles as he licked and nibbled and teased. His palm slid over her stomach, massaging it with strong circular strokes that sent electric shocks to her pelvis. She could feel the hot moisture flooding her and she wanted to pull his hand down to her need, but she trusted his love and his skill, having learnt that anticipation only heightens pleasure and makes the final release so much sweeter.

He played her like an instrument; his lips, tongue and hands roaming and stroking, revelling in her beauty and in her generosity;

and she responded under his skilled fingers. Luna did not hold back. She gave herself up to him, body and soul, relishing each caress, each stroke; urging him on, her body moving sensuously under him, telling him what pleased her most. Her eyes pleaded, her lips begged and he obeyed, but always holding back as soon as he felt she was going to peak.

Now his hands brushed down the inside of her thighs … yes, she had been waiting for that … 'Yes, don't stop,' she half sobbed as the tip of his fingers separated the silken petals and found the swollen nub. She parted her legs wide, and wider still, panting and arching her back, letting her body speak.

So he bent over and took her in his mouth, his tongue exploring the secret hollows that sheltered her womanhood, probing and licking until she was shuddering, entreating him to put her out of her misery.

'Do you want me now, *querida*?' he whispered between caresses.

Luna groaned incoherently and he lifted himself over her, his kisses moving to her mouth to stop her protest, becoming deeper and more insistent. Their limbs tangled wildly and Ruy let her roll him over on to his back. Luna boldly straddled his hips, now almost frantic to feel him inside her. His eyes were feverish with the same raw urgent need as he stared up at her face.

'I want it to be as thrilling for you as it is for me,' she whispered, feeling his heated masculine hardness strain against her in a desperate need to penetrate her.

He sought her secret treasure with his naked flesh and, at first, he moved her up and down along his rigid length, feeling her slick, saturated heat, slowly at first and then faster, guided by her moans. Then, without him needing to guide her, she sank down on him, making them both gasp as he penetrated her fully.

They moved rhythmically together, kissing, sucking, caressing and touching each other intimately, every limb, every inch of their flesh revelling in the pleasure they were giving each other.

Now they were shivering and rocking, breath accelerating and moans growing louder as their senses spiralled out of control into an ocean of sensations where nothing existed but the whirlwind of ecstasy that enfolded them.

Ruy's hands spread over her hips while his upward thrusts became harder and harder, meeting her frenzied lust, their wild sexuality colliding with such power they felt themselves merging in a fiery stream of desire. He gripped her waist, his features taut, calling her endearing names, groaning his passion and his need for her as he thrust against her, his tip hard and silky inside her, sending flames of delicious pleasure to her core.

Egging each other on, pushing their fever to the brink, the rhythm of their movements escalated as white-hot flames devoured them. They were close, so close to the edge, their breath rasping in their throats as the aching torment built inexorably inside them. She parted her thighs even wider so his rigid length could delve deeper into her, moving sensually but aggressively so every part of her soft moist core teased and caressed him, her thighs clinging to his loins as she rode him, pushing him ever onwards. The hoarse moans of Ruy murmuring her name, his pupils dilated in sensuous agony as his hands moved restlessly over her entire body, only sent her to new peaks of excitement.

Then suddenly she felt him shudder violently and cry out her name as he flooded her with his warm seed, and she felt the rush of fierce rippling spasms rake her body. Her head thrown back, her nails digging into his shoulders, they soared higher and higher in ecstasy and her sobs joined his, louder and louder as every wave of red-hot pleasure hit her, their ever-growing pace and strength rippling in spirals through her body, making her gasp and bringing tears to her eyes.

Now she lay on top of his trembling body, against his pounding heart, every nerve still quivering with the power of the storm that had hit her. His arms enfolded her tenderly and he smoothed a hand over her damp hair soothingly as he whispered loving words into her ear.

'*Dios mio*, Luna, my beautiful, sensuous Amazon,' he murmured, his breathing still ragged. 'No other woman has put me through such exquisite torment and brought me to such a shattering release.'

She rolled off him gently and nuzzled down into the crook of his arm. For a while they lay trembling, bodies still entwined, replete though spent, and chests heaving, drawing air into their exhausted lungs.

Luna's heart swelled with love and tenderness for Ruy as she nestled in his warm embrace, just wanting to be next to him and to bask in the wonders of her new-found love.

Ruy turned his head and gazed at her adoringly. He pulled her even more tightly to him. '*Luna, mi pequeña bruja*, Luna, my little witch,' he whispered, his voice still husky. 'Tell me where you've learnt how to drive a man to insanity in this way.'

'In your arms and under your touch, Ruy,' she whispered. Love flamed in her eyes as she rolled on to her stomach and met his dark-blue tender gaze. 'You've made me feel sensations I never knew existed. I thought I was frigid but you've brought my body to life.' She shook her head, bewildered. 'I often wondered what it was all about and, from time to time, I felt left out in the cold.'

Ruy's eyes turned to blue pools of molten infinity at the frankness of her words. 'I'm not the same person either, *querida*. You've bewitched me.' His fingers caressed her cheek, then trailed down to her jaw, tilting her face to him as he stared into her liquid amber eyes. 'You'll never be out in the cold again, *mi amor*.'

They dozed and, when they woke up, the sun was streaming fiercely on the bright blue sea. On the smooth waters, distant sailboats looked like novelty ships floating over glass. The humid heat of early afternoon simmered around them and, in the torrid stillness, the silver mirage of the town of Conil across the water, white as platinum, shimmered insubstantially in the air.

Luna was the first to raise herself up. Turning over on her side, she rested on her elbow, stared down at Ruy's body sprawled on the towel next to her and listened to the steady rhythm of his breathing. He was magnificent, the sun highlighting the gold of his strong chest and broad shoulders, the narrowness of his hips and his long and lean muscular legs. Her gaze slid back up to where she discerned a faint scar over his right hip that she'd never noticed before. Before she thought to ask about it, Ruy stirred.

He blinked and opened his eyes. They widened as they focused on her, now of the palest blue. He gave her one of his dazzling smiles and stretched out his lithe limbs before springing to his feet with the agility of a panther. 'Let's have a quick dip before lunch,' he suggested. 'Would you like that? The sea isn't deep enough for diving but perfectly adequate for swimming and snorkelling.'

The idea quite appealed. Luna still felt slightly languid and slow after their lovemaking, so a swim would be energizing. She hadn't snorkelled since those far-off summer days in California and it was an exciting prospect to explore the limpid clear waters of the bay with Ruy.

Equipped with fins, masks and snorkels they went down to the sea. Luna gave a strong shudder as she felt the familiar cold grip of the water.

'Would you prefer to wear a wetsuit?' Ruy's brow furrowed with thoughtful concern.

She sucked in her breath, advancing gingerly into the depths. 'No, no, I'll be fine once the first shock has passed.'

As they sank beneath the surface, the cold sensation passed. The visibility was extraordinary, the water a crystalline blue with beds of coloured coral on the floor of the sea. They drifted further down into a magical underwater garden with an infinite variety of textures and shapes. Rainbow-hued fish cruised by, ignoring the newcomers, weaving themselves in and out of the fields of strange grasses that waved in the submarine currents, darting about and feeding off the fronds and ferns of the sea. Pretty variegated fish and other luminous ones came into vision from time to time but they never ventured too close to them. Luna remembered her grandfather saying that in nature the prettier the creature, or the plant, the deadlier it was.

A group of seahorses floated past and a large fish, which Luna couldn't identify, chased a shoal of smaller fry, swimming only a foot away from her. Though life below the surface was lively, she found the great silence eerie.

Just before they started to feel the cold and were preparing to go back, Ruy drew a small penknife and began prising sea urchins from the rocks, which he then dropped into a small pouch he had tied around his waist.

After retrieving their tender from the shore, they made their way back to the yacht. Ruy disappeared into the shower first so that he could start preparing lunch afterwards. Luna then took her turn. As she was dressing in the bedroom, she suddenly felt a moment of unease. The room was equipped with various female accoutrements: hairdryer and sun-cream, even make-up and nail polish. When she opened a drawer looking for a pair of scissors, her eyes fell on a packet of condoms. She froze. For a moment her jealous, fragile self reared its head, thinking about the other women who had been there before her.

Oh yes, Ruy must have a high old time on his magnificent yacht, moving in one girlfriend as the other left.

She gave a harsh shudder and told herself not to be so foolish. That was the Ruy of the past. He was with her now; he was different. She quickly closed the drawer and finished dressing.

When she appeared on deck, Ruy was dressed and had already set out the food under the blue-and-white awning. The table was laid with a coordinating blue tablecloth, white china and immaculately polished silver. An enormous platter of a variety of crustaceans had prime place in the centre of the table, surrounded by great wedges of lemon. A large loaf of crusty warm bread, which Ruy had heated in the small galley oven, lay on a wooden board with a slab of butter beside it on a white dish. He had cut open the sea urchins and added them to the platter of seafood. Next to it, a bowl of crisp green lettuce, tomatoes and chives waited to be tossed in dressing.

Luna had changed into pink shorts and a striped cotton cropped shirt and her newly washed and dried hair was scooped up into a ponytail. The sun had given her cheekbones a healthy glow and, with just a stroke of mascara on her lashes and a tinge of gloss on her lips, she looked cool and relaxed.

Ruy stared at her as he helped her to her seat. 'Every time I lay eyes on you, I'm filled with wonder. I don't know what it is about you, Luna. Maybe it's this ethereal quality you have, a kind of wild, untouchable aura you radiate, but I never get tired of looking at you.'

The admiring words, and the way he looked at her, sent a pink hue of pleasure to her cheeks. He must realize the effect his powerful masculinity had on her ... and on other women, she thought a little ruefully.

'Thank you Ruy, I'm flattered.' Then, before she could stop herself: 'You've had a lot of women, haven't you?' she stated.

His lips gave that familiar quirk that she found so appealing. 'Are you asking me or telling me?'

For some reason, his answer startled her. She wished she hadn't begun this conversation. Shrugging, she tried to sound casual. 'You're such a wonderful lover, I take it you've had a lot of experience.' She wasn't about to mention the feminine accessories she'd come upon in the bedroom, nor the telltale contents of the drawer.

He didn't answer immediately but, instead, poured them each a glass of champagne. 'What there is between us has nothing to do with experience, Luna. I thought that was obvious.' He had spoken without looking at her. Now he raised his blue gaze, a strangely intent look on his face. 'When I make love to you, it's like tasting the nectar of the gods.'

He paused and raised his glass to her before offering her an oyster and taking one himself. 'To answer your question, yes, I've *had* many women in my life. Most of them in my bed, it's true. With some, I don't even remember their names, and I'm not proud of that. But I never wanted to make love to a woman, and I never did, before I met you. It was sex, nothing more.'

He helped himself to another oyster, watching her as he did so. 'When you fall in love with a beautiful woman, she is like this oyster. I believe that if you really want to appreciate her, you need to taste her, like this …'

In one swift move he brought the shell to his lips and deftly tipped the mollusc into his mouth.

'You may find this hard to believe, but I've never done to any woman what I did to you that night on the way back from the gypsy camp. Somehow, it always seemed more intimate than I was ever prepared to be.' He hesitated, as if waiting for her to look at him, but Luna found it impossible to meet his gaze and kept her eyes lowered to her plate. Hearing him talk about his past experiences, imagining him with other women, was almost too much to bear.

'I love you, Luna,' he went on, aware of her discomfort but ignoring it, so imperative was it to put his message across. 'The fulfilment I've felt every time we've touched is indescribable. You don't know what that small oyster at the core of you does to me when I feel it under my lips. You leave me trembling every time we make love, like an adolescent in the throes of his first experience of sex.'

He was stripping his soul bare. Luna flushed bright red and bit her lip, finally raising her eyes slowly to meet his. They fired with love and desire.

Luna's senses nagged at her and she drew in a ragged breath. Rays of gold sun reflected on the glassy surface of the water in the little bay like a million dazzling diamonds; there was glorious azure sky and the only noise was the sound of the seabirds and the gentle clank of the halyards against the mast in the light breeze. As she sat across from Ruy, it seemed to her they were two people alone in a paradisal world. There was still a vestige of confused emotion that battled within her when she thought about Ruy and other women, and her own naïvety about love and sex. Would she ever be enough for this man, who had made such a terrifying conquest of her heart and body?

'I don't think that what I do to you is half as much as what you do to me,' she whispered anxiously.

As though he had tuned into her thoughts, Ruy deftly moved the conversation away, his smiling gaze patient and loving.

'Here, have some salad. I want to know what you think of my salad dressing made of sea buckthorn vinegar and olive oil.'

She raised her eyebrows. Another of his strange concoctions, she supposed, but then checked herself. Given his remarkably effective ministrations after her ordeal in the storm, using who knows what herbs, she wasn't as quick to query the use of this one. Instead, she said mildly: 'I've never heard of sea buckthorn.'

'It's a shrub that grows along the Atlantic coast of Europe, all the way to north-western China. You can infuse it and drink it like a tea, cook its berries in a pie or use its extract to make vinegar.'

'Does it have any medicinal properties?' Luna asked.

'We've found that it does seem to be capable of reducing the incidence of cancer in some of our patients, as part of a wider programme, of course. Definitely it has a place in the armoury as one of the herbs we've singled out that can affect the growth of cancers. It even helps to protect bone from radiation treatment.'

Luna couldn't help her mind moving to its default position and her doubtfulness showed itself in her expression.

'Well?' Ruy prompted. 'You look sceptical.'

'It's a very bold claim to be making,' Luna replied carefully.

'I don't understand why you seem intent on continuing to play devil's advocate, Luna. We both know that a quarter of prescription drugs are derived from plants anyway. Patients shouldn't have to kick their heels waiting years and years until a patent is approved. The regulatory burden, not to mention the stultifying cost of bringing a drug to market, is ridiculous.'

'I just feel alarmed when we know that there are plenty of toxic herbs readily available on the internet if you know where to look. You must agree it's worrying.'

'I do, but at the Institute I hope you've discovered our laboratory research and record keeping is no less rigorous than what you'd expect from a pharmaceutical lab. We're not cowboys, you know that.'

'Yes, of course ... but you have to admit that side effects and adverse interactions might well be an issue from some plant-based remedies. That's all I'm saying.'

He fixed her with an intently quizzical look. 'Luna, I some-times wonder how you ever decided to come and work for our Institute ...'

There was a silence. Luna gave a wobbly smile.

'You're right, I'm just playing devil's advocate,' she told him quickly.

They had gone through the whole tray of crustaceans. Presently Ruy stood up to clear the remains from the table. 'Let me remove all this, and we'll continue this conversation when I come back.' He took the plates into the galley, leaving Luna milling over her sombre thoughts.

The sense of guilt that had crept over her, almost from the beginning of the conversation, was now hitting her with greater force. She felt hot with shame that she had ever undertaken her assignment at the Institute in the first place. Even if she tried to justify her reasons for doing so, knowing, too, that she had now completed a *volte-face* with her article, it did not detract from the fact that she had been deceitful and a fraud.

Foolish girl, she remonstrated inwardly, what was she thinking of? In her zeal to uncover the dangerous practices of alternative medicine – something she had thought of as a contributing factor in her cousin's death – her conscience had been clouded. She knew that when Ruy found out about her article, it might well sound the death knell to their precious romance, and the thought made her almost nauseous.

Ruy came back up the narrow wooden steps, carrying a large bowl of fruit.

'I hope I didn't keep you long. I washed the fruit,' he grinned. 'You never know what chemicals have been sprayed over it.'

Luna smiled weakly, knowing that he was scoring points, but remained silent. She drew in a deep breath. Was this the opportunity for her to come clean? For a split second, unspoken words seemed to hang on the air, torturing her. What would be his reaction if she told him the truth now? Yet the thought quickly scurried away from her head.

No, it wasn't worth it, not now – she would wait until the article was published.

However, this time Ruy was not tuned in to her thoughts, he was too engrossed in the subject that seemed to mean so much to him.

'Coming back to what we were saying, the work that we do has had extraordinary results. But we must test it,' he went on, still unaware of her feelings. 'We must gather data, we must undertake statistical analyses. How can we do that if scepticism and obstacles are all we ever meet? In my opinion, today's big pharmaceuticals are simply trying to block progress, just as barber-surgeons in medieval times supported the burning of midwives as witches. It's simply not in their interest. There will always be charlatans making fraudulent claims, but I'm not one of them.'

'I never said you were a charlatan, Ruy,' Luna exclaimed, another tide of colour flaming her cheeks.

He looked intently into her eyes. 'I know, *querida*, I know. Forgive me for being unfair but your comments earlier set me off. You know how deeply we believe in the philosophy of the Institute.'

'And I do too, Ruy. I was just using opposing arguments to provoke you. It was silly of me.'

She found his close scrutiny unnerving; she shifted in her seat a little uncomfortably, hoping they would soon get off this very sensitive subject.

'Fine, but let me finish so we can put this subject to rest once and for all. Our Institute does not tolerate people who make false claims. What we produce does no harm. The products we use do real good, and every year we will add more. Our data is available online. We believe in transparency, unlike many Big Pharma companies that would patent the water we drink if they could get away with it.'

He had spoken passionately about a subject obviously close to his heart. Try as she might, however, Luna failed to stop the horde of anxious thoughts that invaded her mind, and she was glad when Ruy had finished his tirade so she could escape downstairs with the excuse of washing her hands.

She needed to steady her nerves before he read something in her eyes that might provoke more discussion.

CHAPTER 15

Night fell, calm and serene, warmly enveloping the two lovers in its bosom as they sailed back to Conil de la Frontera. In the distance, the arm of the bay appeared like a long limb stretching out into the sea, with Conil and its towers outlined like luminous pearls strung on a long necklace. The ships at anchor in the bay were outlined in dazzling brilliance. It was a beautiful evening, peaceful and still. The only sounds were the gentle ripple of water frilling in small waves along the flat beach and the rumble of surf on the reef.

As they made their way to the far end of the harbour, another sound assailed their ears. It came from a tall precipice of granite, its jagged spears of rock outlined darkly against the sky. At its base, the sea gushed through a great hole with an echoing roar. In a relentless rhythm, the water, trying to escape the way it had come in, was caught with a thunderous wallop by the next wave battering its entrance.

'Just listen to it,' Luna said, standing by Ruy at the tiller. 'It sounds so violent, but the night is really calm.'

'Strange, isn't it?' he said. 'It's called the Devil's Cauldron – it's actually hollow in the middle. Up on the headland you can look down into it. The effect is quite spectacular, especially at night when it's bathed in moonlight, though it never fails to make one feel dizzy. Sometimes, if you listen carefully, you'll hear the devil calling.'

Were his eyes gleaming mischievously or was it her imagination? Since their conversation at lunchtime, things had quickly returned to a loving equilibrium between them, but Luna was still alert to every nuance of Ruy's mood.

'I get vertigo very easily, so I'm not sure I'll be going up there,' she confessed, with a shudder.

'There's a legend attached to this place. Apparently, on the night of a full moon, the devil took the shape of a mermaid and lured a sailor, who was lost on the beach, towards the cauldron. As he bent over the precipice to feast his eyes on her beauty, she pulled him into the abyss and he was never seen again. Ever since then, when it's a full moon, the sailor can be heard walking over the shingle on the rocky shore below the cliff. Over there, in fact,' said Ruy, pointing.

'Really?' said Luna, deadpan. She smiled and rolled her eyes. 'Who's actually heard him?'

'Everyone who lives around here.'

'Has anybody seen him?'

'No.'

'So how do they know it's the sailor?' she asked. The romance of the place hadn't completely quelled her logical side.

'He has a rolling gait, like someone trying to keep upright on a sloping deck.'

Luna laughed. 'You always have an answer for everything but you know very well I don't believe in legends. Even the one about the sultan and sultana outfits.'

'How can you say such a thing when our love is the living proof that the legend tells the truth?' he protested, and a cloud seemed to pass over his expression.

Luna felt a sudden frisson and didn't continue the banter. *When I tell him the truth, what if he doesn't forgive me? Then the legend will have been proved wrong*, she thought, and found that part of her secretly didn't want that to happen. This man had offered to spend the rest of his life with her and she was aware of the gnawing thought that soon she might be shutting the door on bliss only to be plunged into a world of torment.

As Ruy wove his way among the anchored boats and floating buoys, the ocean was a placid sheet of glass. Looking back out to sea, Luna could see a mist floating above it. Through it, the lights of vessels making their way out of the harbour to the great unknown were twinkling, formless. It made everything seem suddenly unreal.

Lamps were lit along the wharf and a searchlight was trained on *Vela Gitana* as she moved elegantly, on her motor now, to her mooring. Ruy tied up and helped Luna ashore. Along the harbour front, the bars were already becoming crowded with tourists. Soaked with sunshine and sangria, their cheeks were glowing and they were chattering boisterously. Torchlight flares and lanterns illuminated some of the more chic bars and restaurants; others were bright with electric light. Luna and Ruy walked arm in arm along the pavement, making their way leisurely towards the hotel Ruy had booked for the night.

At one point, outside one of the more expensive-looking restaurants, they strolled past an executive-style black Mercedes with tinted windows. The thought registered briefly with Luna of how out of place the car looked in the beach-town surroundings of Conil. Its engine was running, and through the driver's half-open window a smell of cigar smoke curled its way across the pavement. For an instant, Luna's senses froze. It was like something curtained off in her mind had stirred uneasily, as if a shape had unfurled itself from slumber in a far-off corner of the many-roomed mansion that was her memory. Then the moment was gone. Ruy had bent to kiss her neck, hugging her to him as he did so, startling a soft laugh from her in front of the onlookers seated at the pavement tables.

*   *   *

Susurros del Mar, Ocean Whispers, was a small, twelve-room hotel on the beach, surrounded by its own secluded garden and in walking distance of the drowsy seaside town. Its romantic setting made it a favourite among honeymooners. The suite Ruy had reserved was positioned at one end of the hotel with its own entrance; the rooms overlooked the ocean and the garden, and a massive fig tree hung over their terrace.

While Luna dressed for dinner, Ruy sat in the quiet darkness of the terrace, listening to the night sounds of the ocean and watching the moon through the canopy of fig leaves overhead. The ships had disappeared around the point. Under the moonlight, the sea itself was empty and placid, apart from the tuna boats anchored off the white sandy beach, and the night gave the scene a dreamlike, unearthly quality.

The words of a renaissance poet, Pietro Artino, ran through his head: '*I love you, and because I love you, I would sooner have you hate me for telling you the truth than adore me for telling you lies*' – and the shadow in his heart was like the fig tree above him, dark and irrevocable. While he'd had the distraction of sailing the boat or snorkelling in the ocean, not to mention the exquisite delights of Luna's body to explore, he had managed to block everything else out. It was easier to do so in the carefree hours of sunlight but, now that he was here, alone on the terrace at nightfall, the demons had returned, guilt and fear spreading ice in his heart.

Ruy loved Luna more than life itself; everything about her thrilled him and filled him with wonder. It wasn't just her innate sensuality – though that was an important bonus he'd always suspected existed but had only discovered these past few days – it was also her lively intelligence, and the many fascinating contradictions in her character. He knew he would never tire of her; he was also sure he would never hurt her. Of all the women he had dated, she was the only one he hadn't taken immediately to his bed. In spite of having to fight his own explosive need to possess her completely, he had held off from sex at first, even when she would have willingly succumbed. Other women had given themselves to him – thrown themselves at him, he had to admit – but Luna was different; he always sensed something fragile in her, too precious to be broken.

So many times since they had set off from Cádiz he had nearly told her about the accident; it had been on the tip of his tongue. Then, each time, the words had stuck in his throat and the terrible fear of losing her sapped his courage completely.

When Luna came on to the terrace, breaking into his sombre reverie, there was a dewy look in her beautiful amber eyes and a certain edge of sadness in the smile she gave him that caught at his heartstrings. In that moment, staring at her exquisite face, he almost blurted out the truth.

'Luna, there's something—'

But then she sat on his knees and placed her lips on his with a fervour that took his breath away, and the moment was gone.

Her hand smoothed his hair back and she trailed a finger over his cheek. 'What's wrong, my love?' Her whisper was tender, her eyes searching his. He parted his lips, but what he intended to say remained unspoken.

Taking her hand, he held it tightly in his and then he murmured: 'Whatever happens, *querida*, promise me you will never doubt my love.'

He did not leave her time to answer. With one sweep of his arm he had her around the waist and, picking her up, he carried her to the bedroom and gently laid her on the bed. What better way was there for him to prove to her how much he loved her?

*   *   *

They were up before the birds, showered and ready to attend the *Almadraba*. It was a morning of flat calm with the big blue sky a little hazy, like glass that had been breathed upon. By the time they went down to the beach, the sun was already strong and hot, the sea shining like a carpet of diamonds. There was a clean white brightness about everything and the glare was blinding as they stood at the water's edge, watching the circle of wooden boats off the coast. The smell of iodine hung in the air and a little breeze tempered the great heat of the sun.

'There's a maze of fixed vertical nets stretching for several kilometres from the coast out to sea,' Ruy explained. 'They're attached to floating barrels and corks, kept in place by very heavy anchors. As the blue-fin tuna migrate from the Atlantic to lay their eggs in the Mediterranean, they find their path blocked by the barrier net of the *Almadraba*. As they try to escape, they enter through a funnel into the *cuadra*, the holding net made up of several pens, to end up finally in the central pen, the *copo*, the only one with a horizontal net.'

'It sounds very cruel,' said Luna, frowning. 'Especially since they'd swum so valiantly all that way …'

'The trapping of the tuna is not that cruel when you compare it with other means of fishing. The gruesome bit comes at the end. If you don't want to see that, we don't need to stay. There are plenty of other things to do.'

'I'm happy to stay for now,' Luna smiled contentedly. 'Besides, it's lovely to watch everyone busily at work while we're here holidaying without a care in the world.'

Just then, Ruy realized that he had left his camera on the terrace back at the hotel. 'Look, why don't we get a table at that beach café over there,' he suggested. 'I'll order us a coffee – I'll only be ten minutes or so.'

They ambled over to the café. It had a few unoccupied tables outside, under a red-and-white striped awning. Ruy had a word with the waiter while Luna helped herself to a newspaper from a pile at the counter and took a seat outside.

'He's bringing you a coffee now,' said Ruy. 'I'll order a cup on my return. Don't go anywhere, *querida*. I'll be back shortly.'

'Don't worry, I won't run away,' Luna said, smiling up at him.

She watched Ruy's progress up the beach and along the harbour front, marvelling at the elegant ease he had, the almost panther-like athleticism and grace. She was aware of nothing else but him, so it came as a shock when someone sat down at her table. Luna had the faintest sense of that smell again, the cigar-smoke she'd noticed the previous evening, which had emanated from the parked Mercedes. Recognition hit her like the blow of a sledgehammer. The faintest whiff of memory had tantalized her then; now it came back in a rush, like a lurid flood … Lorenzo.

'Hello Luna, my beautiful niece, how wonderful to see you! It's been such a long time …'

The same arrogant smile she remembered so well greeted her, and turned her stomach. He was still a striking man but his once-blonde hair had now faded to silver and one thing hadn't changed: he carried an aura of the pompous, conceited toreador he had been in his youth. It gave what would otherwise have been handsome features a faintly sneering mien. He was dressed in an expensive cream linen suit that shouted to the world that he was now every bit the successful businessman.

'Uncle Lorenzo …' said Luna blankly, as shock fractured her thoughts. 'What are you doing here?'

'What a lovely surprise,' he continued, evading her question. 'Isabel told me you were staying in Cádiz. Apparently she bumped into you at an exhibition not that long ago and you had dinner together. I think she's sorry she's not seen more of you.'

Luna didn't fail to pick up the rebuke implicit in his words. 'I've been busy at work,' she said shortly.

'Ah yes, at the so-called Institute,' said Lorenzo. 'I heard from Ted Vandenberg that you had taken up an internship there. He says you're a first-rate journalist, by the way, not that I'd expect any less from you, my dear. Anyway, I was highly gratified that the whistle will at last be blown on that appallingly flaky outfit.'

Luna listened to Lorenzo with mounting horror. If he knew, who else did? She felt instantly nauseous and had to steady her breathing before the wave passed. Lorenzo's piercing blue eyes were boring into her and she knew that he was fishing for something. Indeed, she felt uncomfortably like one of the tuna about to be captured in the nets out in the harbour.

'I saw you last night, Luna.' His words were sibilant and soft. 'It didn't exactly seem like a business rendezvous with your boss.' Watching her face, he added: 'I don't know what you've been up to with that gypsy-doctor,' he probed, his penetrating pale eyes fixed upon her, 'but I never thought I'd see you mixed up with a compulsive womanizer.'

'It's none of your business. What I do in my spare time has nothing to do with anybody else, especially you,' Luna snapped. She was feeling fearful and cornered, but not so much that she couldn't turn and bite back at her assailant.

'What you ought to know, dear niece,' said Lorenzo with a caramel silkiness, 'is that your handsome new beau is not exactly a friend of the Herrera family.'

'Oh, for goodness sake! Those old family feuds are ridiculous, they've got to stop!' Luna's eyes were sparking now.

Lorenzo's sharp gaze suddenly glinted in triumph. 'Ah … you don't know …'

To ask what he meant would only sanction the outpouring of more poison, so Luna said nothing; instead, she grabbed her bag in readiness to escape.

'Your bogus doctor,' he enunciated the words crisply and slowly, 'was the driver of the car in which your sister met her death. He managed to sweet-talk his way out of it, never even lost his licence. Your poor mother, my only sister, gave up on life after that. So it's hardly a surprise there's a "family feud", as you put it.'

Luna swayed and clutched the table for support, her face white as the paper cloth that covered it. 'No … no, that's not true. You're lying!' she whispered hoarsely.

'Now why would I do that?' he asked with an oily tenderness, belied by the snappish fury that glinted in his eyes.

'Please, just leave me,' Luna managed to say, in a small, emotionless voice. 'Go now, before he comes back. You've done enough damage. You did a good job ruining my life before. Now you're trying again. It's not going to work, I assure you.'

But even as she said it, she knew her uncle's words had hit home.

Lorenzo pushed back his metal chair with a scrape on the concrete flags and stood up. He paused a moment, and something flickered in his expression before his face became a mask of arrogant pride once more.

'I do hope you're here to see the *Almadraba*. It's a fascinating spectacle, especially when the fish are trying to escape.' He looked down at Luna with a grim smile. 'I highly recommend it.' And with that, he walked off abruptly, as quietly as he'd arrived.

When Ruy returned to the table a couple of minutes later, he was so eager for them to secure a good position with a fine view of the nets that at first he didn't notice that Luna was pale and quiet.

'Shall we get going? I'll forego coffee,' he said. 'You don't want to miss this.'

Luna allowed him to take the lead and, when he grasped her hand, he only mentioned how surprisingly cold it was. She murmured something about the sea breeze having made her feel a little chilled before lapsing into silence again.

Ruy led her to a good vantage point not far from the action. They could hear the fishermen's excited shouts and laughter – '*Anda! Vamonos!*' – as they hauled in their huge nets.

'Look, the fish are trying to get away,' Ruy pointed to the surface of the sea, which was turning white and frothing as though in ebullition, heaving with a multitude of enormous fish, their fins slicing through the water. Luna obediently followed his pointing finger with her gaze but made no comment.

It was as if she were an automaton: there in flesh though not in spirit.

'The mesh of the nets is big enough to allow the younger tuna to escape,' Ruy continued. 'That way the life cycle continues and stocks are maintained.'

Now, men armed with sharp knives were jumping into the *copo* to hook the bluefin tuna, forcing them to the surface and hauling them into the boats, battling for supremacy with the fish, a couple of which looked as if they must be three times the fisherman's body weight. The slaughter had begun.

Now the churning waters had turned blood red. In a frenzy, the huge fish were bucking and roiling, their slithery dark backs arching out of the water in the scarlet urgency of their death throes. Ruy put his arm around Luna's shoulders and gave her an enquiring look, as if to say, *if this is all too much for you, we can leave*, but she was unable to respond, her eyes fixed on the carnage, back and shoulders completely rigid. Instead of leaning into him, she stood perfectly upright, undemonstrative. She felt nothing, her heart encased in ice.

Finally, she turned to Ruy. He saw her lips move but couldn't make out what she was saying, so lowered his head to hers.

'Please take me home.'

*   *   *

Back at La Gaviota Luna undressed and showered, performing the motions of everyday life mechanically. Then she crawled under the cool sheet of her bed with the blinds of the window pulled down, curling up like an animal nursing its wounds.

Ruy had driven her home solicitously, after having quickly thrown things in their two cases at the hotel. Pleading a migraine, she had kept her eyes closed in the car; that way she could block any attempt at conversation and wouldn't have to meet his gaze. She knew it would be full of tender enquiry and she couldn't bear that.

Not now.

As soon as he had parked in front of La Gaviota and turned off the ignition, Luna had grasped the handle of the door, preparing to make her exit as quickly as possible, but he had stopped her with a restraining hand on her arm. She had flinched at his touch and Ruy had then withdrawn his hand and passed it over his eyes.

'Luna,' he said after a moment. 'I can tell something is wrong. It's not just a headache, I know that. Will you tell me what it is?' He waited for her to speak and when she didn't reply, he went on: 'I can't say goodbye to you like this … please talk to me.'

Luna heard the husky warmth in his voice, as well as the fear. She couldn't trust herself to speak but she had to say something.

'Ruy … I don't want to talk … I really need to be on my own right now.' She opened the car door and got out. Then, realizing her case was in the boot, she waited mutely beside the vehicle while he retrieved it.

'Luna, I'm asking you again. Don't leave me like this, not knowing what's wrong. What have I done to upset you? Please … *mi amor* …'

What had he done? How could he face her so brazenly with such a question, as if he were innocent? Finally, stirred from her numbness, she felt colour surge to her cheeks.

'You can honestly stand there and ask what you've done?' she fired back, her amber eyes flashing with anger.

Ruy paled and took a step back, as if winded by a blow to the gut.

But Luna didn't wait for his reply. 'I know about Juliet,' she said quietly. 'And now, would you please leave.'

She could tell from the intense pain she read in Ruy's eyes that her words had hit their mark – it was as if she had plunged a dagger into his heart – but the knowledge caused her neither satisfaction nor triumph. They had both lost something irretrievable, she knew. There were no winners in this game of love and betrayal.

Unable to bear the sight of his suffering face a second longer, Luna had turned on her heels, grabbing her case as she did so. Without a backward glance she let herself into the house, closing the door behind her. A few minutes later, still standing in the hallway, she had heard the sound of Ruy's engine and the scrape of his tyres as he drove away.

Luna lay in bed, eyes closed in the semi-darkness of her room. What did she feel? What did she think? More importantly, what did she believe?

In one conversation, Lorenzo – the same man who had so cruelly destroyed her innocence all those years ago, when she was no more than a vulnerable and defenceless child – had stripped her of everything. At the café, the shock of seeing him had been bad enough and, when he'd told her he knew of her assignment, her mind had begun to teeter on the edge of a precipice. In a terrible flash of realization Luna wondered whether every step she had taken in her career had somehow been orchestrated by her uncle; perhaps he had been the reason Ted Vandenberg had given her a job in the first place. It certainly made macabre sense that Lorenzo should be behind Ted's decision to have Luna write an exposé of the Institute … Then to hear the story of the car accident … it was all too much.

Like scraps of flotsam floating in the sea, her thoughts drifted haphazardly, taking her where they chose without her having any volition of her own.

So this was the secret that Ruy carried. Luna had always sensed there was something wrong. Ever since the night of the exhibition and Isabel's appearance, he'd known who she was … and all the time he hadn't told her the truth.

It had been a cruel delusion to think she and Ruy would be clear of the web of animosity and bitterness that had caught up three generations of their families. What a story it made, she thought miserably. First, Doña Alexandra, Ruy's grandmother, had not only fallen for Isabel's ex-fiancé but had then allegedly used Lorenzo's father, Felipe Herrera, one of the great *toreros* of his time, to achieve her own ends.

During the next generation, Luz, Ruy's mother, had fallen for Andrés de Calderón, the man Luna's own mother, Adalia, had hoped to marry. And now Ruy had caused the death of Juliet, her half-sister, due to his reckless driving. It had never occurred to her that the world was so small that of all the men she could have met, she would fall for the one who had brought tragedy on her family. It came as no surprise to her that Lorenzo had been the one to deliver the death blow to their love; it was only too apt in this horrible, toxic game the two families had been playing for so long.

Luna's throat muscles constricted and her eyes filled with tears. The sobs when they came were deep and hard, her body shaking with their power. Fear, grief and self-pity assailed her; then suddenly she was angry. Angry with her mother for abandoning her; with her father for burying himself in his work when she needed him most; angry with Lorenzo; angry with Ruy because she loved him; angry with the whole world but mostly with herself for her weakness and lack of judgement. It was so much easier to channel all that confusion into one furious ball of emotion.

She had been so happy and suddenly, without warning, everything had changed; it was as if a dark curtain had come down over a beautiful picture. What was she to do? Her head throbbed with the effort of trying to unravel the tangled skein of her life. She knew she couldn't stay here. Not now. But the idea of returning to New York was just as bad. Thoughts turned restlessly in her head in ceaseless counterpoint with the sound of the surf lashing against the rocks in the bay. Finally, the endless rhythm as they crashed and were sucked back repeatedly lulled her fraught mind, and she fell into a half-doze where troubled thoughts continued to plague her.

*　　*　　*

It was mid-afternoon when Luna wrapped a silk kimono around her and went downstairs, where she made herself a cup of herbal tea. She walked outside on to the terrace and sat on the steps, gazing out to sea. The scallop-shaped bay, smooth and green, sparkled like emeralds in the brilliant sunshine. Yachts with white sails moved slowly over the water and colourful flags fluttered from the distant yacht club. A white, lace-like froth edged the water where gentle waves rippled.

How could everything be so beautiful when she herself felt so wretched? Now the pain that had gripped her since she had discovered Ruy's secret refused to ease; the golden moments of her life gone, never to be recaptured. It was as if the whole world of happiness that had thrilled her with such high hopes had shattered into a million pieces at her feet.

'*Buenas tardes, señorita.*'

Luna turned her head towards the voice. Señora Sanchez was walking towards her, black spaniel at her heels, a sunny smile beaming on her face.

'*Buenas tardes, señora.*'

Luna wondered if her friend would pick up on her red-rimmed eyes, and hurriedly wiped her tear-stained face with her fingers.

'So how is life treating you these days?' The jovial Spanish woman stopped a few feet away, her smile replaced by an expression of concern. '*Ay*, not so good, I see. Where were you? I noticed the house was closed and I wondered if you had left. Are you well, *señorita*?'

Luna wasn't in the mood for polite conversation, but the genuine interest of Señora Sanchez and her cheerful disposition got the better of her.

'I went away for a few days, visiting your beautiful Costa de la Luz,' she said, managing a weak smile.

'Alone?'

'No … a friend took me on his yacht.'

'*Il joven*, the young man you had spoken to me about.' She looked knowingly at Luna, and there was such warmth in her gaze that Luna's eyes once more clouded with emotion.

Señora Sanchez came up the steps and sat down next to Luna, taking her hand. 'We have a saying: *Las peleas de amantes son como las lluvias de verano que salen del país más verde y hermoso*, lovers' quarrels are like summer showers that leave the country more verdant and beautiful. I hope you don't mind listening to a meddling old woman, but I've seen some heartache in my time around the ones I love and hope I have a bit of wisdom to call my own … Why don't you go to him, *señorita*? Talk to him.'

'I'm afraid this quarrel has left our love utterly destroyed,' said Luna dejectedly. 'You see, there's something I've discovered from his past … something he kept from me … and it's torn us apart.'

'As the saints are my witness, there is little in this world that can't be mended,' said her friend sagely. 'I'm sure it's just some misunderstanding you can untangle together if you try.'

Luna shook her head hopelessly. 'I'm afraid it's rather more than just a misunderstanding … what I've heard … it's destroyed everything.'

'Just remember, child, *nuestro querido Dios* throws thorns in our path to test us. Maybe this is one of those times.' She paused a moment, sighing deeply. 'So you trusted this young man, yes?'

'I would have trusted him with my life.' Luna wiped her eyes with the sleeve of her kimono.

'And the person who told you about this secret … they were trustworthy too, I suppose.'

Luna froze, her eyes widening a little as she allowed the *señora*'s words to sink in.

As if aware that the younger woman needed to be left alone so that she could ruminate on her problem – where, indeed, she might discover that it wasn't so hopeless after all – Señora Sanchez ruffled the ears of her spaniel, which had been sitting patiently at her side, and made as if to go. However, before she left, she patted Luna's arm and gently offered one last piece of advice.

'Perhaps *il joven* thought he might lose you if he told you his secret,' she said softly. 'For him, it would be a terrible price to pay. That sort of fear makes cowards of us all, *señorita*.'

*   *   *

After Señora Sanchez had left, Luna continued to sit for a while at the table on the terrace, the tears coursing down her face. This time, there was the slightest element of relief to them, a softening, as if her Spanish friend had started the process of untangling and Luna sensed she could now find the strength to continue down that path.

Taking a deep breath, she squared her shoulders. All of a sudden there was more purpose, less hopelessness, in her demeanour. She got up and went inside to her desk, where she opened her laptop. Then she typed a few words into the search bar:

Boston driving accident June 29, 1998, Juliet Perez and Rodrigo Rueda de Calderón

CHAPTER 16

Ruy's mobile rang at the very moment Vaina Jiménez Rivera came into his office, having knocked and entered without waiting for his reply. He ignored the call, letting it go to voicemail.

He found himself looking at Vaina somewhat dispassionately as she breezed over to his desk, her high heels clicking on the stone floor, her trademark Dior scent wafting in with her. If she noticed his lowered spirits, she didn't make any comment. Once he would have found the whole effect of her alluring: the bright lipstick against the whiter-than-white teeth; the glitter of gold and pearls at her neck and ears; the flutter of a silk scarf. Now he found it all too much: the sharp teeth seemed to him almost vulpine, the scent overpowering rather than intoxicating.

After he had called a halt on his relationship with Vaina, Ruy had been persuaded that they were still friends and that she had his best interests at heart. He hadn't expected it of her after their breakup but, when she had seemed determined to remain his most loyal supporter at the Institute, he never doubted her essential integrity. Her next words dissolved that notion once and for all.

'I've just been at a fundraising lunch,' she announced, a malicious edge to her voice. 'It seems your little girlfriend has been a very bad girl indeed.'

He stared back at her, too confused to offer a rejoinder but, as she was positively quivering with the self-righteous need to have her say, Vaina didn't wait for him to respond anyway.

'Yes, a very illuminating conversation I had with Isabel Herrera.' Her eyes gleamed malevolently. It seemed to Ruy that she was taking pleasure in spinning out her news as much as possible.

'Vaina, whatever you think you know, I'm surprised you would credit that woman's gossip with any degree of truth,' he said.

'Oh, Ruy, please! Do I look like a naïve fool? I knew you would say precisely that so I did a little checking for myself,' she replied smugly, her lips contorting themselves into a little moue.

Ruy was not only impatient but also becoming increasingly annoyed. His mood was already dark, plagued by thoughts of Luna and the terrible reproach he'd seen in her eyes. Glaring at her, his next words were curt. 'Get on with it, Vaina! Say whatever you've got to say.'

At this, the perfectly coiffed managing director set aside any vestiges of winsome affectation. 'Luna Ward has been working for us under false pretences, it seems.'

'What do you mean?' His voice was a growl.

She bridled. 'You don't have to use that tone with me, Ruy. I'm not the one who's been writing an exposé on the Institute.'

Ruy blanched, his jaw clenching. 'Go on.'

A more timorous person might have quailed, his tone was so ominous; instead, Vaina seemed to draw strength from it, a triumphant smile hovering on her face.

'Isabel Herrera took great pleasure in telling me that the Institute would soon be called to account. She has been talking to her brother, Lorenzo Herrera, now he's back in Spain, and managed to let slip that our newest recruit, Dr Ward, is working for *Scientific US*. When I probed further, she clammed up, of course.

'I've just rung the editor in New York, Ted Vandenberg, to check if there's any truth in Isabel's story. I spoke to his PA and she confirmed that Luna is indeed employed by him, and that he had sent her to Spain on an assignment. Apparently, she had been briefed to work undercover.' Vaina lifted a disdainful brow. 'Who knows what dirt she's going to dish in her feature. It could finish you, Ruy. Finish the Institute. Everything we've all worked for …'

Vaina's zeal was growing with every second, the words tumbling out of her. Had she noticed Ruy's face was wracked with pain it certainly had no tempering effect on her tirade as she continued to heap calumny on Luna. 'The little bitch! I knew she wasn't to be trusted. What a low-down piece of trash.' Then her parting shot: 'Typical Herrera.'

Ruy could stand it no longer. He stood abruptly, his chair tipping backwards and clattering to the floor. His thunderous response took Vaina by surprise, so that her mouth dropped open. 'Get out!' he roared. '*Le juro a Dios*, I swear to God, if you have any sense, you'll keep away from me.'

For a moment, startled by his fury, fear and humiliation clouded Vaina's eyes as she registered belatedly that she had gone too far. Then, composing herself rapidly, she stalked to the doorway, where she turned and lifted her chin defiantly.

'The hard-nosed womanizer has finally fallen and landed flat on his face,' she mocked. She made a move to say something more but whatever it was couldn't be heard over the slamming of the door in her face.

*   *   *

After Luna had finished reading the online newspaper article about the accident she had collapsed on the sofa, reeling from its implications; ashamed too that she could have so blindly accepted Lorenzo's version of events. Picking up her phone, she'd dialled Ruy's number. It went straight to voicemail. The message she left was hesitant, saying briefly that she was sorry, that there were things they needed to talk about, and would he please come over.

For the next half hour she sat there, her ears pricked for the slightest sound that might indicate he had come.

At last she heard the throb of an engine, followed by the sound of a car door slamming, then the squeak of the gate and footsteps on the path. Finally, the doorbell.

'Ruy!' she cried as she pulled open the door. But the smile froze on her face.

He stared at her blankly. It was the face of a stranger.

'What's the matter?' she asked, eyes wide with alarm.

'*Matter*?' he echoed as he strode into the room and turned to face her.

He knew! Luna's stomach gave a sickening lurch. Disappointment, hurt, betrayal and anger were there, written all over his face. Her glance wavered and fell away from his arctic gaze.

Now for the reckoning …

'It was a bad day for me when I met you. Even worse, when the Institute took you on. Why? What were you hoping for in all this?'

She passed a dry tongue over even dryer lips. 'Who told you?' she asked in a trembling voice.

His laugh was brittle and sarcastic. 'Lies have short legs, Luna, didn't you know? But never mind how I learnt about it, what the hell made you do it?'

Luna looked up at him and felt chilled to the bone, the words freezing in her throat. How contemptuous he was. Enduring the steely look in his eyes was as bad as having her face slapped. She lowered her gaze, unable to witness any longer the blazing scorn she read on his features.

'You don't want to answer? Then let me fill in the gaps. I suggest you were out for publicity, using every nasty little trick in the book. Never mind that you were going to bring down the

Institute, savage my reputation. So long as you got your precious article published. Well, now you can go back to New York and pick up your paycheque. Not a bad month's work. Catching a little sun in Spain, with a bit of romance thrown in.'

Luna heard the words and felt each one cut her like the jagged blade of a knife. She needed to explain, to melt the ice she saw in his eyes, but she was floundering against his onslaught, and every time she hesitated the more guilty it made her seem.

'It wasn't like that, Ruy …'

He wasn't listening; still following his own thread of logic. 'Perhaps you thought you could get away with it,' he accused her brutally, and then added sarcastically: 'Maybe you believed I would never know the truth. *Madre de Dios*, you're such a good actress! All those questions of yours, all that devil's advocate nonsense … you never believed in me from the start!'

Luna felt faint with humiliation. Her fists were shut so tightly, her fingernails dug into the palms of her hands. 'It was never like that … Yes, I took the assignment … I'd been so hurt over my cousin's death. Angelina insisted on alternative medicine over chemo … I felt somebody had to be held accountable. I wanted to do some good, I suppose … But then—'

'Oh, so you wanted to do some *good*?' His mouth tightened at her revelation, his gaze hardening to a cynical expression she had never seen in his eyes before. 'A spoilt little crusading journalist, trampling on other people's hard work!' He ploughed on, the fury gathering in his eyes. 'I'm sorry about your cousin, but I can't see how it's an excuse for destroying everything we've worked so painstakingly to build. All the effort the Institute and its staff put in day after day to help patients … did it mean nothing to you?'

Luna shrank away before the torrent of words but she managed to whisper between stiff lips. 'You've got it all wrong … I was going to tell you. But now you won't listen.'

He drew a deep breath, striving for control, but the hot-blooded gypsy in him had taken over and he was too angry to pick his words wisely.

'We made love together and all along you were lying to me, looking into my eyes, telling me how much you adored me, and the whole time you were betraying me!'

Luna moaned in torment at the cruel lash of his words. Noticing the uncompromising line of his jaw and the glitter of steel in his eyes, she shook her head, bewildered at the viciousness she had never suspected in this man she loved. She steadied her voice to answer, searching for the words to tell him how wrong he was; yet they refused to come and she could only manage, 'But that wasn't a lie … How could you think …?'

'What I think is that getting ahead in this career of yours means so much to you that you were prepared to sell yourself in every way.' He gazed intently into her eyes, scrutinizing the confused depths of the amber pools staring back at him and, for a moment, he seemed to forget where he was and a tiny light flamed behind the blue irises so that they shone brilliantly, and the sculpted lips opened softly in hesitation. Then it passed like an illusion, his eyes hardening as they pierced hers, and he hurled his words at her like sharp stones. 'You use people to get what you want, utterly ruthlessly. How could I have been so mistaken about you? And that aura of innocence you projected … nothing but lies and deception!'

Reeling, Luna put her hands over her face, no longer able to bear the icy fury in his eyes. 'Please, Ruy,' she whispered. 'Please listen … It wasn't like that … I've been trying to put things right …'

But he wasn't listening and now he had turned away. He pulled open the front door with a rough jerk then delivered his parting shot: 'You will tender your resignation unless you prefer to be fired,' he said in a chilling voice. 'I'll get Charo to pack up your things and send them here. You'll not set foot in the Institute again.'

In the still muteness of the room, his words fell slowly with the precision of a church bell tolling.

Deep in her soul, Luna knew that she was beaten. There was nothing she could say: he was determined to perceive the worst in her. She realized in all probability that she would never see him again. Her heart felt bruised, too sore to much care what happened to her. Still clutching at straws, she ran to the open door, hoping against hope that he would change his mind and forgive her at the last minute. Already he was walking down the path but she called out in a hoarse, sobbing voice:

'Ruy, don't go. I can't bear it! Please … it was sheer stupidity. I realized I was wrong … I've been trying to put it right. Give me another chance … please!' Tears rained down her cheeks in an uncontrolled stream.

He paused on the pathway and, for a moment, she thought he was wavering, but he did not even turn round. As he strode away, her heart plummeted, her dreams dashed to pieces, and she was left staring after him. She continued to stand there, sobbing, long after his car had driven off.

Now the dull pain of loneliness settled in her heart. It was too late for regrets. She had reaped what she had sown, and part of her did not blame him. Nevertheless, she felt as if she had been caught up in a tornado that had left her battered and stripped of everything she held dear.

*   *   *

Ruy stepped out of the shower and wrapped a white towel around his waist, using another to rub his hair vigorously. The evening air was warm so he wandered out on to the terrace, drying his muscular arms and torso, and stared into the distance. Dusk had now tinted the horizon like a delicate pink finger, pointing across the sky in the west.

Out in the bay he could see the moving lights of ships drifting into port. In the occasional sweep of the lighthouse lamp, falling across the sea like an ever-watchful eye, there was a reliable steadfastness that contradicted Ruy's turbulent feelings and had a tranquilizing effect on his mind.

For the past half hour he had been on the beach, pounding hard along the edge of the turbulent water near the rocks under the emerging twilight stars. Though his run along the sands had taken the edge off some of his pent-up fury, there was still a smouldering energy to his movements that threatened to burst out of him in howls of rage and hurt, if he were to let it.

How could Luna have done this to him?

Under the heavy, warm weight of the shower water he had calmed down a little and then the doctor in him had begun to search for a reason for Luna's duplicity. Was she so scarred by her childhood and blighted by the curse of the Herreras that she had to ruin the most precious things in her life? Was her self-esteem at such rock bottom that she was driven to acts of destruction for the single reason that it hurt her in the process? Was that what it was all about? He didn't know but, while he savagely cast about for an answer, the pain kept scoring his flesh like the knife-like beak of Prometheus's eagle.

To think, only a few days ago he had been defending Luna to his housekeeper, who loved him like the son she'd never had. Mela had witnessed the harm the Herrera family had caused to his parents and was well aware that his grandparents, too, had suffered viciously at the hands of members of that same family. His mother had laughed at how Mela always spoke her mind no matter the consequences and, until now, it was one of the things he most liked and valued about the robust Spanish housekeeper. However, when she had been so vocal in her assertion that Luna must somehow be tainted by her relationship with the autocratic dynasty, he'd found it hard to hear – to the point where he had been extremely brusque with her. Still, he knew, underneath it all, that Mela always had his best interests at heart and would defend him to the hilt, no matter what.

He could see her now, standing in his kitchen, hands on hips, her bright eyes taking on an almost pugnacious quality. 'At the end of the day, Ruy, that girl is bound to be damaged goods, and that's all there is to it.'

At this he had felt his hackles rise as he watched her scrub the flour from her hands under the tap, as if washing her hands of Luna and the whole blighted Herrera clan in one go. 'No one else is going to say it to you but I've looked after you since you were a squalling baby and I'm too old to care if you rant and rave and go off in a sulk. No, *niño*, the sooner you get out of this ill-fated relationship the better. I've not met the girl, but I know the type. A little minx who has you running to do her bidding, but who will trample on your loyal heart, believe me.'

The most terrible thing of all was that, only three days later, Mela had been proved right.

Ruy went inside, back to the bathroom, and combed his hair, avoiding the reflection of his pale face in the mirror, out of which his eyes glowed dark and thunderous, seething with pain and torment. Every now and again a vision would push its way into his mind unbidden: that of Luna, trembling and fragile, trying to have her say, desperate to make her peace with him. Then the longing to hold her in his arms and soothe away her anguish was so powerful – so visceral – that it was all he could do not to bellow out loud.

He had been hard on her. Ruy couldn't remember when he had been so hurtful to anybody, but he had intentionally struck to wound for the simple reason that he loved Luna with a passion. Vaina's revelations had been devastating and he had sought to rip into Luna, no matter what hurt he caused her, or himself, in the process. Yet, now that it was too late to take back his words, he wished that he had not been so quick to utter them.

How could he have been so self-righteous when he himself had hidden a terrible truth from her?

The searing guilt that he had suppressed in his blind rage at her betrayal returned, adding to his torment. He'd had no doubt that, sooner or later, some do-gooder was sure to enlighten Luna about his car accident in Boston; and fate had cruelly proved him right. Still, what did it matter now what she thought of him? He had been so heartless and savage that she must surely hate him already.

Just then his brooding thoughts were interrupted by the beep of his mobile phone and he strode into his bedroom to check the screen.

It was a message from Charo: *Sorry to bother you on your day off but there's a document in your inbox you ought to look at. An article that needs your approval before it goes to print.*

Ruy went over to his laptop, which was sitting on the dresser, and flipped open the screen. Scrolling through his inbox, he found the message, then clicked open the attachment. He began to read, and was so engrossed in the text that he never even noticed his cat Gitano-Negro rub against his bare calf.

*   *   *

The stars shone like amber jewels over the bay, large and flashing in the darkness. But Luna, sitting on her terrace at La Gaviota, had no interest in the beauty of the night sky. Stars and moonlight were for lovers and they no longer belonged to her now that the romance in her heart had vanished from her life. As that gloomy thought took its bleak shape in her head, the cold white moon seemed to look down on her, its lopsided smile hiding a cryptic message.

The quietude of the night and the freshness of the air eventually calmed her nerves. Since Ruy had left, Luna had been tortured by a host of conflicting emotions. She moved through loss and desperation, fear and self-abnegation, to settle finally on the pure fire of anger. Stronger than before, it consumed her body, wave after wave, like red-hot coals cast at her soul, making their scorching mark like a branding-iron. How could he have said those terrible things to her? Nothing, after the intimacy they had shared, could possibly warrant such a weight of scorn and loathing.

As her fury diminished, so the dream aspect that had clouded everything that had happened in the last twenty-four hours vanished too. Reality stepped in and Luna no longer cared that Ruy hadn't told her about the accident. As Señora Sanchez had so wisely insinuated, it was his fear of losing Luna that had made him hold back, just as the fear of losing him had stopped Luna from telling him about her assignment.

No, she was hurt for a different reason: she reproached him bitterly for not having given her a chance to explain herself properly, for casting aside their beautiful love with a mere wave of the hand. In a matter of minutes he had sealed their fate with a torrent of cutting words, which had pierced her heart again and again, shattering her dreams into a million shards. Nevertheless, anger, as it always will, eventually burnt itself out and now all she had left was an aching gulf, and a vast ocean of tears.

'Ruy, Ruy, my love, where are you?' she cried out into the night, breaking down once again, her body shaking under unrelenting sobs. It was a hoarse, wild cry, ripped from her gut, echoing her passion, her longing and desperate frustration as it tore the darkness, its sound rippling through the intense silence that seemed to envelop the world.

'I'm here, *querida*,' the night answered back.

Luna looked around her as her heart missed a beat. She was hearing voices. Was it her fancy? Was she going mad? She wiped away her tears with the back of her hand.

As if in a dream, Ruy materialized out of the shadows. In the darkness, she couldn't see his face but she watched, mesmerized, as he climbed the steps of the terrace towards her. Holding up her hands defensively, she took two paces back, gesturing for him to stop where he was. She was too stunned to do anything else – her mind numb, her whole being still reacting to his unexpected appearance. When she opened her mouth to say something, no words came out.

His eyes – she saw them now, those hypnotic azure eyes – slid over her with their tongues of flames. He looked at her long and hard, bleakness and vulnerability showing on his face, his irises glittering with intense emotion. Luna could see that, like her, he was confused, hesitant, trying hard to pick the right words, longing to pour his heart out to her but frightened of rushing things. When he spoke, he sounded tense and she sensed that he was deeply moved.

'You came into my life like a comet from the blue. I couldn't let you vanish in the same way. The world would be too dark without your light,' he whispered in a choked, almost inaudible voice. Then he added: 'I saw your article.'

It was all he needed to say. The sorrow, regret – and the hope – was written all over his face.

Luna swallowed hard. Though her mind registered surprise and half-formed questions swirled at the back of her consciousness, she still couldn't answer; yet she was slowly gaining control of herself. How she longed to run to Ruy and put her arms around him, feel herself melt into his strength, but in a flash his cruel words came back to her, hitting her again like shattering blows. There was no doubt that at the time he had spoken from the heart.

How could she trust him now not to hurt her, when only a few hours ago his eyes, which were now filled with love, had only reflected scorn and contempt? How could she accept being treated like an object to be used or rejected at whim?

Luna's chin lifted a fraction, her hands curling into fists. Her amber eyes flamed with a medley of passions, in which love, pain, resentment, desire and forgiveness battled for supremacy.

'How could you have said all those hurtful things? I wasn't the only one bearing the burden of a secret … one that had the power to hurt.'

Though her voice was trembling, she tried to keep the tone cutting.

Ruy paled. Luna's words had flown true to their target. He shook his head and made a bleak gesture. 'No, you don't understand … let me explain, please.'

Once more, flashbacks of his brutal treatment of her assailed Luna; pain rolled over her in sheeting waves as the memory of the contempt in his steel-like eyes cut her heart again and again.

'The way *you* let me explain yesterday?' she accused derisively.

His eyes glittered diamond-bright as he fought his emotions. 'I was out of my mind. I recognize that I'm sometimes an impulsive brute.' His voice was choked and she saw him swallow deeply before he continued: 'I was shocked and hurt. I know it's no excuse for the way I treated you.' He shook his head dejectedly. 'But shock makes you do strange things sometimes. Will you not forgive me?' There was a pause while they stared at each other, not so much enemies as two wounded people.

Luna took a deep breath before answering, trying to stop her voice from quavering. 'And suddenly now, in your magnanimousness, you've decided to forgive me, is that it?' she retorted. 'How do I know that in a week, a month, a year or even ten from now, you won't decide otherwise? How do I know that you won't play Jehovah, verbally striking me down every time we disagree?'

'That's unfair, Luna. I love you more than myself, more than my pride, more than life itself!' he cried, despair written all over him. 'Just hear me out, for both our sakes. Don't do this to us.'

Ruy took a step towards her.

'Just stay where you are,' she flared, leaning against the balustrade to prevent her knees from buckling under her. He was getting to her: she could feel herself wavering. The despondent expression in his eyes, the obvious distress in his voice, his pleading demeanour as he humbled himself before her … all were conspiring to overcome her resistance, arousing the memories of happy days – so recent – when he had caught her up in a whirlwind of passion. Now his proximity, and the relief she felt knowing he still loved her, was threatening to break through the new barriers she had raised, shakily, in her defence. She turned away, staring out over the dark bay.

'Maybe you should start by explaining,' Luna cleared the sudden croakiness in her throat and continued, 'about the accident in which my sister was killed. Yes, let's start with that.'

His frame straightened defensively, then relaxed a little. 'Fair enough. Listen to me first, Luna, I beg of you, before judging me.'

'More than a little presumptuous, don't you think, after the way you refused to listen to me earlier?' Luna forbore telling him that she had already discovered, through the Boston newspaper article, that his part in the accident had been – from what she could tell – completely blameless; and she continued to ignore the voice of reason inside her urging her to stop torturing him.

There was silence behind her, then Ruy's tone was stiff. 'How much more do I need to beg?'

The bitter question shocked her. 'I'm not asking you to beg …' She turned to face him now, trying to ignore that his eyes had become remote and cold, his face like chiselled pale bronze. 'I'm simply pointing out the irony of your request.' Folding her arms, she stared at him. 'Go ahead, I'll give you the opportunity to say your piece, which is more than you gave *me* when I asked to defend myself.'

He took a deep breath; calmed himself. 'Thank you,' he said quietly, and went to lean on the opposite side of the balustrade. He took a packet of cigarettes out of his pocket. 'May I?'

Luna frowned. 'I didn't know you smoked.'

'Very occasionally. Only when I'm stressed.'

'You're a doctor, you should know better.'

He gave her a wry smile. 'Do you care?'

'That's not the point.'

He sensed she was weakening. 'Stop fighting me, *querida*. You love me … I know you love me. A love like ours can't die in a breath.'

She winced, but she wouldn't allow herself to be beaten. 'Let's get back to the subject.'

He lifted the cigarette to his lips. 'You don't mind?'

She shrugged. 'Your funeral.' She gave a shrug and turned back to gaze at the sea.

Ruy shook his head desolately, lit the cigarette and puffed on it silently for a few seconds. Though she was not looking at him, Luna knew that he was watching her profile outlined in the shadows. She could feel the intensity of his burning gaze upon her and sensed he was fighting the same tidal wave of passion that was threatening to engulf her at any moment, should she let it. It was almost as if electric crosscurrents of emotion spun and spread between them with the intricacy of a spider's web.

'I was twenty-one at the time, a student in Boston. My best friend Carlos was also there, part of a student exchange programme, and was dating Juliet.' He spoke in an almost inaudible voice and she had to study his mouth to catch every word. 'He was madly in love with her. Well, half the men on campus were but, honestly, the way she treated him. I don't think she cared much about him.' He paused, as if trying to find the right words. 'It's hard, because she was your sister ... and she lost her life that day ... but she could be so self-centred at times. Completely heedless of anyone's needs but her own. She could be fun too, and Carlos, poor man, was utterly besotted.'

Luna could just imagine her sister using her looks and charm to get her own way, delighting in the power she discovered she had over boys. Poor Carlos, he wouldn't have stood a chance.

Ruy cleared his throat. 'That said, and I'm sorry if I sound insensitive, you need to know that there's not a day that passes without stray pictures flitting in front of my eyes like a film, and I think of my friend and your sister, wondering if there was any way at all that I could have prevented the accident.'

Emotion caught in his throat; he paused and gave a sigh that lingered in the night air, so sad that it crushed the strings of Luna's heart.

He pulled himself together and gave her a rueful smile. 'I'm sorry. I haven't talked about this for a very long time.'

'Ruy,' she whispered in the gentle, low voice he was accustomed to. His eyes remained steady but they were glowing once more like blue stars, no longer cold as steel. Now she could sense the hope that burned in his heart, the rekindling of the twin flames of love and desire. His hard features softened and his mouth grew tender.

The night was quiet around them. There were flashing stars in the sky and, on the hills, the lights of the quaint *Pueblos Blancos* glimmered upon the slopes. A turn of the head, and the lamps of the port grew visible with their watery reflections; the dim outlines of Puerto de Santa María in the distance beyond them.

Luna and Ruy both knew there were still words they needed to say. Their eyes met in sudden charged silence, but neither of them moved.

Time passed while Ruy smoked silently, gathering his thoughts as he watched her, his blue eyes dark with emotion. It was clear to Luna that this conversation was deeply painful for him. After years of silence and repressing his feelings, she acknowledged it must be hard for him to suddenly have to talk about them, especially to her. After all, she had a part in this tragedy.

Finally, Ruy threw his cigarette away. In the moonlight Luna saw his jaw tighten. His face remained pale and intense.

'That night, we were going out as a foursome to the end-of-year ball at Juliet's university. Before leaving, Juliet and Carlos had a flaming row because she was taking so long to get ready. Finally, we were in my car, Carlos in the front next to me. He would have sat next to Juliet in the back, only he was still irritated by her. It was then that she refused point-blank to wear a seatbelt. I asked her to buckle up, but she kept insisting that her dress would be ruined because it was made of very delicate silk.'

He paused and rubbed a hand over his eyes. 'It never dawned on me that she would be foolish enough to pretend she was putting her seatbelt on, when she never had any intention of wearing it at all.'

He lapsed into silence again, reliving the tragic last moments of that day, a mask of raw pain etched into his face, darkening the usually cheerful features. When at last he spoke, his speech was slow and laboured, as though every tormented word he uttered cut into him with renewed pain.

'It was raining hard, I could hardly see in front of me. Suddenly, a truck skidded across the road from the opposite lane and headed straight for us, it didn't even slow. Later I heard that the driver was asleep at the wheel. His headlights were full on, blinding me. I had no time to swerve out of its way.'

His voice caught.

'The impact was enough to hurl Juliet into the seat in front with such force that both she and Carlos were crushed. I was okay, just the odd cracked rib and a nasty gash on my hip. The others would have survived if only she had worn her seatbelt … hadn't been fussing about that wretched dress …'

Ruy had his hand over his eyes as though trying to shut out the picture that had haunted him for so long; and then he broke down, tears pouring from his eyes, his body shaking convulsively with every sob.

'He was my best friend ... more than a brother ... We grew up together ... did everything together ... and his promising young life was snatched away in one violent second.'

Like an injured beast Ruy howled his anger and despair into the night, thumping the balustrade with his clenched fists, fighting demons that had been lying low for so many years and had suddenly raised their heads to taunt him viciously again.

It was more than Luna could bear. She'd never seen him like this, never seen anyone in such despair. She flew to him, her heart overflowing with love and compassion, and wrapped her arms around his shoulders, cradling him in her embrace with passionate gentleness, whispering soothing words against his wet cheeks. Her heart bled for him, and like a helpless child he wept in her arms, begging for her forgiveness.

'Ruy, don't blame yourself,' she whispered, trying to keep her voice level and struggling to ignore the lump in her throat. 'I know you weren't to blame. Anyhow, Juliet and my mother were almost strangers to me. It all happened such a long time ago.' She wiped away his tears with her fingers. 'Come, let's sit down inside. I'll make you a herbal tea with some of that verbena you left in my kitchen.' She gave him a comforting smile and he managed a pale one in response, shaking himself roughly to regain his composure.

Under the electric light Luna saw how gaunt his features were. Purple shadows under his eyes testified that here was a man who had been to hell and back. How could anyone seem to age so much in such a short time?

He threw himself down on the sofa while she went into the kitchen and prepared them both an infusion. When she came back, he was lying against the cushions, eyes shut as though it had been days since he'd had any rest. Luna gazed down at him. He looked so vulnerable, his defences lowered. Her heart ached for him and swelled with tenderness.

Ruy opened his eyes; she had never seen them so blue. He smiled apologetically.

'I think I must have dozed off. Come, sit next to me.'

He stretched out his hand and pulled her down beside him. She tumbled, falling on to his lap, and he drew her against his chest, his face nuzzling at her warm neck, buried under her long, sweet-scented hair.

'Luna, oh my beautiful, gentle, wonderful Luna … I thought I'd lost you,' he whispered, nibbling at the lobe of her ear. His warm breath fanned her temple; he smelt of sea air and tobacco and she breathed in his potent fragrance.

She pulled away from him and started to speak, hesitantly. 'Ruy, I need to tell you everything—'

Ruy placed a finger on her lips, looking deeply into her warm amber eyes. He sighed. 'Your turn next, *querida*. But first, let me finish. There is something else you must know.'

Luna's breath caught in her throat and a cloud shadowed her eyes. All at once she was afraid; suddenly she didn't want to know. What other dark secret was he about to reveal? Maybe he had a child. Maybe … She shook her head.

'Ruy, nothing you can tell me can change my love for you.'

She was still sitting on his knees and he took her hands in his and kissed them. 'I know, *querida*.' He drew her closer, against his chest, and hugged her. 'Nothing that serious, don't worry … but I still feel you need to know.'

Luna sniffed, took a tissue from the box on the side of the sofa and blew her nose. She smiled. 'I'm listening,' she said obediently.

'After the accident I was riddled with fear and guilt and I fell into a deep depression. I had to be hospitalized. There were long periods of sanity interspersed with times of deep despair where I could do nothing, refused to see people and hated myself. Doctors all but gave up on me, saying with time the wound would no doubt heal and, in the meantime, they upped the doses of antidepressants and tranquilizers. When my father came across La Pharaona, she assured him she could cure me without the need for pharmaceutical drugs. That's when I was introduced to the wonders of hypnotism, as well as her herbal remedies.'

'She hypnotized you?'

'Yes, we had many sessions. And her remedies were so effective too. She concocted them using oil extracts from all sorts of wild plants, and she pulled me out of the dark pit into which I had been sinking daily, and for so long. She succeeded where conventional doctors and accepted medicines had failed. I haven't needed to take any medication since, I assure you.'

She gently brushed a stray wisp of hair from his forehead and met the deep blue pools of his eyes, which gazed back at her apprehensively. 'How you could think that I would worry, or hold it against you,' said Luna, wonderingly, 'when you have been so helpful to me about my own childhood trauma. We both have wounds from our past.'

She paused, suddenly remembering. 'You have a scar …'

He nodded. 'I suppose I was lucky to get away with just that.'

'But I think you suffered in ways that were more than physical.'

He smiled at her tenderly. 'Funnily enough, though, after having to get through the pain and grief following the accident, I feel the stronger for it. I think it's just that I know how to deal with the ups and downs of life now. If it hadn't been the case, I would never have asked you to marry me.'

'Marry you?'

'Yes, have you forgotten?'

She smiled awkwardly, guilt chasing along her features. 'No, but after what I did …'

'But I told you, I've read your article, Luna.'

'How did you get to see it?'

'The sub-editor emailed the text, wanting it copy-checked before they went to print. They needed to be assured the details were accurate, so it was passed to me. It's going to be the cover story,' said Ruy with a grin.

'Oh, Ruy,' exclaimed Luna, excitement radiating from her face, 'everyone will hear about your amazing work! Think about the Institute. All the boundless efforts of your staff and researchers.'

'I couldn't be happier,' he said. 'Thank you, *querida*. I should never have doubted you.'

'You were right to be furious,' said Luna. 'I came to Cádiz with the intention of discovering just how scientific your clinic's programme was, and I was convinced that much of it would be hocus-pocus. But very soon I realized that what you're doing here is extraordinary, and I was so happy to be part of it,' she added, her eyes glowing with earnest appeal.

'I so wanted to tell you the truth, but I needed to finish what I'd started, and was determined to deliver a feature that helped you … helped the Institute. It seemed the least I could do.' She paused, suddenly apprehensive. 'Won't your family object to our getting married? They hate the Herreras.'

'They'll love you, don't worry,' he said. 'You've already made an impression on them. Anyway, we could elope. Let's have a gypsy wedding. We'll take off together, just like *gitanos* do.' He grinned. 'You know, the *novio*, once he has decided to marry his chosen one, carries her off from the tribe. A mock fight often takes place to bring the girl back to the camp, and the ceremony is performed the next day.'

Luna looked thoughtful. 'I must admit that I do find gypsies a very romantic people. I suppose all that passion inevitably engenders very strong feelings and hasty behaviour.'

Ruy looked at her with laughter in his eyes. 'Ah, my ever-analyzing Luna!'

She grinned back at his teasing. 'Well, I guess that's one of the things that attracts me to you. You're so different from the other men I've met. So uncompromising and intense ... spontaneous, too.' She threw up her hands. 'Why not? Let's do it. Let's have a gypsy wedding!'

He squeezed her to him. 'That's my girl! You'll see, it'll be fun, and that way we don't need to wait to get married.'

'And I'll truly be your wife?'

'You'll be my wife gypsy-fashion to start off with, but we can have a church wedding later, a grand affair with family and friends. In Spain or in the States ... wherever you like. You must have your day, *querida*. I want to show you off to the whole world.'

But Luna wasn't listening. She didn't care about big weddings and what other people thought, she was too busy listening to her body clamouring for him to seal their promise by making wild and passionate love to her.

Blinking back tears of happiness, she hugged him. 'Oh, Ruy, I love you so much!'

The belt of the thin robe she was wearing loosened and a naked thigh peeped out from the folds.

'It's getting late,' he whispered huskily, 'and I want to make love to you.' His hand slipped through the slit in the robe and met her satiny skin. 'I've missed you. You can't imagine how much.' He pulled her to him and, this time, the garment fell open, revealing her beautiful nakedness.

His eyes turned such a pale blue she thought she could see right into the mysterious depths of his soul. She gave a tremulous sigh, his name fluttering from her lips as flames of need instantly scorched their way along her nerve endings.

'Let's go upstairs,' he murmured. 'It'll be more comfortable for what I have in mind for us tonight.'

'Oh, and what's that?' Luna raised an eyebrow coquettishly.

'I think you can guess.' Hunger gleamed in his gaze, shooting a current of pleasure straight to her core. 'You are my beloved fiancée, the woman with whom I have chosen to spend the rest of my life, the woman who will be the mother of my children. The most desirable, generous and loving woman I have ever come across, and I want to eat you … drink you … fill you, *querida*.' He cupped her face in his hand. His eyes, so blue and full of promise, met hers. 'Then, in three or four weeks, I will make you mine. The generous, loving, intelligent, beautiful woman I've been waiting for all my life.'

She looked up at him, her heart shining in her eyes. 'How can you arrange a wedding in three or four weeks?'

Ruy's lips quirked. 'Easy,' he answered beaming. 'Just watch me!'

'But …'

'No buts, *mi novia hermosa*,' he cut in, eyes like twinkling sapphires. 'Do you trust me?'

'Yes, yes, of course I do … But what shall I wear? What do gypsies wear? What …?'

'Leave it all to me, *querida*. I have it all in my mind.' He chuckled. 'And now, first things first,' he added as he picked her up to take her to the bedroom, his eyes gleaming with mischief. 'We have better things to do.'

She gave a tremulous laugh and wound her arms around his neck.

'How I want you, my beautiful siren!' he sighed and pressed her closer to his chest.

She felt his heart race, an answering statement to all her questions. Warmth spread through her and, as she snuggled against him, letting her head fall on his shoulder, she closed her eyes in the ecstasy of the moment.

Chapter 17

One week later a large parcel arrived for Luna bearing a Californian postmark. She was sitting on her terrace, having breakfast with Ruy, when the postman drove up in his yellow van; she signed for the box as Ruy used his penknife to slice open the tape.

'It's from Grandma Ward,' said Luna, studying the address label. 'I recognize her writing.'

She opened the lid of the enormous box, catching the scent of lavender as she did so. Lifting a fold of tissue paper, she glimpsed underneath it the sheen of pure white silk, gleaming with a pearly iridescence like the moon on a cloudless night. Feeling overwhelmed, and more than a little emotional, she replaced the tissue carefully and picked up the letter that was lying on top of it.

My darling Luna,

I was so happy to receive your wonderful news. Your father rang me sounding highly delighted. We are both absolutely over the moon that you'll be having a second wedding in California. That your fiancé should suggest the plan spoke enormously in his favour, especially as his family and friends will have such a long way to travel. He is undoubtedly a very kind and thoughtful man. Bless you both!

I have sent you my wedding dress with all my love. I was always a little disappointed – having borne three sons – there was no one to

*wear it again. Now you will have something of your family's – a special
heirloom – for your gypsy wedding. We'll be thinking of you on the
big day. Aunt Bea sends her love too. May the sun shine on you both!*
Your loving Grandma xx

'Ruy, this is so perfect! You don't think it will look out of place?'
asked Luna breathlessly. 'I can't wait to try it on! You can't see it
of course, so don't so much as peek!' Then her forehead creased.
'What if it doesn't fit?'

'Don't worry, *querida*,' Ruy assured her, a warm, indulgent
smile curving his lips. 'Firstly, of course it won't look out of
place. There's nothing our gypsy friends appreciate more than
something that's been passed down through the generations.
If it's old and has a story, then it is all the more romantic and
meaningful to them – and to me. And you don't need to worry
about it not fitting, *mi amor*. Mela is very handy with a needle
and thread. She'll be able to adjust it for you, I'm sure.'

He glanced at his watch. 'In fact, why don't we go over to her
cottage and you can ask her yourself? It's high time you met her
and it's only ten minutes on foot from here. She'll probably be
back from walking her dog by now.'

The tiny *casita* was one of three on a stretch of beach Luna
knew well from her walks. Covered with red bougainvillea, it was
white with a terracotta-tiled roof and encircled by a picket fence.
It looked much like the sort of house a young child might draw,
with one window either side of the front door. A table and chairs,
decorated with shells, sat on the tiny patio to the left of the door,
and there was a small bird table near it, on which a couple of
finches were squabbling. Then the front door opened and Luna
could take in nothing else, so amazed was she by the woman she
saw at the threshold.

'Señora Sanchez!'

'*Señorita!*' The Spanish woman's eyes widened in disbelief.

Ruy looked from one to the other in mute enquiry. A second later, the two women were hugging each other, laughing delightedly.

'I take it you already know Carmela Sanchez, then,' Ruy remarked, watching the two women with amusement.

'She's my friend. You know, the dog-walking lady I told you about,' Luna explained to Ruy, once she had pulled away from Carmela's embrace and caught her breath.

'*Santa Madre!*' exclaimed the *señora*. 'What is the world coming to next? So, *niño*, this is the nameless lady you didn't want any gossip about.' A multitude of thoughts and emotions flashed across the Spanish woman's face as she gazed at Luna, realization dawning. Her frown then melted into a wide smile before she tutted and flung up her hands.

'*Ay!* I should knock your two heads together for all the time I've spent worrying about the pair of you. One day talking to a tearful Luna, then Ruy banging his head against the wall. And all the time I needn't have bothered. Ah, *perfecto*! Made for each other; like sugar and flour in my *churros*!'

They sat outside at the little shell-encrusted table while Carmela brought them coffee and some freshly baked *almendrados*, crispy almond cookies, and soon the three of them were talking animatedly.

At first, Carmela was not impressed by the idea of a gypsy wedding and she was quite candid about it. To her mind it was not befitting for the grandson of a count and the daughter of a tycoon to be married in such an inappropriate way. She had her own ideas about gypsies and their traditions, many of which, in deference to Ruy, she kept to herself. But when he explained that there would be another wedding – a *boda correcta* – a proper church wedding in the United States, and Luna assured Carmela that hers would be the first name on the invitation list, she embraced the idea wholeheartedly.

'I will come over this afternoon to La Gaviota and we'll sort out this dress of yours,' she said, looking Luna up and down critically. 'I think you've lost weight worrying about *el joven* here, so I may have to take it in. Anyway, enough of that.' She laughed and reached out to squeeze Ruy's arm, her voice softening almost to a whisper as she did so. 'I'm so happy for you, *querido niño*. After all you've been through, you deserve this joy. If only my Pedro were here to see it.'

*   *   *

Brightness filled the air on Luna's wedding day. The view that morning was a sight to dream of. Summer had set in, and the great flood of sunshine was almost blinding. A few beautiful sailboats were racing each other in the breeze, like colourful paintings on the scintillating sea.

Luna sat in the shade on her terrace, savouring a plate of freshly baked *churros* as she sipped a cup of chocolate. Never, she reflected, could there have been anyone as happy as she was. That morning, as she opened her eyes, she had been greeted by the delicious aroma of baking, mingled with an almost overwhelming fragrance of flowers. Slipping out of bed, she'd padded down to the kitchen to find the house bursting with white blooms of all kinds of flower imaginable. Every bouquet, posy and basket had a small note pinned to it with loving words and poetry, each one of them different: '*If I could give you the stars, I'd gather them in my heart, and wrap them with my love, to brighten your day*'; and '*I used to think that dreams did not come true. That changed the day I laid eyes on you*'; and again, '*Do you know that men and women are angels created with one wing? They need to embrace each other to be able to fly away. You are my angel and together we will fly through the world*'.

Ruy must have spent hours writing those romantic and passionate words.

Carmela had come to La Gaviota early to bake *churros* for breakfast. She'd stepped out of the kitchen when Luna came downstairs. 'Just look at all these flowers! Ruy *está loco por ti*, Ruy is crazy about you,' she'd told her. 'Legions of women have run after him, even when he was sixteen. Doña Luz, his mother, used to confiscate his mobile phone because it never stopped ringing! But he's never given his heart to anyone until you came along, *señorita*.'

She paused and there was a wicked twinkle in her eyes.

'You know, Doña Vaina moved heaven and earth to make him love her. *Dios mio*, that woman was a piece of work! But he kept his heart untouched *para la mujer de su vida*, for the woman of his life. Now he has given his heart to you.'

She smiled warmly at Luna, who was both touched and amused by the Spanish woman's gushing approbation. '*Usted es su primer amor*, you are his first love. I know you'll be so happy together.'

There was no doubt that Carmela doted on Ruy, whom she'd helped look after from birth. She had witnessed the days of depression that followed his accident and it was understandable that his family's housekeeper should feel protective towards him. Luna was aware of the secret message in her dark eyes that read: *Take good care of this man. No one will ever love you the way he does.*

She went up to the *señora* and put her arms around her. 'Ruy is my first love too, Carmela, and I know that I could never live without him. I remember once reading a quote that said: "Some people come into our lives, leave footprints on our heart, and we are never the same." That's exactly what has happened to me. You need not worry, *señora*. Without Ruy, life wouldn't be worth living.'

Carmela sighed with pleasure and patted Luna's cheek affectionately. 'I knew you were special when I first saw you on the beach. You two are good together; I have seen the way you look at each other. Maybe God has done this to end the feud that has been tearing apart your two families for generations,' she mused. 'Go upstairs now, and I will bring you a real Spanish breakfast, like the one I used to make for Doctor Ruy and for Doña Luz when she was a young girl. You must relax. It will be a long day; the festivities don't start until the evening.' She gave a mischievous smile. '*El Medico* has a surprise in store for you.'

'A surprise?'

'*Sí, sí, señorita*. It's a big one but you'd better go now in case my tongue runs away with me. *Ay*, may the saints sew my lips together for my prattling! I've said too much already ... He'll be very cross if I let the cat out of the bag.'

As Luna was not allowed to see Ruy before the evening, she decided to sit in the shade on her bedroom terrace and have a quiet morning. She was trying to take in everything that had happened to her since her arrival in Spain; it was incredible to think it was still not that long ago.

She smiled inwardly. Now that she came to think of it, Ruy had never really asked her to marry him. In his usual way, he had been very autocratic, just stating they would be married, almost as if he was not giving her a choice. Coming from anyone else, she would have been offended at such a proposal, but not with Ruy. It was so like him, this spontaneity: an almost childlike innocence that made him believe in the magic of the moon and the stars and the *One Thousand and One Nights* fairy tales, in legends and in fate; and that, of course, included happy endings. For him it was a foregone conclusion that they were meant to be together, not out of arrogance but because he knew that now she believed it too.

So was she apprehensive about the wedding itself? She had never really given it much thought. Well, perhaps a little. Everything had happened so quickly. There was one thing about which she was sure, though: she didn't ever want to relive the despair she had felt when she thought she'd lost him.

Ruy was exciting, intelligent and fascinating. In just a few weeks he had introduced her to so many novel things; most of all he had introduced her to her true self, a self that had lain dormant and that she might never have discovered had she not met him. In fact, she liked this new Luna, a woman freed of inhibition, who felt feminine and good about herself because she knew she was loved and wanted by a man like Ruy, a man she admired and respected more than any other in the world.

Watching the waves surge up the sandy beach below and the white foam recede with a gentle hiss, Luna's heart swelled with joy. Love! Passion! She had never imagined what they were like until she had met him, until he swept her off her feet and helped her defeat her fears. He had a zest for living, the like of which she had not encountered in anyone before.

But it was not only Ruy's flagrant masculinity, his expertise at most things and his knowledge of life that she loved. The man behind the mask had touched her most: the kindness and vulnerability that hid beneath the outer shell of competent doctor and accomplished womanizer. He had stirred feelings inside her that went well beyond admiration, physical attraction and respect. It might sound crazy, after such a short time of knowing each other, but the truth was she could scarcely imagine life without him now.

'Do you really want to live in Spain?' her father had asked when she had called to tell him the news. 'You'll be away from your family, all your friends … everything you've been familiar with the whole of your life. It's a huge step, one that should not be taken lightly, Luna.'

The answer to that question was also clear. She loved Spain and its smiling, vibrant people who, it seemed to her, contained the essence of the country's sunshine and light. Not the hard-nosed society types like the Herreras, the polished upper classes found in any part of the world, whom she had never much cared for. No, she was talking about the ordinary folk – the Carmelas, Morenas and Chicos – the passionate, spontaneous, happy-go-lucky men and women who formed the core of this ardent and colourful country. Besides, travelling was so easy nowadays. She could go back to visit friends and family at any time.

No, she had no misgivings; she really wanted this.

*   *   *

Restless from sitting about, Luna spent the afternoon running on the beach and going for a swim, much to Carmela's disapproval.

'You'll tire yourself out with all this exercise. … Just like Luz was always doing at your age,' she tutted, shaking her head.

Then, two hours before Luna was due to leave for her gypsy ceremony, she and Carmela, who was about to begin the painstaking task of getting the bride ready, heard the sound of the doorbell. 'Who could that possibly be?' wondered Luna aloud. 'Ruy knows not to come over before the ceremony.'

'Maybe a delivery of flowers or some such thing,' said Carmela, leaving Luna at the dressing table and walking down the stairs.

Luna heard the housekeeper's questioning tone, then the sound of a man's voice: the deep resonant American drawl she knew so well. In seconds, she had run down the stairs, tying her kimono around her as she went.

'Dad!'

Montgomery Ward, tall, broad-shouldered and built like a rock, stood in the hallway of La Gaviota and scooped up his daughter as if she weighed no more than a feather, whirling her round as he used to when she was a young child. All at once Luna felt overcome, her heart so full she felt it might burst, and tears of joy flooded her eyes.

'You came!' was all she could stammer, her mouth quivering with emotion.

'I couldn't let my little girl get married without her old pa there to give her away,' said her father, a gruffness in his tone betraying the strong feelings he too was experiencing at their reunion. 'There were times in your childhood, my darling, when my work took me away from you – many, many times, to my eternal shame. Well, here I am … and I wouldn't have missed this day for anything.'

'Yes, here you are, and I couldn't wish for more. I still can't believe it!' Luna exclaimed ecstatically, clasping her father's hands, her eyes shining with happiness.

'I rang that young man of yours and we decided to keep it a surprise. He likes surprises, I can tell. Told me there's another up his sleeve but he didn't say what it was.'

Carmela, who stood beaming at the door, gave him a look and he put a hand to his lips. 'There goes my big mouth again! I won't say another word.'

'Well, this is just the best. It couldn't get any better, it really couldn't!'

Montgomery smiled as he placed a large arm around his daughter. 'I don't know what's in store for us today. A bit of a mystery, this gypsy wedding. I won't be walking you up the aisle, I presume.'

'We'll just have to play it by ear,' said Luna laughingly. 'I was a little nervous about the whole thing before but, now I've got you, I'm not worrying about a thing!'

'That's just the way it should be,' said Montgomery. 'Until I hand you over to the arms of your new husband, you're all mine. I intend to make the most of it, I assure you, and look after you very well indeed.'

*   *   *

As Luna made her way with her father and Carmela to the gypsy camp, the summer sun was sinking, a ball of fire set in fleecy crimson clouds. It was as if a magician had extended his golden wand over the stunted countryside and now the sky, sea and hills were ablaze at its touch. The landscape was enrobed in flames of cinnamon and vermillion, with shades of pale yellow and pink that melted and mingled together.

The journey was a silent one, each passenger lost in deep thought. Luna's father held her hand clasped gently in his and, every now and then, Carmela would check a tendril of Luna's hair with careful fingers or ask Mr Ward to mind his daughter's dress. By the time the white limousine had reached its destination, darkness had fallen and nothing was left in the vaulted, studded sky but the silver crescent of the young moon and the stars, flashing brightly in attendance.

There was an earthly radiance about the camp, an atmosphere of high revelry. Tonight the gypsy settlement was in festive mood, lit by a thousand torches and braziers and great blazing fires. Tents, wagons and cars were decked with green oak leaves, willow branches and a kaleidoscope of wild flowers from the surrounding hills. Everywhere there was bustle and movement. Large pots and cauldrons bubbling with *piria* – the aromatic stew of the gypsies – hung over man-made clay stoves, smoke floating up in thin wisps. A suckling pig and other meats were being turned on spits by stout women in cheerfully coloured dresses, who seemed oblivious to the fat that trickled out, spluttering on the red-hot coals beneath.

Ruy, magnificent in a white suit, was waiting for Luna in front of one of the brightly lit caves. As he strolled to their car with long, panther-like strides, she saw that his glossy, jet-black hair was slickly pushed back from his forehead and drawn into a short ponytail. She had never seen him wear a ponytail before and she felt her heart pound suddenly in her breast. It definitely added to his roguish look and enhanced the mystery and sex appeal emanating from him. More than ever his sculpted-bronze face reflected the passion and the pride, the strength and that tinge of gypsy arrogance that characterized everything he did.

He threw open the door of the car and extended his hand to help Luna out. A tint of rose flushed her cheeks when she read the blunt message in the cobalt-blue eyes that studied her elegant, tapered silhouette as it emerged from the car. She looked every bit the Queen of the Night in Grandma Ward's pure-white wedding gown. It was made of embroidered chiffon over satin and its high, French-lace collar showed off her graceful shoulders and enhanced the slenderness of her swanlike neck. The boned bodice moulded her bust to perfection and ended in a wide V-shaped waistband that added definition to her hourglass figure.

The dynastic dress made Luna feel both stylish and unique; she was acutely aware of the fact that she was wearing a little piece of history and Ruy's intent gaze told her everything she wanted to know: that tonight he found her ravishing, sexy and unforgettable.

Carmela had done wonderful work with Luna's hair, which she had twisted and knotted, Spanish fashion, at the nape of the bride's neck. The veil was secured by a floral ring encircling her head like a crown; entwined on its stem were three orange blossom flowers fashioned out of pearls, each with a diamond at the centre of the five petals and leaves made of tiny emeralds – every bit a jeweller's work of art. The teardrop diamond earrings that swung from her ears gave the last glamorous touch to the ensemble. Coiffed in such a way, Luna's Castilian genes shone through. Carmela had cleverly brought out her Spanish characteristics for what was to be, gypsy or otherwise, a uniquely Andalucían ceremony.

'My beautiful goddess of the night,' Ruy murmured hoarsely as he lifted her slim hand and touched it to his lips. 'I am so proud of you.' He then turned to Montgomery Ward and paid his respects like a true *hidalgo* with a slight, aristocratic bow. Luna could tell that her father was charmed.

She stood for a moment, taking in the beauty of the scene, arm in arm with the two most important men in her life, one on each side of her. Then two little girls with huge, laughing black eyes appeared from nowhere, dressed in frilly pink dresses. With great care, they picked up Luna's train. The entourage made its stately way to where two throne-like chairs made of caoba wood had been set up under the plane trees.

Gypsies from all over the camp gathered behind the couple as they walked; Luna caught sight of Ruy's family in their midst, Alexandra arm in arm with Salvador, Luz holding Andrés's hand; she saw Charo beaming with happiness next to Miguel, whom Luna had finally met, and whose quiet, steady demeanour seemed a perfect foil for her gregarious friend. On the other side of them, Morena walked with Chico, whose wink to the bride and groom could be seen by everyone because he stood a head taller than anyone else in the entourage. Then there was the sound of cannon and a flock of pure-white doves flew into the air and over their heads.

Luna was exhilarated; intoxicated by the buoyancy of the people around her and the flamboyant personality of the man she loved. It was as if a fever were running through her veins. She was in a dream, an extraordinary, weird but wonderful dream.

As the bridal pair sat on their royal seats, the chief of the gypsies, a tall, surprisingly straight-backed old man with a wispy white beard, whom Luna recognized from the christening, followed by his helper, came forward, bearing a loaf of bread, some salt and a glass of wine. In the sudden silence that fell on the camp, the only thing she could hear was the distant whinny of a horse, carried on the soft sea breeze.

The old man, his swarthy sun-baked face taking on a serious countenance, broke the loaf in two, sprinkling salt on the portions with his knobbly fingers before handing the pieces to Luna and Ruy. 'The day you tire of this bread and this salt will see the day you tire of each other,' he said in a cavernous voice that echoed sonorously in the night. 'Before eating your share, you must exchange it with your partner's,' he explained more quietly.

When they had done this, the chief poured some wine into the glass. He offered it first to Luna, asking her to drink just half before passing it to Ruy.

'This bread and this salt are the symbols of your love, of richness and of prosperity, with which I hope your marriage will be blessed.' He turned first to the bride. 'Luna, you now belong, body and soul, to Ruy.' Then, looking at the bridegroom, he said: 'Ruy, you belong, body and soul, to Luna.'

It all seemed to happen in the briefest moment and, almost before Luna could register what had happened, the chief was bringing their heads together as a symbol of their union, with the simplest of phrases: 'You are now married.'

Luna's and Ruy's eyes locked, and there was an ocean of meaning in their twin gaze, an eternity of love so freely and willingly bestowed. For a short while it was as if there were no one else present: they were conscious only of each other, alone under the moonlit sky, in silent and mutual exultation.

The chief had a final word of warning for the bride and groom, and his eyes glinted ominously as he delivered it. 'Unlike *gajo* marriages, that of the gypsies is sacred and dangerous to break. Infidelity by either man or woman is not tolerated. Any infringement of our laws by either party will be heard before a tribal council.' Then the old man's gaze softened and his face – which until then had worn a serious expression – broke into the widest of smiles. 'Go in peace now and be happy.'

As people gathered around them, Luna turned and smiled at the old man, who clasped her hand in his strong brown fingers. 'This is a very unusual ceremony,' he said. '*Gajos* hardly ever marry *Calés* and only once before have I seen it, with Ruy's father. Like him, your husband is not a pure gypsy but, as the grandson of the very beautiful and gifted Marujita, he is a valued member of our tribe. She was the queen of it for many years, and this wedding is homage to her, as well as to her son, who still helps us in every way he can. I hope you will be very happy together. We know Ruy well – he is a good man.'

Luna smiled again, demurely. 'Thank you for this honour. Ruy is more *Calés* than *gajo*. I know we will be very happy. He's wonderful and we love each other very much.'

Just then Morena appeared at her side, her striking sable eyes gleaming with affection. 'You see, Luna, *El Destino* caught up with you after all.' The *gitana* embraced her warmly and kissed her on the cheek, whispering: 'The Queen of the Night has emerged from the dark at last and into the light.'

Luna's smile trembled slightly with emotion. 'I know, Morena. You were right, of course.'

The end of the ceremony had been greeted with lunatic merriment as the guests wished the married couple luck. Grains of rice were showered over the pair, and the gypsy camp erupted into singing and dancing. Huge plates of food and enormous gourds of wine were passed around. In the light of the flickering fires the riotous celebration, in which all ages took part, had begun. Luna was taken up in a fantastic whirlwind, joining wholeheartedly in this outlandish merriment.

She looked over at her father. Montgomery Ward was standing with the men of Ruy's family and Salvador was laughing at something he had just said, clapping the powerful-looking American on the back in a genial fashion. Her father's face seemed entirely smoothed of care, Luna noticed: gone were the habitual frown lines scoring his broad forehead and the vertical creases either side of his generous mouth. She couldn't remember ever having seen him look so happy.

Being in charge of a business empire, its balance sheets and staff, certainly had its downsides – Luna knew that more than anybody. But to have denied himself so much, all his adult life, so many simple pleasures ... and, most damaging of all, almost missing his only daughter grow up – that was a terrible loss that she could tell he felt keenly. He could never get those years back but she was determined that things would be different from now on. Maybe, he might be able to have a more hands-on, carefree relationship with his grandchildren, she mused, and she found herself growing warm inside at the thought.

She went over to him and he put an arm around her waist. 'Ah Luna, you've got one heck of a Spanish family here,' he said, smiling broadly. 'I no longer have the slightest worry about your living here. Not if you have this lot to watch your back.'

'Oh, we will most certainly look after her,' said Salvador graciously, his English impeccable, though with a strong accent. 'In fact, you won't be able to keep Alexandra and Luz away if you're not careful, Luna. They're fearful meddlers.' This was said with a wink at Luz, who had just walked over to their group.

'*Papá*, that is really not true,' said Luz, laughing. 'Don't believe it, Luna. He's just teasing.'

Montgomery Ward broke in now, hugging Luna close and giving her a resounding kiss on the cheek. 'Well, all I know is what I see,' he said, with a wink at Salvador. 'Just look over there, Luna – your husband can hardly bear to have you out of his sight. I don't think your in-laws will get much of a look-in, to be frank. Ruy will want you all to himself.'

'I've no complaints about that,' remarked Luna contentedly.

She looked over at Ruy, standing with his grandmother, Alexandra, and Chico, who were helping themselves to food from a trestle table under the plane trees. As if sensing her eyes upon him, he looked up and locked gazes with Luna. Then he raised an enquiring eyebrow, as if to say, *I hope they're behaving themselves.* She gave a happy flash of a smile in return.

'Ah, young love!' Andrés spoke now. Luna reflected that his

gypsy good looks must barely have weathered in all the years since he had met Luz. One could have taken him for Ruy's older brother, rather than his father.

'Oh, come on. You're making me feel old!' said Luz, laughter lighting up her eyes. She turned to Salvador. 'As you always so rightly say, *Papá*, you're as young as you feel.'

'Oh yes, there's plenty of life in this old goat yet,' Salvador grinned. Luz laid a hand on her father's arm and he bent his head to receive a feather-light peck on his cheek.

'You will always be eternally young in my eyes, *querida*,' Andrés said graciously. 'You look as ravishing as you did when I first laid eyes on you.'

Luz dimpled, accepting the compliment happily. 'Still, I can't believe our little Ruy has just got married,' she sighed. 'It only seems like yesterday that he was making *almendrados* with Carmela at the kitchen table, creating all that mess. She was always so patient with him.'

For a moment her eyes wore a far-off look of nostalgia as she glanced across at her former housekeeper, who was deep in conversation with Morena. 'Excuse me a moment, I'm going to join them. To be honest, I'm somewhat intrigued. Carmela's never been entirely polite about our *gitano* friends, but she seems to be getting along like a house on fire with Morena. I'm so delighted.'

'There's nothing like a wedding to bring people together,' said Montgomery, nodding sagaciously. 'There's not a person under the sun who won't get along, given the right circumstances. Although I'm extremely glad, Luna, you haven't asked your uncle and aunt Herrera. I never was enamoured of those two.'

Luna nodded. 'You and me both,' she said simply.

'You can take it as read that all of us agree on that,' Andrés couldn't help adding. 'Although I'm not sure Lorenzo Herrera would have been free to come anyway.'

'Go on,' said Montgomery, curious to know more.

'Well, not that I want to spoil the mood of our celebrations, but I heard this morning that Herrera's been arrested for some rather dubious financial practices. The word on the street is that this time his tax lawyers won't have a hope in hell of getting him off. He'll almost certainly do time.'

Luna couldn't help a snaking feeling of jubilation winding its way through her. Maybe there was such a thing as divine justice after all, she reflected, although she swiftly berated herself for her superstition. No, the man had got his just desserts; it was no more or less than that. Lorenzo had no doubt been the cause of his own undoing, as many a crook before him. *'Truth will out, and right will prevail'*, wasn't that what Grandma Ward always used to tell her?

Added to that was a feeling of relief, which surged through her suddenly. If her uncle had caused his own downfall, there would be no need for Ruy to get involved in a vendetta. Luna had felt sure that, true to his impulsive gypsy blood, he would conceive of some act of *venganza* when the occasion presented itself but, as she knew only too well, at the end of the day it wasn't necessarily the worthy or wronged party who succeeded in coming out on top. All she wanted now was never to have to see or talk of the Herreras ever again. Then, as if everyone else was in perfect accord with her sentiment, the conversation moved smoothly on to other, happier, matters.

Luna moved to join Ruy, drawn to his side with a compulsion that she found so exciting, as if an invisible elastic string joined her to him irrevocably. At her approach he turned, as if he too could sense her presence with that almost supernatural power that bound them together. Alexandra had broken off her conversation at Luna's approach and the old lady's eyes twinkled with unrestrained joy as she looked at the bridal pair.

'Thank you for making my grandson so very happy,' she said, clasping Luna's hands in her own. 'I knew from the moment I saw you in your silver moonlight costume that you were sent, almost by some divine providence, to bring joy into his life.'

'*I'm* the fortunate one,' said Luna simply, locking eyes with her husband, whose azure gaze held a wealth of tenderness. 'I didn't know what love or joy was until he showed me.'

'That is just how I felt when I met Salvador,' Alexandra happily exclaimed. 'It is a gift not bestowed on everyone, so we all have a good deal to be thankful for.'

Ruy gave his grandmother an enormous hug that took her breath away.

'Thank you for receiving Luna into our family with such openheartedness, *Abuela*. I told her everyone would love her.'

'Ah, Ruy!' exclaimed Alexandra, with a tinkling, almost girlish laugh that could not have changed at all over the decades, Luna supposed. 'Our family may have got itself into various scrapes and blood feuds over the years, but there's one thing for certain: we've always known how to love.'

The festivities were still going strong when, at three in the morning, Luna and Ruy decided it was time to take their leave. As custom required, Ruy had parked his car away from the festivities, in Cádiz; and so the couple clambered into the bridal gig, festooned with flowers and drawn by two beautiful white horses. Followed by *gitanas* snapping their fingers louder than castanets and *gitanos* dancing and singing at the top of their lungs, the procession marched down the hill and through the narrow streets of the sleeping town until they reached the decorated vintage Austin.

The convoy of merry gypsies waved them off and, when it was out of sight, Ruy stopped the car. Silently, his eyes met Luna's, intent and glittering; her glossy lips parted invitingly, her honey-brown gaze hot with desire. He pulled her towards him almost savagely, his strong arms wrapping possessively around her, and took her mouth avidly.

'I've been wanting to do this all evening,' he murmured finally, his burning lips still against hers. 'But I'm afraid we're going to have to wait a little longer, *querida*. There's a surprise waiting for you, and unfortunately, it's three hours' drive away. Do you mind?'

Luna laughed. 'A few hours more shouldn't hurt too much. Haven't you always told me pleasure is enhanced by anticipation?'

He dragged her back to him, his mouth on fire against hers, his tongue invading the soft wet warmth rapaciously. She moaned and he felt her melt beneath his onslaught.

'Incredible,' he muttered as he drew back, shaking his head. 'What you do to me is unbelievable.' He looked sheepishly at her kiss-bruised lips and trailed his fingers over them. 'You turn me into a wild beast, Luna. Forgive me if I've hurt you.'

She looked up at him, cheeks fiery, eyes glazed with desire. 'Do I look like someone who's hurting?' She smiled. 'Let's go now or we'll never get to my surprise. Where is it? *What* is it?'

'As one of your poets once wisely said, Longfellow, I think it was: "All things come round to him who will but wait."'

Her eyes sparkled mischievously as her hand went to the back of his neck to stroke it. 'And as our former President, Woodrow Wilson, said: "All things come to him who waits – provided he knows what he is waiting for,"' she retorted with a grin, pleased with herself for being so quick off the mark.

Ruy laughed, a deep, hoarse sound tinged with a raw kind of hunger. 'You're so bright, so beautiful, so wonderful, so sexy,' he said. 'And if you don't stay still in your seat and go to sleep, we'll either have an accident or I'll have to stop the car and put myself out of my misery.'

'All right, I'll try to get some sleep, but promise to wake me when we arrive.'

'Of course!'

Luna took off her veil, undid her hair and pushed her seat back to settle herself comfortably. Though excited, she was nevertheless tired. Perhaps Carmela had been right about her relaxing more before the wedding. The movement of the car rocked her as she let her thoughts wander happily, and she drifted off into a deep sleep.

*   *   *

As the vintage Austin glided elegantly through the peaceful night towards Jaén the roads were deserted. Sleepy moonlit towns and villages fled by like ghosts, one after the other, under the pearly gaze of the thin, lustrous crescent moon. In the indigo sky, stars trembled, yet their music was strong like the voice of love and passion travelling through darkness from some unknown world.

Ruy drove fast but carefully, lost in thought. It was by a stroke of luck that, shortly after Luna had told him wistfully about her childhood memories of an old mill surrounded by olive trees, he had come across an advertisement in *El Periodico de Andalucía*, which was offering an olive grove for sale in Jaén. When he had enquired about it, he'd found that it was actually Olivar, the property of which Luna had spoken so longingly.

For some time he'd been thinking of buying an olive grove, but one closer to home. However, when he'd seen the advertisement, because he was already obsessed with Luna, the idea of buying something that had left such an impression on her as a child excited him; it was like owning a little piece of *her*, he told himself.

So, in the week before little Luis's christening at the camp, he'd flown down to Jaén to have a look at the property, which nestled peacefully at the edge of a small village on the outskirts of the town. He had been charmed by the quaintness of the place and, though it was slightly neglected, he had at once seen all the possibilities it presented. True, it needed work, but the challenge was part of the attraction. The vendors were foreigners – Australians – and were eager to sell, and when he'd put in his offer, it had been accepted immediately.

His eyes slid across to the woman sleeping soundly beside him. A glow of warmth and pride washed over him and his heart swelled at the thought that one day soon she would bear his children. For him, there was no greater thing in life than having the woman he adored bring the fruits of that love into this world.

EPILOGUE

They had arrived at the old millhouse just as dawn was breaking. With his usual thoughtfulness, Ruy lifted the half-asleep Luna out of the car, carrying her into the house and up to the bedroom. Gently he relieved her of her clothes and pulled up the covers, making no move to make love to her, even though she would have fought her exhaustion had he done so. She slept all night in his arms, barely stirring.

Now Luna opened her eyes. A pleasant languor suffused her body and she stretched her arms contentedly. Ruy was sitting beside her on the bed, already dressed. He had brought her a cup of coffee.

'Good morning, Señora Rueda de Calderón,' he said with a lazy grin.

'What time is it?' she asked, smiling sleepily and sitting up to take a sip of the hot brew. Her eyes focused on the warm, exposed-brick walls, oak beams and charming rustic wooden furniture. 'Where are we?' she added, putting her cup down on the bedside table.

'Here, put this on and I'll show you,' said Ruy, passing her silk kimono. She could sense that he was barely able to suppress his excitement.

A moment later, he had scooped her up in his arms and was carrying her to the window.

'See for yourself.'

It was a wonderful, white summer day, the sky clear and cloudless. Clasped in the golden light of morning like the sweetheart of the sun, the millhouse bricks glowed a rich terracotta, kissed by its warm beams. Night dew still clung to the soil and made the plants glisten. Birds called to one another and the butterflies and bees were already at work.

The glorious lamp of heaven washed the roofs and hillsides with clarity, in a kind of dreamy and magical light; the countryside stretched to infinity in all the freshness of a new Eden.

At first, Luna didn't realize where she was, imagining that Ruy had booked them into a hotel. Yet when she looked outside, she slowly recognized the hilly landscape with its endless olive trees, their boughs black and crooked. The sun streamed down, creating bright patches between the trees, its light streaking across the silver-green groves. She instantly burst into tears.

Olivar. The place of her happy childhood memories.

'Don't cry, Luna.' Ruy gently wiped her cheeks with the back of his hand. 'I bought it for you, *mi amor*. For *us*,' he told her, with stars lighting his eyes.

How had he remembered? How had he found it? *He'd bought it?* Ruy was amazing! Life was wonderful.

'But what if it hadn't worked out between us?' she said, sniffing, too stunned to think.

He dropped a kiss on the tip of her nose.

'That was never an option, *querida*, you know that. Legends never lie. It worked for my grandparents and, after that, for my parents. I had no reason to think it would not work for us too. I always knew you were my love, my destiny.'

His eyes darkened as his hand went to her hair, which hung loosely around her shoulders, running his fingers through its pale softness. Nuzzling into it, he bent to kiss her throat as his hand sought hers. Luna sighed with pleasure as her pulse accelerated, and she let Ruy lead her to the bed. Her kimono slipped to the ground and she lay back, heat suffusing her body.

He stood there motionless, staring down at her. He could have been a statue but for the gleam of raw desire glittering in his ocean-blue eyes, watching the pink hue flush her naked body as it came to life and bloomed with her need for him. Oh, every inch of her flesh knew that look and was instantly reacting to its fire, each nerve-ending in her body sparking into life.

A ripple of sensation made her shiver and she stared up at him, burning for his lips, desperate for his touch; yet still he made no move, his eyes ranging over her in a sweet, teasing torture, commanding her thighs to quiver and her breasts to harden to aching points, the core of her begging for his possession.

Gazing intently into her eyes as she lay so vulnerable in front of him, her body denuded of all inhibition and pretence, he was ignited by the flames of her desire and, unfastening the buttons of his shirt, proceeded to strip himself of his clothing.

One by one he removed each item, purposely taking his time, his movements slow, erotic, intentionally making her wait. He watched her pupils dilate with excitement until her irises seemed almost black, the amber in them having very nearly disappeared.

She felt exquisitely feminine under his masterful gaze, a restless urgency to be possessed by him burning between her legs. It was his usual game of anticipation, a most powerful aphrodisiac that worked each and every time.

This would be their first time as man and wife and the thought made Luna almost sigh with joy. How much longer was he going to make her wait? She could see the swell of his arousal rising as expectancy grew stronger in both of them. He was flaunting the stark evidence of his desire for her shamelessly, knowing full well what it was doing to her. She could see that he was hard, *so* hard; he wanted her just as much as she wanted him and, instinctively, she parted her thighs to receive him.

She was naked and wanting, her eyes pleading. Couldn't he see that her breathing was accelerating, every limb quivering?

And then suddenly, with a groan, he was near her. '*Dios, Luna*, you drive me insane!' he rasped silkily. 'I'm going to touch you, kiss you, taste you, relish every part of you and then, when your need for me is so overpowering and you can't stand it any more, I will possess you in every way I know until I fulfil your every need and you're completely saturated with my love.'

The images his words conjured up almost devastated the last vestiges of Luna's control. She parted her legs, desperate for him to fill her, and he started to move deliciously against her silky wetness with his rigid arousal, driving her wild until she moaned against his mouth, pleading wordlessly for relief.

But Ruy hadn't finished with her yet. He moved away from her moist feminine curls, tearing a sob of protest from her throat and, with the febrile need of an addict, his lips, tongue and hands began their sensuous and audacious exploration of her lean and graceful body, his touch alternating between tenderness and fierce, demanding passion, sending shivers of agonizing pleasure racing up and down her spine. Drunk with arousal, she surrendered to his voluptuous onslaught, trembling, her amber eyes glazing over with the power of her desire, relishing his caresses; delighting in his love.

His eyes wild with feverish longing, Ruy trailed a path with his predatory tongue down to her breasts, where he left the peaks of them wet and taut, then moving from her cleavage down the middle of her, kissing and murmuring words that were unintelligible now, his hot breath fanning the fire that already scorched her satiny flesh as he sought the burgeon of her need.

'I want to take you in my mouth, I want to taste your sweet nectar, savour each bit of you until you lose your mind,' he whispered roughly as his hands continued their decadent journey over her sensitized breasts, moving with teasing caresses over her slender waist and tracing her quivering curves as his head worked its way downwards.

Then he found the engorged heat between her thighs. Again and again, waves of pleasure flooded over her as he inched her many times to the brink, making her cry out his name and rave and squirm, responding like a puppet under the command of his masterly, wicked tongue.

As her hands fisted in his dark hair, Ruy suddenly rose up and pinned her wrists above her head, eliciting from her a fresh gasp of surprise and pleasure. The molten look in his eyes told Luna that he could no longer contain himself. He slid over her and positioned himself between her already parted thighs. With one smooth glide, he thrust into the slick opening of her body, burying himself to the hilt in her velvet heat, making her cry out. She moaned in sensual delirium as he pushed deeper and longer into her and her hips rose to meet him, knowing their mutual hunger was building with a galloping momentum, the heat coursing through their veins as they devoured each other, body and soul, giving and taking in perfect unity.

At last, letting go, he drove them both to a rapturous climax, staggering in its raw potency as an astonishing deluge of pleasure surged through their bodies, splintering their senses and leaving them exalted.

Ruy pressed his forehead to Luna's, panting for breath. 'You're all mine. *Te amo, mi hermosa esposa*, I love you, my beautiful wife.'

Her arms curled around his neck, tears springing to her eyes. '*Te amo, mi marido querido*.'

*   *   *

A few hours later, after they had made love many times over and basked in the pleasure of each other's bodies, Ruy and Luna finally dressed and left the sanctuary of their bedroom to explore the grounds of Olivar together.

They went down to the part of the garden that was bordered by a lake, which Luna had talked about with such emotion. It was a day in which mere existence was a delight and they sat on the grass, leaning against the gnarled bark of an olive tree heavy with summer foliage. As they breathed in the pure air, Ruy and Luna gazed in silence over one of the most magnificent prospects the eye ever looked upon, asking themselves if they were not in some kind of wonderland.

A smiling, green and fertile valley stretched to infinity with line after line of silver-green olive trees and the deep, dreamy Guadalquivir River scintillating like a necklace of blue diamonds under the azure sky. The outlines and undulations of the hills and slopes, which rose and fell boundlessly to the horizon, were lit by the incandescent smile of the bright sun.

Ruy broke the silence. 'I bet you can't guess what I found when I first came here to look at this place,' he whispered in her ear.

'No, tell me.' Luna turned her head and met the twinkle in his eyes. 'What did you find?'

'Come, I'll show you.' He helped her up and led her towards the house, walking around to the back. The previous owners must have kept a few chickens because there was a broken-down coop; there was also what appeared to be an old kitchen garden, almost entirely overgrown.

'Gitano-Negro would like it if we kept birds, I'm sure,' Ruy chuckled, crouching to pull at the wire netting as he peered into the cage.

'I remember this,' said Luna, wide-eyed with delight. 'We used to steal cherries when no one was around. They had an old gardener, who was a bit of a terror, I seem to remember.' She smiled at the memory, her gaze travelling around the rambling potager.

'But look over here,' said Ruy as he straightened up, gesturing towards an area next to where they were standing. Surrounded by a dry-stone wall, the emerald-green patch was alive with a profusion of herbs. 'Mint, verbena, rosemary, thyme, echinacea, chamomile ... they're all here.'

Luna breathed in the heady fragrance. 'That smell is heavenly. Oh Ruy, we can have our very own herb garden!' Her eyes danced with excitement.

'That was exactly my thought, too. We can plan it together, tend it together. I inherited the other herb garden from La Pharaona but it never felt truly mine. We can take cuttings and plants from it, anyway. You know, maybe in time we might create something as wonderful as the famous, seventeenth-century Chelsea Physic Garden in London.'

'Just think how many of your beloved infusions we can make,' said Luna, laughing.

'Did your friends tell you the legend of the olive tree?'

'If they did, I can't remember it.'

'When I bought the grove, I did a bit of research. The legend says that Zeus promised to gift the peninsula of Attica to the god who would bring to him the most valuable and useful present. Poseidon, god of the sea, and Athena, daughter of Zeus and goddess of wisdom, both came to present their gifts. Poseidon struck the earth with his trident and produced a horse, which was considered a powerful instrument of war. With the touch of her spear, Athena brought forth an olive tree, a symbol of hearth and home, vital for cooking and light, health and fertility. With this more peaceful gift, Athena beat Poseidon and, from that moment on, the humble olive tree has represented peace and prosperity.'

'I do feel so safe and peaceful here,' Luna whispered with a tremulous sigh of contentment, as she leaned back against her husband's firm chest.

He smiled down at her, hugging her into the warm circle of his arms.

She trembled slightly and they sat in silence for a few moments, both lost in reverie, reflecting on their happiness and the sway of fate.

The atmosphere was full of love: Luna's and Ruy's love. From the undergrowth, a few cicadas chirruped lazily. Somewhere on the lake came the pleasant sound of rushing water – the cascade was soothing and gave a sense of coolness after the day's heat.

'Isn't this perfect?' she said, snuggling deeper in his embrace.

'It'll be even more perfect once we've filled this place with the laughter of children.' He spread his palm over the flat plane of her stomach lovingly. 'One day, not too far off, we'll be sitting here with our little Rueda de Calderón heir, the fruit of our precious love.'

She looked up at him, her amber eyes glittering with excitement. 'Then let's make a baby tonight.'

He buried his face in her fragrant hair and chuckled. 'Always impatient, *querida, ey?*'

But Ruy didn't need a second invitation. His lips closed over hers with tender passion. After all, why not? It seemed the most fitting culmination of their whirlwind romance.

About the author:

Q AND A
WITH HANNAH FIELDING

Viva España

What is it that inspires you about Andalucía?

In my lifetime, I have been fortunate enough to travel to all manner of places around the globe, but Andalucía remains one of my favourites. That sultry, sunny Spanish region so fired up my imagination that I set my Andalucían Nights Trilogy there.

There are so many things I love about it: for one thing, how people come together, often over food … what amazing meals I've had in Andalucía! The spirit of the people is also captivating. I found a real sense of 'fiesta' in the places I visited, and an intensity; as Salvador says in *Indiscretion*: 'Everything we Andalucíans do, we do with intensity.' Andalucía is an autonomous community, so there are many people who are very proud of their Andalucían nationality.

The art and architecture have always drawn me to the region and it's a place where the Moorish influence, in particular, has left its mark. My favourite example is the Alhambra, the amalgamation of fabulous Arabesque palaces and a fortress complex built by the Moors on a steep wooded hill during the mid-fourteenthth century in Granada, Spain. It's straight out of the exotic tales of *The Arabian Nights* and is startling for its beauty.

The stunning scenery is another thing: I love the colours of the landscape. Andalucía is known for its *Pueblos Blancos* –

white villages – and the sky and sea are so beautifully blue. The temperate climate makes for such a wonderful life, enjoyed in the warmth of the Mediterranean sun and beneath glorious blue skies (the dry area of Andalucía enjoys some three hundred days of sunshine per year!).

Family is an important theme in the trilogy (the title *Legacy* hints at this), and so where better to situate the story than in a place where roots are a source of great pride – and, sometimes, friction. For me Andalucía is the heart of Spain. The opening of the trilogy begins with: *En la sangre hierve España sin fuego* – 'In Spain, blood boils without fire.' The proverb says it all: this is a land of deep passions, the perfect setting for fiery, dramatic romance. *Olé*!

Flamenco features prominently in the Andalucían Nights series. How did it inspire the romance and passion in the trilogy?
Flamenco is an integral aspect of the Andalucían culture and is so ardently passionate. As I wrote *Indiscretion*, *Masquerade* and *Legacy*, I listened to flamenco music and found myself transported to the south of Spain. It is so vibrant, evocative, stirring and soulful.

You never forget your first flamenco show. I remember how I felt, in my early twenties, entirely captivated by the strumming guitars and raw vocals, the shoes tapping in time to the rhythm of my heartbeat. I remember the mesmerizing grace of the dancers, their stunning sensuality, their naked emotion and the sheer spectacle of it all: the swirling, vivid colours of the beautiful costumes.

I adore the fashion of flamenco; the beautiful red-and-black dresses the women wear, in particular. What young woman isn't intrigued upon discovering a new fashion? When I saw my first *traje de flamenco* (flamenco costume), my first thought was: 'Wow – beautiful!' My second: 'I want one!' The flamenco attire I saw was novel at the time, and alluringly exotic to me. Nowadays, flamenco fashion is big news, capturing the imaginations of fashion designers the world over.

Most of all, I love the music – what Federico García Lorca called 'the weeping of the guitar'. In *Masquerade*, the hero Leandro is of gypsy decent: the history and culture of his people and their home, Andalucía, define him. So it stands to reason that he is a talented and passionate guitar player. In *Legacy*, Ruy inherits his father's ability and develops it even further, becoming an impressive musician who can move between mandolin playing, flamenco and classical guitar. Both Leandro and Ruy, in their own ways, embody the wild and beautiful spirit of flamenco. There's no other music like it in the world, and no other music so raw and moving.

Would you say Luna Ward is the most complex of your heroines so far?

Absolutely. Luna is the least adventurous of the three women in the Andalucían Nights Trilogy, but she is the one who probably has the longest way to go to reach emotional maturity because of the baggage she carries. Therefore, she is definitely the most complicated of my heroines, compared with Alexandra and Luz, who both share a reckless propensity to follow their passions. Like Alexandra, however, Luna knows what it is to have tragedy and division in her family, and that unspoken connection is perhaps what instinctively draws these two women of different generations together when they meet in *Legacy*.

With Luna, her intellect often obscures the intensity of her feelings and she finds it safer to maintain the façade of the cool, proficient, level-headed scientist. She is an idealist and that's why she accepts the controversial assignment she is given, and remains in it until she is convinced that her assumptions are wrong. Self-reliant where her work is concerned, her self-confidence wavers when it comes to men and love, though. Luna is deeply scarred by a traumatic childhood experience, which colours all her reactions to the opposite sex; and this is the challenge that Ruy must face with her when he helps her to conquer her internal demons.

Independent, orderly and reserved – almost an introvert – Luna is nevertheless courageous and passionate once she decides to trust and her emotions are unleashed. When she finally accepts her feelings for Ruy, her love has no bounds and she gives herself without restraint, also liberating herself from her 'tunnel vision' as Ruy calls it, as well the fear of her past.

You seem to be fascinated by the idea of fortune telling – where does this theme come from?

I have long been intrigued by fortune telling. When I was a young woman I visited plenty of fortune tellers and became quite persuaded that some people really do have the gift to see into the past and future. My experiences set me on a path to finding out about divination across various cultures and throughout history. Although the methods of divining the future are varied and fascinating – from tarot cards and astrology to palmistry, rune-casting and crystal balls – I have always found pyromancy wonderfully evocative; imagine telling the future by staring into flames – so dramatic!

Including fortune telling in my books allows me to build on three key themes.

Mystery: confusing and troubling the heroine until all is revealed at the climax. *Control:* each of my main characters is independent and strong, and wants to feel a good measure of control over her life. In *Burning Embers*, *Indiscretion* and *Masquerade*, in particular, the heroines are asserting their right to equality with men, testing their wings in worlds with expanding freedoms for women. Falling in love can feel like losing control, and each heroine must work to establish her own identity while surrendering to love's course. *Taboo:* fortune telling is frowned upon by some. It is taboo and, in any love story, what is forbidden can be powerful – and attractive. By bringing in this element, I test the heroines. Will they stick to what they feel they 'should' do and think, or will they follow their hearts into the risky unknown?

Packing Up My Suitcase

Who/what inspired you to travel?

As a little girl my parents took my sister and me on trips to Europe, which were magical and inspirational for a romantic like myself. But after the 1956 war in Egypt almost everyone was stopped from travelling. As I grew through my teens, the desire to travel boiled up in me. I don't think I ever recovered. Two or three times a year I reach for my passport and we're off.

Which passport stamp are you proudest of?

Most definitely the Swiss stamp I was given on arrival in Geneva in 1968. My family had been forbidden to travel for ten years under the regime of the time, and this was my first trip abroad since I had been a child.

Which passport stamp would you most like to have?

I am compulsively nomadic – there are so many countries I have still to visit. The romance of travel will never fade for me. I think China is calling next. My father was a great collector of Chinese porcelain and I love it too; and I have always been fascinated by Confucius and his philosophy.

When and where in your travels have you been happiest?

Travelling with my teenage children and a whole bunch of their friends on skiing holidays to Courchevel and Méribel in winter, and to a rented villa in the hills of the south of France, where we eventually bought a house.

A Writer's Life

What is the best piece of advice you could give to someone who wants to get into writing?

First and foremost, write from the heart. Be true to yourself and don't compromise to please the market. Markets change, fads come and go; your work will remain.

Research your facts thoroughly. A writer today has no excuse for not getting his/her facts right. Use all the tools available to you. Travel, internet, books, films, documentaries: they're all there to enrich your experience and make your writing journey easier.

Plan your novel down to the smallest detail. This will make your writing so much easier and 'therefore' so much more enjoyable. A writing plan is your map. Would you set out on a long journey by car without a map?

Read, reread and reread. Edit, edit, edit. Go through your manuscript again and again and edit it. I know that it will break your heart to delete a phrase or even one word you have spent time agonizing over but, sometimes, less is more. Not easy advice to follow but, in the long run, it does work. If you can leave the manuscript alone for a few weeks and revisit it at a later date, reading it as if it were someone else's, then that's even better.

Do not get discouraged. Continue to write whether you think your work is good or bad. There is no bad writing. There are good days and bad days. The more you write, the better at it you get.

Find out more at www.hannahfielding.net